Praise

"The BEST second-chance historical romance with estranged spouses that I've ever read." -triviareads, *Goodreads*

"Victorian Charlie's Angels with ridiculously hot sex is a perfect concept, and Charlie was always the kind of distant, rational mentor waiting in the wings as each of the Angels went on their adventures. Making her story a marriage in trouble take—with, like, a lot of twists—adds a sense of messy drama and humanity and yes, angst. But it remains a ton of fun, with the adventure, heat and sly humor I've come to expect from a Grace Callaway book. This one has my heart!" -Caroline, *BookBub*

"This second chance romance is one of the best (along with The Lady Who Came in From the Cold).... The banter is out of this world delicious and the bedroom scenes are hot!" -Angela, *BookBub*

"I wish I could give this book all the stars! Seriously...absolutely outstanding from the characters and emotion to the intricate plot woven with twists and turns I couldn't see coming, I couldn't put it down." -Alyza38, *BookBub*

"The story has wonderful characters that are vibrant and interesting. The plot is intricate and keeps the reader quickly turning the pages to see what will be coming next. The steamy encounters between Charlotte and Jack sizzle on the pages." -Pinn4139, *Bookbub*

"Charlie and Jack have all the GC magic - connection, passion, angst, and swoon. With a mystery to uncover and a past to work through, Callaway shows why when second chance romances are done well they can be a top tier read." -Sadie Reads, *Goodreads*

"I felt completely immersed in the story, and I couldn't put the book down. Five glorious stars!" -Gloria, *Goodreads*

"Steamy and witty romantic intrigue." -Suzette, *Goodreads*

"This story wrecked me. Without giving too much away, there was the potential for a lot of angst (which I am not a fan of) but honestly it was just the right amount. It was a second chance romance and the passion between Lottie and the H was so hot it scalded the pages. There was also intense feeling and protectiveness that went both ways. I loved that Charlotte finally got her happy ending and that we found out the mysteries behind her past." -hollygolightly_01, *BookBub*

"A novel that sparked joy. It made me smile, it also made me read into the early morning." -Jan, *Goodreads*

"Spectacular. That's the only word I can think of that truly captures the essence of this book. Callaway has crafted a world that is vivid and engrossing and utterly captivating. Hell, at one point I was so involved I thought I might be one of Charlie's angels. And then...there's this incredible loooove story! My gawd!!! The love between Charlotte and Sebastian is timeless. Their energy, connection and love is unparalleled. Neither time nor distance could dim its brilliance." -ilovebooksnschit, *Instagram*

"This story and romance are perfection." -AJ, *Goodreads*

For my parents
whose love story
inspires the ones I write

Also by Grace Callaway

BLACKWOODS
One Kiss to Desire (Fall 2024)

LADY CHARLOTTE'S SOCIETY OF ANGELS
Olivia and the Masked Duke

Pippa and the Prince of Secrets

Fiona and the Enigmatic Earl

Glory and the Master of Shadows

Charlotte and the Seductive Spymaster

GAME OF DUKES
The Duke Identity

Enter the Duke

Regarding the Duke

The Duke Redemption

The Return of the Duke

HEART OF ENQUIRY (The Kents)
The Widow Vanishes (Prequel Novella)

The Duke Who Knew Too Much

M is for Marquess

The Lady Who Came in from the Cold

The Viscount Always Knocks Twice

Never Say Never to an Earl

The Gentleman Who Loved Me

MAYHEM IN MAYFAIR

Her Husband's Harlot

Her Wanton Wager

Her Protector's Pleasure

Her Prodigal Passion

Charlotte

AND THE
SEDUCTIVE SPYMASTER

Lady Charlotte's
SOCIETY *of*
ANGELS

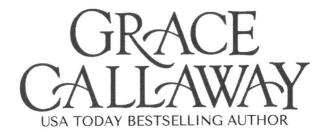

GRACE CALLAWAY

USA TODAY BESTSELLING AUTHOR

Cover Art: EDH Graphics

Typography Design: KM Designs

Formatting: Colchester & Page

PROLOGUE

C harlotte paced before the hearth of her bedchamber with her hands balled at her sides.

"How long have you been sleeping with her?" she said in a trembling voice.

"For the last bloody time, Charlotte, I am not having an affair."

In contrast to her agitated movements, her husband Sebastian James Courtenay, the Marquess of Fayne, remained perfectly still, his hands braced on his hips, his expression hard and unyielding. Charlie hated that her rage and despair did not diminish her sensual awareness of him. Tall and muscular, he had a commanding presence that shrunk any room he entered. The light of dusk streaming through the villa's windows gilded his thick chestnut hair, angular cheekbones, and square jaw. Beneath his straight brows, his eyes belonged to a warrior: the iron-black orbs were fierce yet guarded, revealing little of himself.

Charlie, being more observant than most, had learned to read her spouse somewhat during their year of marriage. After they made love, his eyes were as warm and potent as freshly brewed coffee. When they locked horns, his gaze turned unyielding, specks of bronze glittering in those coal-like depths. As they were both hotheaded, their rows were not infrequent, but they usually made up in ways that compensated for the emotional bloodshed.

But not this time—not since he'd betrayed her—and never again.

"Pray do me the courtesy of not treating me like an idiot," she snapped. "I *saw* you, Sebastian. With my own eyes. You were kissing Eleni Pappas—making love to her in the back room of her dashed taverna!"

The memory drove a red-hot spike through Charlie's breast, and she choked back a sob. She'd caught the proprietress and Sebastian *in flagrante*, the former's bountiful curves pressed against the latter's hard edges. And the pair's mouths had been fused together.

How could Charlie have been such a fool, trusting her happiness to a man? One of her earliest memories was of being lost in a bustling Cairo market when her papa, a gentleman with a fever for antiquities, had abandoned her to chase down some relic. Frozen with terror, she'd huddled in the stall of a kindly Egyptian fruit seller, waiting for Papa to return for her. Wondering if he would. To this day, figs tasted to her of fear. From that experience, she'd learned to make herself useful so that Papa would not leave her behind again. So that she might claim some of his attention, maybe even some of his affection.

An invisible hand fisted around her heart. *I should have known better than to trust a man.*

"It wasn't what you think," Sebastian said.

He shoved a hand through his hair, tugging back the heavy front wave which needed a trim. Annoyingly, his casual style suited his outsized virility. Although a nobleman by birth, Sebastian despised foppery. His current outfit consisted of a linen shirt rolled up to reveal his hair-dusted forearms and toast-brown trousers that clung to his long legs. Even in a laborer's garb, he looked like a king. He dressed and lived as it suited him, and devil take what anyone else thought.

From the instant Sebastian had come to her aid at a port in Marseille, Charlie had been drawn to his confidence and power. When he bestowed his attention upon her, she felt as if she'd been given the greatest gift in the world. And when he took it away...

The feeling was all too familiar.

It was an important artifact, Charlie. Papa's impatience had shone in his grey eyes, the only inheritance she'd received from him. *I had to go after it. If you were a boy, perhaps you would have kept up.*

"Eleni and I are...we're just friends," Sebastian said gruffly. "I swear it upon my honor."

Hearing him and the widow paired in the same sentence, Charlie felt sick with jealousy.

"Your honor." Her pain hardened into sarcasm. "We both know what that is worth, don't we?"

"Bloody hell." His flaring nostrils conveyed his growing frustration. "If you were a man, I would call you out for that."

"Go ahead. I know how to use a pistol," she retorted.

Growing up in excavation camps and other rough-and-ready environments, she'd learned to fend for herself. Which was a good thing. Clearly, she couldn't trust someone else to look after her best interests.

"For Christ's sake, Charlotte. I am not going to shoot you—"

"Why not? It would be kinder than what you did," she said bitterly.

A muscle flickered in his jaw. "I didn't fuck Eleni. Why can't you trust me?"

Because you are you, and I am me. I was a fool to think our happiness could last.

Even though her late father had been the Earl of Bembridge, Charlie lacked a genteel upbringing. Her mama had died when she was a babe, and her papa's hobby had consumed him far more than his impoverished estate. Whenever he'd had two pennies to rub together, he would spend it on things he cared about: a shard of Mesopotamian pottery, some ancient religious relic. He wasn't about to waste money on a boarding school for his daughter. He'd simply brought Charlie with him on his travels, the way one might a battered valise.

At two-and-twenty, Charlie was aware of her physical charms; during her travels with Papa, her honey-blonde hair and grey eyes had attracted plenty of unwanted male attention. She felt like a lady in name only despite her lineage. She had few drawing room accomplishments and no experience whatsoever with the polite world. Her main skills pertained to survival and taking care of her father. When Sebastian had proposed after a whirlwind courtship, she'd felt as if she were dreaming: a man like him could have anyone, yet he'd chosen her.

Now she knew why.

"Did you believe that my lack of experience would make me too stupid to see through your deception?" She balled her hands. "While I may not be as sophisticated as the ladies of your acquaintance, I am aware of how the world works. Men like you think they can do whatever they wish. It was my fault for believing that you were different—that your vows meant something."

Anger and something darker smoldered in Sebastian's eyes. "And it is mine for thinking that you would trust in my honor, wife. In *me*."

"Trust?" she scoffed. "That, *husband*, must be earned. And the way to go about earning it is not by lying to me. Because you have been lying—repeatedly. Haven't you wondered how I ended up at that dashed taverna?"

When he said nothing, she enlightened him.

"I ran into your old friend Georgios."

At the betraying clench of Sebastian's jaw, she felt a grim satisfaction. A friend of her husband's, Georgios was a fisherman who also made his living as a guide for tourists. He'd taken Charlie and Sebastian on several excursions around the islands. Last week, when Sebastian had arrived home hours later than promised, he'd told her that he'd bumped into Georgios, and they'd caught up at a taverna, losing track of time.

As it happened, Charlie was in the village on an errand the following day and ran into Georgios. The kindly fellow asked after her husband, saying he hadn't seen the marquess in over a month. At that instant, icy premonition had prickled Charlie's insides.

Why would Sebastian lie about his activities? What had he been up to?

The chill had spread, as one by one, the memories hit her. The times Sebastian had been delayed coming home...or not shown up at all. His excuses had seemed innocuous: his horse had thrown a shoe, he'd been waylaid by an acquaintance, the meeting with his cartography society ran later than usual.

Once sown, suspicion proliferated like weeds in Charlie's head.

Thus, she decided to verify his explanations. She'd hoped to put her mind at ease; instead, she'd smashed her marital happiness to smithereens. The man she loved had been lying to her. Repeatedly. Even worse, some part of her had always suspected that Sebastian was hiding something—that he had secrets.

While I trusted him with my heart, he played me for a fool.

"Georgios didn't see you last week. You lied to me," Charlie said flatly.

Sebastian rubbed the back of his neck. A telltale sign of unease.

"Georgios has a memory like a sieve," he muttered. "If you were to ask him again—"

"After you've talked to him and convinced him to cover for you?" she said acidly. "Why don't you save us both the bother and tell me where you really were?"

Bronze stars glittered in his gaze, but his lips formed a tight, stubborn line.

In the silence, she felt the weight of the truth. It was heavy enough to crush hope. To pulverize her dreams into glittering specks of dust.

"If you love me, then trust me," he said finally. "I did not betray you. I never would."

Oh no, he did *not*.

"It isn't *my* love that is being called into question," she said with quivering fury. "*You* are the one who broke his vows. The one who destroyed our marriage."

"You are being dramatic—"

Her vision flashed red.

"I want a divorce," she snapped. "Is that dramatic enough for you?"

"Don't be ridiculous. We are not getting divorced." He had the *temerity* to glance at his pocket watch. "Look, I have an unavoidable engagement with the cartography society. I wouldn't go unless I had to. But I have been commissioned to do an important map for—"

"Just go." She couldn't bear to hear any more of his lies.

"I will be back as soon as I can, Lottie."

Hearing his pet name for her shredded her heart. He was the only one who'd ever called her by that name, and she loved how feminine and sweet it sounded. Loved that her husband saw her that way. But it wasn't enough to keep his attention, apparently.

She'd given him everything that she was. And it wasn't enough.

When will I ever be enough?

"I don't care if you ever come back," she said rashly.

His countenance hardened. "Nevertheless, when I return, we will continue our discussion."

"There is nothing left to discuss. Our marriage is over," she said in a suffocated voice. "You are dead to me."

Lines bracketed his mouth. His gaze smoldering like a forge, he looked as if he might say something. A heartbeat later, he turned and walked out.

Charlie awakened feeling like she hadn't slept at all.

She was in bed, dressed in the same clothes she'd worn before Sebastian left. She hadn't wanted to see the maid—to see anyone. She wanted to be left alone with her misery.

She'd gotten her wish. The light slanting through the shutters indicated that it was morning, and her temples throbbed from hours of crying. To no surprise, the place next to her was empty.

He is with Eleni. Probably bedding her right now.

Charlie squeezed her eyes, as if she could shut out the vision. She was done crying over her husband. Before him, she'd been a sensible woman, one in control of her emotions. She had to get back to who she'd been. The pragmatic survivor who always had a plan.

She went to the balcony for some air. The villa was set atop a hill dotted with stucco abodes, the sunrise gilding the terracotta roofs and setting the bougainvillea afire. The vibrant coral and pink sky competed with the rolling azure waves for brilliance.

What am I going to do? She stared at the sea, which looked calm but could suck a woman under. *I have no money or power to petition for a divorce. If I leave Sebastian, where will I go—how will I survive?*

She had no answer to the practical questions, let alone how to deal with her shattered heart.

"My lady?" Though quiet, the housekeeper's voice startled her.

Wiping the backs of her hands over her wet cheeks, Charlie turned. "I beg your pardon, Sophia. I didn't hear you come in..."

She trailed off when she saw the shock etched into the housekeeper's weathered face.

Her heart thumping, she asked, "What is the matter?"

"News just came from the village, my lady. It's...it's the master—"

"Is he all right?" Charlie had to force the words through her numb lips.

"A taverna caught fire before dawn." The housekeeper twisted her apron in her veined hands. "It had closed. Everyone was gone, except for the proprietress, Mrs. Pappas and...and Lord Fayne. They must have... They must have been asleep. The two of them, they did not make it out. I am so sorry..."

The edges of Charlie's vision fluttered, her own words ringing in her ears.

Our marriage is over. You are dead to me.

"Sebastian," she whispered.

Her knees buckled, and she was weeping as she fell.

ONE

The Honorable Francis Devlin braced a hand on the wall next to Lady Charlotte Fayne's shoulder. Framed by his mask, Devlin's blue eyes had a devilish glint as he leaned toward her. Charlie maintained an inviting posture as he traced the edge of her golden mask with his fingertip. She was dressed as Cleopatra. Her wig styled *à l'Égyptienne* and white tunic provided additional camouflage.

"Why don't we have some fun, *chérie*?" he said with a creditable French accent.

"Aren't we doing that now, my dear sir?"

Although she shaped her lips into a coy smile for the benefit of anyone watching, Charlie gave her employee a warning look as his touch traveled lower, following the slope of her jaw. For the evening's mission, she and Devlin were pretending to be strangers meeting at this sprawling mansion tucked away in Hamstead Heath. The host, Ellsworth Rigby, had amassed a fortune through import-export and investments and was rumored to be richer than Croesus. His wealth afforded him and his wife Isadora the freedom to carry on as they pleased. At their masquerades, it was rumored, anything could—and did—happen.

The Rigbys' guest list included celebrated artists, louche blue-bloods, and everyone in between. A propensity for salaciousness appeared to be the main requirement to gain entrée. The party-goers sported costumes to conceal their identities (or sometimes to flaunt them—as in the case of an opera singer whose famed twin assets were on full display in her sheer Grecian tunic). A secret phrase was required to gain entry; through her sources, Charlie had learned that tonight's was "Shakespeare's Brave New World."

Isadora Rigby had spared no expense recreating the forest from *A Midsummer Night's Dream*. Lush potted greenery, silky emerald carpets, and hanging lanterns created the illusion of a magical woodland. Masked guests carried on the theme in a scandalous fashion. A gentleman wearing a donkey's head and a loincloth sprawled on a chaise longue. Beneath the skimpy piece of fabric, the outline of his member was clearly visible as he flirted with a trio of faeries bedecked in a few strategically placed flowers.

Devlin reclaimed Charlie's attention, his breath warm against her ear.

"Do you see the target?" he asked softly.

Arching her neck as if in the throes of passion, Charlie scanned the room from beneath her lashes, which she'd thickened with a paste made of ash. The grey of her irises was unusual, and the last thing she needed was to be recognized. To the polite world, she was Lady Charlotte Fayne, widowed marchioness and paragon of propriety. A lady who used the fortune left to her by her dead husband to do good works. She, along with the young ladies she'd recruited for her charity, the Society of Angels, undertook projects that served women in need.

What people didn't know was that her group did more than write pamphlets, sew clothing, and distribute food baskets. Charlie's true objective was to mentor her charges to become investigators, and she'd succeeded beyond her wildest dreams. In the past three years, the Angels had assisted a score of female clients with every kind of peril, from blackmail to murder. While Charlie was inordinately proud of her team, she'd personally taken on tonight's case.

You are the only one I trust to discover the truth. As much as I adore the Angels, the fewer who know of my husband's perfidy, the better. Amara Quinton's liquid brown eyes had beseeched Charlie. *Find out what Gilbert is up to. I must know what secrets he is hiding.*

Monitoring the room of cavorting guests, Charlie felt empathy tighten around her heart like a rusted wire. Time had dulled, but not entirely diminished, her pain. She knew all too well that a husband could destroy one's happiness. One's very soul, if one allowed it.

Whatever the night reveals, Amara deserves to know the truth. No matter how grievous reality turns out to be, I will be there for her. The way she has been there for me.

Charlie slid her fingers through Devlin's dark wig. The younger son of an earl, Devlin also had a reputation to protect. He had, however, worked covertly on behalf of the Crown years before he'd entered Charlie's employ. With the skills he'd honed through espionage, he was proving a worthy addition to her organization, and Amara had agreed to his participation this eve.

"No sign of him," Charlie whispered back. "We'll search the other rooms."

They ventured deeper into the mansion. Beaded curtains took the place of doors between the public rooms, and wooden pearls slithered over Charlie's bare shoulders as she passed into the library. This room was darker, lit only by a fire in the large stone hearth. As the light waned, so did inhibitions.

Before the blazing hearth, guests occupied the seating area, watching as two couples rutted on the Aubusson. A woman with long brown hair and a crucifix around her throat—Juliet, perhaps? —perched upon a hirsute fellow lying on his back. Beneath her Renaissance-style mask, her lips formed a scarlet *O* as she sank onto his rigid shaft. Her Romeo's groan echoed that of a nearby fellow whose pointy ears and curly, leaf-adorned wig identified him as Puck. He was pounding vigorously into a nymph on her hands and knees.

Thankfully, neither male was Gilbert Quinton.

"Let's check the back of the room," Devlin said under his breath.

The bookshelves that occupied this part of the library were draped with twisting ivy, creating the illusion of hedgerows. Wanton sounds emerged from the stacks: slapping skin, wet sucking, animal mewls. Charlie led the way down the arterial aisle, scanning the shadowy passages between the shelves for her friend's husband.

"Bloody hell, that's sweet."

Did that deep male voice belong to Gilbert?

Pulse racing, Charlie halted so abruptly that Devlin collided into her. She twisted her head, pressing a finger to her lips, pointing another at the next row. She edged closer to the location of the baritone. Peering around the bookshelf, she saw two masked figures. The naked female was leaning back against the wall of books. She stood on one curvy leg, the other hooked on the wide shoulder of the man kneeling before her.

"Do you like being gamahuched, wench?"

Thickened with lust, his voice was difficult to identify. With a cold pang, Charlie saw that his build was similar to Gilbert's.

"Your tongue is divine." The woman wove her fingers through his hair. "I want it deeper. Yes, like *that*..."

An unbidden memory shivered through Charlie. Of Sebastian performing this act upon her. She could still see the hunger in his gaze, feel the hot swipe of his tongue against her most intimate part. He'd kissed her there the way he'd kissed her everywhere: with ferocious greed and possession, as if he wanted to devour her whole. As if he could never get enough of her. He'd owned her with his tongue, made her shake and moan as she climaxed the way the woman in front of her was doing.

I love your pussy, Sebastian had once growled. *I want to eat it for breakfast, lunch, and supper.*

Despite being a nobleman, he'd never been polite about his pleasure. About anything. He eschewed refinement in favor of being himself, and she'd adored his confidence, his knowledge of who he was beyond his wealth and titles.

If only he hadn't been a lying, cheating bastard.

Charlie shoved the past back where it belonged and focused on the couple. The man rose, swiping the back of his hand over his mouth, and removed his mask. His sharp features were not those of Gilbert Quinton.

Having seen enough, Charlie jerked back, accidentally bumping into Devlin. He steadied her by the waist and pulled her into an empty row. Through her thin tunic, she felt the unmistakable shape of his arousal poking into her backside.

When she turned on him with narrowed eyes, he released her, his grin decidedly unapologetic.

"Don't take it personally," he murmured. "You can't bring a man to an orgy and blame him for reacting."

"Remember you are a professional," she said sternly.

That only deepened his grin. Dashed rake.

Straightening her shoulders, she headed into the aisle, Devlin dogging her heels. Their next stop was the billiards room...or what had been the billiards room, at any rate. The place was now a forest, the billiards table covered in a swath of watered blue silk that continued to wind through the room in an artistic rendering of a brook. Upon the table was Ophelia, the death she was suffering far less tragic than that of The Bard's original heroine.

Her dampened shift clung to her slender form as she shuddered with the *petit mort* given to her by the masked man thrusting between her thighs. If Charlie wasn't mistaken, she was observing a public display of marital relations between her hosts, Isadora and Ellsworth Rigby. She wasn't the only one watching. Guests surrounded the heaving pair, some inspired to act out carnality of their own with a partner or two. The air was humid, ripe with perfume and sex.

"I think I've spotted the target," Devlin said under his breath. "To the right, by the potted palm. With the blonde in feathers."

Charlie swung her gaze in that direction, her pulse speeding up. The man with the blue mask had Gilbert Quinton's burly build and face shape, and she saw with a wisp of rage that his eveningwear bore the stamp of his wife's inimitable artistry. He was with a buxom blonde wearing a red dress trimmed with matching feathers, and she was leading him toward the exit.

Charlie followed, pushing past leering offers and grasping hands. In the packed corridor, she saw no sign of Gilbert or the blonde. She and Devlin pushed through the throng, and they arrived at the atrium just as Gilbert and the blonde reached the top of the staircase and vanished from view.

To avoid looking suspicious, she said to Devlin in a throaty voice, "You naughty fellow. That deed you suggested is *far* too wicked to try in public. Let us find some privacy upstairs, shall we?"

As she pulled Devlin toward the staircase, people gave knowing chuckles and let them pass. On the first floor, they found themselves in a corridor lined with oil paintings. Flickering sconces illuminated a line of closed doors—bedchambers. Occupied, if the muffled moans and grunts were any indication.

Charlie marched toward the door at the end of the hallway. "We'll go through each chamber until we find the suspect."

"Shall we do *lovers stumbling into a room*?" Devlin inquired. "If you prefer, I can carry you over the threshold."

"I prefer that you keep your hands to yourself. Now follow me."

"To the ends of the earth, oh fearless leader."

Quelling her amusement at the rogue's charm, Charlie grasped the knob and turned it. The heavy door swung open, releasing a swell of moans. She straightened her spine and headed to the over-sized tester bed. The candlelight revealed a tangle of limbs and writhing bodies. In their frenzy, the participants had shed their masks (and everything else), making Charlie's job easier. Gilbert was not part of the *ménage à*...well, however many it was.

As she turned to go, a hand reached out and snared her wrist.

"Don't go, darling." The blonde winked first at her, then at Devlin. "Join us."

Charlie tugged free. "Some other time."

"Spoilsport," Devlin murmured.

They continued their methodical search through the rooms. No sign of Gilbert or the woman in red feathers. Turning a corner, Charlie came upon the master suite. The double doors were open, revealing a dozen guests cavorting about. The chamber had a suffo-cating exoticism with its jungle-green paper, heavy mahogany furnishings, and jewel-hued upholstery. Large gilt-framed looking glasses hung on every wall...and on the ceiling above the occupied bed.

Devlin gripped her waist, steering her into an alcove adjacent to the door. He buried his face in her neck, appearing to be a fervent lover, but she understood his ploy: he'd positioned her so that she was sheltered from passersby and, thanks to the many mirrors, could monitor the room from all angles. A neat trick, that. Perhaps Devlin deserved the raise he'd been pestering her about after all. As his mouth coasted lightly along her neck, she felt an unexpected flutter in her belly, which she ruthlessly quelled.

The fact that she hadn't had a lover in years was no excuse for her lack of professionalism. She composed herself. Then she gave a practiced moan, writhing against Devlin as if she were in the throes of passion. All the while, she scanned the room's occupants.

The four on the bed...heavens, she recognized them. The Prices and the Kendalls, two blue-blooded couples whom she avoided like the plague. The ladies, in particular, enjoyed using their social clout to bully others over perceived improprieties. Yet here they were, tupping at a party, and not with their own spouses. The hypocrisy was galling but typical.

As for the trio on the chaise...all women.

Reviewing each component of the human train on the Aubusson, Charlie did not see her friend's husband. She focused next on the spectators to the debauchery, and her attention snagged on a tall, broad-shouldered fellow with dark hair. His back was to her, and his build was too lean for him to be Gilbert, but for some reason, she couldn't look away. Needed to see his face with an urgency she couldn't explain.

She directed her gaze to the looking glass on the opposite wall. The stranger's mask hid the upper portion of his face, yet her breath stuttered at the sculpted angles of the man's cheekbones, the stubborn square of his jaw. Her gaze met his in the reflection. Her heart catapulted into her ribs, a keening sound leaving her as midnight eyes stared back and sucked her into the past—

"Bloody hell, my sweet," Devlin muttered against her ear. "I want you too."

Suddenly, his mouth covered hers. Past and present crashed over her in a disorienting wave. She was being kissed, her lover's lips smooth and practiced, his tongue as sly as a thief. He coaxed her lips apart, slipping inside with an experienced sweep. He tasted like spiced wine, dark and sweet...but he did not taste like her husband. He did not taste of whisky and mint and the unique male flavor that was Sebastian's alone.

Sebastian is dead. Devlin is kissing me. What in blazes am I doing?

Regaining her senses, Charlie pulled on Devlin's hair, enough to separate his lips from hers.

"Focus," she mouthed.

His eyes widened. The nod he gave was quick, abashed.

Drawing a breath, she peered around him, needing to verify that the man she'd seen was not, in fact, the husband she'd buried.

To reassure herself that it was just an uncanny resemblance. Once she got a better look at the stranger, she would see the differences between him and Sebastian.

She didn't get a chance, however.

The stranger had vanished.

Two

"Did you find Gilbert?" Amara Quinton's voice held a betraying quiver.

It was eight o'clock the next morning. Despite the ungodly hour, Charlie had made the journey to her friend's celebrated Bond Street dress shop. She had another client to see later that morning and didn't want to keep Amara in suspense. They were in one of the back rooms, seated at a worktable. Dressmaker's dummies stood guard along one wall, a massive wardrobe occupying another.

Known by the chic moniker "Mrs. Q," the African modiste was wearing her trademark black, the superb cut of her frock showcasing her lush figure. Her neat chignon gleamed like a raven's wing. Her snowy lace collar contrasted with the smooth brown perfection of her skin, and the only jewelry she wore was her wedding ring. Seeing that gold band and the anxiety in Amara's eyes, Charlie felt her chest knot.

Get it over with. Sugarcoating helps nothing.

She took a breath. "Yes, I saw him at the Rigbys'."

Conveying bad news was the worst part of Charlie's job. Yet the truth, no matter how painful, was better than not knowing.

Hating the pain in her friend's eyes, she proceeded to convey the events of the bacchanal as matter-of-factly as she could.

"This woman. With the red feathers." The quiver traveled from Amara's voice to her bottom lip. "Did she and my husband..."

"Not that I saw," Charlie said. "Devlin and I searched the house top to bottom and could not find them again. That doesn't mean, however, that nothing happened."

It was her policy to be as truthful as possible. Personal experience had taught her that there was nothing to be gained, and much to be lost, by the withholding of facts. Her papa hadn't told her that he'd used the small inheritance her mama had left her to fund his expeditions, thereby leaving her penniless. Her so-called guardian, Sir Patrick Swainey, had hidden his lustful intentions. And Sebastian...well, her husband had been a master of hiding the truth. He'd been so good at it that even now, a dozen years after his death, she still didn't know what was real and what wasn't.

The questions that had stolen her sleep now threatened her sanity.

Did that stranger just bear an uncanny resemblance to Sebastian? He was masked, after all, and I only saw him for an instant. But those eyes...

"Do *you* think something happened?" Amara pressed.

The desperation in her friend's tone focused Charlie.

Your husband is dead. Amara's is not. Concentrate on the case.

"Quinton was at an orgy." She counted off the incriminating facts on her gloved fingertips. "He had a woman on his arm. Moreover, he lied to you about where he was going."

"He said he was going to a friend's home for a game of cards. How stupid does he think I am?"

Amara's voice had a different sort of quiver now, and it matched the spark in her eyes. Charlie knew what her friend was feeling—knew the powerful rush of rage. She also knew the feeling afterward: when that inner fire burned out and only ashes remained. That acrid aftermath of emptiness.

Nevertheless, a broken heart did survive, even if it bore scars; Charlie was living proof of that. And of the fact that those damaged walls could be rebuilt stronger, hardier than before. Once upon a time, she had believed that love was the key to happiness. Now she knew the opposite to be true. Contentment stemmed from independence. What a woman truly needed was the ability to determine her own destiny. Once she discovered her own strength, she could do anything, be anything.

The first step toward freedom was the truth.

"You could talk to him," Charlie said bluntly. "You could present him with the evidence you have and demand an explanation."

"No." Amara clenched her jaw. "I have given him that option too many times. A month ago, he began acting strangely—and by strangely, I mean he was testy and secretive. I asked him what the matter was. Repeatedly. We do not quarrel, except occasionally over the parasites on his side of the family, yet we did over this. Every time, he insisted that he was fine, that I was imagining things. But a wife *knows*."

Charlie nodded with bleak understanding. In the weeks leading up to her discovery of Sebastian's infidelity, he had been acting more distant. She'd secretly fretted that he was losing interest in her; when she'd worked up the courage to address the topic, he'd told her to stop being silly, then *proved* his interest with such vigor that she couldn't sit comfortably in a saddle for days.

The perfidious scoundrel.

"I let it go because I trusted him. Because I...I love him. Fool that I am."

Hearing the hitch in Amara's voice, Charlie held out a hand-kerchief. "Having a trusting heart does not make you a fool, my dear."

"Being delusional does." Amara waved away the scrap of lace-trimmed linen and drew back her shoulders. "Even now, I cannot believe that he would throw away seven years of marriage for...for what? Some *doxy*?"

Hearing her friend's anguish, Charlie remained silent. There was nothing to say. All she could offer was the willingness to listen.

"If I tell him I know he was at the Rigbys' bacchanal, he could still deny that anything happened. He could turn the tables, accuse me of not trusting him, and cast me in the role of the villain for having him followed." Amara's hands balled in her lap. "No, when I confront him, I will do so with proof of his infidelity. I want you to continue tracking him, Charlie. I know this is asking a lot. Whatever the cost, I will pay it."

"Since you and that dangerous parasol of yours saved my life all those years ago, I would say the debt is mine."

As Charlie hoped it would, the memory earned a faint smile from Amara. The two had met before Charlie had started the Angels, when the society was still a germ of an idea in her head. On that fateful night, she'd taken a wrong turn and found herself cornered by thieves. Even with her trusty pistol, there had been too many for her to fight off alone.

Like an avenging angel, Amara had waded into the fray, her weapon a parasol equipped with a retractable steel blade. Together, she and Charlie had dispatched the vermin and sent them scurrying back into the shadows. Afterward, Charlie had taken her rescuer to supper, and over a meal of meat pies and ale, their friendship had taken root.

When Amara had decided to open her shop, Charlie had been her primary investor. When Amara had met Gilbert not long after, Charlie had stood as her matron of honor and later became godmother to the couple's newborn daughter. When Charlie had decided to stop her futile inquiry into Sebastian's death and divert her skills toward establishing a female detective society, Amara had been a staunch supporter. She'd even designed clothing and tools to help Charlie's Angels carry out their investigations.

Through thick and thin, Charlie and Amara had been there for each other. Kindred spirits who trusted one another with the secrets of the past and present.

"If it is your wish for me to continue following Gilbert, then I will," Charlie said simply.

Amara's nod was somber. "I want the truth. Even if it brings pain, not knowing is far worse."

Eyes of fathomless midnight flashed in Charlie's head, and her throat cinched. Unanswered questions surfaced to haunt her. After Sebastian's death, she'd been besieged by grief...but also by what she could only term a niggling intuition. A sense that something about his death hadn't been right.

Her doubts had begun with the note she'd found. Going through her dead husband's belongings, she'd found the crumpled scrap in an inner pocket of his coat, the words written in a feminine hand. Eleni's, she'd presumed.

We're in danger. We need to meet.

What sort of danger? Was someone threatening them?

Despite Charlie's anguish over Sebastian's infidelity, she had loved him. He had smashed her heart to pieces, yes, but he had also rescued her. From those ruffians in Marseille and from her guardian. He had married her, giving her the protection of his name.

Before the fighting—and, presumably, the affair with Eleni—had begun, Sebastian had been adoring and passionate. Devoted, even. He'd showered Charlie with gifts and what she'd craved most of all: his attention. With him, she'd felt cherished for the first time. He'd been everything she could want in a husband...until he wasn't.

Soon after, he was dead.

If his death hadn't been an accident, Charlie owed it to him and herself to find out the truth.

Thus, she'd dedicated herself to finding out all she could about Eleni, her husband, and what had happened the night the taverna burned. This would turn out to be her very first investigation. In this case, each question she'd asked had led to more questions. What had started as a simple need to know whether her husband's death had, indeed, been the accident the local authorities concluded it was became something else.

An obsession. An unrelenting desire to uncover the truth.

Ultimately, she hadn't been successful. All her inquiries had led to dead ends. She finally recognized that her fixation on her husband's death was doing more harm than good. It kept her mired in the past, spinning her wheels in the emotional muck of rage and despair. For her own good, she had to let him go. And she had, using the skills she'd acquired toward a more meaningful cause. She thought she had moved on...until last night.

Who was that dashed man I saw?

"Charlotte, what is the matter?"

She hastily returned her gaze to Amara's. "It is nothing."

"Let me be the judge of that." Amara's expression was shrewd. "You're preoccupied, which is not like you. Either there is something about Gilbert that you are not telling me, which would be even more out of character...or something else happened. Whatever it is, it must be significant indeed to compromise your focus."

"With your powers of observation, I always said that you would make a formidable Angel," Charlie said ruefully.

"I prefer to deal with fashion rather than fiends. Although, between you and me, my ten o'clock appointment is a terror in her own right. She wants to murder my creation with an excess of flounces."

Charlie smiled, glad that her friend's sense of humor remained intact.

"Now what is going on, my dear?"

With a sigh, Charlie gave in. "You are going to think I've gone mad."

Amara shrugged. "Did I blink an eye when you told me you wanted to recruit and train debutantes to become investigators?"

She had a point.

"Last night I saw a man. He...he looked like Sebastian," Charlie admitted.

Amara stilled. "Sebastian, the Marquess of Fayne? Your *dead husband*?"

"It sounds ridiculous, I know. It had to be an ungodly similarity. The man was masked, so I didn't see his entire face. Only his jaw and his eyes..."

Eyes that had looked as startled as mine. Eyes that I've never forgotten.

"Did you interact with this man?"

Charlie shook her head. "I saw him in the reflection of a looking glass. From across the room. By the time I tried to look for him, he'd vanished."

"A bizarre resemblance, then." Amara lifted her brows. "Unless Fayne had a twin brother he neglected to mention?"

"While my late husband neglected to mention a great number of things"—Charlie did not bother to hide her sarcasm—"I know for a fact that he had no siblings. He was the last of his line. After he passed, the title and its entailed properties reverted to the Crown."

Sebastian's family tree was a sparse one. Charlie had never met any of his family; his papa had died when he was a child, his mama the year before he met Charlie. Perhaps this familial lack of longevity had led him to make arrangements for her in the event of his own untimely demise. In this regard, her husband had taken care of her generously. His will had stipulated that his considerable personal assets, which included a townhouse in London, were to go to her, free and clear. While he'd failed to make good on his promise of love, he had given her security and freedom.

Perhaps I got the better end of the bargain after all.

"It must have been a coincidence." Amara sipped her tea, her astute gaze glinting over the porcelain rim. "Or not."

"What do you mean?"

"Perhaps in tracking down my demons last night, a few of your own were stirred?"

The insight hit an unwelcome nerve of truth. Charlie felt a spasm of anger—at Sebastian, who had the ability to make her act like a fool even from the grave. At herself, for giving him that power.

"It is only human, my dear, to have memories resurface in such a situation," Amara said gently. "Do not blame yourself."

"But I do."

Charlie's smile was bitter as she smoothed a wrinkle from her skirt. Amara had designed the azure satin walking dress, the attention to detail evident in the glove-like fit of the bodice and exquisite fullness of the skirts. The dress was trimmed with lace handmade by Benedictine nuns, and the contrast of pristine white and vivid blue suddenly reminded Charlie of Greece.

Of those giddy newlywed days.

Of Sebastian leading her out onto the balcony of their villa for the first time. He'd insisted on covering her eyes, even as she'd laughingly told him she'd seen the view as they'd driven up the hill.

The best is still to come, my Lottie.

His husky voice had sent an anticipatory shiver up her spine. The beauty of the sunset had been eclipsed by that of her husband's passion. He'd taken her there, against the railing of the balcony. As always, his lack of inhibition had unleashed her own wantonness. Gripping the stone balustrade, she'd pushed back on his driving cock, his pleasured growls filling her ear as they came together...

"Charlotte, dearest, forgive me. I did not mean to stir up a hornet's nest."

At her friend's worried tone, Charlotte shoved aside the memories.

"I am a professional, Amara," she said tightly. "I cannot—*will* not—let my personal affairs affect my ability to carry out my duty as an investigator. That stranger distracted me from the case, but I promise you I will not allow it to happen again."

"You have helped so many women, my dear. And not just your clients. You've been a tireless mentor to your Angels, teaching them the power of independence and giving them the skills and confidence to navigate the world however they wish." Amara paused. "Yet sometimes I think you allow yourself to be trapped by that very notion of self-sufficiency."

Charlie frowned. "Self-sufficiency is hardly a cage."

"It is when it bars you from happiness."

"I am perfectly happy."

"Are you?" Amara tilted her head. "In our years of friendship, you've only spoken of one man with any seriousness. And he's been deceased for twelve years."

Charlie waved her hand dismissively. "The stranger's resemblance to Fayne merely took me aback."

"Perhaps if you spent more time in the company of living gentlemen, you would be less apt to see your dead husband in unexpected places."

"I spend plenty of time in male company," she retorted. "With admirable regularity, I tolerate dance partners who tread upon my toes, supper companions who drone on about themselves, and fortune hunters who think that, as a woman of thirty-four, I should be weeping with gratitude at their offer to deprive me of my freedom."

"What a charming summary of the male sex." Amara's lips twitched. "Yet not all gentlemen are of that ilk. Take your latest hire, for instance."

Charlie was not fooled by her friend's bland tone.

"What about Devlin?" she said warily.

"How is he fitting in with your society?"

Devlin's kiss tickled her memory. During the carriage ride afterward, he'd tried to apologize, but she'd cut him off and told him to forget the incident. The way she meant to.

She made her reply noncommittal. "His presence last night was valuable."

"In terms of the mission?"

Charlie narrowed her eyes. "What other use would I have for him?"

"Devlin is a handsome rake." Amara's gaze had a knowing glint. "From the gossip I've heard, he is well versed at pleasing women and quite equipped to satisfy."

Charlie wrinkled her nose. "Please. Devlin is my employee."

"Having seen you together, I am certain he would like to be more."

"He flirts with all women. It is an affliction of his."

"If so, he has come down with a particularly bad case where you are concerned." Amara leaned closer. "While I understand your aversion to marriage, there is no reason you cannot enjoy yourself from time to time. Especially if you find the right fellow, one who understands discretion."

Is that what I need? Will taking a lover exorcise Sebastian's memory once and for all? If I go to bed with some other man, will I stop seeing my former husband's ghost everywhere?

Once upon a time, she had opened herself up to a man, and she'd learned the error of her ways. She was older now, wiser. She could take care of herself. She did not need a lover to be fulfilled: she had her society and purpose, a circle of trusted friends.

"I have everything I need, my dear." Summoning a smile, Charlie rose. "Now I must be off to another appointment. I will be in touch when I have news."

THREE

"How can I ever thank you, Lady Fayne?" Bernadette Jones breathed.

The brunette sitting across Charlie's desk was American. She was in London pursuing her dream of being a writer. In her late thirties, she was robustly built, plucky, and independent-minded. She worked hard, taking low-paying assignments, scrimping and saving to make ends meet. A year ago, she'd finally landed her dream job as a writer for *The Englishwoman at Home: A Magazine of Fashion and Good Taste*.

From there, things had gone downhill.

Her editor, a weasel by the name of Basil Hargreaves, had started harassing her. It began with unwelcome comments about her appearance and escalated to groping. Then, one evening, he trapped her alone in the office and assaulted her. Luckily, as he was unfastening his trousers, she had the wherewithal to knee him in the groin and escaped.

She'd struggled about returning to work the next day. But she loved her job, and she wasn't about to let some bounder rob her of it. She arrived at the offices...and was given notice. Her fellow writers were sympathetic but too afraid to interfere. She tried making complaints to the owner of the magazine, but he blamed the victim, saying that she'd "enticed" Hargreaves with her "bold manner." Even worse, he refused to write her a reference, without which she could not find another position.

Hargreaves's parting shot to her had been ominous. *You shall never work in Town again, you stupid slut.*

At her wit's end, Bernadette did what any sensible woman would do. She broke down over tea with a friend, sobbing about her predicament. The friend had referred her to Charlotte.

"It was my pleasure to assist, Miss Jones," Charlie said.

The case hadn't been difficult. Men like Hargreaves were often multiple offenders, mostly because they could get away with it. The Angels had simply dug up the skeletons he'd buried.

"I don't know how you convinced those women to come forward." Bernadette's brown eyes glistened. "I wish I could personally thank each of them for writing those letters. For having the courage to share what Hargreaves had done to them. For making me realize that I am not alone."

After the Angels had tracked down Hargreaves's victims, Charlie had spoken to them individually, asking them to help. When they learned they had not been Hargreaves's sole target, they all agreed to tell their stories anonymously. Charlie then tapped a writer for a newspaper—whose mama had been a past client—and the writer published an exposé of "B.H.," the predatory editor for a popular ladies' magazine.

The article created an instant scandal and outrage. Given the male-dominated nature of society, the word of one woman was seldom believed; the stories of a dozen women, however, were difficult to sweep under the carpet. Fearing the court of public opinion, the owner of *The Englishwoman at Home* fired Hargreaves. He begged Bernadette to come back, which she agreed to...for a well-deserved raise and promotion.

"That is the power of sisterhood," Charlie said.

"Well, I am ever so grateful. To them and to you. When my

friend told me you knew investigators who could solve any problem, I wasn't sure they would deliver justice. Please convey my sincerest thanks to these fearless and dedicated gentlemen."

They are not gentlemen, but they are certainly fearless and dedicated.

To protect the identities of the Angels, Charlie had created the fiction that she used a network of male investigators. It never ceased to amaze how readily the clients bought her story. The concept of skilled female detectives seemed beyond the imagination of society, and she used the fact to her advantage.

"I will," Charlie said. "If you encounter further trouble at work, you know where to find me."

"I do not anticipate any problems." Bernadette's eyes held a twinkle. "My employer is allowing me to choose my own assignments, and I have decided to focus on the Great Exhibition. It is opening in less than three weeks, and I will be granted early access so that I may write articles about the latest innovations in home furnishings and fashions."

Designed to showcase the progress of industry in England and around the world, the Great Exhibition was to take place in Hyde Park. According to the papers, it had taken five thousand navvies to erect the sprawling glass-and-steel building designed by famed architect Mr. Paxton. He'd cleverly incorporated nature into his modern "Crystal Palace" by enclosing trees within the structure, including a giant elm dubbed "Prometheus."

Charlie, herself, planned to attend the exhibition.

"I know of no better candidate for the job," she said sincerely.

"Thank you, my lady. I won't take up more of your time."

Bernadette rose, but her gaze lingered on the chair she'd just vacated as if it were a long-lost lover. Charlie didn't blame her. The chair, and the three matching others, were divine, with curved backs, gilt frames, and cerise silk cushions embroidered with pastel birds and flowers.

"Out of professional curiosity, may I ask where you found these exquisite chairs?"

"Rather lovely, aren't they? They were a recent gift from a friend."

The "friend" was an appreciative client whom the Angels had freed from a blackmail scheme.

"She mentioned the upholstery was handwoven in Spital-fields," Charlie added.

"I am partial to handmade fabrics." Bernadette stroked the chair wistfully. "Whilst machine-made goods are all the rage, I prefer things made the old-fashioned way. Subtle imperfections have a charm, I think."

"In people and furnishings."

Bernadette laughed. "You're a sharp one, my lady. Sharp taste too, if you don't mind my saying. This chamber was designed by a woman who knows herself and has the confidence to show it. When it comes to decorating, there is no greater accomplishment than that."

After the client departed, Charlie took a moment to appreciate her domain. For it *was* hers. Whilst Sebastian had left her the townhouse, he'd apparently never lived in it. From the moment Charlie had stepped over the threshold, she'd felt like she was coming home.

She'd never had a home before. Not with Papa, who'd dragged her from one makeshift camp to another. Definitely not with her guardian Sir Patrick Swainey, who'd afforded her nicer lodgings but expected her to pay for them with sexual favors. Not even with Sebastian, who'd given her a place of belonging, only to destroy it.

No, this was her first true home, the symbol of the life she'd designed for herself.

When she'd first arrived, the place had needed work, and she'd spared no expense in transforming her new residence. She had modernized and used the finest materials—Italian marble, Chinese rosewood, and French fabrics—to turn the tired Georgian edifice

into a feminine retreat that suited her lifestyle. The drawing room
had a gallery of statuary featuring Greek goddesses. Her suite
boasted a dressing room that was fit for a queen. Behind the main
building, the carriage house had been transformed into a training
center for the Angels, including a sparring chamber and a room
dubbed "Backstage," since it stored the Angels' costumes and
disguises.

Bernadette was right: Charlie was her own mistress, and her
home reflected that.

As fond as she was of her house, however, what gave her the
greatest satisfaction was the group of four presently trooping into
her study. The Angels did not bother to knock, for this was part of
the ritual. Whilst Charlotte interviewed clients, they observed
through squints from an adjacent room. This was done to preserve
the Angels' anonymity. Not only were investigations best carried
out in secrecy, but these particular ladies also had reputations to
protect.

Leading the way was Lady Olivia McLeod Wodehouse, the
young Duchess of Hadleigh. Livy was a petite brunette with
looped braids and jade-green eyes. Behind her was the former Lady
Glory Cavendish, daughter of the Duke of Ranelagh and
Somerville, who had recently become the wife of martial arts
master and healer Mr. Wei Chen. The glow on Glory's freckled
cheeks and sparkle in her hazel eyes conveyed that newlywed life
was going well indeed. She was accompanied by her constant
companion, Ferdinand the Ferret II, who had a comfortable perch
on the shoulder of her mint-green walking dress.

Trailing Glory was Fiona Garrity Morgan, the Countess of
Hawksmoor. A ravishing redhead, Fi had been experiencing
morning sickness for the past few weeks, and Charlie was relieved
to see that the lady's constitution appeared much improved. Fi's
eyes were as vivid as her cerulean promenade dress, which was cleverly cut to conceal her early pregnancy.

Last, but not least, was Pippa Hunt Cullen. The pretty blonde had shadows under her eyes. This was hardly surprising given that she and her husband had recently welcomed a darling baby girl whom they'd named Gavina.

Fiona let out a gasp, dashing over to the chairs.

"These are even more exquisite up close," Fiona breathed.

"During the interview with Bernadette, all Fi could focus on were the chairs." Livy's grin was teasing. "I doubt she heard a single thing that was said."

"I was paying attention," Fi protested. "We closed the case. What more is there to do, other than toast ourselves with champagne?"

"Count me out." Pippa plopped into one of the seats. "One sip of champagne and I shall be snoring in this excessively comfortable chair."

"Rough night with Gavina, dear?" As Livy was the mama of a toddler, her voice was filled with empathy. "Hadleigh and I didn't sleep for the first month after Esme was born. But don't worry, it gets better."

Glory's russet-brown ringlets swayed as she canted her head. "Can't the mudlarks help look after Gavina?"

Pippa's husband, Timothy Cullen, was a mythical figure in the London underworld. Known as the Prince of Larks, he was the leader of the mudlarks, urchins who'd once made their living scavenging the banks of the Thames. Thanks to his and Pippa's efforts, the mudlarks' compound was now a school that trained the children in various trades. Charlie couldn't imagine a better partner for him than sweet Pippa, who adored the larks and was adored in return.

"They can, and that is the problem." Pippa stifled a yawn. "The larks want to play with her *all the time*. Between them and my papa, who is the dotingest grandpapa who ever lived, Gavina doesn't have a chance to sleep."

Livy furrowed her brow. "I don't think *dotingest* is a word."

An expert in words and anagrams, Livy would know.

"Well, *nurse* is." Fi patted her midsection. "And you, my dearest daughter, are going to be looked after by an army of them."

"How do you know you're going to have a girl?" Glory asked.

"I want my child to be bosom friends with Livy and Pippa's girls," Fi said complacently. "Therefore, I've added the wish for a daughter to my nightly prayers."

Although Charlie didn't think it worked that way, she didn't want to burst Fi's bubble. Watching the young women banter, she felt maternal pride mingled with burgeoning awareness. She had trained the Angels well, building on their natural intelligence, loyalty, and adventurousness. She'd honed their investigative skills and supported them to become the powerful women that they now were.

At the same time, they were...outgrowing her.

During their cases, the Angels had all found love. Initially, Charlie had feared that a husband would interfere with the ladies' ability to carry out investigations. Yet the Angels had wisely chosen mates who not only accepted but cherished them for their independent ways. The husbands knew about and supported their wives' work. When a male presence helped a mission, it wasn't unusual for the men to offer assistance.

Charlie's goal had always been to empower her charges to be the best versions of themselves. To find the kind of happiness that came with choosing one's own destiny.

And my dear Angels have succeeded. Far better than I have. The recognition was bittersweet. *For as content as I am to be my own mistress, am I truly happy?*

"Well, Charlie? What do you think of our plan for the Snelling case?"

She reached for her tea, washing down the unpleasant taste of self-pity. She'd only listened with half an ear as the Angels had strategized their next case, which involved discovering who was behind the supposed haunting of Mrs. Harriett Snelling. She trusted them—knew that her Angels had their wings and could soar without her.

"Follow your instincts," she said. "I trust your judgement."

The Angels beamed at her.

A knock sounded, and Devlin sauntered in as if he owned the place. Despite the fact that he couldn't have gotten much sleep, he looked as fresh as a daisy...the benefit of being a rake accustomed to late nights and debauchery, no doubt. His copper hair gleamed in debonair waves, and the slight hollows under his eyes heightened the vivid sapphire of his irises. The crisp knot of his cravat complemented his blue frock coat and charcoal trousers.

Devlin made a leg. "I hope I am not interrupting anything of import, ladies."

"As our society deals exclusively with vital matters," Charlie said tartly, "I would say that you are."

Devlin's mouth twitched. Undeterred, he strolled to the hearth near Charlie's desk, draping an arm over the mantel. "Any recent developments I should be aware of?"

"We were discussing our newest client," Livy told him. "A widow who believes she is being haunted by a ghost."

"Is she wealthy? If so, my money is on the 'ghost' being a greedy relation."

"There is a nephew," Glory said. "But there are other suspects as well."

"Let me know if I can be of assistance," Devlin replied.

"We were considering posing as servants to investigate her household." Fiona arched her brows. "How is your disguise as a footman, sir?"

"At the risk o' sounding boastful, your ladyship." With startling ease, Devlin switched into the persona of a cocky manservant. "Ain't much I 'aven't done in my previous line o' work. I reckon I can pull it off."

"Splendid." Fi clapped her hands together. "Charlie, if you

could let Mrs. Snelling know to expect a new footman and maids—"

"Unfortunately, I have need of Devlin elsewhere," Charlie said. "The four of you will have to handle the Snelling case on your own."

Livy angled her head. "Are you putting him on another case?"

"It is a private matter. One I am not at liberty to discuss."

Charlie did not like the speculative glint in the Angels' gazes as they looked between her and Devlin. Nor did she approve of Devlin's smirk, which was intended, no doubt, to further the wrong impression. Straightening papers on her desk, she rose.

"If there is nothing else, ladies, I have a professional concern to discuss with Devlin." Her tone was as warm as a Siberian breeze. "It concerns his employment."

The Angels' eyes widened.

"Well, then." Livy cleared her throat, jumping to her feet. "We shan't keep you."

Once the ladies had exited, Devlin came over, facing Charlie over the desk.

"If I didn't know better, I would think I am about to get sacked," he said.

Beneath his insouciance was a darker undertow of anxiety. The rigid tension of his shoulders betrayed him as well. Charlie thought she knew why. When she interviewed him for the job, he'd disclosed a dishonorable act he'd committed during his previous job. But he had redeemed himself, and moreover, taken a bullet for Fiona's husband, the Earl of Hawksmoor, the colleague whom he'd wronged.

Hawksmoor had obviously forgiven Devlin, recommending him for Charlie's position.

In Charlie's book, Devlin had done penance enough.

"I am not firing you," she said. "On the contrary, I was thinking of making your position permanent."

Devlin blinked. "You want to keep me on?"

He looked like a child who had just received a surprise gift. Entirely unlike the urbane rogue he wanted the world to think he was. Something inside her softened.

"You have proved your worth. If you wish to take the position, it is yours. With a caveat."

He quirked an eyebrow.

"You will stop flirting with me."

He cleared his throat. "I, er, beg your pardon?"

While calling a spade a spade was not the most comfortable approach to solving a problem, it was effective.

"You know precisely what I am referring to," she said bluntly. "You are in my employ, and there are boundaries that should not be crossed. Last night being a prime example."

He had the grace to flush.

"Things got out of hand," he muttered. "I pray you will forgive me."

"As I said in the carriage, we both bear some responsibility. But I will be on guard in the future, and you must be too." To indicate that the matter was put to rest, she sat, gesturing for him to do the same. "Now on to business."

Devlin's gaze bounced between her pretty pink chairs. A furrow appeared between his brows. Gingerly, he lowered himself onto an embroidered cushion as if he feared it might collapse beneath his weighty masculinity.

She refrained from rolling her eyes.

"Meet me tonight at the Boar's Head," she said. "Nine o'clock."

At the mention of the popular Covent Garden pub, he cocked his head. "What are we doing there?"

"Hunting," she said succinctly.

FOUR

"Guv wants you to know the cove ain't budged for the last 'alf hour," the street urchin known as Billie whispered. "'E's swilling ale and palavering with 'is cronies. Guv wants to know if you've instructions for 'im."

The "guv" Billie was referring to was Devlin, who was presently inside the Boar's Head monitoring Gilbert Quinton. Charlie was outside, surveilling the back of the pub. Disguised as an old mort selling flowers leftover from the morning market, she sat on the foggy street corner, a rusty lantern illuminating her bucket of wilted blooms. She'd hidden her hair beneath a scraggly wig, blackened some teeth, and used paint to make her complexion sallow and wrinkled. She had proof of her disguise's success: when she called out to toffs to examine her goods, they averted their eyes and hastened along.

For the night's mission, Charlie had enlisted the help of Billie and her sister Lindy. Lindy was watching over the pub's front entrance while Billie acted as the go-between. The girls' mama had, for some inexplicable reason, named them both "Belinda"; to circumvent confusion, they went by their nicknames. Billie was fourteen and the taller of the two. Lindy was a year older, shorter, and wider, with a shock of red hair and freckles. Both preferred male garb, which gave them protection in the streets and allowed them to make quicker getaways.

The girls had crossed Charlie's path a year ago when they attempted to pick her pocket. She didn't know what had surprised the pair more: the fact that they'd found themselves at the end of her pistol, or that, instead of handing them over to the authorities, she'd offered them honest work for honest pay.

She'd given the girls various assignments, and they'd proved so talented and discreet that she now hired them on a regular basis. They drew the line, however, at becoming her salaried employees. The notion of permanent lodgings and meals made them turn up their pert noses. Apparently, they'd once been recruited to a charity school, and the experience had so scarred them that they refused to obey any authority but their own.

Charlie had learned to respect this even as she plotted to win them over. She'd had a few small victories. A fortnight ago, she'd convinced the girls to have a bath, and they'd departed her home squeaky clean, wearing new jackets and trousers and lugging a large hamper of food between them.

Unfortunately, the layer of grime on Billie's narrow face suggested that she hadn't bathed since then. Lindy hadn't looked, or smelled, any better.

One step at a time.

"Well, missus?" Billie scratched her ear, her brown eyes expectant. "Anyfin' you want me to pass on to Lindy or the guv?"

"Tell them both to stay put," Charlie replied in a low voice. "My intuition tells me the target will make a move soon, and we must follow him when he does."

Billie tapped the brim of her battered cap. "I'll give 'em the message."

"Be careful—"

She'd already loped off, her thin figure melting into the drifting fog.

Charlie continued her watch. Moonlight fell through the mist and shattered in luminous shards upon the cobblestone. From her position on the corner, she could see down the length of the street. Connected to the thoroughfare was a maze of smaller passages between the buildings.

The back door of the Boar's Head opened, and her gaze sharpened, taking in the figure that stepped out. Too skinny to be Quinton—just an employee of the pub out to relieve himself. He disappeared into one of the dark offshoots, returning moments later, buttoning his fall as he reentered the premises.

Investigative work, Charlie reflected, required stamina and patience. Most of it was quite tedious. At the start of her journey, she had spent countless hours sifting through Sebastian's belongings. Trying to find any clue that might be related to his death, she had gone through every journal, every map he'd drawn, every item of his personal effects.

Finding nothing of note, she'd tried to learn more about his background. A private sort, he'd rarely spoken about his past and had a subtle yet masterful way of deflecting her curiosity. He was so good at it that she hadn't even realized how little she knew about the man she'd been married to for a year. Even his few friends—Georgios and members of the cartography society—had rather superficial knowledge of him. While he was admired and well-liked, no one seemed to *know* anything significant about him.

She had resorted to hiring investigators. They'd charged her an arm and a leg to tell her what Sebastian had already shared. Because he had been a frail child, his mama had kept him at home. He had grown up on their remote Devonshire estate and didn't attend boarding school like most males of his class. Eventually, his weak constitution improved, and he traveled the world, exploring his passion for cartography. Then he met Charlie.

The facts were simple and shed no light on who Sebastian was. On why he would marry Charlie, why he would have an affair, why he would end up burned beyond recognition in his mistress's bed.

Some of the investigators had preyed upon Charlie's desperate need to know the truth. They'd made up facts to tantalize her, bilk her of her money. One had even tried to "comfort" her with his advances.

Life had taught her repeatedly that she had to count on herself to get things done. There was no reason she couldn't do what these investigators did...and do it better. She had a natural talent for observation, organization, and planning. As for the rest, she sought out experts to train her. She'd learned combat skills from a talented female fighter named Pearl Peabody, and tracking, lock-picking, and other handy techniques from a man named Hawker. Mrs. Peabody and Hawker had served as her housekeeper and butler for years until they fell in love, married, and moved to York-shire. Whilst she missed her friends dearly, Charlie couldn't be happier for them.

Yet at times like these, she realized how alone she was. Everyone around her had found love. And here she was, still haunted by her dead husband.

Even now, she couldn't shake the feeling that she was not alone. That someone was watching her. She twisted her head, scan-ning the clusters of people passing by. A trio of toffs wove by arm-in-arm, belting a drunken ditty. Two whores posed beneath a lamppost, their sateen dresses yellowed by the gaslight. A hawker sold pocket watches of dubious origins displayed on the inside of his jacket.

It was business as usual in Covent Garden, and no one was paying any attention to Charlie, let alone monitoring her. Her imagination was simply running wild. Perhaps Amara was right, and Charlie did need a distraction. After tonight, she would indulge herself—not with a man; that was hardly worth the trou-ble. She would take matters into her own hands and do it better.

The back door of the Boar's Head opened again, and Charlie's focus shifted to the familiar brawny figure stepping into the alleyway.

There you are, Gilbert. What do you have planned this eve?

He cast a furtive glance around, and Charlie kept her head down, pretending to arrange the drooping flowers in her bucket. When she looked up again, he was heading down the street. She waited a heartbeat before going after him. The swirling fog gave her cover, but she stayed back as far as she could whilst keeping him in sight. When he suddenly twisted around, she ducked into an alley to avoid being seen.

Reaching into her skirt pocket, she took out a piece of chalk, drawing a quick *X* on the brick. When Billie found her gone, she would alert the others; Charlie's trail would help the team find her. Hearing Quinton's footsteps start up again, she peered around the wall and saw him head left, down a narrow offshoot between two buildings. She followed, taking a parallel alley to avoid being spotted. She dashed through the fetid darkness, rats scurrying across her path. Reaching the next street, she looked to her right; heartbeats later, Quinton emerged. He glanced at the alley behind him but not in her direction. Then he crossed the street and headed down another alley.

She counted to ten before following.

Sandwiched between tall buildings, this alley seemed darker than the others. Or perhaps the fog had thickened, blocking out the sporadic moonlight. Charlie squinted, her senses on alert as she heard a squeal...of door hinges in need of greasing. The veil of fog suddenly lifted, and she saw the row of back doors ahead before the alley hit a dead end.

Three doors. Quinton could have gone through any of them.

She started with the closest door. Lighting a match, she held it up to the small sign: an apothecary...an unlikely establishment for Quinton to visit this time of night. The next back entrance was to a pawn shop. A possibility. She reached the following door, which was unmarked. Interesting. As were the large, fresh footprints in the dirt.

She tried the handle—locked.

As she reached for the lock picks in her skirt pocket, her nape stirred. She turned, her pulse ticking up as four hulking figures advanced toward her. Even in the shadows, they had menacing miens, those of cutthroats looking for easy prey. She shifted her grip from the picks to her pistol. Since shooting the bounders would draw attention, it would be her last resort. She would try other means first.

"Looking fer company, gents?" She flashed them a smile that flaunted her blackened teeth.

"We ain't interested in an upright, you filthy old hag." The biggest brute, the leader, had mean eyes in a meaner face. "Hand o'er your coin, and be quick about it, if you want to keep what's left o' your gnashers."

Faking a whimper of fear, she gave him her coin bag. If he wasn't a greedy bastard, there ought to be enough in it to satisfy him.

He dumped its contents onto his palm, sneering. "That ain't enough for an evening's entertainment."

Quelle surprise. He is a greedy bastard.

She made her expression placating. "That's all I 'ave—"

"Search 'er, boys." He gave the order to his trio of lackeys. "If you don't find nofin' more, give 'er a beating for wasting me time."

Last resort it is.

Charlie whipped out her pistol and fired. The bullet struck as she'd intended: in the blackguard's shoulder, missing his vital organs. Not a lethal injury if he was smart and heeded her warning.

He howled, grabbing his injured arm. "Bleedin' bitch. You're going to pay fer that."

Unfortunately, intelligence was not a common trait amongst brutes.

"'Ave your way wif 'er, fellows," he bit out. "Then slice 'er goddamned throat."

Grinning with sadistic anticipation, his companions prowled toward her.

Charlie dropped into a crouch, grabbing the knife tucked inside her boot. As one of the bastards made his move, she surged upward, slashing her blade in an arc. He screamed, blood spurting where two fingers had been and the severed digits thunking onto the ground.

The remaining pair attacked as one. The taller one lunged with a knife, and Charlie leapt back, the tip of her foe's steel tearing into the padding of her bodice. Before her attacker could regain his stance, she kicked him in the groin. Groaning, he fell to his knees, and she punched him in the face with the hilt of her blade. He dropped his knife, grabbing at his broken nose as it spouted blood.

She kicked his knife out of reach and faced the other scoundrel, twirling her blade. He charged at her, and she side-stepped, at the same time swiping out with the knife. The brute ran into her weapon, his momentum shoving the steel deep between his ribs. He staggered away, gasping and grabbing at the hilt embedded in his torso.

Suddenly, Charlie was grabbed from behind in a chokehold. A burly arm tightened around her throat, cutting off her air. She struck out, her blows ineffectual against the bulk at her back.

"You ain't no mort," the leader snarled in her ear. "Who the bloody 'ell are you?"

She gasped, grabbing at the arm crushing her windpipe. The man whose fingers she'd cut off came over and backhanded her. As metallic pain flooded her mouth, he ripped off her wig, and golden tresses cascaded down.

"Looks like we found ourselves a pretty piece." Sneering, her captor grabbed a fistful of her hair. "We're going to fuck you dry before we gut you like a fish."

She clawed at the tightening noose of his arm, but he was stronger. Even as she fought, the lack of air drained her strength. Her vision wavered and dimmed at the edges as she felt the other bastard tearing at her skirts. Darkness sucked her into its abyss, her body heavy and numb, and she no longer felt anything—

A shout sounded. A shadow bolted in front of her blurry eyes. The pressure suddenly left her throat, but there was nothing to hold her up.

As she tumbled, she glimpsed bronze stars flashing in the darkness.

FIVE

K *eep moving. Act confident. Do not let them see your fear.*
Charlie repeated the mantra as she navigated the dark labyrinth of Marseille. In her haste to escape her guardian, she'd left behind her map and couldn't find the docks she was looking for. After several turns, she ended up in an abandoned alley that ran into a brick wall. She turned around...and found her path barricaded.

Sailors, three of them. On ship leave and soused.

"Lost, luv?" The wiry fellow in the middle spoke with a Cockney accent.

Panic prickled her neck at the opportunistic glint in his eyes, but she maintained a calm demeanor. In her twenty-one years, she'd dealt with her share of predators.

"Not at all," she said glibly. "I am meeting some friends at the restaurant around the corner. They are waiting, so if you'll excuse me..."

She made to move past them, her panic turning to terror when the largest sailor closed a beefy hand around her arm, yanking her so that her back hit his front.

"No need to hurry off, *chérie*." His French accent oozed into her ear, and she cringed when he ground his aroused member against her. "We'll give you all the company you need."

One of the others sandwiched her against his comrade. She acted on instinct, jerking her knee up into his groin. He doubled over, but the bastard behind her kept her restrained. When he gagged her with his hand, she bit him. The brute swore, tearing his hand away, and she screamed for help.

The third assailant slapped her. Pain stunned her senses. Through the ringing in her ears, she heard a new voice.

"Release the lady," the deep tones commanded.

Dimness masked the newcomer's face, but his silhouetted figure was tall, lean, and powerfully built. His wide shoulders stretched his linen shirt, and his trousered legs bulged with sinew.

"*Mêle-toi de tes affaires*," the French sailor spat.

In a lethal blur, the stranger moved. He beat the sailors to a pulp, and they stumbled off whimpering, their tails between their legs. Then he came to her, stepping into the moonlight...and her heart quickened. It was as if something within her came alive. Recognition hummed through every fiber of her being. Her blood rushed and her heart thumped madly against her ribs.

It wasn't just that this man was beautiful, which he most definitely was. His face deserved to be immortalized by a sculptor, the symmetry of his bones lovingly chiseled by nature. No stone, however, could capture his raw male energy. His thick, dark hair gleamed with health, the open vee of his collar revealing his corded throat. Normally, such outrageous masculinity would put her on edge. But the stranger did not seem aggressive. Rather, he looked...concerned?

"Clearly, the blackguards picked the wrong lady to meddle with." He smiled slowly, the hard line of his mouth relaxing into a sensual curve. "Are you all right, miss?"

Transfixed, she managed a nod. "I am, sir. You have my gratitude—"

"It was a trifling matter and my honor to assist." He said it like he meant it. Then he bowed. "Apologies, I have forgotten my manners. Sebastian Courtenay, Marquess of Fayne, at your service."

An English lord. With the smile of a poet and battle prowess of a knight.

"Pleased to make your acquaintance, my lord." She hoped her curtsy would pass muster. "I am Charlotte Danvers. My papa was the late Earl of Bembridge. He..." She chewed on her lip, uncertain if she should share how alone in the world she was. "He, um, passed away last year."

"Condolences, my lady." In the silvery light, the color of Fayne's eyes was difficult to discern, but his sincerity could not be mistaken. "I presume you are here with friends, then, and have gotten separated. May I escort you to your destination?"

How would Fayne react if she told him that her only "friend" in the world was her guardian, Sir Patrick Swainey, whose lecherous advances had led to her current flit? What would the marquess say if she shared that she'd laced Swainey's port with a sedative this eve and run away with a valise of essentials and the money she'd managed to filch from him? That her plan was to buy passage on a ship to somewhere, anywhere, and start a new life working as a governess or secretary?

No man has ever proved worthy of your trust. What makes you think Fayne will be different?

"I...I am not certain," she said haltingly.

"Not certain if you want my assistance? Or not certain if you can trust me?"

Surprised by his acuity, she admitted, "Both."

"Do you like seafood?"

She blinked at the non sequitur. "Um, yes. I do."

"There is a bistro on the next block that serves an excellent *bouillabaisse.*" He held out his arm. "Will you allow me to take you to supper whilst you come to a decision?"

After a moment's hesitation, she took his arm. That evening, over *bouillabaisse* (which was indeed delectable), she proceeded to do something she'd never done before: she confided her secrets. Fayne's response was equally novel, for he listened. Afterward, he insisted on situating her in a hotel and hiring one of the maids to attend to her. The next day, he took her to see her guardian, whose face had reddened with rage.

"How dare you question my honor." Clearly, the sedative hadn't worn off completely, for Swainey's words were slurred. "Taking the word of a lying, scheming little slut."

Fayne requested that Charlotte wait in the carriage. When he emerged a quarter hour later, he possessed a document signed by Swainey relinquishing his guardianship. She took the precious proof of her freedom, and as she did so, noticed Fayne's bruised knuckles. Her throat tight, she impulsively took his hand, running her fingertips lightly over the damaged skin.

He didn't flinch, his eyes a brilliant night sky riddled with stars.

"How can I repay you for what you've done, my lord?" she'd whispered.

"Have lunch with me."

"Lunch?" she'd said stupidly.

"Otherwise known as the meal between breakfast and supper."

Seeing the smile lurking in his eyes, she couldn't help but laugh.

"You've given me back my freedom. And all you want in return is lunch?"

"That isn't all I want, my lady."

The golden blaze around his pupils stole her breath. His hand engulfed hers in a warm, callused grip. His touch was both foreign and familiar, and it took her a moment to recognize what it felt like.

Home.

The slow, wicked curving of his mouth made her heart hammer and belly flutter. Suddenly, she felt anything *but* safe, and her soul, that of an adventurer's daughter, shivered in anticipation of discovery.

His voice was husky with promise. "It is merely a place to start."

Six

"Do you want to tell me what happened back there?"
Devlin said.

Charlie, who'd been staring blindly out the carriage
window, turned her gaze to him. He occupied the opposite bench.
With his cap and wig removed, his curls gleamed in the dim light
of the carriage lamp. His countenance was strangely mutinous.

"I told you," she replied. "I was beset by scoundrels who
caught me unawares, and I took care of them."

She wasn't about to share the ignominious truth: she'd fainted,
and someone had come to her aid. Even worse, she had a crazed
notion that that someone was her dead husband. When she'd
recovered from her brief swoon, incapacitated cutthroats had
littered the alleyway. Her rescuer, however, was nowhere in sight.

*It was just a Good Samaritan. But why did he leave before I
could thank him?*

Her temples throbbed. She told herself not to think about it.
To focus on the job.

"Unfortunately, I lost Quinton," she said.

"Devil take Quinton."

Devlin's vehemence surprised her. He usually gave the impression that little could disturb his devil-may-care equilibrium. Yet now he was glaring at her.

She frowned. "Why are you angry?"

"I'll give you three guesses, Madam Employer."

At his unmistakable sarcasm, her temper flared.

"I do not play guessing games, Devlin."

"Fine. You took off. Into an alley full of brutes without reinforcements. Without alerting"—his voice grew louder as he jabbed a finger at his chest—"*me*."

"Whilst I do not answer to you, I did leave a trail of chalk," she reminded him.

He shook his head. "You literally chalked your well-being up to a few ephemeral marks. Marks that could be erased by the fog or brushed off by the sleeve of any passer-by."

"The Angels and I have been using that system for years. It is tried and true."

"You need a better system."

"If you do not like the way I run things, you are welcome to leave my society."

"Goddammit, Charlie. I do not want to leave." He raked a hand through his hair. "I want you to take better care of yourself."

"Must I remind you that you are in my employ and not vice versa." She narrowed her eyes. "You are not my keeper, Devlin."

"What if I wish to be?"

She stilled. "I beg your pardon?"

"That came out wrong. What I meant to say is that I would like to be more than your employee."

In a blink, he moved to her side of the carriage, taking one of her hands.

She was so stunned she didn't stop him.

"We make a good team, you and I." His gaze was earnest, his voice devoid of its usual irony. "Why should that not extend into our private affairs? You must know that I am attracted to you. For some time now, I have wanted to know you as a woman. As a lover."

She pulled her hand free. "Devlin—"

"At least hear me out before you sack me," he said with a lopsided smile. "Having worked for you these past months, I would be an idiot not to realize that you are a woman who values her independence. I admire that about you, Charlie, and would not dream of undermining your freedom. At the same time, we are both unattached, consenting adults. If we play by agreed upon rules, there is no reason we cannot have some harmless fun, is there?"

Harmless fun. The words might have been uttered in a foreign language. Except for those first blissful months with Sebastian, she'd never been a playful sort.

As if sensing an opening, Devlin pressed on. "As your reputation is above reproach, I know you conduct your private life with discretion. I give you my word that your honor is safe with me."

Charlie was not surprised that he assumed she carried on discreet affairs. After all, taking a lover was a perk of being a widow. She'd tried it once, years ago, and found it wasn't worth the bother. Moreover, a man was hardly a prerequisite for pleasure (and sometimes he was an impediment).

"I have not always been, ahem, as prudent in safeguarding my own reputation." Evidently mistaking her silence for doubt, Devlin looked slightly abashed. "But I promise you that I can—and will be—circumspect when it comes to you."

As Charlie made it a policy to research the backgrounds of all who worked for her, she knew the gossip about Devlin's rakish escapades. He was a regular guest at house parties like the Rigbys', and his appetites were rather legendary. She did not judge him for his predilections. In fact, his experience had uniquely qualified him for a position in her society. Thus far, she had no complaints about how he carried out his assignments. He was loyal, dependable, and knew how to keep his mouth shut: rare qualities in a man.

"I do not doubt your discretion," she said. "But I am not interested in an affair."

"Even if there were no strings attached?" There was a boyish charm to his persistence, the way his blue eyes were both guileless and wicked. "I would ask nothing of you, my sweet. No commitments, no expectations. Just the pleasure of your company."

He took her hand, then turned it gently as he raised it. When he brushed his lips against the tender underside of her wrist, she felt that quickening again in her belly. Then he tucked her hand back onto her lap with a self-assuredness that spoke volumes about his skill as a lover. He was a man who knew when to push and how far.

She shook off the sensual net he cast. "Look elsewhere for a lover, Devlin. Our relationship will remain a professional one."

"Ah. You admit we do have a relationship."

At his incorrigible grin, she had to press her lips together to prevent them from twitching.

"We won't for long if we keep failing on our missions," she said severely.

"Failure is not in my vocabulary." He gave her a measuring look. "If I find out what Quinton is up to, will you consider having an affair with me?"

"When *we* discover the nature of Quinton's activities, the answer to your question will still be no." Sighing, Charlie decided honesty was, as usual, the best policy. "Don't ruin this, Devlin. I have grown to respect you as a colleague. Let us not muddy the waters with romantic nonsense."

"Who said anything about romance? I just want to go to bed with you."

At her narrowed gaze, Devlin held up his hands.

"All right, you win. No more talk of an affair...for now."

"Forever," she corrected.

"In the meantime," he said smoothly, "I suppose we could

concentrate on something else. Such as what I learned about Quinton this eve."

She arched a brow and waited.

"When Quinton left, I headed after him, but first I had a quick rendezvous with Billie and Lindy. I told them to keep eavesdropping in the tavern in case Quinton's cronies had any useful information to share."

"And?"

"And I was right," he said with satisfaction. "Before you and I headed off, Billie told me what she'd heard. Apparently, Quinton's been leaving the pub early for the last month, and his cronies were speculating where he was off to. One of the fellows mentioned that he'd spotted Quinton with 'a fair rose near the Strand.' Claimed Quinton had his arms around the woman, a pretty redhead with doe-like eyes."

"A mistress, likely." Charlie ached for Amara. "I wonder if it was the same woman who was with him at the Rigbys'. The blonde, who was likely wearing a wig. Did Billie pick up anything else about her?"

"Just that this rose has, ahem, generous twin assets."

Charlie cast her eyes heavenward. "Red hair, dark eyes, and a large bosom—not much to go on. But I suppose you could start by canvassing the Strand and see if anyone saw Quinton and this woman."

"I am at your disposal. Will you be accompanying me?"

Charlie shook her head, already dreading the task ahead. "I will be apprising Amara of our discovery."

"Right."

"After that, I have a new client to interview, followed by social calls all afternoon." She sighed. "This evening, I am expected to make an appearance at the Kendall Ball."

"Bloody hell, I'd forgotten it was tonight. I'd rather have a tooth drawn." Devlin's antipathy matched her own. "Having seen more of Lord and Lady Kendall than I ever wished to see at the Rigbys', how am I supposed to endure their moral rectitude?"

"With discretion," Charlie reminded him. "You cannot let on that we were there. Doing so would compromise the case and our society."

He slid her a look. "If I am on my best behavior tonight, will you reward me with a dance?"

She couldn't help but smile at his roguish maneuver.

"Find me the fair rose, Devlin," she said. "And I shall think about it."

SEVEN

"Christ, yes, Lottie," he growled. "Take my cock deeper."

She whimpered, gripping the coverlet, digging her knees into the mattress to brace herself for her husband's driving cock. This was the first time he'd taken her from behind, and she loved it. Loved the primal feeling of being possessed by the man she loved. His muscular hips slapped her bottom in a disciplined rhythm, the erotic sound unraveling her inhibitions.

"You're so deep this way." She sounded tipsy. Felt as giddy as if she'd imbibed a bottle of champagne.

"I want to be deeper. I want all of this pretty quim," he rasped. "All of you."

She moaned as he made good on his word, thrusting inside. So deeply she felt him at her center, so powerfully that he touched her heart. Still, he pounded into her with unrelenting force. Her desire turned into desperation, need clawing at her insides.

"I bloody *love* how wet you get," he gritted out. "Like silk around my cock."

At first, she'd been shocked by his bedchamber talk, but she'd grown to adore his harsh tone and filthy words. When they made love, he shed the skin of a gentleman, and she reveled in his rawness. In the realness of who he was when they were skin to skin.

Not a marquess, not a lord, but a man. Her mate.

It untethered her from her fears and insecurities, and she was free to soar toward the dazzling pleasure. She could feel how wet she was, hear the slick sounds as he sheathed his thick length inside her, stretching her to her very limits.

But it wasn't enough for him.

"Give me more," he said.

He arched over her. The hairy ridges of his chest abraded her spine, making her arch. When he gently fisted his hand in her hair, pulling her ear to his lips, she shivered with feral delight.

"The next time you come, Lottie"—his promise scorched the rim of her ear—"I am going to make you not only drench my cock but the bleeding *sheets*."

She moaned as he made good on his vow.

Charlie came awake, her heart pounding.

She wasn't disoriented. Her constant travels as a girl had given her an uncanny ability to instantly recognize her surroundings. Moreover, every inch of this airy, high-ceilinged bedchamber bore her personal stamp. She'd selected everything from the mahogany half-tester bed she was lying in to the rose velvet settee in the sitting area.

The reason her heart was banging like a fist in her chest was because she'd had another erotic dream. About Sebastian, damn his eyes. Always about him.

Perhaps if he'd cocked up his toes in his dotage, he wouldn't be forever immortalized in her memory as some virile, insatiable sex god. But, oh no, Sebastian could never do anything like a regular husband. He had to die in his prime in a fiery death whilst tupping his mistress.

I hope it was worth it.

Yet even anger failed to quell the energy pulsing through Charlie. She needed to take care of herself. She kept a box in her wardrobe that contained equipment to aid her self-pleasuring, but she was too close to the edge to require more than her own touch.

Closing her eyes, she fell back into her head. Into that place where dark desires ruled the imagination. When the fantasy that emerged starred her husband, she was too needy to fight it. At least he was good for something. Her hands became his, roving under silk to find her breasts. He knew just how to touch her, rubbing the velvety-hard tips, making them throb between the pinch of his finger and thumb.

"You've the prettiest tits," he murmured. "I could worship them all day."

He took his time and palmed her breasts in his big, rough hands. He kissed the full curves, working his way toward the straining peaks. When he finally put his mouth on her nipple, she whimpered with delight. His tongue did wet, magical things. He went back and forth, sometimes sucking, sometimes blowing, always building her pleasure until she was wild with want.

Then he gave her more.

His tongue traced a winding path down her body, over the bumps of her ribs, the dip of her belly. She shivered when he kissed the crease of her thigh. Then, with a rough movement that set fire to her blood, he spread her legs.

"Christ, look at you." Embers of lust blazed in his eyes, his nostrils flaring. "I won't ever get my fill of this sweet pussy. I don't know if I ought to fuck you or eat you first. Lucky bastard that I am, I don't have to choose."

Spreading her with his thumbs, he lowered his head. She moaned as he licked his way up her slit. He found her pearl, his tongue working it with expert strokes, her spine bowing as the wet, hot friction sent fire streaking up her legs. The low, hungry sounds he made in his throat fanned the flames, and when he slid two fingers inside her, pumping as he licked, a climax began to quake.

Sebastian lifted his head, his smoldering eyes holding hers.

"I love you, Lottie," he said fiercely. "You and only you. Now and forever."

A moan lodged in Charlie's throat as she trembled with release.

Afterward, as her heartbeat steadied, she felt a tear slide down her cheek. The lust had subsided, leaving too much awareness in its wake.

Of the power the past still held over her. Of her weakness. Of her stupid, traitorous longings.

This has to stop. I have to let go of Sebastian once and for all.

And she knew what she had to do.

EIGHT

When Charlie arrived at the Kendall residence that evening, the ball was in full swing. Crystal chandeliers cast sparkling light over guests dressed to the nines. The dance floor was packed as the orchestra launched into a lively polka. The bright, swirling skirts and humid air laden with perfume, powder, and sweat created an ambience that Charlie found suffocating.

"Lady Fayne, there you are," a voice trilled. "Have you been hiding from us?"

Why, yes, as a matter of fact.

As Lady Kitty Kendall and Lady Agatha Price cornered her, Charlie put on the smile she'd perfected in front of a looking glass.

"Good evening, ladies," she replied.

She exchanged air kisses with them. Lady Kendall was rail-thin, with inky hair and painted-on eyebrows. Lady Price's sandy-brown ringlets framed her round face, her mouth puckered as if she were perpetually sucking on a lemon.

"May I congratulate you on this splendid event, Lady Kendall?" Charlie said. "It is certain to be the talk of the town."

Lady Kendall's close-set eyes glittered with triumph. "Thank you, my dear Lady Fayne. Given your impeccable taste, I take your compliment to heart. However..."

Here it comes...

"I am quite distraught at the behavior of a certain aging roué."

Lady Kendall cast an arch look in the direction of the champagne fountain, and with an inward sigh, Charlie looked over as well. The target of Lady Kendall's vitriol this eve was Sir Hewitt Lancaster. He was in his sixties, a heavyset fellow with craggy features and bushy grey eyebrows. A wealthy merchant, he had a reputation for being a drunkard and a fool but was quite harmless.

Which was more than Charlie could say about the ladies gossiping about him.

"He looks to be enjoying himself," she said neutrally.

"He's been by the fountain all evening," Lady Kendall announced. "One of my footmen says he's had the equivalent of three bottles of champagne."

"Such immoderation," Lady Price agreed. "An appalling display of excessive appetite."

"His behavior at the buffet table was equally vulgar." Lady Kendall's eyes lit with spite. "I suppose one cannot expect more of a fellow whose fortune comes from trade."

As the ladies sniggered behind their fans, Charlie bit her tongue. In her quest to become a respectable lady, she'd mastered the necessary evil of small talk, but she could never get used to the maliciousness and hypocrisy. For these two to accuse Sir Lancaster of displaying an excessive appetite was beyond galling, given their own public carnal indulgences.

"Oh, there is Mrs. Rigby. Do come join us," Lady Kendall called.

Isadora Rigby, wearing a violet gown that flattered her brunette coloring and slender form, glided over. She was an attractive woman with a triangular face and green eyes.

"Lady Fayne, have you met our dear friend Isadora Rigby?" Lady Kendall gushed.

The vision of Ophelia floated through Charlie's head.

"Charmed," she murmured.

Mrs. Rigby inclined her head, the plume in her coiffure bobbing gracefully. "It is a pleasure to make your acquaintance, my lady."

"We were just talking about Sir Lancaster," Lady Price said with eager glee. "Have you seen such intemperance, Mrs. Rigby?"

Mrs. Rigby flicked her eyes in his direction, looking bored. "Surely we can entertain ourselves with something more interesting than a man making a pig of himself?"

The Ladies Kendall and Price giggled.

"Lady Fayne, we've been looking for you!"

Charlie turned to see Livy and Fiona waving at her from beneath a towering palm.

Thank heavens. My Angels have come to the rescue again.

"Please excuse me," she murmured. "I have some pressing matters to discuss with my charity."

"Charity must come first of course," Lady Kendall said piously.

Charlie escaped and joined Livy, Fiona, and their respective spouses, the Duke of Hadleigh and the Earl of Hawksmoor. While both men were tall, dark-haired, and handsome, Fi's earl had a scholarly mien whilst Livy's duke exuded a jaded air, a remnant of his wild and tragic youth. When Hadleigh looked at his duchess, however, his eyes softened, and there was no mistaking the healing power of their love.

"You look resplendent this evening, Charlie," Fi said.

Given that Fi looked like a princess in peach satin, her flame-red hair arranged in a pearl-studded coronet, Charlie accepted the compliment with a smile.

"As do both of you, my dears." She included Livy, who exuded freshness in a buttercup-yellow gown with frothy skirts. "I have Mrs. Q to thank for my fine looks this eve."

Tonight had seemed the perfect occasion to debut the wine-colored taffeta Amara had made for her. The dress had little in the way of ornamentation, the daring cut drawing the eye to Charlie's bare shoulders and cinched waist. The full skirts were overlaid with sensual black netting, and she had completed the ensemble with black gloves and a simple black ribbon and cameo tied around her neck.

"Your gown, while lovely, does not explain your exceptionally fine looks." Tilting her head, Livy studied Charlie with acute eyes. "Fi is right. You have an extra...sparkle. Or something."

Years of practice allowed Charlie to control her blush. Wryly, she supposed that she ought to congratulate herself on a job well done. She'd trained the Angels so well in the art of detection that now she could get away with nothing.

Nonetheless, she wasn't about to divulge the reason why she'd taken extra care with her appearance. Why she'd had Jenny, her lady's maid, artfully apply cosmetics to highlight the shade of her eyes and fullness of her lips. Why she'd downed a flute of champagne and yet her nerves still felt shot.

Seducing a gentleman for the first time in years was a private matter, after all.

"A sparkle or something." His dark-blue eyes crinkling with amusement, Hadleigh bent and chucked his wife under the chin. "You are quite the poet, little queen."

"I was going to say *glow*." Livy wrinkled her nose at him. "But that can imply a certain female condition, if you know what I mean."

"*I* know what you mean," Fi said with feeling.

"The queasiness hasn't come back, has it, dear?" Livy asked.

"I am perfectly well." Fi slanted an impish glance at her husband. "Hawk is too."

The earl sighed while the Angels giggled and Hadleigh tried manfully to hide a smile. Fi had shared with their intimate circle that Hawksmoor was the most doting of husbands during her pregnancy. He was so attuned, in fact, that he'd started sharing some of her symptoms.

"What is the problem then?" Livy asked.

"Now that I'm back to my normal self, I have the appetite of a horse. I want to eat everything in sight. And I have the strangest cravings."

"She wanted pickles and a Gunter's praline ice," Hawksmoor muttered. "At two in the morning."

"You were such a hero to have it fetched for me."

Fi batted her eyelashes at her earl, whose wry expression didn't quite hide the fact that he was besotted with her.

The way Sebastian once was with me.

Charlie swatted away the thought like it was a pesky insect. The fact that she was being plagued by memories solidified the necessity of her purpose. To let go of the past, she had to live fully in the present. She was not ashamed to admit that she was a hot-blooded woman who had needs. Her paucity of bedpartners since Sebastian was likely the cause of her unwelcome fixation on him. It explained why she was seeing him everywhere, dreaming of him, obsessing over him.

In other words, she was randy, and all that energy was being channeled into the past instead of where it should be focused: on finding a living, breathing male who could satisfy her appetites.

As if Fate agreed with her assessment, Devlin joined the group.

"Ladies, gentlemen." He made an elegant leg. "Enjoying your evening?"

As the others made chitchat, Charlie objectively admired his good looks. The chandeliers illuminated the copper sheen of his hair. His chiseled features looked rested, his jaw freshly shaven above his dark silk cravat. His forest-green tailcoat molded to his broad shoulders, his waistcoat to his trim torso, and his pantaloons looked as if they'd been painted onto his muscular legs.

He was an attractive fellow. Moreover, he was experienced and available.

Which made him perfectly suited to her purpose.

His blue eyes met hers. "You are in exceptionally fine looks, Lady Fayne."

"You are too kind, sir. You look rather well yourself."

His gaze widened slightly at her praise. Or perhaps it was the fact that she smiled at him, giving a subtle wave of her fan as she did so. Really, he oughtn't look so surprised: she was fully capable of flirting, even if she seldom bothered.

"Fi, Glory, and I have made some progress on our, um"—Livy glanced around, making sure no one was eavesdropping—"charity case. Now that Mr. Devlin is here as well, perhaps we ought to find a quiet corner to discuss it?"

"I think Charlie may have other plans this eve," Fi murmured.

Seeing the perceptive glint in the redhead's eyes, Charlie suppressed a sigh.

I really did teach them too well.

"Which is just as well, because I would love to dance." Fi aimed a frolicsome smile at her spouse. "And my favorite dance partner appears to be available."

Hawksmoor gallantly offered her his arm. "For you, my dear, always."

The pair headed for the dance floor. Livy and Hadleigh followed suit, Livy casting a speculative glance backward.

Alone with Devlin, Charlie told herself it was now or never.

"Would you care to dance, my lady?" Devlin asked.

"Not particularly."

His face fell.

"I would, however, like a moment with you in private." She lowered her voice. "Meet me in the orangery."

She walked off, smiling as she felt Devlin's surprised stare upon her.

Having attended other affairs at the Kendalls' stately townhome, Charlie knew her way to the orangery. As she'd hoped, the waltz was keeping the guests occupied, and the lush, glass-walled room was empty. In the candlelight, the orangery had a magical feel, the greenery arranged into winding walks and cozy nooks that seemed an extension of the dark garden beyond the windows. Notes of jasmine and citrus hung in the sultry air.

Charlie selected a niche by the window with a wicker settee. Surrounded by a hedge of lemon trees, the space offered privacy and intimacy, which she would need whilst making her proposition to Devlin. Recognizing his footsteps against the tile floor, she felt a flutter in her chest and chastised herself for being silly.

She was no virgin in her first blushes. She was a widow of thirty-four, and one who had witnessed more than her fair share of depravity. Devlin, furthermore, was an experienced rake. He had made the first move; he was hardly going to judge her for taking him up on it. They were both consenting adults with something to offer the other.

She straightened her shoulders as Devlin rounded the hedge and entered the nook.

"Cozy place you've found," he remarked.

While his tone was casual, curiosity glinted in his eyes.

"I thought it suited the nature of what I wished to discuss." Striving to make her manner more seductive and less businesslike, she patted the cushion beside her. "Why don't you have a seat?"

Devlin did not have to be asked twice. He settled next to her, his leg brushing her skirts. His cologne, a blend of spices, was pleasing.

"What are we discussing? Business or could it possibly be..." His tone took on a husky edge. "Pleasure?"

The man caught on fast. It was one of the reasons she'd hired him.

"That depends."

He cocked a brow. "On?"

Taking a breath, she went for it. "On how discreet you can be."

His gaze grew heavy-lidded but not before she saw the flash of triumph there.

"Darling," he drawled. "You have but scratched the surface of my discretion."

She leaned closer. "What about your ability to keep your emotions out of an affair? The last thing I want is complications."

"I am so uncomplicated that one might call me simple." He bent his head toward her, so close that she could see the moonlight reflected in his eyes. "As for feelings, who needs them, I say."

"And we must both promise that this will not affect how we perform in our professional capacities."

"Sweeting, my performance shall exceed anything you've known."

"I mean it," she said seriously. "I value you as a colleague. I don't want to compromise our working relationship over this."

"If it really bothers you, I'll quit."

She knitted her brows. "You would leave my society in order to sleep with me?"

"There are numerous positions available for a fellow with my particular set of skills." He ran a fingertip along her jaw. "However, there is only one you. And, sweeting, the positions we could try..."

Intrigued by the dark seduction in his eyes, she tilted her head back.

Devlin's kiss was as she remembered: smooth and skilled, objectively delightful. He took his time, and she appreciated it. Appreciated the courtly pressure of his lips, the practiced glide of his tongue. Yet something was missing, she was vexed to realize. That spark, that feeling of ungovernable hunger that Sebastian's kiss had always unleashed in her. Perhaps Devlin was just warming up, and she needed to move things along.

Boldly, she slid her fingers into his hair, pulling him closer. He swept his tongue into her mouth, tasting her with undeniable finesse. He smoothed a palm down her neck, her shoulder, cupping her breast. Yet her heart didn't race, and she didn't feel as if she'd fly from her own skin if she didn't get more.

Instead, she was...thinking.

Dash it all. This is Sebastian's fault. What will it take for me to be free of him—

The smashing glass jolted her from her thoughts.

An instant later, she was pushed to the floor, Devlin on top of her.

"Stay down." His gaze was focused and alert. "Until I find out what's happening."

"I know what happened."

Heart thudding, she pointed, and Devlin twisted his head to look behind him. A large rock sat against the pot of a lemon tree, a comet of glass bits in its wake.

Devlin lowered his brows. "Who the devil would throw a rock through the window?"

The answer crashed into Charlie's head. It shattered her denial, reducing it to shards smaller than those of the broken window. As the truth blazed, she realized that she had always known.

NINE

It was nearing one in the afternoon, and the man sitting on a bench upon the grassy knoll knew the nearby ships, naval and merchant alike, were waiting. Biding their time, just like he was. He'd come every day for the last three days, hoping for a sign. He told himself that if she did not come, she had forgotten him— and he would leave things be. He would continue protecting her from the shadows, staying where he belonged.

Staying away from her was a wise strategy. The right one.

The one his mentor had told him in no uncertain terms that he must abide by.

Unfortunately, when it came to her, he'd been neither wise nor right in his actions. Nor was he particularly good at following rules. Which was probably why he'd ended up on the path he was on.

The ships' ochre sails formed an autumnal forest as they sat anchored in the Thames, the telescopes of their navigators trained upon the bright-red ball hovering above the Royal Observatory. He'd been seventeen the first time he saw the time ball. Seventeen and so miserable that he'd almost changed his mind about coming, but the family's kindly gardener, knowing his interests in maps and ships, had urged him not to miss the opportunity.

It had turned out to be the best day of his young life.

Even now, he felt anticipation build inside him as the ball rose halfway up the thin steel mast the way it always did five minutes before the hour. In another three, the ball would rise all the way to the top. Then, at precisely one o'clock, the ball would drop, verifying the time, an essential measurement that allowed navigators to chart their courses.

It was the reliability that captivated him. The idea that no matter how lost one was, how forsaken, one need only find the red ball to right one's path. Too bad the rest of life didn't work that way.

The ball climbed to the pinnacle. It was as exposed as he was, quivering in readiness for the fall. In those anxious moments, he doubted everything. All the choices he'd made, the decisions that brought him to where he was now, sitting alone atop a hill, hoping for something he had no right to hope for. For something he'd destroyed. For something he'd longed for every moment, every second of too many years.

The ball dropped, and his hopes plummeted with it.

A couple joined him on the knoll in time to catch the ball's descent. Husband and wife, he guessed, by the way the gentleman placed a hand on the small of the lady's back. The domesticity of the gesture pierced him with bittersweet yearning. What he wouldn't give for the right to stand in the light with his beloved, to have her lean against him with trust in her eyes, a smile on her lips. Before the couple left, they nodded politely in his direction, and he nodded back, careful to keep the brim of his hat angled low, his face obscured. A habit in his line of work.

A new presence stirred his nape. The shadow that fell upon him felt like a caress. He shot to his feet, turning.

His heart thundered as he faced her. It was like staring into the sun, a dazzlingly painful sensation, one that he could never grow accustomed to, not even if he lived to be a hundred. Charlotte Elizabeth Anne Danvers Courtenay was the most beautiful woman he'd ever laid eyes upon, and nothing would change that. Not years, not distance, not even mistakes beyond redemption. Nothing could change a beauty that ran as deep as hers, that was rooted in intelligence, passion, and indomitable pluck.

Only a fool would let such a woman go. Even if the fool had reasons for doing so.

Reasons that remain.

It was difficult to hold on to his convictions as she regarded him with grey eyes that starred in his every fantasy. Unsurprisingly, they weren't smoky with desire the way he'd imagined them but cold as steel. How the goddess Athena's eyes might look before a battle. Yet it was her indifference that chilled him to the marrow. The Charlotte he knew was a woman of strong feeling, who never pulled her emotional punches, who'd fought and fucked and loved him with everything that she was. He expected a goddess's wrath at being betrayed. God knew he deserved that from her.

Instead, she gave him...nothing. Ashes instead of fire.

And it pulverized his last stubborn pebble of hope.

"What a surprise." She sounded almost bored. "Hello, husband."

Ten

He's alive. Sebastian is alive. I knew he wasn't dead.

For an instant, her heart felt like it might burst from her chest in some ridiculous parody of joy. Reality slapped the traitorous organ back into its cage, locking it inside for its own good.

Splendid. He's alive. That means I can bloody murder him.

Despite her inner turmoil, Charlie managed to maintain her composure. She refused to give Sebastian the satisfaction of knowing that he affected her—that he had any power over her. For his own reasons, he'd seen fit to abandon his naïve young bride after a year of marriage. Left her to grieve under the most heinous of circumstances. Now he had returned, again for his own reasons, and he would not find that same girl any longer.

That girl was dead. The woman who stood in her place had been through too much to believe that his return had anything to do with her. What Charlie needed to discover was why he'd come back...and how to minimize the damage. If her heart was thrashing against her ribs, her skin prickling with goosebumps, and her lungs straining for breath, she told herself it was because of shock.

It's just like Sebastian to do as he wishes. Fake his death one moment, return twelve years later. Selfish bastard.

She harnessed her anger and used its power to keep herself in check.

Dispassionately, she allowed her gaze to roam over Sebastian. Taking his measure not as a wife but as a seasoned investigator. She concluded, with no little irritation, that the years had been more than kind to him; they'd doted upon the scoundrel. He would be thirty-five now, and whatever he'd been up to these last dozen years had honed his outsized masculinity, hardening his youthful vitality and forging it into something more dangerously attractive.

Beneath the brim of his hat, she glimpsed a scar on his right temple. The pale line said that he had wrestled death and emerged victorious. There were other new lines, too: fanning his eyes, bracketing his mouth. His face was leaner and his jaw as strong and stubborn as ever. He'd packed on some muscle, if the subtle bulging along the arms of his frock coat and long line of his trousers was any indication.

The only thing that hadn't changed were his eyes. That dark gaze was regarding her with the same intensity it always had. The bronze flecks glittered, coalescing around the pupils, flaring in a bright star of...

Hunger?

Her breath jammed in her throat. Her skin tingled with rage.

How. Dare. He.

She balled her hands and strove to keep calm. "No greeting for me after all these years, my lord?"

"Hello, Lottie," he said gruffly.

"Do *not* call me that," she snapped. "That name is no longer yours to use."

"Beg pardon." He acknowledged her point with a curt nod. "I did not mean to offend."

"Then perhaps you should have stayed dead."

"You are not wrong." The grooves deepening around his

mouth, he took a breath. "I wasn't sure you would remember. This place, I mean."

She hated that feeling of exposure, what it said about her that she'd remembered too much—everything—about their time together.

Yet how could she forget the first time he'd said that he loved her? It had been about two weeks after they'd wed. They'd just finished making love, and she'd lain blissfully in the crook of her bridegroom's arm, thinking the moment was almost perfect. Almost...because the intimacy of their bodies had made her want to share what was in her heart. The love she was too afraid to put into words first.

She knew her husband admired and desired her. But he had yet to say that he loved her.

"Do you know what you remind me of, Lottie?" he'd suddenly asked.

"What?" she'd asked eagerly.

Maybe he would compare her to a jewel, a flower. Maybe that would turn into a confession of love.

"A time ball."

When she'd furrowed her brow, he said, *"Do you know what that is?"*

"Yes." The one advantage of having an explorer for a father.

"Have you seen the one in Greenwich, at the Royal Observatory? As much as I detest London, it is the one place I always visit when I am in the area."

He'd looked at her as if he expected her to swoon with joy at the comparison.

"Unless I'm misunderstanding," she'd replied primly. *"Are you saying that I remind you of something that is round, red, and constantly falls?"*

He'd blinked, letting out a roar of laughter.

Then he'd gathered her close, looking into her eyes.

"You remind me of a time ball because you are my constant,"

he'd said tenderly. *"You are the reason I do not feel lost in this world. You are my way home, Lottie, and I...I love you."*

Emotion swelled, and Charlie had to push it back. To not dwell on how readily she'd trusted him. How eagerly she'd responded with her own profession of love.

Taking a breath, she parried his move. "Why the games, Sebastian? I questioned my sanity when I saw you at the Rigbys' affair and in that alleyway. But after that rock conveniently interrupted my *rendezvous*, I knew I wasn't going mad. You always had a possessive streak."

Although Sebastian lowered his brows, he didn't deny it.

"None of this has been a game." He spoke in a tight, controlled fashion. "Whatever you may think of me and of everything that has happened, I want you to know that I never intended to hurt you. I left to protect you. And I am here now for the same reason."

She couldn't hear over the roar in her ears.

"*Protect* me?" Despite her best efforts, her voice shook in the gale of her emotions. "How is letting me believe that you died a fiery death whilst in the arms of your mistress protecting me? What reasons could you possibly have for betraying our marriage, for abandoning me, for making me grieve you, you bloody bastard?"

He stared at her with the eyes of a warrior who knew he was fighting a losing battle. Eyes filled with a mix of resignation and resolve.

"I know you want answers," he said. "But I cannot give them to you."

Fury such as she'd never known whipped through her.

"Go to hell," she said through her teeth. "And this time, *stay there.*"

She turned and made it three steps before she felt his hand circle her arm.

In the next heartbeat, she twisted around, her pearl-handled pistol in hand. She aimed it at the area where an ordinary man would have a heart.

"Don't touch me." Her voice trembled, but the hand holding her weapon did not.

"I'm sorry." He released her but did not back away. "For everything, Lot—Charlotte. But please heed me: you must stop following Gilbert Quinton."

An icy rivulet trickled down her spine. At his knowledge of her activities and the reasons why he might be warning her about Quinton.

"Why?" she said with frosty hauteur.

"Quinton is involved in something dangerous. Something beyond the domestic problems you are investigating," Sebastian replied.

She thought about denying her covert operation, but the glint in his eyes told her he already knew too much. With pointed slowness, she slid the pistol back into the pocket of her skirt.

"What makes you think I am investigating him?" she asked stiffly.

He cocked a brow. "Your secret society specializes in private inquiries, does it not?"

Damn the man. How does he know about the Angels?

Theories flitted through her head about how Sebastian had gained knowledge of her activities. Not that she cared how he spent his time. What he did, who he did it with...none of that was her concern any longer. She had, however, spent the last dozen years establishing her own life, and she was not about to allow him to destroy everything she'd worked to build.

Reminded of all she had to lose, she cast a surreptitious glance around. The grassy hill was a secluded spot and sparsely attended. Yet she spotted another gentleman making his way up to the summit, his striped frock coat flapping in the wind, and she did not want to risk being seen in public with her husband who was supposed to be dead.

"What do you want?" she said tersely. "You have a minute to tell me before I leave."

"I want you to be safe." The ore in his eyes glowed as if it were molten. "That is the only thing I have ever wanted, Charlotte. Promise me that you will stay away from Quinton, and you will never see me again."

Her pulse fluttered like a trapped butterfly. If she were an objective observer, she would report that he seemed earnest—that he was truly concerned about her well-being. Yet experience had taught her better than to believe anything Sebastian Courtenay had to say.

"What I do is no concern of yours," she said.

"You will always be my concern." He braced his hands on his hips, the familiarity of the gesture wringing her heart. "Whether or not you like it."

Sudden fear spiked through her. Although his death had legally ended their marriage, what if he wanted to reclaim his life? She did not trust the courts; when it came to the legal system, men gave themselves all the advantages.

"If you are planning on resurfacing from the dead, I'll have no part—"

"Rest easy, wife. Your widowhood is safe with me."

His crooked smile made her heart clench, memories slamming into her. She'd always loved this smile of Sebastian's; the boyish uncertainty of it was absolutely at odds with the rest of him. The juxtaposition was even more pronounced now with his harder, wearier features.

Don't be seduced by his smile like some feather wit. He's a liar. Get him out of your life—for good this time.

"Do I have your word of honor that you will not try to reclaim what you abandoned twelve years ago?" she asked.

"Does my honor still mean anything to you?"

His quiet words punctured the bubble of her anger. For the first time, she regretted her perspicacity and wished she couldn't see the remorse and self-recrimination glittering in his eyes. Yet what did it matter if his conscience suffered over his betrayal? He'd abandoned her in a heinous fashion, betrayed every vow he'd ever made to her. Now he was back, and he was still keeping secrets. Still lying. Still completely and irrevocably unworthy of her trust.

"I want your promise that you will stay dead," she said flatly.

After a moment, he said, "If you want me dead, I am dead."

"Splendid."

"But I will not stand by and watch you come to harm." The softness of his tone did not diminish its ferocity, nor the fact that he was suddenly crowding her, his smoldering gaze holding her captive as surely as if he'd put his hands on her. "If you will not stay away from Quinton, you are inviting me into your life. Is that what you want, Lottie? Think about that the next time you have the impulse to follow that bastard into a bloody orgy or alleyway."

She balled her hands, not backing down. "Interfere in my business, Sebastian, and you *will* regret it."

"I say."

At the new voice, they both spun around. A dozen yards away, the fellow in the striped coat had emerged upon the knoll, his face sheened with sweat. He mopped at his brow with a handkerchief. His affable countenance conveyed his obliviousness to the crackling tension he'd interrupted.

"Quite a climb, eh?" the newcomer said.

"Quite," Sebastian replied.

While his response was cordial, Charlie noted that he kept his face averted from the other man's view. Then he addressed her like one would a stranger.

"I hoped my directions were helpful, ma'am. If you follow them, you will find your way." He bowed. "Good day."

Without another word, he walked away from her.

Something, she silently fumed, that he had no trouble doing.

ELEVEN

The next morning, Jack stepped into a bath. Since he'd killed off Sebastian Courtenay, Marquess of Fayne, he'd gone by the name Jack Granger. It was less refined, less noble, and it truthfully suited him better. But he hadn't told Lottie of his new identity. Didn't know how to or if he should. Scratch that. He *knew* he shouldn't. His superior would undoubtedly have his hide for letting her know he was alive; if he told her the rest...

Draping his arms over the sides of the tub, he tried to relax. Steam lifted from the lukewarm surface, and he stared broodingly at the wisps rising toward the yellowed ceiling. He had a few moments to unwind before the water grew cold.

Not that he found it easy to relax in London. The cacophony of Spitalfields filtered through the thin glass panes: hawkers conducting their trade in booming voices, carriage wheels clattering, and babes and animals squalling. Even indoors, the air held a distinct pungency of coal smoke, brine, and rotting things. The efforts taken to ameliorate the odors—in this instance, a vase of wilting flowers left by Mrs. Clooney, the annoyingly coquettish widow who operated the lodging house—made matters worse.

The stink was only one of the myriad reasons why Jack hated London. For him, the place unearthed memories best left buried, and he avoided it as much as possible. Since his work kept him abroad, this had not been a problem...until now.

Now the lethal, faceless enemy he'd been hunting his entire career was here.

And so was Charlotte.

My Lottie. His gut twisted with a familiar ache—a torturous longing that he'd learned to live with. But she wasn't his any longer. If he were honest, she'd never really been his. He had deceived her at every turn, and even if he'd done it to protect her, he knew he was not deserving of her trust.

Not deserving of *her*.

Thus, he'd done the best thing for her and left.

But Fate had crossed their paths once again, and he would do everything in his power to keep her safe, even if she wanted nothing to do with him. Agitation and desire stirred as he considered how the years had changed her. She'd always been intelligent, passionate, and far too willful for her own good. Since their parting, she'd obviously shed some of her youthful insecurities—the baggage that her papa had selfishly heaped upon her—and now she radiated feminine confidence as well.

Jack remembered how she'd once bemoaned her lack of genteel accomplishments. She had feared disappointing him—feared that she wouldn't make him a proper marchioness. The irony of it had knifed him in the chest. He, of all people, would never judge another for their upbringing. Moreover, he'd always known she was a lady, not just by birth, but in the ways that mattered.

From the moment he saw her fighting off those brutes in Marseille, he'd been awestruck by her resilience. Learning how she'd escaped her dastardly guardian and planned to take charge of her own destiny had deepened his admiration. To top it off, he'd discovered that her indomitable spirit was tempered by uncommon care and compassion for others. She was not the sort of woman to stand by when she saw others being victimized. Whether it was a shopgirl being harassed or a street urchin being bullied, Lottie would not hesitate to step in, even at her own peril.

He wasn't surprised that she'd started a "charity" to help those in need.

Society of Angels, indeed.

He would have found her brazen thumbing of her nose at societal conventions amusing if it weren't for the fact that her investigation was leading her directly to a nest of vipers. With smoldering rage, he relived the attack in the alleyway.

What if I hadn't been there to help her? What if I'd arrived even a minute later?

After taking down those bounders, it had taken all his self-control to leave her when his every instinct clamored to hold her and never let her go again. He'd had to tear himself away right before help arrived...in the form of that bloody Adonis who worked for her.

His hands clenched on the tub's edge as he flashed to the too-handsome bastard kissing Lottie in the orangery. Another man's mouth on his wife—

No, don't go there. She's not yours any longer. You made sure of that.

Nonetheless, Jack couldn't stop the demon of jealousy from eviscerating him. It didn't help that, twelve years ago, he had left Lottie to shield her from the very group that Quinton was leading her to like a lamb to slaughter. For fifteen years, Jack and his team had been hunting the shadowy anarchist organization known as the First Flame Society. The group had an insidious agenda: to foment chaos and violence and destroy the established order at any cost. It knew no borders and was behind riots, mobs, and assassinations. The blood of countless innocents stained their hands.

Jack was part of a team brought together by international interests to root out the First Flame and put an end to its reign of terror. Whilst he and his group had foiled several plots, they'd never managed to bring in a member of the First Flame alive. The anarchists were zealots, ready to sacrifice themselves for their cause. The chameleon-like society shifted in its location and sometimes went quiet for extended periods. Their latest dormancy had lasted three years, and Jack had begun to hope that perhaps the group had disappeared for good.

He ought to have known better. They were like weeds, their spread vigorous and underground. The only way to fight them was to think and act like them. Jack had lived in so many places, under so many assumed identities, that sometimes he forgot who he was.

But it was easier that way. Burying himself in work, even if it was dangerous, posed less of a threat than allowing himself to remember who he was and what he wanted. To recall the one taste of happiness he'd selfishly taken—that had tormented him ever since.

Seeing Lottie again had made everything worse. Because she wasn't just a memory: she was a living, breathing woman...who, by some miracle, was still free. For reasons he would not allow himself to examine, she had never remarried.

And she remembered the time ball.

He'd had to hide so much of his past from her, but she'd obviously tucked away what he'd said about the Royal Observatory all those years ago. As if what they had shared meant something to her. As if *he* had mattered.

Even though he had no right to it, hope burgeoned in his chest...and other places as well.

Beneath the cooling suds, he was already hard. It was a common condition whenever he thought about Lottie, as was what he did next. The water rippled as he fisted his erection, closing his eyes and pretending that the hand surrounding his rock-hard shaft wasn't his but hers. His wife's. Fantasy and memory wove seductive images, and he lost himself in the pleasure-pain of it.

Of remembering...and wanting.

The day after their wedding night, he'd awoken with a substantial cockstand. Although that was not an unusual way for him to greet the morning, matters had been exacerbated by the fact that his prick had found an enviable home nestled in the soft, sleek crevice of his sleeping bride's bottom. That had left him with quite the dilemma.

He'd deprived Lottie of her maidenhead but a few hours ago. Having never bedded a virgin before, he hadn't known what to expect, but he should have known his new bride. Inexperienced but intelligent, prudent but passionate, Lottie had taken to lovemaking like a bird to the skies. In fact, her enthusiasm had moved him to take her twice...which meant she was undoubtedly sore.

While Jack hadn't always been a gentleman, he'd sworn to himself that, with his new marchioness, he would be. He would be an ideal husband, the version of himself he'd always wished to be. He would cherish his exquisite lady by showing some bloody restraint. Something he'd never been good at, but for Lottie, he would try. Even if his cock was throbbing like the devil betwixt the plump mounds of her arse, he would do the right thing and let her rest.

When she shifted in her sleep, caressing him with her crack, he had to stifle a groan.

Then he heard her giggle.

"Are you always, ahem, an early riser, my lord?"

Lottie twisted her head to look at him, and the naughty glimmer in her goddess's eyes told him she'd been awake for some time. Her teasing undid his good intentions, tossing them aside like a used cravat.

"You little minx," he growled.

He pounced on her, claiming her mouth until she had no breath left for laughter.

Kissing her until all she gave him were soft sighs and whimpers.

When he judged she was ready for more, he continued his feast down her body. All sleek lines and soft curves, Lottie was everything he found alluring in a woman. Her downy skin and female scent fed his hunger, threatening his resolution to be a courteous lover. Luckily, his bride seemed to be similarly lost in the heat swirling between them, clenching his hair as he licked her breasts, moaning when he sucked one candy-pink nipple into his mouth.

Pleasure flushed his skin, his fist jerking harder as he trailed kisses down Lottie's torso. He traced the elegant curve of her ribs with his tongue, teased the dip of her belly. Even though she was new at this, she was his match in every way, arching into his caresses, panting for more. Her wantonness set him afire and incinerated his resolve to act like a proper gentleman in bed.

Clamping his hands on her thighs, he spread her wide, his nostrils flaring at the sight of her golden fleece and the plump, pink secrets beneath. He ran a finger up her slit, marveling at how wet she was. How ready. He'd been with lusty women before, but none of them had Lottie's sweetness. None had made him feel desired the way she did. None of them had been his—his woman, his wife.

"You are so lovely, Lottie," he said raggedly. "I *have* to taste you."

He dipped his head, delving his tongue deeply. Christ, she was delectable. His first taste of his bride's pussy, and he was hooked for life. To her womanly flavor and her intoxicating response. No prim and proper marchioness was his Lottie. She bucked against his mouth, her needful whimpers urging him to lick deeper into her succulence. He found her pearl, rubbing it as he ate her. She cried his name when she came, and he groaned at the decadent squeeze of her passage around his tongue.

He crawled up her body and claimed her mouth, sharing the taste of her pleasure with her. It wasn't the sort of thing a gentleman would do, but he was too far gone to care. Especially when Lottie swirled her tongue against his, stretching against him like a cat.

"Make love to me," she whispered.

"Greedy chit." Looking into her soft-as-smoke eyes, he asked, "Aren't you sore from last night?"

She bit her lip.

He smiled tenderly. "As tempted as I am, sweeting, we'll wait another day or two before we have another go."

"As you've just demonstrated, there is more than one way to make love, isn't there?"

She reached between them, and he shuddered, feeling her tentative caress against his cock, which lay like an iron bar against her belly. She stroked him, watching his face, the desire to please him shining in her eyes. Although her touch was that of a novice, her rhythm too leisurely, she aroused him more than any woman he'd ever known.

"Like this." Shifting onto his side, he wrapped her hand firmly around his cock. "Touch me harder and faster."

It didn't take his bride long to figure out how to drive him mad. She was the most capable lady he'd ever met, even in this. His blood pounding, he watched her frigging his engorged prick. Her delicate fingers barely enclosed his thick, veined shaft as she stroked him like he'd instructed. As she worked her fist up and down, her exquisite touch wrung a drop of pre-seed from his flared tip.

"Oh, you feel slippery," she breathed.

He groaned at the note of excitement in her voice, the glint of discovery in her eyes. In the next heartbeat, he rolled atop her again, thrusting his prick against her hot, slick furrow.

"Not as slippery as you," he said huskily.

She gasped when he drove his hard length against her sensitive bud. Lubricated by her dew, the sensation sizzled down his spine. He shoved his cock against her, his breath rasping when she wrapped her legs around his hips, allowing his stones to drag against her wet petals. She moved with him, their joining natural and perfect. Her soft sighs and lush cunny brought him to the edge, ripping off his mask of civility.

"Come for me, Lottie," he gritted out. "I want to feel your honey on my cock."

It was the first time he'd used such language with her...and he felt a surge of satisfaction when she *liked* it. She came with a sweet little squeak, gushing dew that made her crease even more deliciously slick. Panting, he fucked her wetness, the heat in his balls building and building until it shot up his shaft. He jerked his fist, the water rippling as he found his release.

Afterward, he lay in the cold tub, emptied but nowhere near satisfied. Nowhere near sated. Over the years, any relief he'd found had proved temporary. There was only one cure for what ailed him...but he couldn't take it.

The best is still to come, my Lottie.

He'd never forgotten the promise he'd made her. Back then, he'd intended to give his bride the world. Instead, he'd had to abandon her for her own good.

He told himself it was for the best that Lottie hated him. It would make it easier for him to carry out his plan. A few months ago, Jack's superior had picked up rumblings that the First Flame had become active again, resurrected by a new leader. The last time the First Flame had come out of hibernation, it had incited a clash between a mob and authorities in Spain; hundreds were killed, an entire village burned to the ground. Then, a few weeks ago, Jack had followed a lead to Calais and met a fellow connected to the First Flame. The man had agreed to help Jack...but then he disappeared.

Jack's search for the suspect had brought him to London. He had to find the cove, discover what the anarchists were planning now, and put a stop to it before more lives were lost. At the same time, Jack had to protect Lottie. He did not, for a single second, believe that she was going to heed his advice. She planned to do exactly as she pleased, which meant her loyalty to her friend Amara Quinton would land her right in the middle of whatever the First Flame was scheming.

Whatever the case, Jack would protect Lottie. He would bleed, lay down his life, before he let her come to harm. Dying, however, would be easier than the other part of his plan: he could guard her, but he could not get close to her. He couldn't act on his desires, couldn't open his heart the way he yearned to, couldn't be... himself.

That had always been the problem with him and Lottie.

The hairs stirred on his nape, cutting through his brooding. Years of training put his senses on instant alert; he heard the subtle, unmistakable click of his door being picked. He was out of the tub in a flash, grabbing the pistol he never left out of reach. Water sluiced from his muscles as he leveled his weapon at the opening door.

"Hello to you too, darling." The blonde who entered smirked, dipping her gaze briefly to his groin. "Did you miss me?"

Jack grabbed a towel, knotting it around his waist. He did not like feeling exposed in front of a woman. Even if that woman was a spy under his command and he knew she was merely trying to get his goat.

"You shouldn't be here," he said curtly. "If Mrs. Clooney sees you, I'll have to find new rooms."

"As if I would be seen." Maria Delaney examined herself in the cracked looking glass, adjusting her wig. "Besides, that blowsy old mort won't throw you out. She wants you in her bed too badly."

He yanked on a shirt. "What do you want?"

"Primus called a meeting." She picked up a neckcloth from a chair, tossing it to him before sauntering to the door. "Three o'clock, the usual place. Don't be late."

Twelve

Although not the most pleasant location, the butcher shop on Skinner Street provided a secure and inconspicuous place to meet. Mr. Campbell, whose family had owned the shop for three generations, was an old friend of Primus, the leader of Jack's team. As Campbell's brother had been killed in a riot instigated by the First Flame, the butcher was an ally. He was short and brawny, his tea strong enough to melt teeth and his stew some of the best Jack had ever sampled.

Jack entered through the back door, which was heavy and had multiple locks to keep thieves out. As the back room was used to store and cure the carcasses Mr. Campbell bought from the nearby market, it had no windows, and the door separating it from the front of the shop was extra thick. This had the benefit of preventing anything discussed in the room from being overheard. The smell, however, was trapped in along with the sound. Luckily, it must have been before market day because there were only two sides of beef and a few yet-to-be defeathered fowl hanging from hooks.

Nonetheless, Maria Delaney complained. Short and curvy, she

gave the impression of softness until one looked into her eyes. She had a spy's gaze, hard and assessing. The gathering included the two other spies who answered to Jack, Jean-Paul Laurent and Luis Calderone, and the team's head spymaster, Primus.

"All of us here are rich." Delaney addressed the group, giving her fake blonde locks an irritable shake. "We've traveled across the Continent, been in some of Europe's finest places. And *this* is the best we can do for a meeting place?"

She had a point. Primus not only paid them an exorbitant salary, but he was a financial genius who'd taught them to invest their money well. He was motivated by pragmatism as well as generosity: a rich spy was less likely to be bought off by the enemy. As a result, all of them could have retired...but none of them did. They were too dedicated to the cause. For Jack, the work also kept his demons at bay; he didn't know who he would be without it.

"You owe me five pounds, *mon ami*," Laurent said to Calderone.

The Frenchman and Spaniard were both dark-haired Adonises, the former a shade taller, the latter a bit more muscular. Women loved them, and they sometimes loved women. Mostly, though, they saved their true affection for one another.

"I should have known better than to wager with a Frenchman."

Sighing, Calderone handed over the money.

Delaney narrowed her eyes at them. "What did you bet on?"

"How long it would take before you started complaining," Laurent said smugly.

Although Laurent and Delaney were not related, they fought like they were. Not that Jack had much experience when it came to family. In fact, this group was the closest thing he had to one... which wasn't saying much.

Delaney curled her hands. "I'll give you something to complain about—"

"Enough." Primus spoke, and everyone listened. "We have work to do."

The spymaster's ability to pull the wool over people's eyes never ceased to amaze Jack. When Primus was out and about in London, he played the part of Sir Hewitt Lancaster, a bumbling well-to-do drunkard. No one took him seriously; few cared when he was around. His money got him through doors, and the snobs enjoyed having him around as a target for their condescension. It was the perfect disguise, day and night from the man he truly was.

Exacting. Calculating. Ruthless when required and sometimes when it wasn't.

He was also Jack's mentor. He alone knew the disgrace of Jack's past, and he'd given Jack a chance anyway. An opportunity to start over again, to do something good, to make something of himself.

"Give me your reports," Primus said.

They did, in turn. Delaney had picked up a rumor that a new and violent gang had taken over a flash house. She'd infiltrated it to determine if it was the First Flame; it wasn't. Similarly, Calderone had ruled out a workhouse as a potential First Flame headquarters. Laurent had investigated a society that called themselves anarchists, but according to the Frenchman, they were the "good kind."

"True revolutionaries," he explained. "Who want to make a difference in the world, not tear it down."

"Granger?" Primus inquired.

"I haven't found the suspect from Calais yet," Jack said. "But I am confident the two leads I'm following will yield results soon."

"Very well. Keep at it, all of you." Primus nodded, his jowls wobbling slightly. He was a stocky man and stronger than he looked. "I know you need no reminding, but the Great Exhibition opens in just over a fortnight. Visitors are flooding the city, as are foreign dignitaries. Crowds are everywhere. It is no coincidence that the First Flame came out of dormancy a few months ago and are rumored to be in operation in London. If the First Flame is planning to strike, there is no better time to create mass destruction than during these next few weeks."

Calderone crossed his arms over his broad chest, his head angled. "Have you picked up any information regarding the new leader, *señor*?"

"I have not. Whoever is in charge now is keeping his head down."

"Or her head," Delaney said. "The anarchists have had female leaders."

Primus acceded the point with a nod. "He, or she, is doing a damned fine job of keeping their plan under wraps. In the past, if the First Flame had an Achilles heel, it was the need to flaunt their prowess. Someone would brag about their scheme, and we would get wind of it and act. But this time around, the First Flame is being as silent as the grave, and it...it concerns me."

Jack's nape prickled as Primus was not a fellow who was easily concerned. Looking around the room, Jack saw Laurent widen his eyes, Calderone shift on his feet, and Delaney chew on her lip.

Laurent broke the silence. "You have warned the local authorities, *non*?"

"I have informed domestic security of my concerns, but they are stretched thin managing the influx of people into the capital. The police will not act unless I can give them proof of a credible threat or an imminent attack." Primus sighed. "Which, as of now, I cannot. That is why I am counting upon you to uncover the First Flame's plot. Before it is too late."

"Yes, sir," they all chimed.

"Granger, stay behind. I want a word."

The other agents left, Delaney mouthing, *Good luck. You're going to need it*, before exiting.

Primus cut to the chase. "Did you reveal yourself to her?"

Jack took a breath. "Yes, sir."

"How much does she know?"

"Just that I am not dead. I didn't tell her the rest."

"You had better keep it that way. Our mission cannot be compromised. I can feel it in my bones that the First Flame is plotting something on an unprecedented scale." Beneath his bushy brows, Primus's gaze was as sharp as a hawk's. "There is no going back, Granger. You knew this when you left her. When you came to me for help and I devised the plan to protect her, you knew it was irreversible. You gave me your word that you would not contact her again—that you would keep your secrets from her. For your own good and the good of our team."

"I know."

Jack remembered his panicked state when he'd asked Primus for help. Primus had presented him with an agonizing choice: stay and risk Lottie's life...or leave and keep her safe. He'd made the excruciating decision to abandon the only woman he'd ever loved. The fact that he'd done so for the right reasons didn't make his actions feel any less wrong. Over the years, he thought the pain had dulled, but seeing her again brought his regret and yearning rushing to the fore. He would never get over the loss of his wife, not if he lived to be a hundred. There would never be a day when he didn't want her, pine for her, burn for her.

She, meanwhile, hated his guts. Deservedly so.

"You must not make the wrong choice because of a woman. Not again."

Primus's words knifed Jack's gut. The reminder of his shame focused him. Even before he left Lottie, he'd never been worthy of her. She was better off without him...then and now.

"I won't, sir," he said tightly.

"Good." Primus's countenance relaxed. "I am heartened to know that the effort I have invested in you has not gone to waste. You have proved yourself a capable spymaster and second-in-command, Granger. When I retire, I expect you to take over my position."

"Surely that is many years away, sir."

"I am not getting any younger." Primus inclined his head, signaling the end of the small talk. "I will not detain you. Next time, I shall expect a successful report."

Thirteen

"Do you have plans for the evening?" Devlin asked.

Charlie braced, not because the carriage was bumping over a rough patch on its way to the Strand, but because she knew where the conversation was headed. Given all that had happened over the last two days—namely, the reappearance of Sebastian—she needed to nip things in the bud with Devlin.

The change of plans irked her. If she were honest, it wasn't that she regretted not taking Devlin as a lover. Even before Sebastian had broken the orangery window—she'd kicked herself multiple times for neglecting to take him to task for acting like a Neanderthal—she'd known that the spark was missing with Devlin.

His kiss had been agreeable. Like the lover before him, he was attractive, pleasant, and discreet. She liked him, but she didn't desire him.

At least, not in the way she knew she could desire a man.

Not with a feverish, all-consuming need that exploded through every cell of her body, that melted her brain, that made her feel reckless and safe and alive.

The way she'd felt with Sebastian...and, regrettably, only him.

The recognition stoked her smoldering anger.

Once again, he had upended her life. This time, not by dying, but by being inconveniently alive. And, after all this time, did he have the decency to offer an explanation for falsifying his demise?

I know you want answers. But I cannot give them to you.

It was a wonder she did not hunt him down and murder him in his sleep.

"I was going to see if you would like to have supper."

She started, realizing that Devlin was observing her, his brow creased. Wondering, no doubt, as to the cause of the emotion she couldn't quite conceal.

"But if you are busy, perhaps another time," he said.

His casual tone didn't mask the awkward tension between them. She knew she had to address it to preserve their collegial relationship. She smoothed out a wrinkle in her trousers—for the day's mission, she was disguised as a man—and collected her thoughts. She hated that Sebastian had the power to affect her. She was no longer a naïve miss to be swept off her feet, yet he was still turning her world topsy-turvy. Making her question her choices and change her well-laid plans.

"About that." She forced herself to focus on Devlin. "After some deliberation, I do not think we ought to pursue a relationship beyond the professional."

"May I ask why?"

She wasn't about to tell him—or anyone—about Sebastian. Knowing her former husband, he wasn't going to linger anyway. He would probably stay long enough to wreak havoc before taking off to do...well, whatever it was he did. In those early years after his "death," when she'd started digging into his past and came up with remarkably little, she'd begun to suspect that he was not the carefree lord he made himself out to be. Or not just that, anyway.

What that scoundrel does is none of my business. Whatever danger he is involved in does not concern me...although it is curious how much he knows about me. About the Angels and what we do. Should I worry that he was able to access such private information? Will he try to use what he knows about me to his advantage?

The problem was that she had no idea what Sebastian wanted. He claimed his goal was to protect her—from what she didn't know—but having been burned to a crisp before, she wasn't about to trust him. She would have to stay on her toes where Sebastian was concerned. She turned her attention back to Devlin, who actually deserved it.

"It has naught to do with you," she said honestly. "I have had a…a change in circumstance. This matter requires my attention, and I cannot in good conscience start an affair knowing I have neither time nor energy to devote to it."

"It's not me, it's you?" Devlin grimaced. "Interesting being on the receiving end of that line. Can't say that I like it."

"It is not a line, Devlin." Sighing, she said, "Truth be told, I have grown rather fond of having you around. I should hate for anything to threaten our working relationship."

He studied her with sharp blue eyes. "Nothing I say will change your mind?"

Obviously, he knew her well. Looking at the fellow, who possessed brains as well as looks, she felt a pulse of regret at closing this door. Yet it would not be fair to involve him in her complicated situation.

"No," she said. "I would like, of course, for us to remain friends."

"As you wish."

He inclined his head in a courteous manner, and she was relieved by his easy acceptance. Perhaps their kiss hadn't made much of an impression on him, either. At any rate, the blow to her vanity was vastly preferable to a messier outcome.

"Now that we've dealt with that." She adjusted her hat. "Tell me about your progress with Quinton."

Devlin's gaze glinted with amusement before he responded.

"With the help of the erstwhile Billie and Lindy, I have canvassed the Strand from Trafalgar Square to St. Clement Dane's. Haberdashers, milliners, clergymen—I've spoken to them all. No one recalls seeing a couple matching the description of Quinton and his doe-eyed, buxom redhead. All hope is not lost, however. We have Holywell Street on the agenda today, and if that turns up no leads, we can always procure some reading material."

Holywell Street, a lane off the Strand, was known for its book-shops featuring erotic works.

"I didn't take you for much of a reader," Charlie said dryly.

"Oh, I'm not, sweeting. I just like to look at the pictures."

At Devlin's smirk, she felt her lips twitch and was thankful that their relationship had resumed its normal course. Arriving at Holywell, they split up, each taking a side of the street. In addition to searching for the redhead, Charlie had to keep a lookout for Sebastian. The memory of his harsh promise quivered through her.

If you will not stay away from Quinton, you are inviting me into your life. Is that what you want, Lottie?

Her cheeks flushed. Although she did not want him nosing about in her affairs, she wouldn't put it past the arrogant bastard to do so anyway...for what reasons, she could not fathom. If his purpose was to protect her as he'd claimed, why had he betrayed and abandoned her?

None of it makes sense. And I've wasted enough time mulling over the bounder. I must focus on the life I've built for myself—on helping Amara and the clients who count on me.

When she entered the first bookshop, the absence of any reaction from the other occupants confirmed that Vera Engle, the Angels' mistress of disguises, had done her job well. Charlie blended in with the other patrons, padding and tailoring giving her a portly male silhouette. A salt-and-pepper wig, sideburns, and mustache completed her look as a prosperous middle-class gent.

Selecting a random unmarked volume from the shelves, she went to the counter and spun her prepared tale to the clerk. She pretended to be a merchant looking for his "niece"—which everyone knew was shorthand for a mistress—who'd run off after a tiff. Charlie described her supposed redheaded paramour, adding that a friend had seen the woman in the company of a dark-haired, brawny fellow, likely, she said mournfully, to be a new "uncle."

The clerk was not unreceptive to her questioning, especially when she pushed coins across the counter for his trouble. He had not seen the redhead in question but mentioned that there was a club tucked away on the next street where Charlie might wish to make further inquiries. Apparently, the exclusive "Academy of Venus" catered to patrons of both sexes and was known for its unique salons.

"If your *niece* cannot be found"—the clerk waggled his brows —"there are plenty of other fresh young ladies in need of protection."

Thanking him, Charlie continued on her way.

She learned nothing new at the next eight establishments. By the time she arrived at a storefront that a faded sign proclaimed as "Wallace's Bookshop," the mission was starting to feel as productive as the proverbial search through a haystack. Opening the door, she hoped Devlin was having better luck—

"Let me go!"

At the fear infusing the female voice, Charlie tightened her grip on her walking stick. A quick glance revealed a cramped space with an unattended counter to her right and a maze of teetering bookshelves. She followed the raised voices toward the back of the shop.

"Stop fighting me, dove." The menacing drawl raised the hairs on Charlie's nape. "I'll pay you for the slap and tickle, something I'm certain you give away for free—"

"Get your hands off me, you bastard!"

"You bit me, you *bitch*."

Charlie arrived in time to see a man slap the brunette he had pinned to a table. He yanked up her skirts as she kicked out, screaming bloody murder. Charlie did not hesitate.

"You will unhand the young lady," she said in her lowest register.

The man looked up, and Charlie narrowed her eyes at the chiseled features and blond hair slicked over a high widow's peak. She knew the blackguard: Ashley Lowell, rake, profligate, and youngest son of a wealthy countess. He was the apple of his mama's eye, which was how he'd managed to harass half the maids in London without repercussion.

Unsurprisingly, his behavior with shopgirls was no better.

"Who the devil are you?"

Lowell gave Charlie a once-over. Even though she'd had to tolerate dancing with the bounder on several occasions, there was no sign of recognition in his pale, slitted eyes.

"Who I am is of no import, sir," she said evenly. "But as a gentleman of honor, I cannot allow you to molest this woman."

Lowell's mouth edged into a sneer. "Rather a high horse you're perched on, *sir*, given the nature of your reading habits."

"My choice of reading material harms no one. Your actions, however"—Charlie gestured at the brunette he still held down on the table—"are not only reprehensible but criminal. Release her, or I shall make you."

To prove her point, she held up her walking stick. A quick twist of the knob revealed a glinting blade at the end.

Lowell's face reddened. "You dare to threaten *me*? Do you know who I am?"

"If you are someone with a reputation to protect, I would suggest you depart this instant. Before I summon the police."

At her calm words, Lowell's visage turned thunderous. He released the woman with a vicious shove that made her head smack against the table.

"You will regret this," he snarled at Charlie.

He stormed out.

Charlie turned her attention to the woman rising from the table.

"Miss, are you all right?" she asked with concern.

The shopgirl reached for a pair of wire-rimmed spectacles that must have flown off during the assault. She untwisted the mangled frame, donning the glasses with hands that shook slightly.

"I...I'm fine."

She did not look fine, not with her swelling cheek, bleeding lip, and the way she swayed on her feet. A few strands of coffee-brown hair straggled from her tight topknot, curving against her cheek. Although her spectacles and severe hairstyle aged her, Charlie saw that she was young—in her early twenties perhaps. Her voice had a natural, sultry rasp that was at odds with her prim exterior.

"Here, take this." Mindful that the other had just been assaulted by a strange male, Charlie kept her distance, pushing a handkerchief across the table. "For your lip."

"I'm much obliged to you, sir. For this"—the woman took the scrap of linen, wincing as she dabbed her lip—"and for coming to my aid. I must look a frightful mess."

"Through no fault of your own."

"You can say that again." The shopgirl pulled her shoulders back and lifted her chin. "I knew that bloke was trouble from the moment he set foot through the door. But Mr. Wallace, the shop owner, is a skinflint and refuses to have more than one clerk working at a time. Even though I've told him *repeatedly* that some patrons think more than books are for sale, if you know what I mean."

Charlie nodded with empathy. At the same time, the gears were turning in her head. She noted the other's petite yet curvy frame, which included a plump bosom hidden beneath a drab and ill-fitting dress. Behind the spectacles, the woman's eyes were big and brown...and oddly unjaded given her occupation and what she was presently sharing. Although she took pains to hide it, she was also quite pretty.

She fit the description of the woman Quinton had been spotted with. The only thing missing was the red hair. But hair color could be changed easily enough.

Sensing the shopgirl's skittishness, Charlie proceeded with care.

"Perhaps you would like me to speak with Mr. Wallace, Miss...?"

"Loveday. Xenia Loveday," the girl said after a brief hesitation. "While it is awfully nice of you to offer, Mr. Wallace won't listen to you any more than he does to me. And I need this job."

"Perhaps we ought to summon the police—"

"*No.*" Miss Loveday's vehemence was paired with bona fide panic. "That is, Mr. Wallace won't want police nosing around here. He'll sack me if I cause trouble, and like I said, I need the wages. Now, sir, would you like assistance selecting reading material? I could make recommendations based on your, um, interests."

Miss Loveday offered to help select a dirty book the way another shopgirl might show a range of gloves. Matter-of-factly and without even a blush. She was a most curious young woman. For an instant, Charlie contemplated revealing her true purpose and asking Miss Loveday outright if she was involved with Gilbert Quinton...but she discarded the strategy. Beneath her pragmatism, the shopgirl was a bundle of nerves. What secrets was she hiding?

I won't find out if I scare her off.

"I will browse on my own," Charlie murmured. "Thank you."

Miss Loveday looked relieved. "Let me know if I can be of assistance."

As Charlie wandered to the shelves, Miss Loveday disappeared through a tattered curtain at the back of the shop. When the bell over the front door tinkled a few moments later, she re-emerged, her hair once again neatly restrained. Smoothing her skirts, she went to greet the new customer.

Charlie made a beeline for the curtain. Behind it was a tiny storage room crammed with books and a table that held a small bag. A quick search of the bag's contents revealed a coin purse containing two shillings, a rusty key, bread and cheese wrapped in a napkin, and a hairbrush. There was also a folded handbill: an advertisement with a silhouette of a voluptuous woman reading on a chaise. "Scheherazade's Salon" was written in flowing letters above the drawing, and below was a banner announcing, "Wednesday evenings at the Academy of Venus."

Taking what she needed, Charlie exited the back room and returned to the shelves. Not a moment too soon, for Miss Loveday popped her head into the aisle.

"Still doing all right?" she asked.

Charlie pulled a stack of books at random. "Indeed. I've found what I am looking for."

After making her purchase, she departed the shop and met up with Devlin.

"I hope your luck was better than mine," he said as the carriage rolled off.

Taking out a long, dark strand that she'd plucked from Xenia Loveday's brush, Charlie held it up to the light. The root of the hair was bright, glinting red.

With a surge of triumph, she said, "I believe it was."

FOURTEEN

On Wednesday evening, Charlie arrived at the Academy of Venus, a tall brick building tucked at the end of a cul-de-sac. Masked guests were ushered through the front gate by a pair of strapping footmen. As Charlie followed the flow, she looked up at the three rows of windows; a rosy glow slipped through the crack of the heavy curtains, but there was no other indication of what was happening within.

After her visit to Wallace's Bookshop, she'd assigned Billie and Lindy to follow Miss Loveday. The girls had reported that, after finishing her shift at the bookshop, Miss Loveday had made a stop at the present house of ill repute. She hadn't stayed long, but she'd left with a garment box, bidding farewell to one of the prostitutes with a cheery, "See you at the salon!"

Given the handbill Charlie had found in Miss Loveday's bag, she'd deduced that Miss Loveday was referring to Scheherazade's Salon. Her instincts also told her to surveil Miss Loveday this eve; the shopgirl had secrets, and one of them likely involved Gilbert Quinton. Accordingly, Charlie secured a ticket to the event. She was solo tonight as Devlin was monitoring Quinton. She wanted to keep an eye on both; if her hypothesis was correct, the pair's paths would dovetail, and she could provide Amara with the answers she deserved.

Entering the Academy of Venus, Charlie saw that it was packed with patrons, male and female. Apparently, the club offered something for everyone, and after depositing her cloak, Charlie performed a quick reconnaissance. The brothel had three stories: the top floor contained private chambers, the second larger areas for group activities, and the first held a series of public rooms offering the opportunity to mingle and enjoy refreshments.

Charlie returned to the drawing room. Decorated in burgundy and gilt, the space could have belonged in any fashionable home. The night was about excess, and the well-heeled patrons were dressed in lavish costumes and jewels. With a frisson of unease, Charlie recognized Lord and Lady Kendall and Isadora and Ellsworth Rigby sipping wine together. The Kendalls appeared twitchy and titillated, the Rigbys rather bored. Charlie reassured herself that they would not recognize her with her auburn ringlets and purple mask, the padding beneath the violet taffeta altering her shape. Nonetheless, she would steer clear of them.

Mingling with the crowd were the "students" of the academy, male and female. Their attire was a carnal mockery of boarding school uniforms. The men were shirtless, their wide Etonian collars and schoolboy cravats bringing attention to their sinewy shoulders and chests. Their black trousers molded to their lower halves, showing off their bulging wares. Similarly, the women were dressed like depraved schoolmisses. They wore pinafores with no dress beneath. The apron-like garment, constructed of translucent linen, provided glimpses of rouged nipples and generous derrieres.

As one of the male prostitutes approached, Charlie pasted on a smile.

"Good evening, madam." The fellow was sandy-haired and handsome. "My name is Thom. First time?"

Playing the part of a silly matron, Charlie said in breathy accents, "How can you tell?"

"You are as fresh as a garden rose," Thom said with practiced gallantry.

Charlie giggled, patting her auburn wig. "I wager you say that to all the ladies, sir."

"Only the ones with whom I'd like to get better acquainted." He leaned toward her, his sandalwood cologne making her nose itch. "As a matter of fact, darling, I've a sandwich I think you would enjoy."

"Thank you, but I am not hungry."

"You'll have an appetite for this, I assure you."

Thom nodded toward a fellow whose back was to them. As if he sensed he was being discussed, the man turned and appeared to be identical to Thom. Down to the smirk he aimed at Charlie.

"That's my twin brother. When we were young, we liked to do everything together." Thom's voice lowered suggestively. "We still do...for the right price."

Cheeks flaming, Charlie realized the kind of sandwich he was referring to.

"Bidding starts at five hundred pounds for an experience you shan't forget." Thom took her hand, expertly grazing his lips over her skin. "Come find us after Scheherazade's reading."

As he strolled off, Charlie pondered his offer with wry amusement.

If a lover didn't help me get over Sebastian, perhaps what I needed was two.

The thought of Sebastian sobered her, and she scanned the room. She'd seen no sign of him but wouldn't put it past him to interfere. She had to stay on alert for him as well as Miss Loveday.

A bell rang, and it was announced that Scheherazade's Salon was about to begin. Charlie followed the herd toward the library, a high-ceilinged room with emerald-green walls. Clusters of chairs faced a dais, upon which was a large silk screen. The seats filled quickly, but she managed to secure a chair at the back of the room.

Anticipation crackled through the crowd as the overhead lights dimmed. Lanterns had been placed behind the screen, illuminating a silhouette: Scheherazade, in all her exoticized glory. The shadowy woman had long, wavy hair cascading down her back and pooling on the ground beside her. She was provocatively reclined on a large floor pillow. Her outline suggested that she was nude with high, rounded breasts, a nipped-in waist, and curvy hips.

Could she be Xenia Loveday?

"Good evening, ladies and gentlemen."

Charlie recognized the warm, sultry voice immediately. It *was* Miss Loveday.

"I am Scheherazade, here to entertain you with a bedtime story. I have famously entranced a sultan, the passion of my tales unleashing inhibitions and making imaginations run wild. As you fall under my spell, you may begin to see the stories come to life on this screen. Now sit back, relax, and enjoy this rendition of *The Fishwife's Tale or A Lady in Need of Discipline*."

A hush came over the crowd as Scheherazade/Miss Loveday began to read. The plot was unabashedly silly and depraved: a headstrong lady leaves her tolerant husband in a fit of pique after their latest argument, seeking refuge at a convent. There, she finds she has jumped from the frying pan into the fire—or in her case, from her marital bed into an orgy. Forced to submit to the lascivious nuns and priests, she discovers her own true desires.

Nonetheless, Miss Loveday's storytelling mesmerized the audience. Her voice brimmed with emotion, passion, and humor. As if she conjured them to life, figures materialized behind the screen, performing every lurid act she described. The shadows writhed and arched and thrust like a primal fever dream; the fact that they were silhouettes heightened the mystery and titillation.

"Lady Analise did not know how long she lay there, naked and strapped face-down to the punishment bench," Scheherazade said in husky tones. *"The abbess had stopped birching her, and she could feel the raised hot stripes upon the trembling hills of her bottom,*

*exposed to the rapacious eyes of the novices and priests. To Lady
Analise's shock, it was no longer pain she felt but throbbing pleasure. Her nipples pulsed against the rough wood, and the place
between her thighs wept with dew.*

*"'You have a wanton cunny in need of correction,' the abbess
said.*

*"Lady Analise shuddered when the abbess ran the handle of the
birch up between her thighs, teasing her opening until she quivered
with need.*

*"Why did I run away from Robert? Lady Analise thought
miserably. He was kind and loving, but I did not open my heart to
him. I did not trust him."*

A spasm gripped Charlie's throat at the authentic quiver in the
narrator's voice. As Lady Analise wriggled her shadowy rump in
rhythm to the abbess's stroking rod, Charlie berated herself for
being affected by what was mediocre erotica at best. Yet it seemed
like the universe was hell-bent on resurrecting the demons of her
past. Even in this godforsaken brothel, she had to listen to a
parable of a wife who wrestled with trust.

If you love me, then trust me. Sebastian's gruff words, the
desperation in his eyes reached out from the past and grabbed her
by the throat. *I did not betray you. I never would.*

Yet how could she trust him when she'd caught him lying?
From the day they met, he'd had secrets; she'd always known that
he kept parts of himself hidden. She'd let herself be blinded by
desire and the need to believe that her husband loved her above all
else.

I left to protect you. And I am here now for the same reason.

Sebastian's bleak resignation hadn't seemed feigned. But after
years of grieving and anger and pain, how could she possibly
believe him? Moreover, why would she wish to? Before his reappearance, she'd been about to move on with a new lover, and a part
of her believed that was still the wise choice. She was young

enough to enjoy passion whilst having the maturity to not let it rule her.

Awareness stirred her nape. She trawled the room with an alert gaze. While several men leered back at her, none of them was Sebastian. She couldn't shake the feeling that he was near. Perhaps it was her imagination or the bawdy story, but she would not put it past him to show up out of nowhere. Her gaze caught on a man entering the room, and her pulse quickened for a different reason.

Quinton.

He seemed ill at ease—*and so he should, being here when he has a loving wife at home,* Charlie thought indignantly. His big shoulders were hunched, his mask stretched awkwardly across his broad features. He remained close to the doorway, as if he wanted to bolt, but his gaze was trained upon the silk screen where Scheherazade/Miss Loveday appeared to be reaching the climax of the story.

"'Do you need a good ramming, my dear?' she inquired in a cruel, throaty voice.

"The abbess came to stand beside Lady Analise's head, stroking her cheek with a cold, hard object. Lady Analise let out a gasp when she saw her tormentor had traded the birch for an ebony phallus of enormous proportions."

Even Charlie had to blink at the shadowy cock, roughly the size of a forearm.

"'Is this what you want?' the abbess said sternly.

"'No.' The protest came out as a moan, for the abbess had begun to rub the bulbous head against Lady Analise's pulsing love-knot. 'I know now that what I want...what I truly want...'

"'Say it,' the abbess commanded.

"'My husband,' Lady Analise sobbed. 'I want Robert.'

"'Then you shall have me,' a familiar male voice declared.

"One of the priests threw off his cassock, revealing himself to be Robert. He stepped to his wife's head, cupping her cheek with such gentleness that she sobbed harder. He was naked, his muscles gleaming, his instrument bigger and harder than she'd ever seen it. Never in her life had she been so glad to see another.

"'Did you miss me, my love?' her spouse said softly.

"'Yes,' she whispered.

"'Then show me.'"

Murmurs rose from the crowd as the silhouette of Robert presented a truncheon even larger than the dildo to Lady Analise's penitent lips. He pushed, and she appeared to swallow it in the manner of a sword-eater. Unbidden, Charlie's throat flexed with a remembered sensation: of Sebastian's cock entering her in the same way. He had introduced her to fellatio and was the only man she'd ever done it with. She'd loved it, loved the taste and feel of him in her mouth, loved the heady power of unraveling his control. In those moments, she had owned him as completely as he owned her...

Her forehead damp, she swatted away the memory. Dash it all, the past was proving a potent distraction this eve. She sent a covert glance in Quinton's direction, making sure she hadn't lost him... and was relieved when she saw the grey-haired fellow with a black mask standing close to him.

Good old Devlin. I should have known he would come through.

Although Devlin didn't look at her, his smug grin conveyed that he'd noted her presence. He appeared absorbed by Miss Loveday's reading, the prose growing more purple by the moment.

"After making rough use of his fair lady's mouth, Robert withdrew his machine, its tip a weeping tribute of his love.

"'Will you untie me now?' Lady Analise asked shyly.

"'Not until you have learned the fullness of your lesson,' he said, a twinkle in his eye.

"She lost sight of him as he strode behind her, but a moment later, she cried out as his enormous rod skewered her insides with pleasure. He rode her, sending her into paroxysms of delight. Soon her lord joined her, flooding her with his forgiveness. Aroused by the spectacle of conjugal bliss, the nuns and priests formed a naked ring around the lovers and gave in to frenzied abandon of their own. That evening, no desire was left wanting and no orifice unfilled.

"From then on, whenever Lady Analise was tempted to mistrust her husband, he brought out the punishment bench to remind her of his commitment, and they lived happily ever after."

"This concludes the reading of *The Fishwife's Tale or A Lady in Need of Discipline* by Sir Piers Bottom," Scheherazade said. "It may be purchased at the fine booksellers of Holywell Street. Until the next time, I bid you adieu. May all your fantasies be fulfilled tonight."

The light winked out behind the screen as the audience exploded into applause. Amidst the foot stomping and whistling, Charlie saw Quinton duck out. She made eye contact with Devlin; he gave a subtle nod and followed his target. She followed hers, who hadn't emerged from behind the screen. Wading through the buzzing crowd, Charlie reached the dais and saw a door behind it. Going through, she found a small antechamber on the other side. Costumes and wigs were piled upon a settee, along with a leather-bound volume of Sir Piers Bottom's literary masterpiece. There were no doors other than the one Charlie had come through.

Where had Miss Loveday gone?

Examining the room's perimeter, Charlie found the answer: a servant's passage hidden behind a bookcase. She slipped into the corridor and discovered that there were hidden doors and peep-holes into all the chambers on the floor. A quick survey of the public rooms revealed no sign of Xenia. She took a flight of stairs to the top floor, where the private rooms were situated.

Pressing her cheek against the wood, she peered into the first chamber.

The room had been transformed into a garden with potted greenery and plaster sculptures of the Roman gods. A half-dozen participants were cavorting. A fellow wearing the head of a satyr howled with delight as a naked nymph rubbed against his back whilst another sucked his rampant member. Another trio made use of a stone bench. A woman lay on her belly upon it, moaning as a fellow pushed his cock into her mouth, another plowing her from behind.

Seeing no sign of Quinton and Miss Loveday, Charlie moved on. The action seemed more frenzied and abandoned with each successive chamber, and the air in the corridor grew stuffy and humid. As Charlie continued around a bend, a door opened several feet ahead. She quickly retreated, peering around the corner. Her heart sped up when she saw Miss Loveday and Quinton exit the room. Had she caught them in the act at last? Trepidation and anticipation filled her as she caught their whispered words.

"We have to go to Hastings," Miss Loveday said.

"This is dangerous business." Quinton's tone was dour. "If my wife finds out—"

"He is depending on us," she insisted.

He? Who are they talking about? What is going on in Hastings?

Miss Loveday took Quinton's arm, urging him along. They disappeared into another room, and the instant the door shut behind them, Charlie followed. She was halfway to her destination when she heard the click of a door opening to her right. An arm reached through and yanked her inside. She was hauled against a large, hard form, a hand muffling her gasp of surprise.

FIFTEEN

"It's me, Lottie. Screaming will endanger both our purposes. Nod if you understand."

As Jack murmured the words against his wife's ear, he had to keep himself in rigid check. Intellectually, he understood that she wasn't his wife any longer...but holding her like this, for the first time in years, made rationality fly out the window. The truth was that he'd never stopped thinking of Lottie as his and probably never would. The way their bodies fit, like two pieces of a puzzle, bolstered his delusion that they were somehow meant to be together.

She was tall for a woman, her head tucking against his chin, her lush backside pressing against his front. Beneath her perfume, he could smell her natural scent: lavender and clean linen, like a freshly made bed. Or perhaps he just thought of bed whenever he had her in his arms. He wanted to root for more of her fragrance. To nuzzle the pretty curve of her ear, suck the plump lobe. He wanted to strip her bare and feast on her like a man who'd been starved for years...twelve, to be exact.

Most of all, he wanted to fall on his knees and beg for forgiveness.

But he couldn't. After the pain and destruction he'd caused, he couldn't undo the only noble thing he'd ever done. The only right thing in his entire benighted life.

She struggled angrily, writhing against him in the most torturous of ways. Nonetheless, he kept a firm grip on her. When she stomped on his foot, he gritted his teeth; at least the pain distracted him from his raging erection.

"Your hen has already flown the coop," he whispered against her ear. "And I have taken precautions to ensure that you will not catch her this eve. Accept that, and I will release you. Agreed?"

After a moment, she stopped struggling and nodded.

The instant he released her, she spun around and slapped him. While he could have stopped her, he figured he owed her that much.

"You bastard," she hissed.

She wasn't wrong. The light of battle flashed in her goddess's eyes. No matter how deserved her fury was, he couldn't allow her to unleash it here, not when they would likely have an audience. Voyeurism and exhibitionism were draws of the club, and this room, like the others, was peppered with peepholes. Indeed, after tonight's chef-d'oeuvre, this chamber, which looked like the abbess's punishment dungeon, would be a sought-after one. The stone walls and wooden straw-covered floor had a distinctly medieval feel...as did the rack, stocks, and flogging net made of rope. On the wall directly behind the machines hung a variety of whipping instruments placed in direct view of the victim. To heighten the anticipation, no doubt.

The image of Lottie bound and panting for him sizzled through his blood. They'd never played in this manner...or any, really. Their passion had burned so hotly that they'd just ripped each other's clothes off and got to it. If they hadn't been separated all these years, he wondered what avenues they might have explored, what inventive delights they might have discovered together.

Once her fires were burning, Lottie had no trouble letting go of inhibitions. He'd tupped her in a public place more than once—on a balcony in Paris, a beach in Greece. Each time, she'd come so hard around his cock that his eyes had rolled back in his head. Had his wife been as sweetly wanton with other lovers? The hot sap of jealousy trickled through his veins.

He shoved aside the possessiveness, which he knew he had no right to. Instead, he focused on his goal: to prevent Lottie from ruining his carefully laid scheme. His hard work was finally paying off, and he couldn't allow her to scare off Xenia Loveday.

For the sake of any audience they had, he adopted the languid tones of a louche blueblood.

"Is that the game you wish to play this eve, darling?" he inquired. "*The Fishwife's Tale* was rather diverting, and the chamber is certainly set up for a rendition of Sir Piers Bottom's *pièce de résistance*. Are you to play the part of tempestuous Lady Analise whilst I take the role of long-suffering Robert?"

Her eyes narrowing in the holes of her mask, Lottie studied their surroundings...and did he detect her breath quickening at the sight of the stocks? Christ, the things he could do to her there—

Stop it, man. Concentrate. Don't get distracted by the idea of screwing her from behind whilst she screams your name in pleasure.

He knew Lottie was buying time to analyze her options. He saw the moment she accepted that Miss Loveday was out of her reach this eve. Praise God she was as intelligent as she was beautiful. Then again, a lady couldn't run a highly successful secret investigative society without brains. He'd always admired her analytic prowess, even when it had led her to conclude that he'd been sleeping with another woman. As if he would ever betray her in that fashion. As if he would even have the stamina to do so, given the frequency of their conjugal activities.

He watched with no little fascination as his wife composed herself in a blink, locking away her emotions the way another lady might her jewels. This was new. The Lottie of the past had worn her every reaction on her sleeve. *This* Lottie had learned control, a woman of secrets rather than a girl of passion. It intrigued and depressed him simultaneously.

"That scenario is so done, *darling*." Her honeyed voice sent a thrill up his spine, even though he knew better than to believe she had any sweetness of feeling for him. "I thought we would engage in a variation on the theme."

"What do you have in mind?"

He burned to know. It was an ungodly curiosity given that the only reason she would put her hands on him would be to strangle him. Was it wrong that the notion aroused him?

He was a damned fool. Yet what was more important: to live intelligently or die happily? All his life, he'd survived by his wits, but when was the last time he'd been happy?

You know when. Twelve years ago.

Longing escaped its cage, gripping his lungs, making it hard to breathe. *God*, he'd missed her. She was everything he'd ever wanted: then, now, and always. The force of her was beyond resisting—like gravity. Essential and inescapable. She made the blood plunge from his head and land in his other head. The one that wasn't capable of thinking. That knew only instinct and desire and was harder than an iron pike.

He saw her gaze drop to his groin, her eyelashes flickering when she registered his state. Was she going to put a stop to their game, perhaps endanger their situation after all? He waited with bated breath...

She licked her lips.

Christ.

In that heart-pounding instant, their smoldering antagonism burst into a different kind of flame. The kind that was as dangerous and unpredictable as a runaway train. He was powerless to stop it—and, more to the point, he didn't want to. Savage satisfaction surged through him because *this* was the way it had always been for them. Passion and feeling beyond reason. Even if it led to pain. Even if it destroyed you and ruined you for anyone else. Even if it made you suffer every minute you were apart, every heartbeat, every breath of twelve endless years.

"Strip," Lottie said.

Die happily it is.

Aiming for nonchalance, he managed not to sound desperate. "What will you do with me when I am naked and at your mercy?"

Whatever you want. Do it. For the love of God.

"That is up to me." She arched a brow in challenge. "Stay or leave—that is your choice."

Charlie didn't know what game she was playing.

She could blame the overstimulation of the club. All this depravity was bound to affect anyone, and she was a sensual woman who hadn't had a satisfying bedding in years. She was, unfortunately, also a woman who made it a rule not to lie to herself.

It wasn't the dashed club that riled her up. It wasn't listening to salacious stories or watching those same fantasies played out in the flesh that made her blood rush hotly under her skin. It wasn't even the years of celibacy.

It was Sebastian, damn his eyes.

He infuriated and aroused her to such a degree that she didn't know what she was feeling. All she knew was the *intensity* of her state, the years of pent-up emotions, the feeling that if she didn't discharge the energy coursing through her, she might explode. Her head buzzed. Her skin tingled. She felt reckless and out of control, and for once she did not care.

Sebastian did this to me, and he's going to face the consequences.

Just because she issued the challenge, however, didn't mean that her former husband would take it. Well, she'd given him a choice, which was more than he'd given her when he interfered with her mission this eve. The thought threw tinder on the flames, but she would deal with Miss Loveday and Quinton later...if Devlin hadn't already.

Right now, her mind was on one thing.

Retribution.

She was going to get her satisfaction in whatever form she desired. And there were so many ways to choose from. She ran her gaze over the options, letting it linger upon the stocks before returning it to Sebastian.

"Well?" she said blandly. "Are you staying or going?"

Bronze stars glittered in his midnight eyes. "I am still here."

She lifted her brows. "Yet you are still dressed."

His gaze locked on hers, he began to strip. He did it without any pretense of modesty, and Lord knew the bastard had plenty to be proud of. As he tugged his shirt over his head, revealing a rippling expanse of muscle, she felt a quiver in her belly. Dash it, but the years had treated him well. His youthful virility had hardened and roughened, turning him into what he was today: a man in his prime.

His torso looked as if it had been hewn from granite, from the blocks of his chest to the delineated ridges of his abdomen. The memory of lying beneath that broad chest, the delicious weight of those honed edges and soft scratch of his dark chest hair, set off a tingle in her nipples. His eyes glittered, and his mouth curled up as if he knew what she was thinking, the arrogant bounder. He removed his footwear, and it irked her that even his feet were sexy, large and masculine. When he reached for his waistband, he paused, a slight tilt to his head.

She realized he was asking for confirmation that this was what she wanted, and anger mingled with lust. Did he think she was the same naïve miss he'd married? That she couldn't handle the sight of his nudity?

"Keep going," she said coolly. "A naked man is nothing I haven't seen before."

The smile left his eyes, a dangerous smolder taking its place. Was he *jealous*?

Serves him right.

His jaw clenching, he unfastened his trousers, removing them with swift tugs. There was defiance in his dark gaze as he stripped off his smalls and tossed them aside. Ah, his lower half was just as impressive as the top. The lean hips with the arches of muscle, those sinewy legs. That thick, long cock. He stood, his hands loosely curled at his sides, his bold posture daring her to look her fill. As if a woman could do anything else with such a bounty before her.

It made her remember that hers were likely not the only female —or male—eyes taking in Sebastian's splendid masculinity. For some reason, the public nature of their playing made her feel safe. It wasn't just the masks and disguises; it was the fact that she knew this was merely sexual. A one-time carnal encounter to exorcise her demons once and for all. This wasn't about intimacy and love and trust, the things that had landed her in trouble the first time around.

This was about lust. About using her former husband for what he was good for—and paying him back for his interference tonight. Judging from the size of his erection, he didn't mind one bit.

As she eyed that raring beast, she felt a molten trickle between her thighs. It wasn't possible for a man to get bulkier there as well, was it? Perhaps her memory hadn't managed to capture his larger-than-life manhood, the bulging veins on the huge burgundy shaft, the glossy sheen on the broad tip. His bollocks swayed like a plum too ripe for its branch.

"Will I do?"

His eyebrows rose above his mask, his arrogance restored. Just because she found his confidence attractive didn't mean she wouldn't challenge it.

"Looks are not everything," she said haughtily. "The question remains if you are ready to accept a punishment of my choosing."

"I would take anything you chose to bestow upon me."

At his fierce reply and yearning gaze, her heart thumped in a way that she didn't want to examine. Instead, she swept a considering look over the instruments of sensual torture. She was squeamish when it came to pain and derived no pleasure from inflicting it. The idea of locking Sebastian in stocks, even in play, held no appeal, and the punishment bench seemed rather pedestrian.

She made her decision. "Step up to the flogging net, then, and be quick about it."

"Yes, ma'am." Sounding amused, he strode to the net made of rope, the top corners suspended from the ceiling and the bottom two rigged to the floor. "What next?"

"Face the net. Spread your arms wide and grab hold of the ropes."

He did as she instructed, turning his back to her and fisting his hands around the hemp.

"How is that?"

His voice sounded a bit strained—probably because the twisted twine was rough against his aroused cock. But he stayed as he was, his back a masterpiece of rippling hollows and grooves, his arse high and tight. She came over to inspect him and noted that he had new scars. Apparently, he hadn't just been gallivanting and enjoying the life of a privileged rakehell. The four-inch red line below his left shoulder had been made by a blade, and her chest tightened as she realized how close that weapon had come to ending his life.

There were other assorted hurts: what appeared to be a healed bullet wound close to his hip, another mark made by a blade, this time a jagged one, a few inches higher. Sebastian's powerful body was a canvas of pain. Whatever he had been up to, it had been dangerous...literally life or death. What was so important that he would risk himself in such a fashion?

None of this has been a game. Whatever you may think of me and of everything that has happened, I want you to know that I never intended to hurt you. I left to protect you.

Perhaps he hadn't been lying. That did not excuse anything he'd done to her. At the same time, the realization reached beneath her anger, uncovering her desire to know the truth.

"Not as pretty as you expected?"

He was trying to sound casual, but she was surprised to hear the gruff undertone of uncertainty. It made her want to laugh. Beneath his arrogance, did he harbor doubts about his attractiveness? When scars only served to heighten his virile appeal?

Not that she would give him the satisfaction of knowing. After all, he'd been keeping secrets from her for years, and now she knew what she wanted tonight, what she was determined to get: answers. The public nature of the scenario made interrogation difficult, but she was a skilled investigator. One who would make use of all the tools at her disposal.

She headed to the wall behind the net where the devices of punishment were displayed on hooks. She felt Sebastian's eyes on her as she ran a finger over a birch, a cane, then a leather whip, making the handles swing and clack ominously against each other. Did she imagine it, or did she hear his swift intake of breath when she selected the gleaming black riding crop?

His gaze followed her until she went to stand behind him. Knowing that they might have an audience, she trailed the tip of the crop along the scar beneath his shoulder blade, and he shuddered.

"Oh, darling," she purred. "Wait until I'm done with you."

SIXTEEN

J ack was so hard he feared he might spill over the ropes. Even the chafing roughness of the hemp did not dampen his arousal. Looking down, he was treated to the shameful sight of his cock jutting between the ropes, a milky bead clinging to its tip.

"Spread your feet shoulder-width apart."

At Lottie's command, which was followed by swift taps of the crop against his inner thighs, his bollocks tightened, the drop of seed splattering on the ground. He bit back a groan and did as she asked, exposing himself to her mercy. He hadn't lied: he would take what he could get from her. After he'd blocked her from following Xenia Loveday, the last thing he'd expected was for Lottie to play a sexually charged game with him. Or perhaps she merely meant to torture him. But he'd take his chances.

This was the woman he'd fallen in love with: spirited, unpredictable, and bold. Maturity had honed her independent spirit into something rare and intoxicating. When he felt the edge of the crop sliding up the crack of his arse, he shivered, wondering just how far his little spitfire would go.

"You've been a naughty boy, haven't you?"

Because of his past, his desires did not typically involve being dominated by women. Even now, shame flirted at the edges of his consciousness, but he was able to push it back. Because he was with Lottie, and with her, everything was different. Everything felt right in a way that nothing else in his life did. Even when she was playing this part, her manner that of a cool schoolmistress, he felt the heat of their connection, and it burned away his numbness.

It was as if he'd been sleepwalking all these years, and the presence of his wife awakened him. Made him feel alive again. Alive and randy as hell.

Despite her well-deserved anger, he knew that she would not hurt him. She was not that kind of woman. It was one of the reasons why he'd fallen head over heels for her: the care and compassion that was at the core of who she was. He trusted Lottie. More than anything, he yearned to win back her trust. If that meant giving her control over the situation, then he would play along.

"Yes, ma'am," he said steadily. "And I'm sorry for it."

"You'll be sorrier yet."

Her sensual threat, coupled with the sensation of the crop tracing up his spine, sent another sizzle up his prick. Hearing rustling behind the walls, he knew they were being watched. He felt an illicit thrill at the idea of others seeing him with his beloved. If things were different, he'd give them a real show and take Lottie up against the stone wall. Their fucking required no enhancement, was pure beauty in its rawest form. Him and her, skin to skin, his cock buried inside her tight, wet pussy—

Smack.

He jerked, the sting on his right buttock making him grunt.

Lottie circled around the net to face him, and he roved his gaze hungrily over her bounty. He saw clearly what others could not: the magnificence that lay beneath the wig and padded frock, the mask and paint. He wanted the world to know that she was his...if only for this game.

"Am I boring you?" she inquired.

The idea was laughable.

"Never."

"Then give me your full attention."

When she tapped the tip of the crop against the dome of his cock, his breath hitched. For the first time, unease nudged him— or maybe that was just her torture device. His heart pounded like a fist when she pushed the crop through the net, caressing his cock from the base to the dripping head.

He had to clear his throat to speak. "You have my attention."

Understatement of the year.

"I'm going to ask you three easy questions: a *yes* or *no* will suffice."

Before he could appreciate her clever stratagem, she left his field of vision. When she next spoke, it was from behind him.

"If you answer me truthfully, you will be rewarded. If you don't..." She used a pause to splendid effect. "You will be punished. Do you understand?"

He twisted his head, wanting to see her eyes. "Yes—"

"Keep your hands on the rope." Her reply was crisp. "If you let go, the game ends."

He tightened his grip.

"First question." She brought her lips to his left ear, and he shuddered at the warm caress of her breath. At her words, which only he could hear. "Did you betray me with Eleni?"

Easy.

"No," he said firmly.

Lottie went in front of him and studied him keenly. She rapped the handle of the crop against her palm, the *tap tap tap* accelerating his pulse. Would she believe him? He didn't care if she flogged him—maybe with her, he would even like it—but he realized with sudden clarity that her distrust would destroy his denial.

His helpless fantasy that somehow, some way, he could win his wife back. That, despite everything, she would give him another chance. Even when he had no right to ask for one. Even when it might compromise his mission. Even when it was wrong of him to consider the possibility of endangering her—when that was the reason he'd left her in the first place.

But Lottie is different now. Stronger and more formidable. She always had the mettle of Athena, but now she has the wisdom—the control and confidence—too. Maybe she could handle what I do... who I truly am.

Her eyes were still stormy, but perhaps there was a hint of warmth. Like the sun veiled by thunderclouds. And relief flooded him.

She believes me. Even after everything.

She leaned in, and his mouth watered at having the slender column of her neck so close, just on the other side of the net. He remembered all the times he'd nuzzled the groove above her collarbone, tasting her skin. He nosed the rope, sniffing hungrily for her scent, and his cock did the same, stretching eagerly toward her.

When she wrapped her free hand around his shaft, a guttural sound raked up his throat. From the moment she'd touched him, she had ruined him for anyone else, and it was no different now. Her satin-covered fingers worked his straining rod. She pumped him once, twice, enough to make him pant and thrust his hips into her pretty fist. Then she let go.

"Is that supposed to be a reward?" he managed.

Her lips curved. Then she leaned toward him, her next question feather-soft against his ear.

"Is your interest in Xenia Loveday personal?"

He hesitated. Lives depended upon his ability to keep secrets. Yet he would not be divulging any information by answering Lottie's simple question.

"No," he said.

Lottie began frigging him again. This time she cupped his stones, squeezing the weights that swelled in her palm until he groaned. She milked him to the tip, drawing forth wetness that she thumbed over his sensitive head. Fire danced along his spine as she stroked his cock, the roughness of the rope against his bollocks making him even hotter. He thrust his hips...only to find himself fucking air yet again.

He let out an oath of frustration.

Lottie tilted her head. "Ready for your final question?"

"Bloody right I am. And if I give you the truth, you'll finish me off..."—he recalled himself enough to push through his clenched teeth—"...*ma'am*."

She smiled like a cat, then pounced, depositing a hushed query in his ear.

"Are you a spy?"

Bloody hell, she knows...or she's guessed, anyway.

His mind was a vortex of conflicting wants. Admission, denial —neither came readily. After a lifetime of silence, of bottling everything up, he didn't know how to release the truth. Didn't know if he could allow his desires to overrule his duty.

His gut clenched, his hands gripping the ropes. "I cannot answer that question."

"You have a habit of saying that." Lottie's eyes flashed with judgement. "Punishment it is, then."

He expected to feel the lash of her anger on his skin. He didn't bother to brace himself because he was getting what he deserved. Thus, he was totally and wholly unprepared for what she did next.

When Charlie took hold of Sebastian's cock, his big body lurched against the ropes as if he'd been tossed by a tempest. She saw the surprise in his eyes, and grim satisfaction filled her that he still hadn't caught on. There was more than one way to get the answers out of him. Her mind felt as overrun as Covent Garden on market day, a chaotic collision of questions and emotions. Yet a single truth blazed.

Sebastian did not betray me twelve years ago. At least not in the manner I assumed.

She believed him. The truth had been there in his eyes when he answered her first question. Of course, his response blew the lid off Pandora's Box. Who had Eleni been to Sebastian, if not his lover? What had he been mixed up in? What was he up to now, and what did Quinton and Miss Loveday have to do with it?

I am sick of his secrets. Sick of not knowing why he ruined our marriage. Why is he back now, and why does he think he has the right to protect me? From what?

She pumped him with the smooth, firm strokes he used to like. That much hadn't changed. His eyes smoldered beneath their heavy lids, his cock thick and long in her fist. He gritted his teeth, the tendon on his neck cording the way it used to just before he spent. She released him abruptly, and his cock toppled like a felled tree. They both watched as the stiff crimson length bobbed under its own weight. Rather like a heavy branch...but a cock couldn't break, could it?

He made a sound like a snarl. *"Bloody hell."*

"You can finish yourself off if you like. If you let go of the rope, however, our game is over," she said sweetly.

"I'll finish this damned game if it kills me," he bit out.

Just like she knew he would. The fellow had always been as stubborn as an ox.

"Do you think frustration can kill a man?" She tilted her head. "Let's find out, shall we?"

She gripped him again, squeezing his turgid length, her own breath quickening as his cock burgeoned further. He'd always been big, but it was more than his size. His eyes were as hungry as his body, his desire for her immutable, bordering on desperation. To be the focus of such intensity had always thrilled her and unleashed the strength of her own passion.

It was, she suddenly realized, the reason why her other lover hadn't satisfied her the way Sebastian had. He hadn't needed her as much. Hadn't come close to owning her and being owned by her in return.

"Maybe a woman isn't immune to frustration either." Bronze embers glowed in Sebastian's eyes. "I'd wager that you're as aroused as I am, Madam Torturer. That beneath those skirts, your pretty cunny is wet and wanting, aching to be filled by my cock."

At his wicked words, she squeezed her thighs together. Heavens, she *was* wet.

"Are you sure it's your hand you want me to be fucking?" he asked.

From any other man, she would have disdained the crudity. Sebastian, however, had a way of making her feel beyond his lust to the yearning beneath. An unspoken need in him that she knew instinctively was about more than sex even though he'd just used the word *fucking*. She worked her fist, her pussy clenching as if it could feel that bulging length too.

The moment she felt him stiffening, thickening, she cupped his mushroomed dome and squeezed.

He gnashed his teeth. From behind the wall, she thought she heard a commiserating groan.

"I could do this all night," she said.

His gaze was mutinous. "Do it then."

When she took up the challenge, he muttered something under his breath.

"What was that?" She leaned closer.

"I reminded myself that frustration can't kill a man." His voice rasped against the sensitive whorl of her ear. "Otherwise, I'd have died years ago."

She ought to leave that provocative remark alone. Yet when had she ever been wise where this scoundrel was concerned?

She said with a scoff, "When have you ever suffered from frustration?"

He looked as if he wanted to say something. Instead, he set his jaw.

Two can play at that game.

She tossed aside the crop, using both hands on him. She palmed the smooth heft of his balls while using her other hand to work his turgid shaft.

"Answer me," she said.

"If you want to bring me to my knees, there is an easier way." He consumed her with his battle-fierce eyes. "I'd go down readily for a taste of your sweet pussy. I would kneel before you, put my mouth on your cunny, lick your pearl until you came. I would feast on your dew, get every drop of it, and I wouldn't stop until you screamed my name. Then I would do it all over again."

Heavens.

Her breathing hitched, her body seized by the pleasure he promised. She *felt* him there, his hands covering her thighs, spreading her for his delectation. He would eat her exactly as he described—savoring her as if she were a banquet, driving her mad with his greed. His thoroughness.

"I'd push my tongue so deep inside you that I would feel you clench." Against the rope, his cheeks were flushed with arousal. "Would you like that, darling? Coming in my mouth that way? Would you go wild and rub your sweet quim against my face and beg for more?"

Heat roiled beneath her skin, her face sweaty against the mask. Her nipples pulsed against her bodice. She pressed her thighs together, trying to quell the ache of emptiness, but all she felt was how wet she'd become. The dampness of her pussy, the throbbing of her swollen pearl...

"Christ."

Sebastian's groan snapped her back. Too late, she realized that he'd mesmerized her with his fantasy, making her frig him harder, faster with each dirty word that had rolled off his talented tongue. She released him immediately...but it was too late.

Visible pulses traveled up his jutting shaft. His torso flexed, every muscle on his chest and abdomen rigid with tension. He came, shuddering, his seed shooting from him in thick, creamy arcs. Before she could react, he reached through the net, hooking her by the nape. He pulled her close, his lips claiming hers through the rope, his kiss hot and greedy and possessive.

Her mind fogged. Her knees quivered.

He broke the kiss, sliding his mouth to her ear.

"I've been frustrated for twelve damned years." His molten whisper scalded her insides. "From the day we met, there hasn't been anyone else—only you."

She staggered back, and he let her go. Her heart knocking against her ribs, she saw the truth blazing in his eyes. It was too much, all of it.

As applause broke out from behind the walls, she turned and walked out.

SEVENTEEN

That night, Jack dreamed.

Of Lottie and him, back in that room. Only this time they didn't have an audience. They didn't need to disguise themselves—could bare themselves fully to one another. She was as naked as he was, and this time, he had her against the ropes. She was the one gripping the hemp, her blonde tresses cascading down her back, her face turned to the net. He palmed her lusciously rounded arse, giving her a proprietary smack that he knew would annoy her.

He didn't care. Sometimes he irked her on purpose because a riled Lottie was also an uninhibited Lottie. And he loved nothing better than his wife's complete surrender.

He spanked her again, but before she could scold him, he dropped on one knee. Spreading her firm cheeks, he licked her drenched slit. Bloody hell, she tasted fine, and her gasps of pleasure were even better. He found her opening, stabbing his tongue inside. To his delight, she pushed back against him, taking him deeper, moaning his name when she came like the hot little wanton she was.

He took her hands and placed them on her quivering buttocks.

"Spread yourself for me," he said thickly. "You're mine. All of you."

He ate her until she was shaking, moaning, begging for more.

Only then did he surge to his feet and push his cock into her tight passage. He sheathed himself, groaning as her slick tunnel clenched around him. Gripping her by the hips, he began to plow her.

"Yes, yes," she moaned. "Fuck me harder. Drill your big cock into me."

Even through his haze of lust, he felt an odd twinge. As if there was something he was supposed to remember. But her sex milked him insistently, and with a groan, he gave her what she demanded.

"You're an animal. An absolute beast," she crowed.

Her voice had changed. Shaded not just by desire but something else... Something that he'd never heard from Lottie.

"Ram your cock inside me. Do it. Make me spend," she screamed.

She came, and he felt it. Even though the sensation was pleasurable, another feeling churned inside him: shame. A sense that what he was doing was wrong. But why? Lottie was his...his wife, his love. He was too far gone, the climax overtaking him...

She pushed him away and twisted to look at him with glittering green eyes.

"Never spill inside me, you jackanapes! We cannot be discovered—"

Jack's eyes flew open. His heart was racing, his hands knotted in the bedclothes. Sweat dripped off his brow, and to his mortification, the sheets were sticky with more than perspiration. He sat up, raised his knees, and dropped his head into his arms, waiting for his gut to stop roiling. Willing the sickly feeling to subside.

The memories pierced his brain like a red-hot spear. The biggest mistake of his life. The mistake he could never come back from, no matter how hard he tried to atone or outrun it. His disgrace stained every fiber of his being, and he felt it every time he looked in the mirror. Every time someone called him by a name that he had no right to. Every time he wanted to go back in time, change history, do everything differently with Lottie.

He scrubbed his palms over his eyes, trying to focus. To think. Last night, he'd fallen asleep on a euphoric cloud. It wasn't just the climax Lottie had given him, splendid as that had been. It was the fact that she'd trusted him enough to play the game with him, and when he'd told her the truth, that he hadn't been with another since her, she'd *believed* him.

She'd obviously been shocked, which was understandable given how voracious his appetite had been with her. Yet she still had sufficient faith in him to believe that he'd honored their vows over the last dozen years. Broodingly, he considered that she likely hadn't done the same; why would she, when she believed he was dead? When he'd staged his demise in such a way that no woman would wish to remain faithful to her philandering husband? If she'd fucked someone else on his freshly dug grave, he would probably deserve it.

Rationally, he knew this. Yet reason had never applied to Lottie, and it didn't stop jealousy from gnawing at him. He couldn't shove aside the question of how many she'd lain with. How many men he would need to beat to a pulp for touching his wife. This despite the damnable fact that he had no right to ask or care.

Yet he did bloody care, and he hated himself more for it.

He told himself that the encounter between him and Lottie last night meant nothing...to her, at least. She'd walked away without a word. Their sexual play didn't mean that she would take him back. It didn't mean that his deepest fantasy would come true: that he would win her love and hand again, this time forever.

There is no going back.

Primus was right. Even if Jack could go back, he wouldn't, for Lottie's sake. There was too much at stake, and the danger was rising with the tides of people flooding London. The best thing he could do for her was to stay away—and keep her out of the First Flame's path.

Whilst he'd kept Lottie occupied last night, Delaney had followed his order to track Xenia Loveday. Delaney had caught snippets of a conversation between Miss Loveday and her partner-in-crime, Gilbert Quinton. They'd been searching for Anthony Quinton (Miss Loveday's paramour and Gilbert's younger brother) who'd gone missing. At the academy, they'd found an acquaintance of Tony's, who'd mentioned that he had a friend in Hastings, and they were planning to go to the coastal town to look for him.

Jack would follow them, for Tony was the missing link to the First Flame.

Two months ago, Jack had picked up rumors about anarchists operating in Calais. Posing as a fisherman, he'd infiltrated the community. He'd had no luck getting anyone to talk...until a young Englishman showed up at the portside *brasserie*. The cove had been nervy, despondent, and clearly terrified. Jack had acted the part of the friendly local, inviting the other to share his table, buying drinks. He'd bided his time; eventually, the man's tongue had loosened.

Tony had used an alias, claiming he was a sailor in town for a few days. The cove was a shoddy liar, which made it easy to sift out the pieces of the truth. After a few more drinks, he admitted that his fondness for gaming had landed him in terrible debt.

"Have you ever made one mistake after another"—Tony's voice had hitched as he knuckled his reddened eyes—*"until you've dug a hole so deep that there is no escape?"*

Jack answered truthfully. *"I have."*

His hole was a crater so vast that he'd lost himself completely. At times, he even forgot his real name, who he was. His mistakes had cost him his best friend and his wife.

"Then you understand." Tony looked at him with glazed,

desperate eyes. *"I never wanted to hurt anyone. I am not a bad person."*

"We all make mistakes." Experience guided Jack's words. *"But you can still redeem yourself."*

"I can't." Tony drained his glass. *"It's too late. They won't let me."*

Despite his thudding pulse, Jack asked calmly, *"They?"*

"They're everywhere. Watching. Listening." Tony's gaze jumped around the smoky room, panic piercing his inebriated state. *"I shouldn't be talking. I've said too much already—"*

"I can help you."

"No, you can't. No one can."

"I can." Jack leaned in, his voice low and urgent. *"I have the power to protect you from the First Flame. If you are willing to do what is right—what I know is in your heart. For yourself and your country."*

Tony gawped at him. *"Who...who are you?"*

"A friend, if you'll let me be."

Jack had spent the rest of the evening gaining Tony's trust. They'd stuck to lighter topics—their hobbies, interests, families—and even if the details were not real, the camaraderie was. By evening's close, Tony had seemed hopeful and agreed to meet with Jack the following night. He'd said he would bring "evidence" that would help Jack bring down the First Flame.

Tony never showed.

Jack had been looking for him ever since. Tony had said he was from London, and although he made his living as a sailor, his dream was to be a writer. He penned what he called "stories for the masses" whilst he worked on an epic masterpiece about the plight of the working class. He mentioned having a muse: a Scheherazade, who breathed life into his stories and made them so popular that they sold out at bookshops in the Strand.

Those clues had eventually led Jack to the infamous Scheherazade at the Academy of Venus...whose real name was

Xenia Loveday. During Jack's search of her tumble-down flat, he'd found a keepsake portrait of a fellow matching the sailor in Calais to a tee. The name "Anthony Quinton" had been written on the back, surrounded by doodled hearts. From there, Jack discovered that Tony Quinton had gone missing, and Miss Loveday had enlisted the help of his older brother Gilbert to look for him.

With any luck, the pair would lead Jack to Tony. Then he could discover what the First Flame was plotting and put an end to it. He would fulfill his duty and protect his beloved. After that, he would get the hell away from London. He didn't trust himself around his wife. With her, he had a primal urge to bear his soul, including his ugliest secrets...which would only result in disaster.

The only solution was to get away.

From the temptation of Lottie and the life that had never been his.

"Charlie, we weren't expecting you!" Fiona exclaimed the next morning.

Charlie could see that this was true. Fi's fiery curls looked disheveled, and the skirts of her leaf-green walking dress were wrinkled, as if they'd recently been bunched by an impatient hand. Behind her, Hawksmoor was discreetly adjusting his crumpled cravat. It did not take a seasoned investigator to deduce what the pair had been up to before Charlie had shown up unannounced on their doorstep.

The couple's marital bliss reminded Charlie of her own encounter last night.

From the day we met, there hasn't been anyone else—only you.

Sebastian's revelation had wreaked havoc upon her senses. She'd barely slept or eaten, too consumed by his admission. Why had he been faithful to her? Why had he left? How had he managed to remain celibate for *twelve years*...and what did he want from her now?

What do I want?

Obviously, time hadn't diminished their physical attraction. Desire was one thing, however, and emotional entanglement another. While she couldn't deny that Sebastian affected her senses like no other, she knew better than to trust him.

Then why do I still feel a pull toward him? As if he were gravity and I some hapless object inexorably drawn toward him? I burn to know all his secrets even though I shouldn't care.

She also had to face the discomfiting fact that she'd allowed her personal feelings to get in the way of the case. Because of Sebastian, she had lost track of Xenia Loveday. Luckily, Devlin had picked up the trail, following Quinton and Miss Loveday to one of the group rooms. A whore had planted herself in the spot nearest to them, barring Devlin from eavesdropping. However, he had tracked Quinton afterward to a coaching inn. The latter had secured a pair of tickets for Hastings, a village near the Sussex coast, leaving in two days' time. He had expressed interest in visiting a pub there that a friend had recommended, one owned by someone named Simon Legg.

"That would be the Legg & Arms," the innkeeper had replied. *"On All Saints' Street and a treat not to be missed."*

Was this a tryst Quinton was planning? Away from London, from the life he'd built here with Amara, would he show his true fickle colors? Or did this getaway have another purpose? Last night, Miss Loveday had mentioned that some fellow was depending on her and Quinton; who was this mysterious man?

Charlie would get the answers to those questions. Yet she knew that Sebastian had an interest in them too. She had to be prepared to deal with his interference, and the best way to do it was to arm herself...with knowledge.

She air-kissed her protegee's cheeks. "I apologize for my

impromptu and unfashionably early visit. I have a confidential matter I wish to discuss."

"You are welcome any time," Fi said.

She exchanged a look with her husband.

"Splendid to see you, Lady Fayne." The Earl of Hawksmoor bowed. "I shall leave you ladies to—"

"Actually, it is you I wish to talk to, my lord," Charlie said.

"Me?" The earl furrowed his brow.

Fi looked equally surprised. "What business do you have with Hawksmoor?"

"I should like to consult him on a matter involving his professional expertise."

Fiona and her lord shared another look before she closed the door and led the way to the sitting area. She and Charlie shared a settee whilst Hawksmoor folded his long frame into an adjacent wingchair. Fi distributed the tea, and Charlie took a breath before plunging in.

"This matter is a personal one," she said. "I trust you can be discreet?"

"Knowing what you do of my profession," Hawksmoor said wryly, "do you doubt it?"

The earl had done an excellent job of convincing Society that he was an unassuming scholar. Fiona hadn't suspected his covert activities—nor he hers—when they'd agreed to a marriage of convenience. Then they'd fallen in love, and their professional and personal lives had collided in a most spectacular fashion.

"Not at all, my lord," Charlie said. "The question was more for Fiona's benefit."

"I can be discreet," Fi protested. "I'm an investigator, too."

"And an excellent one at that." Charlie gave her protegee a pointed look. "But I am asking you not to divulge what I am about to share with the other Angels."

While Charlie would trust Fi with her life, the dear did love to gossip with her bosom friends.

Fi's forehead pleated. "You wish me to keep a secret from Livy, Glory, and Pippa?"

"For the time being. I am sorry to ask that of you, but the fewer who know, the better."

Fi nodded slowly.

"Then I will get to the point." Charlie aimed her gaze at Hawksmoor. "What do you know about the foreign specialty in your line of work?"

Hawksmoor's grey gaze revealed nothing, which likely accounted for his success as an agent of the Crown.

"Could you be more specific, my lady?" he said in neutral tones. "If I am at liberty to provide an answer, I will. I am certain you understand that I am bound by rules similar to those that govern your own society."

"If I said a name, could you tell me if he was engaged in your sort of work abroad?"

"I can neither confirm nor deny the existence of any colleagues, ma'am. To do so would compromise their safety."

She'd had a feeling that the earl would respond in this way. Which left her no option.

"Even if the man I am interested in is my own husband?" she inquired.

The earl frowned. "Lord Fayne passed away some time ago. I don't understand why—"

"I have recently gained some information which suggests that all was not as it seemed where my husband was concerned. As a result, I am looking for answers."

She skimmed over the fact that Sebastian was still alive, cursing her instinct to keep him that way. If he was a spy, she did not want to compromise whatever mission he was working on. Or, more importantly, his safety.

"Specifically, I would like to know if he might have been working for the foreign specialty twelve years ago when we first met in Marseille. And later in Rhodes—"

"Greece, you say?" Hawksmoor sat up, his visage sharpening. "And before that France?"

"Yes." Her pulse accelerated. "What do you know?"

His brows knitted, Hawksmoor was obviously sifting through what he could and could not reveal.

Charlie clasped her hands in her lap and tried to calm her nerves.

"Darling." Fi leaned forward, touching her husband's sleeve. "You can trust Charlie. She will keep whatever you say in confidence. Given the circumstances under which we met, our respective organizations have working knowledge of one another anyway. Why, one could say we are nearly collegial."

Despite her tension, Charlie had to hide a smile. Amongst Fi's many talents was her ability to charm her way through any situation.

Hawksmoor gave his lady a sardonic look. "We're colleagues now, are we?"

"More than that, I should say." Fi's demure smile was decidedly flirtatious.

His mouth twitching, the earl said, "Minx. I was going to tell Lady Fayne what I know...which, candidly, isn't much. My focus has been domestic, not foreign. I do know that those involved in foreign espionage must practice extra discretion: if they are captured, they will not be protected or, indeed, claimed by the institution that sent them."

"That sounds rather heartless," Fi said, wrinkling her nose.

"It is how the game of politics is played. Everyone spies, and everyone knows it. But no one acknowledges anything, and if you're caught..." Hawksmoor shrugged.

With a shiver, Charlie contemplated why Sebastian would sign up for such a perilous and, frankly, thankless job. She couldn't deny that he had all the makings of an excellent spy: from his physical prowess to his daring nature, he was a man who didn't balk at breaking the rules. She'd always sensed he had his own moral compass, guided by secrets she'd never managed to unearth whilst they were together.

From what he'd told her of his past, he'd been sickly as a child. Bullied by the neighboring lads and swaddled by his mama, he hadn't been sent to school or allowed to do the activities enjoyed by young boys. He'd grown up in relative isolation on the family's remote Devonshire estate. While he'd eventually outgrown his weak lungs, perhaps something of his past lingered: the need to prove himself, to show the world that he could do whatever he set his mind to.

"What else can you tell me?" Charlie asked.

"If your husband was indeed involved in the foreign branch, it would have made sense for him to be in France and Greece during the time you specified. There were rumors of a highly secretive anarchist group at play—a phantom organization whose members lived in various nations with a single purpose in mind: creating chaos and bringing down the establishment at any cost. They'd cloaked themselves so well that their existence had never been proved, but it was believed that they were behind assassinations, violent mobs, and acts of terror across the Continent. France, being a hotbed of revolution, was believed to be the headquarters of this group, with sects located in Germany, Italy, and Greece."

Charlie let the chilling information sink in. "And there was a group working to counter these anarchists?"

Hawksmoor propped his elbows on the arms of his chair, his hands steepled. "No official group. But I have heard—purely rumors, you understand—that there was a select team of agents from different countries collaborating to fight the anarchists. They, too, were 'ghosts.' No country would officially acknowledge their existence or sanction their purpose, despite the speculation that this group has prevented multiple attacks on the public."

Pieces of a puzzle fell into place: Sebastian's absences and lies, his nebulous past, the shadows and secrets in his eyes. It ought to have been shocking to discover that one's former spouse was, most likely, part of an elite espionage team, but what Charlie felt was... relief.

Silly, irrational, overwhelming relief.

At least now she understood that Sebastian's betrayal had been for a greater purpose and not just because he'd had an itch for some voluptuous taverna owner. She didn't have all the answers yet, but she had sufficient knowledge to decide that she wanted to know more. Even if she couldn't forgive Sebastian for abandoning her, she needed to know why he'd done it. Needed to know the man she'd married—who he'd been then...

And who he is now.

Recognition tremored through her. She'd felt more last night with Sebastian than she had in twelve dashed years. It hadn't been just physical: their emotional connection had somehow survived the wreckage of their parting. Before and after Sebastian, she hadn't met a man who could match her in tenacity, passion, and wit, and that hadn't changed. They were two sides of the same hot-blooded coin. Beneath her fury and hurt, another feeling crept into her awareness.

Gladness. She was glad that the man she'd once loved with her whole being wasn't dead.

Even if at times he made her want to resort to bloody murder.

"Do you know anything else about this ghost team, my lord?" she asked.

Hawksmoor shook his head. "As I said, anything I've heard is a rumor. This team is mythical amongst espionage circles: a legend that proves even a small group can change the world for good."

"We Angels believe that as well," Fiona put in. "Don't we, Charlie?"

"You and the others have proved it," Charlie said with pride. "Your dedication to our clients and each other has demonstrated the true power of sisterhood."

Fi tilted her head. "You are part of the sisterhood, too."

Too late, Charlie recognized the trap. Fi's charm was like a candy coating over her keen intellect.

"The business with the Marquess of Fayne is not entirely in the past, is it?" Fi studied her with earnest blue eyes. "Won't you bring us into your confidence, Charlie? You can trust me and the other Angels to help."

Charlie didn't want to hurt Fi's feelings, but she recognized now that Amara's predicament was about more than infidelity. Sebastian had tried to warn Charlie that Gilbert was involved in something dangerous...but what, exactly? The blacksmith was a monarchist; he and Amara had named their child in honor of Her Majesty the Queen. Charlie could not imagine him involved in a radical organization.

Miss Loveday was a different story. She was unpredictable and ingenious; there was no telling the kind of mischief she was capable of, and Sebastian had obviously been tracking her for a reason. What was going on between her and Amara's husband? Did she have him in her sexual thrall...or was her hold on him a different sort altogether?

Until I have the answers to these questions, I must honor my promise to Amara. I must solve her case with discretion...and deal with my own problems after.

"It is not about trust but timing, my dear." Charlie patted Fi's arm. "I have things in hand for the time being. If I need assistance, however, you and the Angels will be the first to know."

"Promise?"

"You have my word. Now I must be off." She stood. "Thank you for the information, my lord."

Rising, Hawksmoor bowed. "It was little enough, my lady."

"I will see you out," Fi said.

As they exited the drawing room, Charlie said, "How is the Snelling case progressing?"

"We are wrapping things up." Fi's smile was a bit smug. "As I suspected, the butler did it."

"Very good. Now I must ask that you and the others keep an eye on the society for a few days."

"Where are you going?" Fi asked immediately.

"To Hastings. I have an old acquaintance to catch up with."

It wasn't a lie. Charlie knew that she would not be the only one tracking Quinton and Miss Loveday to the coastal village. In fact, she was counting upon it.

Eighteen

Despite its fame as the site of the eponymous battle of 1066, Hastings had a sleepy ambience that Jack associated with seaside towns. The sky was gently bruised by dusk, and the lulling crash of waves, salt-laced air, and higgledy-piggledy buildings had a lethargic charm that he would have found relaxing in other circumstances. As he headed down the narrow cobbled All Saints' Street, a thoroughfare that ran from the ancient parish church to the town gate, he kept an eye on his quarry.

Xenia Loveday and Gilbert Quinton were several yards ahead, making their way through the throng of townsfolk out to spend their hard-earned wages. The pubs lining both sides of the street were packed, spewing light and laughter. Loveday and Quinton paused in front of several establishments, peering at the signs before moving on.

Their fifth stop was a half-timbered building with diamond-paned windows. A squeaky wooden sign above the doorway pronounced the premises as the "Legg & Arms." The pair entered; Jack counted to ten before following. Ducking to fit under a low beam, he was greeted by a blast of raucous voices and steamy air scented with smoke and hops.

The crowd inside was a rowdy mix of local working class, tradesmen passing through the port, and a few adventurous tourists. Tables were packed, barmaids weaving through the crowd to deliver foaming tankards and plates of fried fish, pickled trotters, and pies. Spotting Loveday and Quinton waiting by the long wooden bar, Jack casually went over to join the queue. He'd styled himself as a merchant vacationing by the seaside. He'd padded his striped waistcoat to give himself extra girth and added silver to his temples and a thick mustache. A pair of wire-framed spectacles sat upon his nose.

Three patrons ahead of him, Loveday was whispering to Quinton.

Jack read her lips.

"I think that's him," she said. "Tony's crony."

Loveday pointed at the lanky ginger-haired fellow behind the bar—the publican, Jack would guess, by the familiar way he greeted the patrons. The proprietor was popular, the queue to see him winding the length of the bar even though another barman was also taking orders.

His profile grim, Quinton muttered, "Let's hope he knows where the wastrel is."

Anticipation simmered in Jack. *I bloody hope so too.*

Time dragged, the publican palavering with the folk ahead of Loveday and Quinton as if they were long-lost relatives. Finally, it was the pair's turn. Jack edged as close as he could, receiving grumbles from the patrons ahead of him.

"New to the establishment?" Below a shock of ginger curls, the publican's thin face creased with a friendly smile. "I'm Simon Legg, the proprietor. I'd be happy to recommend a fine ale—"

"Actually, we would like a word." Quinton cast a nervous glance around. "In private."

Although Legg's smile didn't falter, his eyes narrowed. "Afraid I ain't got time."

"It is about our mutual friend To—" Loveday began.

"Busy night, as you can see." Legg cut her off. "Now I'd be obliged if you'd state your order or let the good folk behind you do so."

The waiting patrons muttered in agreement. Jack's attention was snagged by the brunette serving maid who'd joined Legg behind the bar. On her right cheek, she had a large purplish birthmark that made people avert their gaze—typically to her bosom, which was distractingly ample in the low square of her neckline. Jack, however, studied her face more closely, peeling away the heavy eyebrows, deceiving contours cleverly created by paint, and thickened lashes.

When he found her glinting gaze, disbelief and awe struck him at once. He'd known she would show up—had dreaded and anticipated her appearance in equal measure. He couldn't deny that her disguise was top-notch, and the fact that she'd managed to stay one step ahead of him, securing employment here... Torn between irritation at her reckless risking of her own neck and admiration for her ingenuity, he could only shake his head.

The tiniest of smirks touched her painted lips. Then she bent her head, appearing to be fully occupied by the task of loading drinks onto her tray while she eavesdropped on the increasingly heated conversation.

"We must speak to you about my brother," Quinton insisted. "We came all the way from London—"

"Don't give a rat's arse if you came from Timbuktu."

"It's a matter of life and death, Mr. Legg." Loveday's phrasing was rather dramatic, but given her literary performance, this was no surprise. "We need to find Tony, and I believe you know where he—"

"Get a drink or get out." Legg sheathed his amicability in unexpected steel. "If it's the former you're wanting, Betty 'ere—" he gestured to Lottie—"will take care o' you. I've other patrons waiting."

When he turned to the next customer, Loveday and Quinton

exchanged frustrated looks. Clearly—and wisely—they didn't want to reveal more of their business publicly. They mumbled their orders to Betty/Lottie, who informed them in brassy tones that she would bring their drinks over.

Unable to help himself, Jack stepped up to the bar.

"Pour me a drink, love?" he asked.

"Ain't your love," Lottie retorted.

Oh, darling. If only you knew.

"But if you ask nicely," she amended, "I'll bring a drink to your table."

He eyed the beer on her tray; it looked like piss. Nonetheless, he gave her his order and coin, and she took both with the careless aplomb of a woman who'd worked her entire life behind a bar.

His Lottie. Was there anyone else like her in the world?

He chose a booth next to Loveday and Quinton. The latticed partition gave them a false sense of privacy, or perhaps it was desperation that fueled their whispered conversation. Jack discreetly observed them through the slats.

"I'd wager my smithy that this Legg fellow knows where Tony is," Quinton muttered.

Jack agreed. Legg's reaction to the mention of Tony—stiffening shoulders, increased respiration, dilated pupils—gave him away. The publican knew something, all right.

"What if he won't talk to us?" Loveday bit her lip. "Do you think we should try again—"

"If my fool brother doesn't want to be found, he's sworn Legg to secrecy. Legg won't talk unless we threaten him—"

"Threaten?" Loveday squeaked.

"Or we can follow him."

God save me. The last thing Jack needed was the bumbling pair of amateurs scaring off Legg when the man could lead him to Tony Quinton.

"'Ere you go, lovelies." Lottie arrived, thumping drinks on Loveday and Quinton's table. "Anything else I can get for you?"

"I don't suppose you could..." Loveday peered up at her hopefully. "Get Mr. Legg to speak to us?"

"About this missing friend o' yours? Thomas, was it?"

Jack had to respect his spouse's smooth interrogation skills.

"Tony," Loveday said eagerly. "He's my, um, friend. And Mr. Quinton's brother. Maybe you've seen him? He looks a bit like Mr. Quinton, but he's younger and slimmer. He's ever so handsome, with princely green eyes."

"I may have seen 'im," Lottie said after a moment.

"Where?" Quinton demanded.

"Around." She waved vaguely.

"It is vital that we find him," Loveday burst out. "He may be in trouble."

"What sort o' trouble?" Lottie enrobed her voice with appropriate wariness. "I ain't getting involved in any shady business."

"Some bad men are looking for him," Miss Loveday said in quavering tones. "If we don't find him first—"

"Not a word more." Quinton aimed a scowl at Lottie. "We want to talk to Legg. Can you arrange that or not?"

Lottie pretended to think it over. "All right. But it'll cost you a quid."

Quinton handed over the money, which the shameless minx pocketed.

"Give me a few minutes, and I'll get 'im out to the alley behind the pub," she said.

The pair scrambled outside as if they expected to find Father Christmas there.

Lottie sauntered over to Jack's table. Behind the concealing thicket of lashes, her gaze was sharp and serious. He guessed that she'd pieced a few things together. She deposited his tankard, leaning forward as she did so. The jiggle of her breasts momentarily distracted him.

"Are anarchists after Tony? Is he in danger from them...and from you?"

Her whispered words made him jerk as if she'd shouted.

Bloody hell, she has put more than a few pieces together. She has damned near finished the puzzle.

"Is that why you're visiting the seaside, sir?" Her voice back at its normal volume, she prattled on like a friendly barmaid. "'Oping to catch a few fish?"

He cleared his throat. And his head.

"I was told Hastings has prime fishing grounds," he said. "I am not interested in the little fish. It's the big ones that I'm after."

He wanted to reassure her that he meant Tony Quinton no harm.

From Lottie's considering look, she received his message. "For a price, I will personally show you where to find the largest ones."

He couldn't resist.

"I thought that was my line, dove," he drawled.

She tried to hide her smile and failed. "Now my assistance will cost you double."

"I'd better stop while I'm ahead. What's the price for your wisdom, sweeting?"

"Five quid."

Christ, the woman was raking it in this eve. Yet he found himself intrigued by his wife's offer. Having seen her in action several times now, he was realizing that she was a bloody fine investigator. Although his first instinct would always be to protect her, to shield her from the darkness of the world, he had to admit that she was no delicate flower.

And if what she intimated was true, she knew where Tony Quinton might be hiding. Lives depended upon Jack getting this information. Coming to a decision, he slid the money across the table; when she reached for it, he nabbed her hand, pulling her toward him. To anyone watching, it would appear to be a flirtatious move—and it was—but he also had a message to deliver.

"Get rid of the other two," he said under his breath. "It's too dangerous. Tell them I'll look after Tony."

Her subtle nod conveyed her understanding. She pulled her hand free.

"I'm off in an hour," she said. "We'll discuss plans then."

She sallied forth with her tray. Jack took a sip from the tankard. The beer tasted worse than piss, but the view of Lottie's swaying bottom and the prospect of finding Tony Quinton more than made up for it.

"How much farther?" Jack asked in a low tone.

"We are almost there." Lottie's reply was equally hushed. "Do try to keep up."

She looked down her nose at him—which wasn't difficult because she was leading the way and on a higher part of the ledge. They were ascending cliffs along the shore; they hadn't lit their lanterns for fear of being spotted by Tony Quinton or the people after him. The full moon illuminated the beach and rippling waves a dizzying distance away. A decent climber himself, Jack was impressed by his spouse's agility. She reminded him of the Alpine ibex he'd seen in Italy, gracefully leaping from rock to rock, up the mountain face.

As he didn't think his wife would like to be compared to a goat, no matter how graceful, he refrained from sharing his thoughts. He had to brush up on flirting. Not that he'd ever been good at it. Recalling her reaction to being likened to a time ball, he stifled a grin. Anyway, if he were to pay her a compliment, her nimbleness wouldn't be at the top of his mind. Not with his current view. Lord help him, but she was tempting from the rear.

She'd changed out of her disguise. Beneath her cleverly detachable skirts, she'd had on the present dark breeches, and the way they hugged her narrow waist and heart-shaped derriere ought to be a sin. She'd buttoned a slim, dark waistcoat over her barmaid's blouse and woven her hair into an efficient braid.

She looked like a young Athena, gorgeous and bold, and he flashed back to their first meeting when she'd valiantly defended herself against a trio of brutes whilst escaping her lecherous guardian through her cunning. Her courage and spirit would always lead her to choose peril over passivity. She was a goddess who would not go down without a fight. Jack wanted to shield her, possess her, and worship her at the same time.

On the carriage ride over, she'd demanded to know what he wanted with Tony. Given that the horse had long bolted the barn, he told her about the meeting in Calais. How he believed that Tony wanted to do the right thing and help stop the anarchists. Then he asked her some questions of his own.

"How did you convince Loveday and Quinton to stay behind?" he'd inquired.

"I told them Tony was mixed up in dangerous business, and if they wanted to see him alive, they would leave finding him to the professionals." She shrugged. *"Gilbert knows my work and therefore trusts my judgement."*

Jack had also asked how she had managed to stay one step ahead of him.

"One of my associates followed Quinton and heard him buying tickets for Hastings and inquiring about Simon Legg. I headed to Hastings before his arrival to investigate Legg. As Legg happened to need a barmaid, I made myself a suitable candidate for the position."

Her pleased little grin had caused a quickening in his groin.

It had also caused a quickening of something else. Something he'd tried to extinguish but never could: hope. The voice inside his head whispered, *She's changed, and so have you. Perhaps there is a way to win her back—*

"We're here."

Lottie's whisper jerked his attention back to the present and the gaping hole that appeared halfway up the side of the cliff. It was the entrance she'd told him about—the one she'd seen Legg entering the night before. Without proper reinforcements and knowledge of what awaited inside the caverns, she'd wisely decided to monitor his movements from afar. Legg had emerged about an hour later, minus the sack he'd been carrying. Had he delivered supplies to his old crony...was Tony Quinton waiting inside those caves?

Although Jack believed Tony was feckless rather than felonious, he did not want to take any chances. A fox was at its most dangerous when cornered.

"I'll go in first," he said in low tones.

Even in the moonlight, he could see Lottie rolling her eyes at him. She lit her lantern and waltzed into the mouth of darkness as if it were a ballroom. Sighing, he readied his own light and followed.

Inside was a narrow rocky corridor, and their lamps afforded a small bubble of visibility in the oppressive gloom. Natural rock formations created eerie shapes along the tunnel, which looked like it had been widened by human hands—smugglers, no doubt. The coastline was riddled with secret warrens used to store goods trafficked across the Channel. It made sense that the smugglers had made their hideouts higher up from the beach; the high tides would fill the lower caverns created by nature.

Jack kept close to Lottie. Even in this godforsaken place, her nearness teased him, the whiff of her linen-and-lavender scent freshening the dank passage. Her thick braid was gilded by his lamplight, and he had the urge to sweep it to one side, place a kiss on her nape like he used to...once upon a time.

They arrived at a fork in the path. Separated by a line of stalactites that hung like glittering chandeliers, the two passageways split off in different directions. Crouching, Jack examined the ground. He found traces of sand and mud caked on the path to the left, and they looked fresh.

"Footprints." He took the lead and felt the change in the terrain. "Have a care. The path is sloping downward."

"I can look after my—*oof*."

He turned just in time to catch her around the waist.

"All right?" he asked.

Even in the dimness, she looked adorably annoyed. "I am fine. I just slipped a little."

"Slip all you want. I am happy to catch you."

Truthfully, he wanted to do a lot more than catch her. In her current outfit, he felt every supple line and curve of her pressed against him. They fit like they always had—like two halves meant to be a whole.

"Don't be an idiot." She shoved at his arm. "Let me go."

Was it his imagination, or did she sound slightly breathless? On that wistful thought, he continued to lead them down the passage. When it divided in other places, he identified the path those before them had taken and followed it.

"I hope you know where you're going," Lottie muttered.

"Of course I do. I'm a cartographer."

"Are you really?"

Hearing her skepticism, he cast a glance backward. "Not everything I told you was a lie. In fact, I stuck to the truth whenever I could. You know me, Lottie, better than anyone."

"That's not saying much. Considering I thought you were dead."

He ignored her jibe. "Maps have fascinated me since I was a child, and I've always had a good sense of direction. When I retire, I plan to spend my days charting new territory and drawing maps."

"Hmm." Her reply was noncommittal. "What direction are we headed now?"

"Northeast. On a decline of approximately..." He mentally calibrated. "Seventeen degrees."

"How would I know if you were wrong?"

"I suppose you'll have to trust me."

He flashed her a grin. She snorted.

After several minutes, the path veered to the right, and he

slowed when he saw a glow coming from an opening a few feet ahead. A cavern—possibly Tony's hiding place.

"Let me do the talking," Jack murmured. "I know the cove."

She lifted her brows but didn't argue.

For caution's sake, he kept close to the wall, peering around the opening. The cavern was large, and someone was living there. An overturned crate was being used as a table, a sack and burning lamp upon it. Along the far wall was a blanket and... He heard Lottie's swift inhalation as she, too, spotted the figure lying face-down upon it.

"Mr. Quinton?" Lottie's voice held a thread of hope. "Your brother sent us...we're here to help you..."

The fellow showed no signs of hearing her.

Crossing over, Jack went down on one knee and, with cool detachment, turned the body over. Tony Quinton's sightless eyes stared back at him above the congealed slash on his throat.

"Poor sod's gone."

Obvious, but he had to say it.

"How long?" Lottie asked quietly.

He examined the body. Still warm and flaccid.

"Not long. Within the last two hours, I would guess."

He performed a search of the dead man. He found nothing. Nothing that could be the "evidence" Tony had wanted to bring him. Nothing that could steer him to the First Flame, goddammit—

Hearing a shuffle behind him, he shot to his feet, twisting in time to see moving shadows.

Lottie was faster. "Watch out!"

She flew into him, and they hit the ground with a thud. Jack rolled to his feet, yanking out his pistol. Two shadowy figures stood at the entrance to the cave, and he fired off a shot at the larger one. The man yelped in pain, and Jack readied to fire again, Lottie doing the same beside him. But the second assailant was faster than both of them, his gun already raised to fire.

Jack shoved Lottie behind him, but the attacker pointed his weapon upward. The blast echoed through the cavern, followed by what sounded like hooves thundering overhead. Jack swore, pushing Lottie to the ground, covering her body with his as the roof came crashing down.

Nineteen

When Sebastian's lashes lifted, his dazed, dark eyes staring up at her, relief rushed through Charlie. His head was cradled in her lap, and she had been trying to rouse him.

He coughed. "What happened?"

"Part of the cavern's roof collapsed. You got us out of harm's way...mostly. You were hit by debris and have been unconscious for several minutes."

She tried to sound nonchalant, but her fingers shook a little as she ran them over the gash near his temple, which overlapped with his existing scar. When she'd rolled him off her and seen the blood, she'd feared the worst. Luckily, the wound was superficial, and she'd managed to stanch the bleeding, though he would have a nasty bump.

"Does the injury hurt?" she asked.

"I've had worse."

He sat up before she could stop him. He cupped her face, his thumb skimming her right cheekbone. She winced at the tenderness; she'd probably have a shiner in the morning.

"You're hurt," he whispered.

Remembering how he'd shielded her body with his own, from the assailant's gun as well as the avalanche of rocks, she felt her throat cinch even as she shook her head.

"It's just a bruise. You took the brunt of it." She inhaled. "You shouldn't have—"

"You are my wife." His gaze was fierce, as if daring her to deny it. "God knows I've given you reason to doubt me, but never doubt this: I would do anything to protect you. Anything."

She...believed him.

"And you did the same," he went on. "If it weren't for you, I'd be dealing with a bullet, not just a cut. You acted on instinct, putting your life on the line, because no matter what has happened between us, we are still bound, you and I."

She wanted to deny it but couldn't. Not with the filaments of tension snapping and crackling between them and the truth thumping in her heart. Biting her lip, she changed the subject.

"Do you want the good or bad news first?" she asked.

The intensity didn't leave Sebastian's expression, but his mouth curved faintly.

"Bad," he said.

"We are currently trapped in this cave. The entrance is completely blocked"—she gestured to the wall of rubble where the opening had been—"and it would take us days to dig ourselves out, if we had the proper equipment. Which we don't. We are also so deep inside the cliff that we cannot hear the ocean, which means that no one will be able to hear us calling for help."

He quirked a brow. "What is the good news?"

"We are alive and having this conversation."

"Right."

Amusement flickered in his gaze, and in the next second, he rose before she could warn him to take it easy. As if a man like him would ever take things easy. Covered in dust, battered and bruised, he was a warrior ready for another round. He looked steady enough on his feet, and when he reached a hand to help her up, she took it. Their gazes locked, his big hand engulfing hers, and despite the circumstances, she felt inexplicably safe. Sheltered by his touch, his presence, the connection between them that refused to break.

She jerked her hand free and walked away, ostensibly to assess their situation. She was aware of Sebastian's gaze upon her as she paused by Tony Quinton's body, now covered in a layer of fine dust. She thought of Gilbert, and her heart squeezed.

"Should we do something for Tony?" she said somberly.

"There is nothing we can do." Sebastian's tone was not cruel but matter-of-fact. "Let us focus our efforts on finding a way out, sweeting. We'll come back for the body later."

Nodding, Charlie went to look for an exit. She glimpsed a small object close to the pile of rocks and picked it up. Blowing off the dust, she saw it was a matchbox. The label had the words "Brompton's Finest Lucifers" set within a decorative border of red and white, a drawing of a large tree in the background. Inside were five matchsticks.

She held up the box. "I didn't see this on the ground when we entered, did you?"

Sebastian shook his head. "The attackers must have dropped it."

"A potential clue, then."

Pocketing it, she continued to poke around. As the bag atop the crate held foodstuffs, she shouldered the strap. She noted that the lantern next to it continued to burn.

"The flame is strong," she said. "There is a supply of oxygen coming from somewhere."

Sebastian was prowling along the perimeter of the cave. "First rule of smugglers: have more than one exit. There must be another way out."

She grabbed the lantern, moving in the opposite direction. Her pulse quickened when the flame suddenly leapt. She held the lamp closer to the section of the wall, and the flame flared again.

"Over here." She ran her fingers along the rocky surface, finding a seam. "There is air coming in through a crack."

Sebastian joined her, moving his hands expertly over the surface. "It's not a crack...it's a concealed door. I've seen ones like this before. There is usually a hidden lever somewhere close..."

The nearby stalagmites caught Charlie's attention, and she went to examine them. The formations had the smoothness of man-made plaster rather than the irregularity of nature's hand. Probing her way down the widening column, she felt a loose section and pressed down. A squeal sounded from above, and she glanced up, seeing a pulley hidden in the rock. It turned, pulling the attached rope, and an instant later, the rock wall in front of Sebastian slid open to reveal another tunnel.

"Clever girl. You've located our exit."

She told herself it was the prospect of escaping and not Sebastian's approval that sparked a tingle of delight.

He took the lantern from her and said, "Let's go."

Inside the passage was another bag with a blanket peeping out the top, and Charlie scooped it up as she passed. The tunnel was narrower, the ground less smooth than the one leading to the cavern. In several places, Sebastian had to duck to avoid the stiletto-sharp outcroppings of rock. Professionally, she admired the supreme confidence with which he navigated the way. He hadn't lied about being a cartographer.

You know me, Lottie, better than anyone.

An ember sparked, warming her chest. Her appreciation became a tad less professional as she observed the breadth of his shoulders beneath his linen shirt and the flexing of his taut, rounded buttocks.

If I perish, at least it will be with a splendid view.

"The path is on a decline." His voice reached back to her. "And do you hear that?"

She tilted her head, listening. It was faint at first, but then she recognized the sound.

"Waves," she said with anticipation. "We're getting closer to the water."

Within minutes, the tunnel widened into another cavern. It smelled of the sea, and a small rowboat lay near the passage on the opposite end. A quick check of the passage revealed the boat's function: beneath this cavern was another one, at present submerged by the high tide, but when the water receded in a few hours, they could use the boat to float out.

Meanwhile, the cavern made for a cozy resting place. Sebastian set down the lamp, and Charlie examined the supplies she'd gathered. The bag of foodstuffs included apples, a stack of plum heavies, and two pasties with gathered sides that looked like purses. There was also a bottle of wine. From the bag she'd found inside the passage, she pulled out a blanket...and a small leather pouch tumbled from the folds. Opening the pouch, she found a small glass vial containing a clear liquid. When she tilted it, a few fine white crystals drifted through the solution.

"What is it?" Sebastian came over.

"I am not certain."

Taking it from her, he uncorked it, and they both sniffed. The odor was faint.

"Sulphur?" she guessed.

"Perhaps."

When he put his fingertip to the top of the vial, she stopped him.

"What are you doing?" she asked.

"Taking a taste."

She stared at him. "What if it is poison?"

"I have a high tolerance to toxins."

She decided she did not want to know how he'd come to that conclusion.

"As I do not wish to drag your lifeless body from the cave, please refrain from ingesting the mysterious liquid," she said primly.

"It's probably harmless..."

He trailed off because the liquid began to smoke and bubble.

Hastily, he shoved the cork back into place. Just in time: half the liquid had vaporized.

"We'll figure out what this is after we get out of here," he muttered.

Giving him an *I-told-you-so* look, she carefully stored the vial back in the pouch. "Could this be the evidence Tony Quinton wanted to give you?"

"Hard to say."

Evidently, that was *all* he had to say about it. She was not fooled by his noncommittal tone or bland visage. Yet she decided to let him have his way for the moment, mostly because she was hungry and needed food before arguing with him.

She spread the blanket and arranged the provisions, selecting one of the plum heavies. She sat, munching on the scrumptious currant-studded biscuit. Sebastian joined her, stretching out his long legs. He took a pasty, and they ate in companionable silence. Famished, she chased the biscuit with one of the pasties, which had a savory filling of bacon, liver, and cheese. Sebastian uncorked the wine, taking a swig before passing it to her. It was fruity and light, surprisingly delicious.

They passed the bottle back and forth, their fingers brushing. Each time she pressed her lips to the glass, she thought of his lips being there moments before. If his heavy-lidded gaze was any indication, he was entertaining similar thoughts. Tension blossomed, the humidity of the cave swelling. Her shirt clung to her damp skin.

She took a crunchy bite of apple.

"You're hungry," Sebastian remarked.

"I was on my feet all evening serving drinks." She used her sleeve to catch the sweet juice trickling down her chin. "After which I scaled a cliff and fought enemies, managing a narrow escape. Is it any surprise that I have worked up an appetite?"

"I wasn't being critical. I've always found your enjoyment of food charming."

"I don't care what you think." She took another bite of apple, chewing pointedly.

His smile reached his eyes. "Also a part of your charm."

"If I am so charming, why did you leave?"

The question burst from her. Then again, it had been festering ever since he came back. And she deserved an answer.

When Sebastian didn't respond right away, frustration gripped her. But it was frustration tinged with despair. It was the feeling of banging her head against the same wall again and again, and the only thing that changed was the dent she was putting into her own skull.

Why are his secrets so dear to him? Why are they more important to him than me?

"It was never about you," he said finally.

"I will thank you to have the decency not to lie," she said bitterly. "Of course it was about me. You faked your death to get out of our marriage—"

"I loved you."

Three words, and they were enough to crumble her defenses. She stared at him, her mouth open, not a single word coming out. What was the appropriate response, after all?

"There will never be another woman for me. That is why I stayed true to my vows." His features were fierce and held no embarrassment or shame.

She had to swallow past her heart to get the words out. "Then why did you—"

"They threatened you—the anarchists I was hunting then, the same ones I am after now. That last night we fought, I was supposed to meet with an informant. She'd joined the First Flame Society thinking that they would bring about a revolution for the working class but soon realized that the group's only goal was destruction and chaos. She wanted out and agreed to help my team bring down the anarchists. She was feeding me information but was worried the enemy suspected something."

"*We're in danger. We need to meet*," Charlie murmured.

Sebastian shot her a startled look.

"I found that note in your things," she clarified. "That was from your mole?"

His nod was bleak. "I was supposed to meet her at an old warehouse that night. I arrived too late; the anarchists got to her first."

His jaw tightened, lines slashing around his mouth. Charlie saw clearly for the first time what the shadows were in his eyes: ghosts. She waited, her heart rattling against her ribs.

"They'd left her strung up. Didn't even cut her down after they'd tortured her for hours." Sebastian's tone had a removed quality that Charlie understood—that she'd used herself when describing the horrors of her work. "They did something else too."

He took a breath, and Charlie tensed.

"Her husband and daughter—they were there. The bastards had murdered them in front of her. Slit their throats and she was helpless to stop them."

Bile rose in Charlie's throat. She reached for Sebastian's hand, offering comfort, holding on. Their fingers linked on the blanket.

"They'd left a note too. A warning." His pupils were dilated, darkness snuffing out the light. "*Back off, or your family is next. And I couldn't...I couldn't let that happen to you. The woman I loved. My team and I, we arranged the bodies of the informant and her husband to look like me and a lover. I left some of my hair, and the fire we set at the taverna...well, it took care of the rest."

His fingers spasmed against hers, and while they were callused from countless battles, they were also cold. Her warrior of a husband, whom she'd believed to be larger than life and beyond fear, was terrified...at the thought of her being harmed. Of losing her.

Understanding shifted her perspective, making space for her to examine all the emotions jammed inside her. She was still angry, yes, for his stupid decision—for not trusting her enough to tell her the truth and acting on his own. But she was also filled with sadness and regret and a strange sort of relief now that she finally, *finally* understood what had happened. Even if she wanted to rant at him for the decisions he'd made, his explanation made sense...in a way that his supposed infidelity never had.

All along, she'd felt there was something shady about his death. So much so that she'd investigated it for years. Now she knew why.

Because deep down, deep in the recesses of her soul, she'd believed in his love. In their bond. In the alchemy that had forged them into one from the day they met. A part of her rejoiced in the discovery that she hadn't been wrong about her husband, hadn't been delusional...and another part raged.

"I understand why you did what you did." Her voice trembled. "But you took away my choice, Sebastian. And you did it in the cruelest way possible."

"I had to." His eyes were full of remorse but also resolute. "If I didn't stage my death the way I did, you would have been suspicious. You were already suspicious about my absences. I needed to make you angry—so furious that you wouldn't give a damn about my death. That you would think 'good riddance' and count yourself lucky to be done with your bastard of a husband and move on."

"How could you think that?" Incredulity made her voice rise. "How could you *ever* think I would be happy to be rid of you?"

It hurt her to witness the rawness of his response. After what he'd done, she shouldn't care, but she did. In all the time they'd been together, he'd never been vulnerable with her, and now he was letting down his guard.

"I don't deserve you, Lottie," he said hoarsely. "I was never your equal, and I knew it when I married you. I knew I didn't deserve a lady with your courage, spirit, and intelligence. But when we were together, it made me forget myself. Made me forget everything but how good it felt, how much I wanted to be your husband, one who was worthy of you."

"Why wouldn't you deserve me?" She furrowed her brow, baffled that he would feel that way. That her larger-than-life former spouse would have any cause to feel less than, well, anyone. Least of all her. "You are my equal. In fact, when it comes down to titles and such, you outrank me."

"I've done things, Lottie. Things no gentleman would do."

The shadows were back in his eyes, and this time she saw they weren't just ghosts but demons. Her own experiences provided an explanation.

"Because of your work, you mean? But you were only doing your duty to protect your country and innocent people from harm." When he said nothing, she went on gently, "I understand, you know. I was never a sheltered miss to begin with, but the work I do now has exposed me to the darkness of life. I know what evil is, what good is, and even how each can be mistaken for the other. Nothing you could say would shock me for very long. I am strong, stronger than you think. Stronger than whatever secrets are festering inside you."

He was gripping her hand now, his touch no longer cold but warm. Desperate.

"I am no good for you," he rasped. "No good for anyone. I've endangered the people I care about most—my best friend, he...he died because of me. Because I couldn't protect him. And I won't let that happen to you. The threat isn't over. Now that I know that the First Flame is back, I must stop whatever heinous plot they are hatching."

"I will help you," she said.

"You will bloody stay out of it."

He snapped his brows together, and his hands were no longer warm; they were hot. And she knew this because one had gone to cup her nape, the other holding her jaw so that she had to look into his eyes. They were darker than midnight, all the stars consumed by his ferocity. The time for vulnerability had apparently ended, and Sebastian was back to his dictatorial self.

She wasn't the least bit cowed, shoving his hands away. "I am already a part of it."

"Aye, and I regret letting that happen," he growled. "You should not have found a dead body and been shot at. You shouldn't be trapped in this cave with me. You should be somewhere safe."

Her control over her temper started to fray.

"Like a drawing room, you mean?" Her sarcasm dripped like honey into tea. "You do realize that I haven't been swaddled in cotton since you left? As an investigator, I can assure you that I have been places and done things that would shock even you."

"What you do as part of your society is up to you," he clipped out. "I cannot stop you."

"The great spy is capable of sense, after all."

He ignored the taunt. "But I will not have anything happening to you because of me. Because of *my* bloody business. After tonight, you will stay away from the First Flame, and that is final."

His ultimatum broke the tether on her restraint.

"It is not just *your* business," she snapped. "Has it occurred to you that the First Flame destroyed *my* marriage, took *my* husband from me, made me grieve for *years*? They stole my life, my happiness, and I didn't even know until now. Didn't know that it was them who shredded my heart by convincing you to leave me, even though you stupidly went along with their plan. So do forgive me when I say, with all due respect, that it is *my* bloody debt to settle as well, you dashed idiot!"

She glared at him, her chest heaving. He'd stilled, and if she wasn't so angry, she might have laughed at his open-mouthed expression. Then he firmed his jaw, and the bronze light that sparked in his eyes made her brace. She readied to do battle—to assert her right to be a part of this, to do whatever it took to bring the enemy down.

But when he spoke, they weren't the words she expected.

"You grieved...for years?"

He sounded so genuinely surprised that red coated the edges of her vision.

"What did you expect? I *loved* you." She fisted her hands in his collar, giving him a little shake. "You were my world, and then you weren't, and nothing has been the same since."

He captured her jaw in both hands, his touch as rough and real as his words. "Bloody hell, Lottie, I've never stopped wanting you."

The emotion and desire surging between them was overwhelming. Dash it all, she wanted to *feel* again—feel alive in the way she'd only felt with Sebastian. She couldn't fight it.

Still, she tried. "We cannot do this—"

"One night. I know I don't have the right to ask for anything more. And you have my word that we won't do anything..."—his eyes burned into hers—"irrevocable."

An inner voice whispered of danger. Sebastian was a spy with demons and secrets, a man she could never fully trust. She knew that a future with him was impossible, knew that she had to protect her heart even as she yearned to give in to passion.

I can do this. No strings, no risk. Nothing but pleasure with the only man I've ever desired.

Temptation overrode caution.

She saw his smoldering intent, but she beat him to it. Or, rather, they acted at the same time. Their mouths crashed, years of frustration and longing combusting into uncontrollable need.

TWENTY

In the minuscule part of her not overtaken by desire, Charlie knew this was a mistake. But some mistakes were worth making. Especially after twelve years of being careful, of guarding herself. Of thinking and thinking and thinking.

With Sebastian, there was never much room for thought. The feelings he inspired were too big, too intense, and that hadn't changed. She was engulfed in sensation, in the rightness of the moment as he spun them around so that his back was against the hard cavern wall and she was sitting astride him, her knees bracing his thighs, their mouths fused. His kiss consumed her, ravenous yet somehow tender too, as if he wanted to eat her and savor every bite.

Her own hunger was no less. She took of him as he did of her, feasting on his taste, his rightness. Their lips clung, then parted, his tongue driving inside and tangling with hers. The kiss turned wet and deep, her insides melting. The heat built and built, expanding until she thought she would burst out of her skin. Just from his kiss.

"I've missed this," he growled against her lips. "I'll never get enough of you, Lottie."

And he proved it by trailing hot, open-mouthed kisses over her jaw. He mouthed her ear, and she arched her neck at the bliss. He fisted her braid and held her head in place while he licked her, the scalding pleasure spreading to her nipples and between her splayed legs. She was burning, aching everywhere. Coming out of her skin and needing more.

His mouth claimed her throat, his fingers making short work of her buttons. She helped him tear off her waistcoat, then her shirt, moaning when he put his hands on her breasts, not only because of how good it felt but also because of his expression. The greed and reverence glittering in those warrior's eyes.

He cupped her breasts as if weighing something precious. "Bloody hell, your tits are even more gorgeous than I remembered."

At his coarse appreciation, she felt liquid trickle from her center. She'd always loved the rawness of his desire, how it stripped away the layers of civility and refinement and bared his true self. His primal nature tore away her inhibitions until she was panting, squirming, alive with her own need. He heightened her desperation by fondling her mounds whilst avoiding the throbbing tips.

"Stop teasing," she said breathlessly.

"Is that what I'm doing?" His eyes glinted with wolfish playfulness, and her breath caught as his thumb edged closer to a straining pink crest. "Here I thought I was relishing the moment."

"Well, relish it quicker...*ohh*."

The moan scraped from her throat because he leaned forward and took a nipple deep into his mouth. The fierce suction pulled at her core, releasing a gush of liquid pleasure. With one hand splayed between her shoulder blades, he held her against his voracious kiss. His other hand played with her other nipple, plucking and rolling and pinching until the heat in her became a fever. Too much to bear and not enough.

Then he gave her more.

Clasping her hips, he guided her higher against him, and she trembled to feel the pulsing length of steel inside his trousers. He widened his legs, forcing her knees to spread further, and she gasped at the new alignment of their bodies. Of the feel of him so hard, so thick against her aching flesh.

"Ride me, sweeting," he rasped. "Rub that sweet pussy against my cock."

With a desperate moan, she did. Grasping his shoulders for purchase, she slid her pussy against his erection, the pleasure almost unbearable. She squirmed against the thick ridge, moving her hips up and down, using the broad tip to stimulate her own swollen nub. It was depraved and delicious, and his hoarse pants urged her on.

"I can feel you soaking through my trousers." His nostrils were flared, his features sharpened with lust. "Work that pearl against my prick, darling. Come on me."

At his decadent demand, she whimpered, moving her hips faster. The fever rose and rose, and then he put his mouth on her breasts again. Tonguing her nipples, sucking them deep. When she felt the graze of his teeth, she broke.

She came with a cry, her entire being splintering with bliss.

If a man could expire from pleasure, Jack would have cocked his toes up the instant his wife spent from rubbing her pussy against his cock. He ran a proprietary hand up the silken curve of her spine, curling his palm around her nape. Looking into her cloud-soft eyes, he saw his version of perfection.

"You are bloody magnificent," he said and claimed her mouth.

Their kiss started softly, then caught fire. His surging lust was accompanied by an undertow of gratification. It had always been this way for them, and nothing had changed. They still couldn't get enough of each other.

Her lips sweet and hungry against his, Lottie clearly wanted to take charge. It was only fair that he let her have her turn. She unbuttoned his shirt, and he shuddered to feel her hands on him. She glided her palms over his leaping muscles, the light scrape of her fingernails making his stones draw up taut. When she bent to lick his nipple, he exhaled at the sharp delight.

She slid off his lap, making space for herself between his legs. Her eyes had a kittenish spark as she continued kissing his chest. She seemed intent upon investigating every nook and cranny of him with her tongue, and he had no complaints. The ridges of his abdomen tensed as her lips followed the path of hair that led toward his waistband. When she kissed the rigid curve of his cock through his trousers, his breath hissed through his teeth.

Was this headed where he thought it was?

"Take off your trousers," she said.

Praise God, *yes*.

He rose and stripped. She knelt before him, and the proprietary look in her eyes made him so aroused that she had to pry his prick from his stomach. Her delicate fingers barely circled his veined girth, the sight unbearably erotic.

"You're so big," she murmured.

"You make me this way. I fantasized about you all the years we were apart. Just the thought of you made me hard. Now to have you here...with me..."

His breathing grew harsh as she stroked him with a confident hand, giving him a squeeze at the tip just the way he liked. His wife —bloody made for him.

"What did you fantasize about?"

Her knowing tone told him she knew the filthy content, but he gave her what she asked anyway.

"About you kneeling at my feet just so. You would wrap your hand around my cock and bring the tip to your soft lips."

His lungs burned as she did exactly that. Then she waited, looking up at him with smoky eyes and pink-tipped breasts, better than any goddamned fantasy.

"*You would kiss the head...yes*, like that," he gritted out.

It was almost too much, watching her place a chaste peck on his bulging knob. She milked him slowly with her fist, and when she drew back the skin, seed beaded on his dusky tip.

The command rolled off his tongue. "Lick it off."

Her gaze holding his, she swiped her tongue over his crest, and he felt the swirl of heat everywhere—his prick, his balls, his pounding chest. She coaxed forth another drop and took that one too. Her enthusiasm for fellatio was nothing short of delightful. From the time he'd introduced her to this brand of sport, she'd loved driving him mad with her talented mouth.

Like a thief, a sudden question crept into his head. *Has she done this with other men?*

He couldn't stop jealousy from sinking its claws into him. What made it worse was that he knew he had no right to feel this way. He'd left her, destroyed their marriage, and even now he had nothing to offer her. Nothing but this moment.

"Sebastian?"

Seeing her flicker of uncertainty, he refused to ruin what time they had.

Let tomorrow bring what it may. We've lost too many years. Tonight is ours.

"Suck me, love." He slid his hands into her hair, wrecking what was left of her braid. "Remind me what that talented mouth of yours can do."

Before Lottie, he hadn't always enjoyed this act. He'd liked the sensations but not the loss of control. But when he'd introduced his bride to fellatio, she'd shown him how good it could feel to trust another with his pleasure.

If there was anything Lottie loved, it was a challenge. Her eyes sparkled as she leaned forward and...*fuck*. She took him into her mouth, surrounding him in wet, blissful heat. Sucking him as if he were a boiled sweet. It felt like yesterday when he'd taught her this: back then, she'd been game but a bit shy. Now she didn't hesitate to circle his head with her tongue, teasing the sensitive groove on the underside, before lapping at him again. The fact that she remembered what he liked expanded his longing until he thought he might burst from unrequited lust.

"Bloody hell." He gripped her scalp. "Take me deeper. As deep as you can."

She bobbed her head in reply. With each plunge, she took more of his length. When she came up, he saw the tight stretch of her lips around his shaft, the effort dampening her lashes and brightening her eyes, and he wanted to burn that image onto his brain for all eternity.

"You're so damned beautiful," he rasped.

She hummed, the vibration shooting down his length and weakening his knees. She took more and more, his meat disappearing between her lips. The lush squeeze of her throat was making short work of his self-control.

"Now you're just showing off," he groaned.

Smiling cheekily—something he guessed not many women could do with a mouthful of cock—she went down on him again. Dove on him as if his surrender was sunken treasure she was determined to claim. It was too much; there was only so much pleasure a man could handle. He felt the warning pressure at the base of his spine, the churning in his stones.

"Love, stop. I'm too close."

He dug his fingers into her scalp, trying to pull her away, the way he'd always done in the past.

She didn't budge. Instead, she fisted the base of his prick, frigging him as she sucked. Surely she had to know the inevitable conclusion if she kept this up... Her sultry gaze met his, and he realized that she *did*. This naughtiness was new—not something he'd taught her. The bite of possessive rage amplified his arousal, pushing him over the edge.

"*Fuck,*" he bit out.

If this was what she wanted, he'd give it to her. Gripping her head, he thrust into her mouth. Harder and harder still, harder than he'd ever done in the past. But she took it; she *liked* it, the desire in her eyes turning him inside out. Reminding him that nothing, nothing else mattered but being here with her.

With his Lottie, his bold little wanton—*his*.

Groaning, he came and came, spilling himself on his wife's sweet tongue.

When the last shudder left him, he withdrew his still-hard cock. Her lips were swollen from pleasuring him, and lust licked his belly when he saw traces of his spend clinging to the plump bottom ledge.

When he thumbed it away, she gave his digit a nip.

"Was that as good as your fantasy?" she inquired.

She looked so endearingly pleased with herself that he had to tease her.

"It was not a bad start."

"Not a bad start—"

Her indignation melted into a gasp when he tumbled her onto her back. He yanked down her trousers, his blood pounding when he saw her pretty thatch, a shade darker than the blonde on her head. He ran a possessive finger along her slit, and animal satisfaction poured through him to find her wet and swollen. Holding her eyes, he brought his finger to his mouth and sucked it clean.

A whimper escaped Lottie. Her breasts heaved, the tips flushed and budded.

"We've twelve years to make up for," he told her. "As devilishly perfect as that mouth of yours is, love, we've only begun."

To prove his point, he pushed her thighs apart. His nostrils and cock quivered at the lush pink oasis. Like a man starved, he lowered his head and feasted.

Jack opened his eyes to the semi-darkness of the cave.

At first, he wasn't sure he'd awakened at all. Not because of the unfamiliar setting—he was used to waking in strange places—but because of the woman he held in his arms. Because he'd dreamed of this so often that it was difficult to convince himself that, this time, it was real.

She was here, her hair spilling like silk over his chest. Her scent teasing his nostrils, making him think of fresh linens even though their bed was currently a sandy blanket. Her soft, naked curves tucked against him, his better half, making him feel...whole.

Lottie and I...we belong together.

After last night, there was no doubting it. Not just because of the pleasure—though God knew there had been plenty of that going around. The memory of spending in his wife's mouth, her pussy creaming against his own, contributed to his substantial morning cockstand. By all rights, he should be sated after coming thrice and making Lottie spend more times than that, but she was his obsession.

He could never get enough of her. He'd always known this, even though he told himself she deserved better. That was still true —she deserved more than the bastard he was—but last night had changed things. If twelve years hadn't broken their connection, then maybe...just maybe there was a way to make this work?

Yet how could he come back into her life the way he wanted to —that is, permanently? How could he give her a life worthy of her? How could he be who he was and still be the husband she deserved?

The answer was simple...and impossible. He had to tell her the truth—about his past, his failures, the true nature of the man she'd married. And there was the rub: what was the point of telling her everything when it would only push her away? He'd deceived her from the start, and even though he'd tried to atone, to protect her and do what was right, he'd made things worse.

By walking away from the only woman he'd ever loved.

By making her grieve.

By depriving them both of everything they could have been... for twelve damned years.

"Mm hm hm."

His brooding lifted, and his mouth twitched at his spouse's sleepy mumbles. He used to tease her about talking in her sleep... mostly because he'd enjoyed her haughty denials that she did no such thing. Apparently, she hadn't lost the charming habit.

Cheered by the thought, he felt the call of nature and reluctantly disentangled himself from Lottie. He managed not to wake her, although the sight of her pretty nipple peeping over the blanket almost made him reconsider his plan. He'd like to start the day right by eating his wife for breakfast...he grimaced, looking down at his erection and feeling the pressure of his bladder.

Take care of business first, eat Lottie later.

He pulled on his trousers and coat, shoved a pistol in his pocket, and paused by the leather pouch sitting in the sand. Scooping it up, he felt the promise of discovery in its slight heft. He glanced at Lottie before tucking the pouch into his inner pocket for safekeeping.

He departed for the lower cave. There, he saw the tide was already low, the cave opening to the ocean and pink horizon. He and Lottie could leave now on the lighter. He almost regretted their imminent departure from this cocoon, their return to the outside world with all its problems...

He squinted, seeing something bobbing near the mouth of the cave. He reached for his weapon, aiming it at the object as it came closer and closer. A rowboat with a single occupant.

"Granger? Is that you?"

Recognizing Delaney's voice, he lowered his pistol. He headed over and helped her dock.

"You managed to find me," he said.

"I followed you at a distance last night like you instructed, oh great spymaster. By the time I made it into the caves, the tunnel was blocked."

"Did you see anyone leaving?"

"No." She cocked her head. "Who else was there?"

"A pair of assailants shot at us. Members of the First Flame would be my guess. Unfortunately, I didn't get a good look at them. They could have escaped...or they're buried in the cave." He paused. "Along with Tony Quinton."

Delaney digested the news. "Primus thought you could use extra reinforcements, so Laurent and Calderone are here too. They can start digging and looking for bodies."

"I'll help," Jack said.

Delaney shook her head. "Primus wants to see you. He's waiting at a cottage nearby, and he's *not happy*."

Jack's gut clenched. How was his mentor going to take the news that he'd not only reunited with his wife but wanted to do so for good?

Delaney pressed closer, her voice urgent. "I saw you with your widow last night. What happened? You know your instructions were to keep her out of—"

"Ahem."

He spun around, and his heart seized at the gloriousness of Lottie. Her hair was liquid honey over her shoulders, her slender legs displayed by her trousers, the curves of her breasts playing peekaboo in the vee of her hastily buttoned shirt. Even her slight shiner heightened her fearless beauty. A resilient goddess who did not back down to darkness.

His blood plunged from his head to his cock.

Which was probably why he missed the fury in her eyes.

Until she said in tones of glacial civility, "Good morning. How lovely to see you again...Eleni."

TWENTY-ONE

As Jack entered the cottage on the outskirts of Hastings, he wanted to get the meeting with his superior over with. The most pressing reason was Lottie, with whom he had not parted on the best of terms. Although he'd tried to remind her that nothing had happened between him and Maria Delaney/Eleni Pappas, nor ever would, Lottie had given him the cold shoulder. His fumbling attempts to apologize had only made matters worse since Delaney had been on the boat with them, making no attempt to hide her amused smirk.

Things hadn't improved when he'd seen Lottie to her lodgings.

"Wait for me," he said. "I'll be back after I speak to my superior."

She arched her brows. "You will inform him of my involvement in this case?"

He'd drawn a breath through his nose, his own feelings on the matter going back and forth like a damned teeter-totter. On the one hand, his instinct to protect Lottie was shouting at him, telling him he was an idiot for considering letting her get sucked deeper into this perilous mess. His would-be informant had been murdered, and he and Lottie were bleeding lucky they'd escaped the caves relatively unscathed. If anything had happened to her...

Yet there was another voice in his head, a newer one.

And it said, *"Letting her?"*

No one *let* Lottie do anything. She made her own choices, and woe to the bastard who tried to stop her, even if his intentions were good. The realization struck him that he'd been that bastard in the past...and what had that gotten him?

Years of loneliness, longing, and coming by his own hand.

Not exactly a winning combination, nor one he'd care to repeat. Moreover, he could not deny that Lottie would be an asset to any investigation. She'd proved herself, time and again, tracking down clues and saving his hide. The First Flame Society was a formidable adversary, and with the Great Exhibition creeping closer and closer, his team could use all the help they could get. In fact, keeping Lottie by his side would put him in a better position to protect her.

"I will speak to him," Jack said. "But I cannot guarantee he will agree to bring you on."

"I was not asking for his permission," Lottie said tartly. "I was merely doing him a professional courtesy by informing him that the Angels will be investigating the First Flame. If he wishes to combine efforts, he may contact me."

"Promise you won't do anything without me."

"As I am not a liar, I cannot make such a promise."

"Goddammit, Lottie. After last night, I thought—"

"What did you think? That after an enjoyable interlude, I would become your meek and obedient wife once again?"

He inhaled for patience. "I have, not once, thought of you and the phrase *meek and obedient* in the same sentence. What I was going to say was that I thought last night we worked well together. Made a good team."

We fought splendidly together. And the fucking, darling—that was even better.

"Oh." She sounded suspicious.

"And I hoped that we could continue the positive trend."

"Which trend are you referring to: working or sleeping together?"

That was his Lottie: stunning *and* perceptive.

"Why not both?"

She narrowed her eyes. "You said there were no strings attached."

"There aren't. But that doesn't mean we cannot repeat the experience." He curled a finger under her chin. "I thought you enjoyed yourself as much as I did."

"I did."

Because, as she claimed, she was no liar, twin lines appeared between her brows. She seemed conflicted. Combined with the faint bruising by her right eye, she looked vulnerable in a way that made him want to carry her back to their rocky cocoon and make love to her until every thought of leaving him was vanquished. Yet with Lottie, he knew when to push and when to retreat.

"Then think about what I am offering. Pleasure without commitment."

Until I can find a way to offer you more. To give you everything. To give you a future where all you know is happiness...and the best is still to come.

He tipped her chin up and saw her eyelids lower. He bent his head, and her lips parted. He kissed her on the nose.

"I will see you when I return," he said. "Wait for me."

Now, as he prepared to see Primus, he was far from certain that Lottie would be at the inn when he returned. But he knew where to find her. With simmering anticipation, he realized that for the first time in years, he had something to look forward to.

The door to the parlor opened.

"Sir." Jack bowed.

Lancaster waved an impatient hand. "Come in."

Jack followed his superior into the rustic room. The curtains were drawn, but the shadows suited them both. There was a pair of overstuffed chairs by the fire, but as his mentor remained standing, so did Jack. He was reminded of what Primus told him the day he was recruited.

"The life of a spy holds few comforts. Your life as you know it will come to an end, and you will be asked to give up happiness as defined by ordinary men. From here on in, you will dedicate yourself to doing your duty...even though no one will ever know of your heroism. Is that what you wish?"

At the time, Jack had had nothing to lose. He'd known few comforts in his life, and the few blessings he'd been given, he had destroyed. His most fervent wish had been for his miserable existence to end. Instead, he'd been given an opportunity: to remake himself, find redemption in duty and patriotism, and emerge a different man.

He hadn't yet succeeded in those goals. But he'd done his best to follow in his mentor's footsteps. Primus would stop at nothing to protect his country. With his gritty honesty and self-sacrifice, he'd demonstrated to Jack what was required to be an agent for good.

"How much does she know?" Primus said without preamble.

It spoke volumes that the spymaster asked about Lottie before Jack's progress on the mission. Primus saw her as a threat, setting off a chill in Jack's gut. The last thing he wanted was a clash between his mentor and his beloved...especially when he'd decided to try to bridge both parts of his life. To take a shot at becoming whole.

Given Primus's acuity, there was no point in dissembling.

"Pretty much everything," Jack admitted.

When he finished outlining the extent of Lottie's knowledge, Primus exhaled. "By Jove. She discovered that you were a spy, that you were chasing anarchists, and that Anthony Quinton was involved?"

"Yes." Jack felt a strange sort of pride, for his Lottie was one of a kind. "She also led me to Quinton's hideaway."

"She is a rare creature." Primus's tone implied this was not a compliment. "What did you tell her about our group?"

"As little as possible. I did not reveal your identity." He cleared his throat. "But she met the others when they found us."

Laurent and Calderone had been waiting for them on the shore. Jack's subordinates had appeared quite charmed by Lottie and, he noted wryly, vice versa.

"I take it the meeting with Delaney did not go smoothly."

Primus's expression was ironic. No one understood the situation better than he. Twelve years ago, Jack had gone to his mentor in a panic after finding the murdered informant and his family and the note threatening Lottie.

"Cut ties. Permanently," Primus had instructed. *"That is the only way she will be safe."*

At the time, Jack hadn't doubted his mentor's wisdom. But now...now he couldn't help but wonder if deception had been the only path. Or the right one.

"Let's just say that Charlotte hasn't forgiven me for faking my death," he said somberly. "Or the way I did it."

"You explained, I assume, the motivation behind your actions."

"It doesn't matter." Jack raked a hand through his hair. "The fact is that I abandoned her in the worst way possible and made her grieve."

For years, Lottie had said. His heart hammered with remorse... and hope. If her feelings had been that intense, that enduring, then perhaps he could find a way to fix things.

"There is no going back."

His attention snapped back to Primus, whose visage looked carved from ice.

"I've told you this on three occasions now," his mentor reminded him. "The first was when you insisted on marrying

Charlotte Danvers against my advice. The second when you left to protect her. The third when you recklessly compromised your cover and let her know you were alive."

"I know," Jack said tightly.

Because he did know. Primus had warned him from the start that marrying Lottie was a bad idea—that the life of a spy did not allow for personal ties, and relationships were a liability. He'd followed his heart anyway, and even now, with all the mistakes he'd made, he could not bring himself to regret his choice. Truth be told, he deserved Primus's censure and any consequences the other saw fit to mete out.

Primus assessed him with a hawkish gaze before sighing.

"I understand, you know. I was young once. In love once."

Jack's surprise must have shown, for Primus's thin lips formed a rare smile.

"Did you think I was incapable of folly?" he inquired.

"No, sir. That is," Jack said hastily, "you have always seemed rather...er, logical. In your choices and decisions."

"I think by *logical* you mean *calculated*."

"I didn't mean—"

"One must never apologize for the truth." Primus turned to the window, widening the part in the curtain. The sliver of light highlighted the silver in his thick, grey hair, the harsh lines etched into his skin. "And the truth is I learned to be shrewd because of the mistakes I made. Because my decisions, based on foolish impulses, nearly led to disaster."

Jack blinked, trying to reconcile this with the mentor he knew.

Primus let the curtain fall back into place, turning to face him. "A long time ago, I met a woman. We were married. It did not end well."

For some reason, Jack had always assumed that Lancaster was a bachelor. The other seemed like one: unsentimental and unattached, fastidious in his habits.

"I did not know—"

"It is not common knowledge, and I prefer to keep it that way."

"Of course, sir."

Primus adjusted the sleeve of his jacket. "I trust you with this information to show you that I understand your situation better than you realize. But as I warned you before, decisions have consequences. Sebastian Courtenay, the Marquess of Fayne, is dead. He cannot come back." He paused. "Not this time."

The reminder sucked Jack into a memory: the warm ooze beneath his palms as he put pressure on the gaping hole in his best friend's chest. Sebastian's labored breaths, the pleading in his dark eyes. *It's too late for me. You...you must be Fayne now.* He'd shoved a crumpled, blood-stained note at Jack. *"Promise me... promise you'll finish the job... Show them I'm a hero."*

Jack swallowed. "I know."

"She is beautiful, your widow. Intelligent and capable. A rare female, as I said."

Sensing more was coming, he waited.

"She would be a difficult woman to walk away from. But you did it. And now you must remain committed to the path you chose."

It is now or never.

"What if there was a way back, sir?" he said.

Greeted with Primus's stony silence, Jack nonetheless forged on.

"Charlotte is, as you noted, capable. And she wishes to assist in our mission—"

"Out of the question." Primus snapped his brows together. "We do not involve civilians."

"I was a civilian," Jack pointed out. "And you recruited me."

"The circumstances were different. You merited the exception. Despite your background, I saw your potential, which is why I mentored you personally."

At Jack's lowest, when his sins had come for him and he was

friendless and penniless, Primus had taken him on. The spymaster had given him a fresh start and purpose. He was the man he was today because of Primus. And he could never forget his debt.

"And I owe you for it," he said gruffly.

"You have paid me back." Primus's mien softened a fraction. "You have shown dedication to your duty and made invaluable contributions as my second-in-command. It is only natural that, after a sustained period in the trenches, a man should want for the softer things in life. For companionship. To that end, I know women who specialize in seeing to a man's comforts. Albeit temporarily, but with great discretion—"

"I don't want a whore," Jack said bluntly. "I have a wife."

"You have a widow." Primus returned fire with precision. "Due to the arrangements that I helped you to make—which, I might add, took considerable effort—said widow was left in very comfortable circumstances. For the rest of her life, she will be addressed by a coveted title and will want for nothing. Do you truly wish to take that away from her?"

"No." He hated how he sounded...like a sullen lad. "But she... she grieved for me, sir. You said she would recover and move on. But it took her *years*. And she never remarried—"

"Because she does not know who you are. If she did..."

Primus did not have to say more. Reality sank into Jack like a dagger between the shoulder blades. There was no defending against the truth of who and what he was, and this was the crux of his problems.

"You are an excellent spymaster, Granger. Loyal, bold, and relentless. Yet you have an Achilles' heel: women. Or have you forgotten the circumstances that led you to me?"

Primus's words twisted the blade. They were an agonizing reminder of what Jack had done—the lying, disloyal bastard that he was. Shame churned his gut.

"You betrayed your friend and your honor because of a woman," Primus went on with quiet ruthlessness.

"I know," he said tautly.

"She led you by the bollocks. And you let this go on for years—"

"I *know*."

He felt sick, remembering all the things he'd done with her. How he'd been her bloody sexual lapdog. Panting and hating himself even as he went back for more. Even after he had broken free of her, learning for the first time that he was capable of doing good—of *being* a good man—she had still tried to leash him, this time with blackmail. She'd threatened to publicize the depraved things they'd done—and things they hadn't—if he didn't continue to service her.

Primus had put a stop to that. He'd negotiated for her "tell-all" journal, a twisted mix of half-truths and venomous lies. As high as the price had been, it had been worth it to be rid of her. Jack owed his mentor for more than an education in spy craft: the other had also buried his deepest shame.

"Do you need to read it again?" Primus said quietly. "To remind yourself of what your lapse in judgement cost you? What you must never allow to happen again?"

Although Jack hated that Primus had kept that lurid memento, he also knew why. The diary's existence was Jack's cross to bear. Only when he overcame its power—by proving its contents wrong—could he find his salvation. Only when he conquered the demons within those pages would he be truly free from his past.

"I bring this up as a reminder." Primus spoke in, what for him, passed for a gentle tone. "As spies, we must understand our own vulnerability. Yours, Jack, pertains to women. Your chivalrous nature blinds you to the machinations of the fair sex. While your widow may have given you hope of a reunion, she has also shown her skill at deception and manipulation. In other circumstances, I would say she has the makings of a fine spy. But because of you—because I don't wish the years I have invested in you to be wasted—I see her as something else altogether: a threat."

Jack shook his head. "Lottie would never betray—"

"Purposefully or not, she has power over you, Granger. She is Paris's arrow, and you have no defense against her. You never have."

His humiliation grew. Was he that weak? That incapable of exercising clear judgement?

For Lottie, you would do anything. And you know it.

"However clever your former spouse may be, she is an amateur and out of her depth. No match for a trained professional. She is a liability—to herself, you, and the mission. Make whatever excuses you need to and extricate yourself. Immediately."

He lifted his chin. "Is that an order?"

Primus shook his head slowly. "I trust you, Granger. I have given you my counsel and know you will make the right choice."

Jack's throat tightened. His mentor's trust had not come readily. He'd earned it through years of sweat and, sometimes, blood. It was proof that he'd made something of himself and precious to him...just not as precious as Lottie.

Conflict continued to war within him.

He said curtly, "I will talk to her."

Primus studied him for a moment longer. "Then let us move on to other pressing concerns. Did you find any clues that might lead us to the First Flame?"

Jack grabbed onto the change of topic like a man trapped in quicksand to solid ground.

"I believe so." He reached into his jacket pocket, removing the leather pouch. "We found this amongst Tony Quinton's belongings."

The spymaster took the pouch. Untied it and looked inside.

His forehead creased. "What is special about this?"

Jack frowned. "The liquid in the vial is quite volatile—"

"What vial?"

Primus showed him the contents.

As the realization hit Jack, he choked out a sound that was half-oath, half-laugh. Inside the pouch was not the vial of liquid but sand from the cavern floor. The clue had been nicked...by his amateurish and out-of-her-depth wife.

Twenty-Two

"Who did this to you?" Devlin leaned his hands on her desk, scowling at her.

Sitting on the other side, Charlie strove for patience. After traveling all day, she was tired and in no mood for an interrogation, no matter how well intentioned. But Devlin had ambushed her as she arrived on her doorstep. Now they were in her study, and it was past midnight. All she wanted was a bath and her own bed.

She'd barely slept the night before...and the reason for it caused resentment to bubble. A part of her knew she was being unfair. Sebastian had told her he didn't sleep with Eleni Pappas—or Maria Delaney, rather—and she believed him. She still hadn't liked walking in on the pair looking so cozy. After the soul-melting passion she'd shared with Sebastian, the last thing she'd wanted to see was another woman's hands on him...especially an attractive female like Maria.

Admit it, you're jealous. And for no good reason.

Charlie hated her insecurity. It was something she'd worked hard to overcome, and to a degree, she had: with the society she'd built and her circle of friends, she knew her own worth. Yet Sebastian had a way of making her feel like that girl lost in the market again, desperate to find someone she could trust, to be protected, to be *seen*…

Her chest constricting, she focused on the here and now.

"I understand that you mean well." Seeing the concern in Devlin's eyes, she softened her tone. "As I've said, I am not hurt. We can discuss this further in the morning—"

"I am not leaving until you tell me what is going on. You left with no explanation and were gone for days. Now you return looking like a prizefighter—not a successful one, I might add." Devlin straightened and crossed his arms over his chest. "Does this have to do with the Quinton case?"

Out of professional courtesy, she owed him the truth.

"As a matter of fact, the case is now closed," she said briskly. "Quinton has not been unfaithful to Amara. He is telling her the truth, probably as we speak, and how they settle things from here is their private affair. Our job is done."

Devlin narrowed his eyes. "What was he doing with that Loveday chit?"

"They were both looking for his brother. He didn't tell Amara because of bad blood between her and his family."

"And did they find this brother?"

Tony Quinton's lifeless eyes flashed in her head.

"Yes."

"One other question."

She raised her brows.

"What is the rest of the story you're not telling me?"

Where do I begin?

Like the bottom drawer of her desk, there was simply too much to sort through at present. She was no fool; she knew she couldn't investigate the First Flame Society on her own. As she'd told the Angels, their strength lay in their sisterhood. She would need her society—which included Devlin—to assist her in uncovering the anarchist plot, beginning with identifying the liquid in the vial she'd found.

Yet she balked...because of the perils.

She had no wish to endanger those closest to her. Moreover, she would have to explain the situation, and she wasn't ready to tell them about Sebastian for a variety of reasons. First, things were too unsettled; she didn't know where their relationship, if it could be called that, was headed. What she did know was that her no-strings-attached arrangement with Sebastian had backfired...at least for her.

One carefree night hadn't scratched her itch for him; it had left her wanting *more*.

More of the passion that only Sebastian had ever ignited in her. More of his intensity and fierce desire. More of *him*. A man who had lain his life down for her more than once. Who'd abandoned her (for foolishly noble reasons) yet stayed true to his vows. Who'd said he'd loved her...but seemed surprised that he might be worthy of her grief in return.

Sebastian's vulnerability floored her. She was realizing that the confident and dashing rogue had insecurities of his own. That perhaps he'd kept secrets not merely for the sake of doing so but because he felt he *had* to. It dawned on her that they'd shared more intimacy in the last two days than they had during the first year of their marriage. She admitted to herself that she wanted to get to know him better...to spend time with him, to understand what made the man tick.

Yet their affair would have to be conducted with the ultimate discretion. The fact remained that she would not expose Sebastian, even to her friends, without his consent. His job was a dangerous one and secrecy his best form of protection. She wouldn't put him at risk for the sake of her personal desires.

"For now, you know what you need to know," she said to Devlin. "I will inform you should circumstances change."

"Should circumstances *change*?"

In a heartbeat, Devlin stalked to her side of the desk, moving so fast that she didn't have a chance to leave her chair. He caged her by bracing his hands on its arms. Her pulse galloped with surprise as she looked up into his eyes.

"We have had our fun and games," he said. "When you told me it would go no further, I stepped back—out of respect for you. Now I'm wondering if I made a mistake."

"Move away, Devlin," she snapped. "I am warning you."

"You are too damned stubborn for your own good. It is one thing to take risks and get hurt, but you are courting danger unnecessarily by doing it on your own. The very thing you teach your Angels not to do."

She hated that he had a point. "I said I will let you know when—"

"You have friends, Charlotte. I am one of them. But maybe, in order to curb your recklessness, I need to be more than that."

Reading his intention, she pressed her hands against his chest to stop him. He flew backward, and for a stunned instant, she thought she had underestimated her own strength. Then she saw Sebastian. He was facing Devlin, who'd collided into a bookshelf, sending volumes crashing to the ground.

Devlin staggered but retained his balance. "Who in blazes are you?"

"Charlotte's husband," Sebastian snarled. "Keep your bloody hands off my wife."

"Was that entirely necessary?" Lottie inquired.

Jack didn't answer because the question was so stupid, he didn't think it was worthy of a reply. He glowered, and she rolled her eyes as if he hadn't found her with another man. A man who'd been about to *kiss* her. Luckily, Devlin was perceptive: realizing who of the three of them did not belong, he'd made a hasty exit. Jack didn't mourn the bastard's departure.

Looking not the least bit contrite, Lottie glided over to a rose-wood spirits cabinet, the front inlaid with mother-of-pearl. The furnishing was decidedly feminine, which fit the overall theme of her home. Everything from the pink walls to the delicate details shouted who was mistress here, and the fact eased some of Jack's tension. He liked that his wife enjoyed the house he'd bought her and that she'd turned it into a home.

He contemplated her desk, the front carved with flora and fauna. If he bent her over and tupped her on it, would the carving be too rough against her silky-soft legs? Or would she like being bent to his will and taken from behind?

"Whisky?" she asked.

Relinquishing the provocative image, he nodded, foolishly pleased that she remembered his drink preference.

When she poured two glasses of whisky, he felt his brows rise. Trust Lottie not to drink like an ordinary woman either. She handed him a glass, and he sampled it, savoring the strong, smooth burn. She knew her whisky. He downed his glass, and she poured him another.

"Do stop sulking," she said. "Devlin is not my lover."

"Not for want of trying."

She cast her gaze to the ceiling, where plaster cherubs frolicked in floral fields.

"Given that you made your feelings known the last time by hurling a rock through a window, I thought your next tactic could not be any more troglodytic." She sipped. "Apparently I was wrong."

"This isn't amusing, Charlotte."

"No, it's childish."

"Any more childish than the cold shoulder you gave me over Delaney?"

Immediately, he regretted his tetchy tone. This was how things had always degenerated between him and Lottie. They were both too hotheaded, quick to anger and take offense.

"Touché."

To his surprise, her lips curved over the rim of her glass. She saluted him, then took another drink of whisky.

He stared at her. "That is all you have to say?"

"You made your point. We are both jealous fools. Is there more to add?"

"I suppose not," he muttered.

"Then why don't we sit and discuss our bigger problem."

He joined her in the sitting area and folded himself into a pink wingchair teeming with flora and fauna. The furnishing was so delicately feminine that he feared his bollocks might shrink in protest. But he couldn't deny the chair was bloody comfortable.

Lottie, of course, looked like a queen on her blushing throne. Her hair was twisted in a fashionable knot, curls framing her oval face. The skirts of her burgundy carriage dress cascaded gracefully to the ground. Confronted by her magnificence, he felt like the peasant he was. He bridled at the feeling—at the invisible wall that separated them. He wanted to tear it down with his bare hands.

She does not know who you are. If she did…

His hand tightening around the glass, he tossed back the rest of the spirits. The burn beat back the fire inside, the impulse that would incinerate everything if he let it loose.

"You took the vial," he stated. "I will need it back."

"We will get to that later. The problem I was referring to was Devlin."

"It is about time you realize that he is a problem."

"He is not the problem." Her eyes flashed battle bright. "The problem is that *you* told him we are married. That you are my *husband*."

Perhaps not his finest hour.

"The bounder was about to kiss you," Jack muttered.

"Devlin could have been about to bed me, and you still had no right to do what you did! Now I am obligated to come up with a suitable explanation..."

She kept talking, but he didn't hear any of it. Because his brain was stuck on her words, spinning like a wheel mired in muck: *about to bed me, about to bed me...*

Another man. About to bed *his Lottie*.

"No right?"

The words left him in a roar, and even Lottie started. He slammed his glass on a table, stalking over to her. She remained on her throne, staring at him with arched brows. Not the least bit cowed as he glowered down at her.

"We are married," he growled.

"*Were* married," she retorted. "The marriage ended when you faked your death. When you decided to abandon me for twelve years."

"Christ, we've been over this. I did it to protect you. Because I love you. And I stayed true to my vows because *you*"—he stabbed a finger at her—"are the only woman for me. Ever. Until the end of bloody time. So, if you think I'll allow some sod to put his hands on what is mine—"

"You love me?"

Her question pierced his fog of rage.

"I told you I did," he bit out. "Back in the cave."

"No, you said you *loved* me. You used the past tense."

He braced his hands on his hips, inhaling through his nose for patience. "Now you're grasping at straws."

"I am *not*, you imbecilic man."

She surged to her feet, moving so quickly that her head almost hit his chin. He refused to budge, and they stood toe-to-toe, glaring at one another.

"You love me. Now."

He didn't know why she was insisting on it when he'd just told her.

"My memory is not faulty, woman."

"But clearly your reasoning is. Last night, you told me we were sharing pleasure without strings or commitment."

Her accusatory tone irked him. Especially because he didn't understand it.

"And?" he said shortly.

"And how can we do that *if you love me*?"

He twitched...not just because she'd shouted the words. Her bosom was heaving, and her cheeks were flushed; she looked a lot like she did when he made her come. Simultaneously, he realized he was hard, his shaft stretching the wool of his trousers, and when she dipped her gaze, running it over the visible outline of his erection, he felt it like a caress.

"What do you truly want from me, Sebastian?" she demanded.

Aroused and captivated, he spoke without thinking. "I can't have what I want."

"Why in blazes not?"

"Because I don't deserve it."

She was on him in an instant, her hands curling around the lapels of his jacket.

"Why not, Sebastian? Why would you say such a thing?"

Because I am not who you think I am. I have been deceiving you...

I am not the Marquess of Fayne, and I never was.

Despair and longing howled inside him. He could give it no outlet—save one.

Shoving his hands into Lottie's hair, he crushed his mouth to hers.

TWENTY-THREE

If desperation had a flavor, it was the one burning on Charlie's tongue. Smoky and wild and complex—everything that was Sebastian. She didn't know what he was hiding, but she knew that he needed her. She felt it in the grip of his hands against her scalp, the bulging tension of his biceps trapping her arms, the proprietary plunge of his tongue. His desire for her transcended the physical, his emotions electrifying the air.

He loves me. Present tense. But he thinks he doesn't deserve my love in return.

Confusion and tenderness wrung her heart. There were so many questions she needed to ask—but later. Now he was communicating with a different kind of honesty, and she understood that this was about more than pleasure. The greedy claim of his mouth, the eager stiffness of his cock was about more than lust.

It was about Sebastian taking what he felt he did not deserve. About his need for her being so raw and ungoverned that he couldn't relinquish it even when he thought he should. It was about him losing control because he'd loved her then, loved her now, and wasn't sure what to do about it.

Heaven help me, I might feel the same way.

She wasn't ready for words either. Instead, she grabbed his bristly jaw and kissed him back with all the chaotic, undeniable longing she felt. He groaned, his tongue delving deeper, and she welcomed him, letting him stake his territory while she did the same. She loved the taste of him: whisky and Sebastian, all male, all delicious.

The kiss blurred everything around her. There was only her mate and their vibrant connection. So lost was she that she didn't notice that he'd lifted and carried her until her bottom hit the hard surface of her desk.

His mouth left hers, but only so that it could attach to her ear. She shivered as he traced the delicate rim with his tongue, flicking the plump lobe.

"You have no idea how much I want you."

His hoarse words made her nipples throb beneath her bodice.

"I have *some* idea." She reached out, stroking the thick length of his erection. "Unless you happen to have a truncheon tucked in your trousers, I believe you are quite happy to see me."

"Christ, Lottie." He looked at her, and she *loved* the dancing bronze sparks in his eyes. "Only you could make me want to laugh and tup you at the same time."

Which made her want to tease him even more. "Is tupping me on my desk one of those fantasies you had during our separation?"

"No." He cupped her nape, looking deeply into her eyes, as if he wanted to see down to her soul. "The idea came to me after I witnessed you dallying with Devlin."

"I was not dallying with him."

She sounded breathless because Sebastian's fingers were nimbly unfastening the back of her dress. A spymaster's hands, he had. Able to give him access to whatever he wanted.

"You know you are the only woman for me." Satisfaction deepened his voice as he pushed her frock off her shoulders. "It seems, however, that I must prove I am the only man for you."

"You don't have to prove anything—"

She gasped when he lifted her off the desk, spinning her around and bending her over the surface. His actions were dominant...and arousing. Her cheek burned against the leather blotter as he pressed his palm to her nape, murmuring, "Stay."

As if she were a pet.

On principle, she retorted, "And if I don't?"

"You'll prove you are a spoilsport and forfeit the game."

"Game? What game—"

"The one you started at the academy. When it was my turn to be interrogated, I was up to the challenge. Now that it is yours, can you say the same?"

The dashed man knew her too well. She never could resist a challenge. And why would she now, when she was quite certain they would both end up winners? Her blood rushed with anticipation as he made short work of her corset. She did love their games. And if she played her cards right, she might turn the tables and learn more about him.

Twisting her head to look at him, she said with feigned defiance, "Same rules?"

The glint in his eyes told her he was enjoying this as much as she was.

"Three questions," he acknowledged. "As we are not in public, you are not limited to *yes* or *no* responses. If you lie, I will punish you. Tell the truth, and you will be rewarded. If you get up from this desk, the game ends."

"How do you intend to punish me? I am short on whips and crops at present."

"Cheeky minx. I'll think of something that is fitting to your misbehavior."

His sensual threat gave her a pleasant shiver. An instant later, her petticoats rustled to the floor, leaving her in her chemise, drawers, and stockings. She heard a ripping sound, and air caressed her bare back.

"That chemise was new," she protested.

"Your next complaint is going to buy you punishment."

As a woman used to being in charge, his authority stirred her. The strength of his will matched hers and made her feel safe to let go, if only for this game. The longing that welled inside her was as strong as desire, as physical as the needs thrumming in her body. She was used to counting on herself, and there was something infinitely relieving and arousing in trusting herself to another's care.

Sebastian pulled off her drawers, crouching to remove her shoes.

"Christ." A rasp entered his voice. "That's quite a view, sweetheart."

Her cheeks grew hot as she pictured what he was seeing from his vantage point, which was face-level with her bottom. Her legs were spread and clad in rose-colored stockings secured to a darker rose garter belt. They would frame her pussy, which she could feel dampening under his gaze.

He rose, running a proprietary hand up her leg.

"Pink stockings. Pink garter."

As he touched each item, he named it like a cartographer charting new lands. She trembled when his callused pads explored her inner thigh. With a roughness that made her breath catch, he nudged her feet farther apart. The air exploded from her throat in the form of a mewl when he stroked her wet, aching crease.

"And my favorite pink of all." He stopped just shy of the place where she craved his touch and made a chiding sound. "You've left a wet spot on the blotter, darling. And the game's hardly begun."

His observation, the casualness with which he shared it, inflamed her and made her wetter. Which was no doubt his intent. Her nipples and pearl throbbed against the stiff leather of her blotter, and all she needed was a bit of friction to ease the—

Smack.

She jolted at the impact of his palm against the right cheek of her bottom, the sound of censure echoing through the study.

"We'll have none of that, wicked minx," Sebastian said sternly. "You are not to bring yourself off without permission. You are not in charge; I am. Do you understand?"

To her consternation, she felt herself blush. Like the schoolgirl she'd never had the chance to be.

"Yes."

"Yes, what?"

At his lordly tone, her belly melted, heat trickling into her pussy.

"Yes, sir," she whispered.

"Good girl."

His approval soothed some confounding need even as he rubbed the superficial sting he'd caused. The sensation on her bottom turned into a pleasant burn, one that spread over her skin and heightened her sensitive state. She loved his masterful touch upon her flesh and nearly protested when he drew it away.

"Let's start with the first question." A pause. "How many others have you had since me?"

Embarrassment twisted inside her, anger following swiftly on its heels. Her affairs were none of his business, and he knew it. He was the one who'd left her—made her believe she was a widow. He'd betrayed *her*, not the other way around.

"Tell me. Unless you are still counting the bastards?"

The words sounded gritted out, and she knew he was angry. But not at her. Sebastian, not being a stupid fellow except on specific occasions, understood that he was responsible for any lovers she'd taken. He wasn't punishing her...but himself. She had the sudden insight that he had a habit of doing so. For some reason, he felt undeserving—of her, of happiness—and she wanted to get to the root of it.

"Why does it matter?" she asked softly.

"That is not an answer."

"It is the one you are getting. Whatever happened, happened. There is no changing the past, only what lies ahead."

As she said the words, she felt the truth of them. If she wanted to move forward, she needed to let go of what had gone on before. Of the pain and anger and fear clouding her judgement. Only then would she have a clear vision of the future. Only then could she decide if the passion that burned so brightly between her and Sebastian could lead to something real and lasting.

"Is that your final answer?"

She turned her head, trying to see his face, but he kept out of her view. Unable to gauge his response, she went with her instincts.

"Yes," she said.

"Very well. An omission counts as a lie. Prepare for your punishment."

His severity sent a lick of fire up her spine, as did the roughness of his touch as he brought her hips to the edge of the desk. He spread her wider and positioned her to receive his will. She braced, her palms sweaty against the blotter, her buttocks trembling in readiness for the castigation she'd earned. A heartbeat passed, then another and another, until she thought she could hear the rapid knocking of her heart against the rosewood. Anticipation expanded her lungs, her insides, until she feared coming out of her skin.

Every inch of her tingled with expectation. With need.

When nothing happened, her chest suddenly seized. He was so quiet, so still. Panic came out of nowhere, surrounding her like a crowd of strangers whose language she didn't understand, who took no notice of her as tears leaked from her eyes.

Is he still there? Did he leave? Am I alone again as I've always been?

A warm, hot mouth closed over her pussy, and she choked out a sob.

Of relief, need, and bliss.

Her emotions were tangled skeins as Sebastian's tongue split the heart of her, laying her open with his kiss. He clamped her bottom with his large hands, holding her cheeks apart as he pushed deeper and deeper, and she whimpered at the feel of his tongue sliding inside her. His oral penetration felt almost more intimate than that of his cock. He took his time tasting her, looking into her inner recesses, exposing her with his thumbs as he licked and licked.

Even that wasn't enough for him. He journeyed higher, and she shuddered as he tongued her crack, finding a forbidden rim. Instinct made her shrink away from the unfamiliar sensation, but he wouldn't let her. The tip of his tongue circled and circled that unexplored terrain, laying claim to it, making it his. Shame turned into surrender and surrender into pleasure. The tremors started, and she felt herself climbing, reaching for that peak...

He stopped. Stepped away.

Left her wet and quivering and panting, balanced on a razor's edge.

As she tried to steady her breath, her lover came into view. Given the frustrated state the bastard had left her in, she oughtn't to have found the satisfied gleam in his eyes arousing, but she did. Despite his smugness, his mouth was red and wet from pleasuring her, and there was a wet spot on his trousers. His erection looked ready to burst free.

It cost him to play with her. To be with her.

This game they were playing was more than a game.

It was about more than pleasure. It was about exposing themselves, letting the other in, and in doing so, opening themselves up to the possibility of a real future. Was that what she wanted?

The answer thumped in her heart.

Yes...*yes*.

He trailed a finger along the curve of her cheek. "On to the next question, hmm?"

With the taste of Lottie on his tongue, the rounded curves of her arse quivering like a mouth-watering aspic, Jack had to wrestle with his hunger. He had to beat back that part of him that wanted to grab her by the hips, thrust his iron-hard prick into her tight, wet cunny, and plow her until they both forgot their names.

His wife was right; he did have troglodytic tendencies. Of course, she was the only one who brought them out in him. Her refusal to discuss her lovers had triggered his need to assert his claim. He respected her right to remain quiet on the matter even as he hated himself more for making this an issue in the first place.

No cock but his should have been in Lottie's pussy.

No man but he should have known the bliss of her heat and passion.

From now on, no man touches her but me. She's bloody mine.

In that moment, he knew. The realization was like sunlight shafting through the clouds during a downpour, improbable yet spectacular.

He was going to fight to get Lottie back.

Even if it meant going against his mentor's advice, exposing his worst sins and the ugliness of his soul, he would do it. Because Lottie was worth it. Their relationship was worth it.

The clarity stunned him and came with a burst of optimism. He was going to find a way to win his wife back. Maybe not tonight, maybe not this week or even this month, but he was going to do it. Bloody hell, he'd foiled assassination attempts, stopped an explosive device from detonating, lived under false identities for fifteen years...surely, he could convince his beloved to take another chance on him.

He just had to bide his time. Play his cards right. Starting now.

He ran a finger from the nape of her neck down her spine, loving how she quivered but did not stop him. He needed her open and vulnerable—needed her to tell him one thing. He traced the dip in her back, then lower, circling the pucker still moist from his kiss. Reminding her of their intimacy, of what they allowed one another, the depth of their bond.

Then he fisted her hair, turning her head so that their eyes locked.

"Can you forgive me?" he asked.

Her eyes widened, and he held his breath. Because if she said no...

"Yes," she whispered.

Relief and joy whipped through him, and he turned her over and pulled her to sitting, needing to see the truth in her face. And it was there.

It was there.

"Could you...could you give me another chance?" he said hoarsely.

"Perhaps?" Her expression was somber, thoughtful. "The truth is I don't know, Sebastian."

"I understand. After what I did—"

"Now that you've explained the circumstances that led to your choice, I understand and do forgive you." She drew a breath. "But I don't know if I can open myself up to hurt and disappointment again."

He wanted to say he would never cause her either, but he couldn't promise that, could he? Not when he hadn't told her the truth of who he was. Of what she would be giving up married to him.

"At the same time, there is the way I feel when I am with you." Her eyes had a brilliance that made his breath catch. "Alive, and, I don't know, *free*—well, I haven't felt this way in twelve years. And certainly not with anyone else."

That was something, at least. Something he could work with. Build on.

"Even though I've found a purpose and done meaningful

things, I wonder now if a part of me hasn't been just going through the motions," she said.

"Sleepwalking," he murmured. "I know how it feels."

She touched his jaw, and he clasped her hand, absorbing the warmth of her forgiveness, feeling it flow into him and give him strength.

"My answer is not a *no*," she said. "It's an *I don't know*."

It was a fair response, better than he expected. In fact, it was better not to rush into things this time around. He still had to give her the full truth...and hopefully, do it in such a way that wouldn't send her running for the hills.

"Then we'll take the time to get to know one another again." *And, in some respects, get to know one another for the first time.* "As long as it takes, as long as you need, Lottie, I will be waiting. I love you."

She smiled, so beautiful that he ached.

"Then show me." She linked her arms around his neck, her eyes bright. "In case you've forgotten, I've answered two of your questions. Therefore, you owe me two rewards."

He bit back a laugh. Leave it to his wife to keep track.

He kissed her. Hunger leapt between them like a flame, the tinder of intimacy taking their passion to new heights. He savored her mouth, which was just as sweet as the rest of her. The taste of her pleasure was still on his tongue, and she writhed as he shared the naughty flavor with her. Their teeth collided and breaths mingled as they fought to get closer.

Then he had to have more. He kissed his way to her breasts, flicking his tongue against one beaded tip whilst he rubbed the other between finger and thumb. Her nipples were ripe berries, and he drew one plump morsel deep into his mouth.

Her fingers clenched in his hair. "Heavens, Sebastian, when you do that, it feels..."

"Yes?" He traded nipples, making the second one as moist as the first. "How does it feel when I suck on your gorgeous tits?"

"It feels like...like..."

Her cheeks were as pink as the bud between his lips, and he knew. This had happened before, years ago, and his cock wept at the memory of how he'd aroused his wife to such a degree that she'd spent from having her tits sucked.

Grabbing her hand, he placed it on her breast. "Touch yourself, sweeting."

She didn't argue, moaning as she rubbed her nipple with her slim fingers. At the delicious sight of her pleasuring herself, he felt his prick jerk. What he wouldn't give to see her touch herself all over...a delight for another day. He bent his head over her free nipple while he reached between her sleek thighs.

Her spine bowed as he sucked one bud and diddled another. The slick sounds of his fingering mixed with her breathy pants, and he hoped she was close. Because if she didn't come soon, he might do something he hadn't done since he was a greenling and spend in his pants... He lashed her nipple with his tongue whilst he thumbed her pearl and thrust two fingers into her heat. She gasped, her thighs clamping around his hand, and she came.

Christ, did she ever.

"That's it, darling," he said through harsh breaths. "Clench on my fingers just so."

Each lush contraction, each delicate ripple, reminded him of other good things to come. No pun intended. He kissed her, extending her bliss with long, deep strokes, touching her as deeply as she touched him. Gazing into his goddess's dreamy eyes, her expression pleasured but far from sated, he knew he was the luckiest man alive.

Her next words proved it.

"Sebastian," she murmured. "I want you."

"I'm yours," he told her. "Any way you want me."

"*Any* way I want?"

The way she wetted her lips made his blood pound. His fingers lacked their usual dexterity as he fumbled through an inner coat pocket, removing the device he'd had the foresight to slip inside. Sitting up on the desk, Lottie took it from him.

"A French letter?" She lifted her brows. "Rather sure of yourself, aren't you?"

He gave her his most charming grin. "More along the lines of hopeful."

TWENTY-FOUR

Charlie decided that Sebastian had a secret weapon: his endearing boyishness. This quality didn't surface often, and when it did, she was quite powerless against it. Which was why she hid her response behind a wry smile.

"I'd wager that earnest charm worked well with the ladies."

"There haven't been any other ladies. Only you."

There it was again—that irresistible earnestness in his dark eyes. Like that of a boy wishing to please. Then he tucked a finger under her chin, and he became all man, kissing her until she was pliant and panting, desperate for more.

"You are overdressed," she murmured against his lips.

He smirked as he took a step back. There was arrogance in the way he undressed, his movements unhurried, as if he were giving her a show. As he shrugged off his outer layers, the fabrics rippled with his bulging strength. He unbuttoned his shirt with deliberate slowness, and her pussy fluttered at the memory of how deep those blunt fingers had reached inside her, the feeling of fullness that had taken her over the edge.

He stripped off his shirt, and she wondered if she could ever see his virile physique without that primal tug of possessiveness.

She curled her hands against the desk, resisting the urge to run them over the hair-dusted slabs of his chest and the washboard ridges below. It was too delightful a spectacle to interrupt.

Off went his shoes. When his hands went to his waistband, anticipation quivered through her. As he pushed his trousers past his lean, muscular hips, he had to work the material over the ridge of his erection, baring that thick column inch by inch. Her heart thumped, her pussy clenching at the beauty of his robust manhood, the promised pleasure of having that abundance inside her. He clasped his rod, his large fist barely containing his virility as he worked it from the burgeoned tip to the thick base anchored to his enormous stones.

"Do you want this inside you, love?" he inquired.

It wasn't really a question, and the cocky slant of his lips said he knew it. It was like asking a starving woman whether she'd like a bite to eat or a fish whether it preferred to be in water.

She crooked her finger. "Come here."

She was mesmerized by the weighty sway of his cock as he strode to stand between her splayed thighs. When he chuckled, she darted her gaze up and saw the lazy amusement in his eyes.

"You can touch, you know," he murmured. "It won't bite."

"Maybe I will," she said sweetly.

His eyebrows shot up. "You know I adore your mouth, darling. But mind the teeth."

In answer, she reached out and boldly took hold of him. Their breaths formed an audible rush as she stroked him, moving the supple skin over his iron-hard core. In a fluid motion, she got off the desk and knelt, filling her mouth with his cock. He uttered a hoarse oath as she crammed in as much as she could, her lips stretching toward his base. His salty male taste saturated her senses. She bobbed on him, hollowing her cheeks. When she swallowed, he groaned as her throat contracted around him.

The next instant, he jerked out.

"On the desk," he bit out.

Heavens, she loved his dominant side. She hopped back up, and he grabbed the French letter, grimacing as he struggled to fit the sheep gut over his burgeoned member. If she wasn't so aroused, she might be amused at his predicament; it gave a new meaning to being too big for one's britches. Instead, she shared his frustration, willing him to get that dashed sheath on.

Finally, he did, and he pushed her back on the desk with thrilling impatience. His glittering eyes latched on hers, he fitted his thick head to her entrance and then...oh then...

"Sebastian."

She lost the capacity for speech, the power of his incursion driving the air from her lungs, the thoughts from her head. There was only him, thick and big and long, filling her. Taking away the emptiness in the way only he could.

"Lottie. My love."

His eyes burned into hers from beneath half-lowered lids, his voice gravelly with pleasure. A flush saturated his cheekbones, spilling toward his jaw, which was already shadowed with his night beard. The tendons on his neck stood out as he moved, thrusting into her center, pushing pleasure outward until even her scalp tingled with bliss. With the completeness of their joining.

He withdrew, and she felt the ache of twelve years. Then he drove inside with such determined force that her hips lifted from the desk. She moaned as he opened her up, drilling toward the heart of her, releasing a geyser of pleasure and emotion. He established a pounding rhythm, and she lifted her legs, wrapping them around his hard, flexing hips. Wanting him deeper, wanting no separation between them, not ever again.

Her throat tight, she whispered, "I've missed you."

"There's nothing like this," he said fiercely. "Nothing to rival being with you, inside you. I never want to leave again."

As if to punctuate the fact, he ground against her with his next thrust, the hard root of him grazing her pearl, flaring her pleasure. She tilted her hips, wanting more of that contact, and he gave it to her. Gave her all the sensations that she craved: the plunging fullness of his cock inside her cunny, the weighted slap of his stones against her folds, the tingling friction at the peak of her sensation. And still he found a way to give her more, pushing deep and butting against a place so exquisite that the pleasure bordered on pain.

"Sebastian," she gasped. "It's too much—"

"You can take it, love." Embers flared in his forge-dark eyes. "Take your pleasure from me. Come on my cock."

The climax broke like a storm. Pleasure flashed, bright and pure, and she shook with the power of its aftermath. Bliss tremored through every fiber of her being, and it was centered on her lover, on his deep and indelible presence. On him returning to the place he'd claimed, that had always been his.

Don't leave. Her heart contracted with the rest of her. *Don't ever leave me again.*

"You're so tight, gripping me like you never want to let me go," Sebastian groaned. "You're going to make me spend..."

She touched his jaw. "I want you to, darling."

His muscle leapt beneath her fingertips, his gaze burning into hers. His chest rippled as he drove more forcefully into her, strokes that buried him to the hilt. She realized that he'd been holding back, and she dug her heels in his flexing buttocks, urging him on.

"Give it to me," she whispered. "Everything you've got."

"Christ, Lottie."

The muscles of his neck stretched taut as he slammed into her. He pounded her with his hips, nailing her to the desk, triggering another gush of pleasure. He shafted deep twice more, then suddenly stilled. He threw his head back and roared. She felt him pulsing inside her, the blast of his seed against the sheath.

Shuddering, he lowered himself over her. Took her lips in a slow, drugging kiss.

"I hope you are satisfied with your rewards, wife." He tucked a loose strand behind her ear, exuding male satisfaction. "Although I can't say which of us enjoyed them more."

"I have no complaints whatsoever."

Her smile was equally pleased because she *had* enjoyed her rewards thoroughly.

Especially since he had given her not just two of them but three.

"Yes, yes. Fuck me. Take me for a ride, you stallion."

Judith was on top, her arse slapping his thighs in a demanding rhythm. She was also making noise, too much of it. Especially since they were in the stable, and anyone passing by the stall could hear them.

"We have to be quiet." Even though his voice had changed and deepened last year, it cracked now with panic. "Sebastian could come back from his ride at any time. I think we should stop—"

"I don't pay you to think," she snapped. "You'll do as I say. And I want to fuck."

He didn't understand how it happened, but her beauty disappeared in a blink. As if she'd removed a mask, revealing her true nature beneath. Her disdain churned his gut, reminded him of all the reasons why what they were doing was a bad idea.

Not that he needed reminding. Shame was like a shadow, dogging his every step, reminding him what a bastard he was. He'd tried to put an end to their couplings, but he was weak and could never stand his ground. This time, he'd managed to stay away from her for weeks, but she'd cornered him in the stables this morning. Stripping off her riding habit, she'd fondled her breasts and pussy, and he'd reacted, getting hard. She'd knelt in front of him, her mouth coaxing forth his lust even though he resisted.

Remembering, he felt desire drain from him. He softened and slipped out of her.

"Dash it all, I wasn't done." She pouted. "Hasn't anyone taught you it is bad manners to leave a lady wanting?"

"S-sorry."

Humiliation joined his shame, and he couldn't meet her eyes. He pushed himself to sitting, brushing off the hay that pricked his bare back. "I should be getting back to my duties—"

"*I* say what your duties are. And I want you to do what you do best. Make me feel good, my darling."

She was smiling again. The tenderness in her green eyes confused him, for he wasn't used to kindness. She had a way of making him feel both worthy and despicable. She placed a palm on his chest, pushing him back down with an insistence that said she was getting what she wanted. And he gave in. He shut his eyes, submitting to her skilled mouth, letting her take him to the place where he didn't have to think. Where he was here but not here. Where things happened, but not to him, and it was if he were merely looking on.

Like when his ma took her last breath, her beauty ravaged by the disease that had consumed her flesh and bone.

Like when the older boys at the orphanage had targeted him, bullying him, until he grew big enough to fight back.

Like when the butler had whipped him for accidentally breaking a porcelain plate, and the mistress of the house had tended to him afterward, her touch wandering from the welts on his back to other places, making him shudder in a different way.

Like now. When she had him in her mouth, and it felt good even as it felt bad. How could pleasure feel bad? But it did. It made him feel filthy and used, like the bastard the bullies in the orphanage liked to remind him he was. A whore's by-blow, a nobody, a waste of space who would never amount to anything.

He wanted to escape, to come.

To be anyone but himself.

"What the devil is going on?"

His shame and disgust were amplified a hundred-fold in the expression of his best friend standing in the entryway to the stall.

"Sebastian, wake up."

He didn't seem to register her voice. He rocked his head on the pillow, his forehead sheened with sweat. His powerful body shuddered as if gripped by a fever.

"No," he mumbled. "No...didn't mean..."

Leaning over him, Charlie gave his wide shoulders a shake. His lashes flew up, and the look in his eyes cinched her throat. Anguish —so dark that his pupils pushed out his irises, not a speck of bronze present.

For an instant, he stared at her, unseeing.

Then she saw his espionage skills kicking in. Sitting up against the headboard, he swept his gaze over her bedchamber, assessing his environment. She guessed he didn't spot any danger in her shell-pink boudoir accented with ivory and gilt. By the time his eyes returned to her face, he had locked away whatever demon had been stalking him whilst he slept. His mouth even took on a faint curve as he regarded the ivory satin bedsheets and pillows in shades of blush and coral.

"I feel like I woke up inside an oyster," he muttered.

"Are we really going to discuss my choices in decoration now?" Wrapping the bedsheet around herself, she drew her brows together. "You were having a nightmare. It was so intense that I couldn't wake you."

"It was just a dream."

She was not fooled by his offhandedness. "You are still sweating. Still trembling." She placed a hand on the quivering bulge of his biceps. "Do you wish to talk about it?"

"I don't remember. The dream, I mean." He scrubbed his hands over his face. "It was nothing, Lottie."

"I understand, you know," she said quietly. "I've seen things, too. Experienced things in my line of work that don't go away just because it is time for sleep. In fact, the quiet and dark of night seems to bring out the worst of the memories. I think it is the nature of what we do, and I am convinced that the only way to battle such demons is by sharing them. I've said to my Angels what I am saying to you now, Sebastian: don't go at it alone. Don't keep it inside. Monsters thrive in darkness, but they fear the light."

He appeared to take in her words. "I appreciate your counsel. But there are things that cannot be undone, and talking about it changes nothing."

"Have you tried?" she asked pointedly.

He clenched his jaw, saying nothing. And she couldn't let it stand.

"You asked me last night to give you another chance."

"So I did." His tone was wary. "What does it have to do with me having a nightmare?"

"Secrets," she said succinctly. "They were the biggest problem in our marriage. Even before you left, we fought constantly. I will take responsibility for my jealousy and temper, for assuming you were having an affair when you were not. You, however, bear some responsibility too."

"Not some, Lottie. *All* of it—all the fault is mine," he said with savage conviction.

"You are doing it again."

"Doing what?"

"Taking the blame. Acting as if you alone carry the weight of all mistakes." She narrowed her eyes at him. "Last night you said you don't deserve to get what you want, and I want to understand why you would think such a thing."

She saw she hit a nerve. His chest rose and fell on shallow waves, and his eyes were tempest-tossed.

"I am not the man you think I am," he said finally.

She furrowed her brow. "Then who are you?"

"I...I cannot be Sebastian Courtenay any longer."

He clasped her bare shoulders as if to keep her attention when wild horses couldn't drag it away. Emotion whirled around them like a dust storm.

"When I staged my death, I knew there would be no going back. I killed Fayne to protect you, but also to protect the work I was doing. I made enemies, and if I were suddenly to come back from the dead..."

"You would be at risk," she said slowly. "But that was twelve years ago. Surely you would be safe now?"

"Not until the First Flame is vanquished," he said resolutely. "I also gave my superior my word that I would not come back as Fayne. And I must honor that vow."

"I understand your professional obligation. But what about the vow you made to me?" Her voice quavered. "You asked for a second chance, and now you are telling me you cannot be the man I married?"

"I cannot be the Marquess of Fayne. But I will *always* be your husband, Lottie."

"That doesn't even make sense!" She threw up her hands. "If you're not Fayne, then who will you be?"

"I was thinking a man named Jack Granger." He said it casually, as if he were telling his valet which waistcoat he'd selected for the day. "He's not a lord. He was born a bastard but made something of himself. He's accumulated wealth through his investments, and he can keep you in the style to which you are accustomed...but he cannot give you a title. Doors previously open to you might close because you would be tying yourself to a man who is not your social equal."

She stared at him. "You created this...this entire identity?"

"More than this one, love. Habit of the trade." His smile didn't reach his eyes. "But I like this one for you because Jack, whilst not blue-blooded, is an honest man. One who sleeps well at night knowing he's put in a good day's work. He is loyal, committed, and doesn't harbor secrets because, at heart, he is a simple man. Most importantly, he loves you as much as Sebastian Courtenay did. Perhaps even more, because he knows what you would be sacrificing if you took him on. He knows you deserve better, but he would fall to his knees in gratitude if you said yes."

Her head spun as she contemplated what he was proposing. How it would change her life as she knew it. To be married to him...but not him. She would no longer be Lady Charlotte Fayne, but Mrs. Jack Granger.

"What if someone recognizes you?" she asked. "A friend or even an acquaintance?"

Unreadable emotion flitted through his eyes.

"As you know, I had an isolated upbringing. My health prevented me from making friends, and since I was so rarely in London, I had few acquaintances. Moreover, twelve years have passed, and I doubt anyone would remember me."

"I see." She chewed on her lip, wondering if his plan could work.

"I am sorry." Sebastian studied her. "I am asking too much—"

"No. That is, this is *a lot* to take in, but I am glad you are being honest with me. I want to know what you are thinking, Sebastian. I want to know *you*," she said tremulously. "As for your proposal, I need time to think about it. About the consequences of any decisions I make."

"I hate that you would have to give up—"

"The title is not my concern." She waved dismissively. "It's true that I once wished I could have had a more conventional upbringing, that my papa had seen fit to raise me as a proper earl's daughter. Having circulated in Society for several years now, I realize that I wasn't missing much. Ironic, isn't it? What I truly miss is the freedom of traveling and the world beyond ballrooms."

"I can give you that," he said. "Travel and adventure, whatever your heart desires. As for ballrooms, we shall avoid them like the plague."

His boyish eagerness lifted her heart.

"My biggest consideration is my society," she said, thinking aloud. "My Angels are important to me. I will not do anything to jeopardize them or the crucial work we do."

"Of course not, love. They are your family, your team. I would never ask you to give them up or do anything that would compromise your purpose."

She loved how well he understood her.

"There shouldn't be a reason why I cannot have both you and the Angels in my life," she conceded. "But it will require fore-thought and careful planning."

"You will consider it then?" Hope roughened his voice. "Consider marrying me again...only this time as Jack Granger?"

"I will think on it."

"Christ, you've made me the happiest of men, and you haven't even said yes."

His exuberance rustled a laugh from her. He kissed her, pushing her back on the bed, and the full extent of his enthusiasm, hard and heavy as an iron pike, became evident. Their mouths and hands roamed, and they tangled and rolled in their eagerness to get closer. She ended up on top, but he dragged her by the hips to kneel over his face. She rode his agile tongue, gasping as he drove her to a climax that made her fall forward in a boneless, shivering heap.

"Hold that thought, sweeting," he murmured.

He slid from under her. He was back in moments, and she twisted her head to see him donning another French letter.

"What can I say?" He shrugged, his smile smug. "I was *very* hopeful."

She was giggling when he gripped her hips. Her laughter dissolved as he pushed inside her, thick and strong, filling her up.

She pushed back on him, pleasure bowing her spine as his wide head butted a transcendent place. "Oh *there*, darling. Right there. That feels so fine."

He withdrew and thrust, hitting the exact spot. He did it repeatedly until her insides turned molten, and she spent with another gush. He groaned, the slick sounds of his plowing accompanied by the disciplined smack of his hips. His self-control unraveled, and she loved it, clutching the bedsheets for purchase so she could take the full force of his pounding. Take everything that he gave her.

"I'm going to spend," he grunted. "I want you to go over with me."

She wasn't sure it was possible, but then he reached under her, finding her pearl, working the slippery bud against his pistoning shaft. The waves of bliss rose again as he drilled his cock deeper and deeper, pleasured growls coming from his chest. Like magic, they crested as one, his body curving over hers, her lips turned to meet his kiss.

Afterward, they collapsed side by side, catching their breath. Sebastian laced his fingers with hers and looked at her with warm, sated eyes.

"The best is still to come, my Lottie," he said huskily. "This time, I am going to make good on my promise."

Her eyes dampened, and she knew what she wanted—what she had *always* wanted.

Him...all of him.

TWENTY-FIVE

W hile Jack would have gladly stayed in bed with his wife all day—and for the rest of their lives—they both had responsibilities that rendered that luxury impossible. Over a hearty breakfast of bacon, crisp buttered toast, eggs with herbs, and kippers served in Lottie's sitting room, they addressed their strategy for hunting down the First Flame.

Lottie tilted her head. "Did your superior agree to collaborate with me on this case?"

"He didn't say no to the idea," Jack hedged.

Primus's parting words rang in his head.

"Since your widow has absconded with our only clue, I suppose her involvement is a foregone conclusion," the spymaster had snapped. *"But you will keep her in line, Granger, and her knowledge of our organization to the barest minimum. Above all, you will heed my advice and keep your identity a secret. For your own good as well as that of the team. You must not compromise everything we've accomplished...and for what? The truth is no woman will accept your past and what you've done. Do not set yourself up for failure. Do not let your weakness for a female threaten our cause."*

When it came to Lottie, Jack hadn't heeded his mentor's

advice, and he couldn't bring himself to regret it. Not when exposing what he had of himself had gotten him closer to her. Closer to the possibility of winning her back. It had been a risk, telling her he was Jack Granger. Other ladies, he imagined, would have a fit if the man they'd married told them he could no longer be a marquess, only a plain mister.

But not his Lottie. She'd seemed indifferent about losing the title and its accompanying privileges. Her only concern was how the change in her status would affect her society and ability to help others. If he'd had to design a woman for himself, the result would be his Lottie.

Of course, he hadn't told her the entire truth: that Sebastian Courtenay, not Jack Granger, was his false identity. He told himself it was best to lead up to it, to prepare her and give her time to adjust. Her response thus far was better than he'd imagined, and it gave him hope that perhaps she could accept him, the real him, despite all his failings and flaws.

"But he wasn't precisely overjoyed at the prospect, was he?"

Lottie's dry rejoinder underscored her acuity, and he saw no point in denial.

"My mentor accepts that you will be a part of this investigation," Jack replied. "Whether or not he likes it."

"A wise fellow. All right, let us review our clues."

Going to her escritoire, she brought over the two familiar items, setting the vial and matches on the coffee table. Jack examined the vial first. In the daylight, the clear liquid had a slight yellowish tint.

"Each of the clues poses a different problem," he said.

"How do you mean?"

"Whatever is in this vial is something uncommon, and we must discover what it is." He tapped on the box of *Brompton's Finest Lucifers*. "Matches like these, on the other hand, are rather too common. Tracing them back to the killer will be like finding a specific fish in the sea."

"Keeping to your analogy, at least we know the species of fish we are looking for," she said. "Brompton's has a manufactory on Fairfield Road, where they produce and sell their Lucifers wholesale. Perhaps they keep a record of the match sellers who hawk their merchandise. Based on the design of the box, they may also be able to tell us when it was made and sold. It's a long shot, I know, but may yield a rough location of where the killer purchased the matches. In my experience, pulling on the tiniest loose thread can unravel the mystery."

Damn, but he admired his wife's logic. As beautiful as she was —and even with her fading shiner, she looked like a goddess in her teal dressing gown—her brains were equally impressive.

"Good thinking," he replied. "That leaves the substance in the vial. My group has a contact in the Royal Society who is usually of help in such matters. Unfortunately, he is lecturing in Germany at present. I will have to locate another scientist who is equally discreet."

"Perhaps my friend Amara Quinton can help. She designs investigative tools for the Angels. Below her atelier, she has a secret laboratory where she tests her inventions."

"As one does."

"Her specialty lies more in detachable skirts, hidden blades, and such, but it won't hurt to ask if she can identify the solution in the vial. Anyway, I need to pay her a visit to see how she is holding up after Gilbert's return."

Jack didn't envy the reception the poor sod was likely receiving.

"I would save my concern for Quinton," he said.

"You would." Lottie rolled her eyes. "Although the blunderbuss thought he was protecting his wife, he ought to have known better than to lie to her."

While her comment was pointed, it held more humor than heat. In the early days of their marriage, Lottie had been prone to letting her resentment simmer. For his part, Jack had been sensitive to criticism, his temper flaring like a match. No wonder they'd fought like cats and dogs.

Some things hadn't changed; if stubbornness was an inherited trait, then God help them if they had children (he felt a fierce and unexpected pulse of longing). Yet they had also both matured. The fact that she could make light of his stupidity, and he could feel amused rather than threatened, boded well for their future.

Of course, he hadn't told her everything yet. But his confidence was growing that she might accept him when he eventually did.

"Love can make even a clever man addle-pated," he said mildly.

She sniffed, but he could tell she was as pleased by their banter as he was.

"I ought to talk to Quinton myself," he said. "And Miss Loveday. They might know how Tony became involved with the First Flame. Now that he is gone, they won't have to fear betraying him. In fact, they may want to help us bring his killers to justice."

Lottie nodded, then bit her lip.

He cocked his head. "Is there a problem?"

"It won't be a problem as long as we are a united front." She drew a breath. "How am I going to introduce you to the Quintons? I don't wish to lie to my friends. Moreover, last night you told Devlin that you are my husband. How are we going to manage the situation?"

We'll tell them it's true. You're mine. It doesn't matter if your surname is Courtenay or Granger because you're my Lottie and always will be.

Because he wasn't an idiot, he said, "How do you wish to manage it?"

"I told you I needed time to think on this." She looked perturbed. "I don't wish to be rushed when contemplating something as important as our future."

At least she'd said "our" future. That had to mean something.

"You could introduce me as Jack Granger," he suggested. "Say that I am an old friend."

She arched a brow. "A friend who shows up in my home unannounced in the middle of the night and acts like a buck defending his mate?"

"The bastard had his hands on you. Was about to kiss you." Jack grew incensed again. "What did you expect me to do?"

"Not break into my home, perhaps? Or at the very least stay hidden when you do?"

His withering look conveyed exactly what he thought of those options.

"Old friend, it is." Under her breath, Lottie added, "But no one is going to believe me."

Shortly thereafter, Charlie and Jack—since she was to introduce him by that name, she might as well train herself to think of him that way—arrived at the Quintons' tidy residence in St. John's Wood. She'd sent a note ahead, and Amara and Gilbert were waiting. They stood close together, both dressed in mourning.

After introductions were made and condolences given, the four of them sat down to tea.

"I must begin by thanking you, my dear," Amara said. "Had it not been for your intervention, who knows how long this dangerous charade would have gone on?"

"I said I was sorry, love." Gilbert sat on the settee next to her, shoulders hunched, expression imploring. "I knew how you felt about Tony, but I couldn't leave him in the lurch. He might be a ne'er-do-well, but he's still blood. Or he...he was, rather."

At the snag in his voice, Amara's demeanor softened.

"My feelings about Tony aside, I understand that he's your kin. Your loyalty to those you love is one of your finest traits. I would have supported you if you had confided in me."

"What I did was stupid," Gilbert said hoarsely. "I swear on our daughter's life that I'll never lie to you again."

Amara's lips formed a tight seam. Then, with a sigh, she held out a hand, and her husband grabbed onto her like a drowning man to a raft. Slowly, they leaned toward one another, their foreheads touching, and Charlie felt a surge of gladness.

My friends are going to be all right. Whatever problems they have, they will work through them. Because of the love they share.

She darted a glance at Jack. The embers of hope in his eyes made her heart thump against her ribs. Everything faded, and it was just the two of them, the way they'd been from the very beginning. Drawn together by some inexplicable and transcendent force. It made her believe that they could overcome their past and find happiness, true and lasting, this time around.

"Ahem."

At Amara's delicate clearing of her throat, Charlie forced her attention back to her friend.

"I, um, beg your pardon?" she said, flustered.

"I asked how you and Mr. Granger met." Amara's eyes twinkled. "Since you are, um, old friends."

I knew she would never buy it.

"Abroad," Jack answered. "We were both lost and luckily found each other."

Charlie had to admire his smoothness. The way he offered the truth whilst revealing very little. She was surprised by how readily she was thinking of him by his new name. Perhaps it was because Jack Granger suited him: dashing yet no-nonsense, perfect for a man who lived by his own rules.

"Mr. Granger was in town, and we reconnected." Charlie could be equally suave. "He insisted on escorting me to Hastings for my protection. I hope you will forgive me for allowing it, Amara."

"There is nothing to forgive. Your safety comes first, my dear. Although I am certain you are not telling me the entire story."

Amara gave Charlie a look that said she was going to get every last detail when they were alone.

"We will have tea, Amara, just you and I," Charlie promised. "In the meantime, we need to ask some questions about Tony's murder. We wish to see justice done and stop whoever killed Tony from harming others."

Jack had asked her to be discreet about the First Flame, and she'd agreed. She hadn't wanted to involve the Quintons any more than necessary.

"Tell me one thing first." Gilbert's stare was hard. "Did my brother...did he suffer before he died?"

Charlie knew that the spies under Jack's command had recovered Tony's body and returned it to Gilbert. The bounders who'd shot at her and Jack, however, hadn't been buried in the rock and must have escaped.

"The end was quick," Jack said.

Gilbert jerked his head in acknowledgement. Then he straightened his shoulders and spoke, his deep voice hoarser than usual.

"Tony had a history of getting involved with bad situations. Bad people. Our ma, God rest her soul, used to say he acted first, thought later, and that was the truth of it. But he wasn't a bad man at heart. He was a generous soul who wanted to do the right thing...but he was also easily ensnared by the temptations of life. Gaming was a vice that sunk its claws into him. I cannot tell you the number of times I lent him money, but it was like bailing water out of a leaky boat. That is why Amara made me promise to stay away from him."

"That and the fact that he thought I wasn't good enough for the Quinton name," Amara interjected. "Even though it was my money as well that fended off his moneylenders."

"What difference does it make now, love?" Gilbert's chest fell on a shaky breath. "When Miss Loveday contacted me, saying that she was a friend of Tony's and he was in trouble and had disappeared, I suspected he was at the tables again. I confirmed my suspicions at his favorite gaming hells where he'd lost five hundred pounds in recent months. He'd paid it off, but there was only one way he could manage that. When I visited Tony's usual moneylenders, however, they claimed they didn't hold his vowels."

"Who else would give your brother the money?" Charlie asked.

"I asked around at all the places I knew Tony would go to ask for help, including his cronies—not that they'd have the money. Feckless artistic sorts, the lot of them. But one of the coves knew I was Tony's brother and talked to me. Said that while Tony used to constantly be short of the ready, a few months back he had a windfall and was suddenly flush. Tony claimed he'd quit his job as a sailor and secured a patron for his art. Someone who was going to support him whilst he wrote the great British novel about the revolution of the working class. About how ordinary men were going to rise up and fight for freedom and justice."

Charlie and Jack exchanged a somber glance. Tony's revolutionary bent had likely drawn the attention of the anarchists, and his "patron" was probably a member of the First Flame. If the group had paid off his debts, then he was under their control. Based on what Jack had told her about meeting Tony in France, Tony had been doing their bidding until he realized how dangerous and destructive the group's true agenda was.

He'd wanted to help Jack put an end to the chaos. But the group must have found out about his plan to defect and gone after him. With no other choice, he'd gone underground.

His enemies had found him anyway. Slit his throat and left him to die on a cavern floor.

What kind of freedom and justice is that? Charlie thought with a rush of rage.

"Did Tony's friend have any idea who this patron was?" Jack asked.

"Not a clue. Apparently, Tony had to keep his patron a secret or he would forfeit the money. But my brother lost much more than that."

"And Xenia Loveday, she didn't know who the patron was either?" Charlie asked.

Gilbert snorted. "The chit hardly knew my brother. She thinks she's in love with him, but from what I gleaned from his cronies, he was stringing her along. He had a bad habit of doing that to females."

"Another reason he and I did not get along," Amara muttered.

"Poor girl thinks Tony's a prince. Risked her neck looking for him and doesn't realize he was using her to sell his books," Gilbert said gruffly. "I'm glad she's left Town."

This was news to Charlie. "Where did she go?"

"I'm not sure. Some place to mend a broken heart, she said."

Charlie looked at Jack, wondering if they needed to track down the lovelorn miss. It seemed that she wouldn't have much to add and had suffered enough already.

"We'll leave her be for now," Jack said quietly.

"Do you think that Tony's patron was involved in his death?" Gilbert asked in a strained voice. "That he was killed over money? Or for some other reason?"

"We don't have all the answers." As ever, Jack was the master of evasion. "But we found something in Tony's belongings and believe it may be a clue."

Taking his cue, Charlie removed the vial from her reticule. "When we removed the stopper, the solution within this ampoule spontaneously began to smoke. It also started evaporating. We plugged the bottle immediately, but this is all that is left. Do you think you could identify the substance, Amara?"

Her friend took the vial, examining it in the light.

"Not with great confidence." Amara shook her head. "While I have experimented with some chemical compounds, they are not my forte, and there is so little of the liquid left. If I attempt to analyze it, I might lose what remains of your clue. You need a more qualified expert for this, I'm afraid."

"Thank you, dearest." Charlie returned the vial to her reticule. "We shall find one."

Amara tilted her head. "Are the Angels helping to find Tony's murderer?"

"Not yet." Coming to a decision, Charlie looked at Jack. "But I think it is time to bring them in."

He gave a reluctant nod. She could guess that his superior wasn't going to like more outsiders getting involved. Yet with the Great Exhibition opening in a week and anarchists to track down, the mission required all hands on deck.

"We will be happy to supply any equipment you may need," Amara added.

"When you discover who killed my brother," Gilbert said gruffly, "will you bring that bastard to justice?"

"You have my word, sir," Jack said.

As the men rose and shook hands, Amara ushered Charlie aside.

"Is Mr. Granger who I think he is?" Amara asked in hushed tones.

Charlie blinked. "Um, what do you mean?"

"In all the time I've known you, there has only been one man you've talked about who could capture your attention and heart the way your *old friend* Mr. Granger does." Amara widened her eyes. "Your former husband is even more handsome than I pictured."

By now, Charlie oughtn't to be surprised by her friend's astuteness.

She blew out a breath. "He and I have a lot to iron out, obviously."

"Obviously."

"He left me. For twelve years."

"The scoundrel," Amara agreed, as any bosom friend would.

"I couldn't possibly give him another chance," she muttered.

"I said the same thing not long ago, but extenuating circumstances do exist. As I now know from personal experience, even a loyal husband can make a stupid decision."

"He left to protect me," Charlie blurted. "And he is...well, he's a complicated man."

"To be your match, he would have to be."

"Would it be weak of me to forgive him?" She chewed on her lip. "After all that he's done?"

"Do not mistake pride for strength, dearest. Forgiveness requires as much, and perhaps even more, fortitude. While only you can judge whether you wish to forgive, I will say that when there is love—love that is devoted and passionate and true"— Amara gave a graceful shrug—"nothing else matters."

Charlie swallowed. "I wish it were that easy. But thank you for the advice."

Amara kissed her cheek. "Tea, my dear. *Very* soon."

Charlie and Jack decided to return to her residence to plan their next steps over luncheon. During the carriage ride back, he admired the pen Amara and Gilbert had given him. It was a fine piece, to be sure, fashioned of filigreed brass. What made the Quintons' design special, however, were the lock picks secreted inside the barrel.

"Devilishly clever," Jack muttered over and over again.

Amused, Charlie watched her lover play with his new toy all the way home.

Upon arrival, to avoid being seen, they entered through the back gate and crossed the courtyard toward the main house.

She gestured at the carriage house as they passed it. "When we have time, I will show you the training quarters I designed for the Angels."

"I saw them."

"When did you...oh." She narrowed her eyes at him. "You had time for a tour during your break-in last night?"

"I like to get a lay of the land." He smirked. "A cartographer's prerogative."

She snorted as she led the way through a side door that took them into the main house. She nodded at passing servants, who curtsied and bowed and didn't blink an eye as she brought a strange man through.

"Your staff is exceptional," he murmured as they ventured down a corridor to the front of the house.

"I choose those whom I allow in my personal sphere with care. I met most of my staff through the work of my society, and some of them have been instrumental to the Angels. My previous butler and housekeeper taught me and the ladies combat and other useful skills. I wish you could have met them," she said with a touch of wistfulness. "You would have liked Mrs. Peabody. And you and Hawker would have got on like a house on fire."

Jack cocked his head. "Why did they leave?"

"They fell in love." Charlie smiled. "Hawker, as it turns out, inherited the duchy of Ryedale. Now he and his duchess are managing their estate in Yorkshire."

As they reached the antechamber, Jack said with wry humor, "Only you would have a duke for a butler—"

He was cut off by familiar voices and footsteps approaching the front door. A key turned in the lock, and the door opened before Charlie could warn him. In the next instant, Glory, Livy, Fiona, and Pippa stormed in like avenging angels.

Twenty-Six

"Charlie, your *eye*," Fiona gasped.

"What happened?" Olivia asked.

"Mr. Devlin was right," Glory said in ominous tones.

"Who is he?" Pippa whispered, pointing at Jack.

"Ladies." Charlie tried to rein in the situation. "To what do I owe this unannounced visit?"

"We never announce ourselves. We just show up." Brow furrowing, Livy held up the key that Charlie had given all the Angels. "Your policy has always been that your home is ours, and we are to come and go as we please."

"Perhaps we ought to rethink that policy," Pippa said under her breath. "It appears Charlie has company—"

"We were worried," Glory burst out.

Ferdinand the Ferret II was curled around her shoulders, and when she spoke, he lifted his furry white head, his whiskers twitching.

"Mr. Devlin told us you were hurt and some strange fellow"— Glory narrowed her hazel eyes suspiciously at Jack—"showed up last night, claiming he was your acquaintance."

At least Devlin had omitted the part about Jack claiming to be her husband.

"That is why we came," Fi piped up. "You have been acting strange, Charlie. All your unexplained absences and furtive behavior—don't think we haven't noticed. We had to see for ourselves that you are all right." Twin furrows appeared between her curving auburn brows. "So, um, are you?"

Charlie couldn't bring herself to be annoyed at the ladies. Or at Devlin for enlisting them. She saw the worry on the Angels' faces and knew her friends were only acting out of care. In truth, if she suspected any of them was in trouble, she would react similarly.

She cast a glance at Jack, who shrugged as if to say, *I'll follow your lead.*

"I am perfectly well," she began. "In fact, I was about to contact all of you..."

She trailed off because Glory had prowled up to Jack. With her reddish-brown curls bristling, Glory looked like the protective tigress she was. FF II hissed from her shoulders as she braced her hands on her hips.

"Well, sir?" she demanded. "Are you responsible for our friend's injury?"

To Jack's credit, he did not seem taken aback by Glory's enmity.

"No, ma'am," he said politely.

Livy joined Glory, eyeing him with equal suspicion.

"What hold do you have over Charlie?" she said bluntly. "Are you blackmailing her?"

"Or are you abusing her in some other fashion?" Fi took her place on Glory's other side, Pippa trailing behind her.

"You should know, sir," Fi said, chin lifted, "that we are women of the world. We've met scoundrels who manipulate women for their own nefarious ends and can spot them from a mile away. We will not let our friend fall prey to some unscrupulous fiend."

"Christ," Jack muttered.

"My dears." Charlie cut in. "I appreciate your concern, but it is unnecessary. May I introduce Jack Granger, an old friend?"

Taking the cue, he issued an elegant leg.

"Ladies," he murmured. "Lady Fayne has sung your praises, and I am pleased to make your acquaintances at last."

The Angels looked unmoved by his charm.

"Mr. Granger did not hurt me," Charlie insisted. "In fact, he has protected me from danger time and again. If it weren't for him, my injuries would be a great deal worse."

"If Mr. Granger did not hurt you," Glory said, drawing her brows together, "then who did?"

"I will explain everything over tea," she said.

They gathered around the coffee table, and once the cups were distributed, she filled her friends in on the details of the case. To stop the anarchists, she needed their help, and time was running out. Jack made no effort to stop her, and she took this as his tacit agreement with her strategy. She decided to hold back her past with Jack. She wanted to come to a decision about their future before subjecting their relationship to external scrutiny. She also skimmed over the details of Jack's profession and the group he worked for, saying only that he had been hired to investigate the anarchists and had come to her for help.

The Angels took everything in stride, listening avidly as Charlie explained that she was working with Jack to discover and put an end to whatever plot the First Flame Society was hatching.

"We will help," Glory volunteered.

She turned to Jack, who occupied the adjacent wingchair. "On behalf of the Angels, sir, I must apologize for the earlier misunderstanding. Based on what Mr. Devlin told us, we assumed the worst."

"No apology necessary, Mrs. Chen," Jack said sincerely. "Indeed, I am relieved to know that Lady Fayne has such loyal friends."

Glory beamed. On her lap, FF II gave a *tuk-tuk* of approval.

"It seems to me that the mysterious liquid is the key, and we should begin the investigation there." Livy's green eyes were focused on the vial on the coffee table. "And I know someone who can identify it."

"Who, Your Grace?" Jack asked.

"Harry Kent."

Charlie suddenly recalled Livy's family connection.

Jack's eyebrows rose. "Sir Harry Kent, the president of the Royal Society? The fellow is a genius. Rumor has it that he set a record with the number of patents he holds."

"Aunt Tessa—she's Uncle Harry's wife—had an entire wing added to their home to accommodate his inventions. She says she was tired of tripping over them." Livy's grin was impish. "And of their children playing with explosive devices."

"Your uncle can be trusted to be discreet?" Charlie asked.

"He is a Kent. Discretion is the family motto. I'll bring the bottle to him and explain the situation. If I know Uncle Harry, he will have an answer for us within a few days," Livy said confidently.

Charlie looked at Jack, who nodded.

"On to the matchbox then," she said. "Mr. Granger and I are going to pay a visit to the manufactory to see if we can get information about where this particular box might have been sold."

"May I see the matchbox?" Pippa requested.

Receiving the box, Pippa gave it a thorough once-over. Removing a small notebook and pencil from her reticule, she swiftly copied the design. Her reproduction of the lettering, large tree in the background, and decorative border of acorns and leaves was stunningly precise.

Even Jack looked impressed.

"Pippa is an artist," Charlie told him.

"I will make copies and distribute them to the mudlarks," Pippa said.

Jack furrowed his brow, no doubt wondering how the pretty blonde would be familiar with street urchins. "You have contact with mudlarks, ma'am?"

"She lives with hundreds of them," Fiona said airily.

"My husband, Mr. Cullen, has looked after the larks for many years," Pippa explained. "We run a school of sorts now, teaching the children various trades. But the larks still like to roam the streets and have eyes and ears everywhere. If that matchbox is still being sold, they will find out where. I will also ask my husband if he has heard anything about this First Flame Society."

Jack looked at Charlie. "You have a remarkable team, Lady Fayne."

"I know it," she murmured.

"Speaking of teams, sir." Fi's manner was guileless. "I'm afraid I can't recall who hired you to investigate the anarchists?"

"That is because I did not mention it," Jack said dryly.

"For any particular reason?"

Given that Fiona's earl was an agent for the Crown, she'd probably guessed Jack's line of work. Hawksmoor had said he didn't know Fayne, but Charlie wondered if the reverse was also true. Did Jack know that Hawksmoor ran in espionage circles? It seemed the foreign and domestic branches had little knowledge of one another, which put her—and Fiona—in an awkward position. She knew Fiona would never compromise Hawksmoor's cover without his permission, just as Charlie would never do so to Jack.

Jack seemed to come to a decision. "I am employed in the interests of national security. Particularly from threats from abroad. That is all I am at liberty to say."

"I understand." Fi paused. "Given the potential threat posed by the anarchists, do you think local authorities ought to be put on alert?"

"They have been informed of the heightened risk," Jack replied. "Unfortunately, we don't have substantiated information concerning the threat. Just a murdered bloke, a bottle of unidentified liquid that begins to smoke when exposed to air, and a box of matches."

"Nonetheless, proper precautions must be taken." Glory chewed on her lip. "According to the papers, the opening of the Great Exhibition is expected to draw a crowd of over twenty thousand. Her Majesty the Queen, Prince Albert, and their children will be there, along with dignitaries from around the world. If one were intent on creating mass devastation, on proving that progress is an illusion, it would be the most obvious—and symbolic—place to target."

"I agree," Jack said gravely.

"If the anarchists' aim is to attack the exhibition, we must have a counterplan," Livy declared.

The Angels nodded as one.

"I could surveil the site," Glory said. "And get a copy of the exhibition map. That way, we will be better able to anticipate and prepare for any eventuality."

"A splendid idea," Fiona said. "I will help you, Glory."

"We have a strategy then," Charlie said. "Livy takes care of the liquid, Mr. Granger and I visit Brompton's manufactory, Pippa enlists the larks, and Glory and Fi take on the exhibition. Do you have anything else to add, Mr. Granger?"

Jack shook his head, his mouth curving. "I think you ladies have everything well in hand."

TWENTY-SEVEN

En route to Brompton's, Jack had to make a stop at his boarding house for a fresh change of clothes. Although he told Lottie to wait in the carriage, she would have none of it and followed him into the ramshackle building.

Mrs. Clooney, of course, pounced on them like a cat. She regarded him with the avaricious gleam that he'd always found discomfiting. Then she noticed Lottie, and her eyes turned squinty.

"I run a respectable place, Mr. Wilkins," she said. "No visitors allowed in the rooms. Those are the rules."

Her dyed black curls quivered with outrage, her stubby fingers gripping her wide hips. Her righteousness was rich since she'd intimated more than once that she would enjoy his company in her own room. He'd politely declined each time, but that didn't stop her from making advances, including showing up at his door one night in a flimsy robe, a sight he wished he could unsee.

"We'll be but a moment, Mrs. Clooney—" he began.

"No exceptions, sir." She glared at Lottie. "And fancy pieces ain't welcome in my establishment."

"I am not a fancy piece." Lottie's eyes flashed like a blade. "I am his wife."

"His wife?" Mrs. Clooney looked momentarily nonplussed. "But Mr. Wilkins ne'er mentioned no missus—"

"He also probably neglected to mention the fact that he is giving his notice. Effective immediately." Lottie continued walking toward the stairs as if she owned the place. "Come along, *Mr. Wilkins.* We must pack your things."

"Well, I ne'er," Mrs. Clooney huffed.

Suppressing a grin, Jack followed his spouse up the steps. Even the inconvenience of having to find new accommodations didn't dampen his sudden joy. Bleeding hell, he loved it when Lottie acted like he belonged to her.

"Do you even know where you're going?" he murmured.

Lottie shot him a fulminating glance. "How long has that woman been trying to get in your bed?"

Her acuity never failed to astound him. As he wasn't an idiot, however, he was not about to court trouble.

"I am not interested—"

"I know that," she said in clipped tones. "But she has tried?"

He gave a hesitant nod, uncertain where this was headed. Luckily, he was saved from saying more because they arrived at his room. He focused on getting his keys out and opening the door. Lottie entered first, and her brows elevated. Seeing the space through her eyes—the cracked ceiling, peeling wallpaper, and sagging furnishings—he cringed at the squalor of his living situation.

"Is Mrs. Clooney's cooking exceptional?" Lottie asked.

"Er, not really." With his foot, he nudged an old newspaper under his bed. "Unless you mean exceptionally bland. Why do you ask?"

"Because I am struggling to understand why you would choose to live here."

Because I've lived in worse places. Because since I left you, I haven't cared where I live. Because the only home I've ever had is with you.

He shrugged, opening his wardrobe and rifling through the choices. "It is the sort of place where George Wilkins, traveling actor, would live. It's cheap, conveniently located, and nondescript. It also explains my late hours, absences, and disguises."

Lottie arched a brow. "How many identities do you have?"

"Not enough time for that, love, if we're to get to Brompton's before closing." He selected a pinstriped waistcoat and pair of dark trousers. "Does that say innkeeper to you?"

"I don't see why you get to make the inquiries at Brompton's."

He loved the way she pouted.

"Because you lost the coin toss. It should be a simple in and out." He paused, his hands on the buttons of his collar. "Would you like to wait in the carriage whilst I change?"

"It is nothing I haven't seen before." Lottie rolled her eyes. "And a great deal of, I might add."

"Since you put it that way."

Mouth twitching, he disrobed and gave her a bit of a show. He couldn't help it, egged on by Lottie's reaction. Despite her bold words, she was blushing, looking whilst trying not to look, and the result was altogether adorable. Thus, when he managed to get his trousers off, his cock toppled out like felled timber.

"Heavens." Lottie's voice was delightfully strangled. "Are you always this way?"

"When you are near, yes."

Naked, he stalked toward her, and she retreated a few steps, her back hitting the wall next to the wardrobe. He placed a palm on the other side, caging her. He shuddered at the brush of taffeta against his erection.

"It arouses me when you get possessive," he murmured.

"I am not possessive—"

"Aren't you, *Mrs. Wilkins*?" He nipped her ear, feeling her shiver in his balls. "You staked your claim in front of Mrs. Clooney. Just like I did in front of Devlin."

He looked into her dilated eyes, daring her to deny it. To deny the pulsing and proprietary bond between them.

"That was stupid of me." Lottie blew out a breath. "I suppose...I suppose I don't like the idea of another woman looking at you that way. For heaven's sake, Jack, she was like a butcher's dog salivating at a prime cut."

He would have laughed at her analogy if it didn't trigger a memory.

"You are a piece of meat, Jack, and I shall have my fill of you." Judith's green eyes had glowed with lust and maliciousness. *"If you do not please me, I will tell Sebastian that you forced yourself on me. That you have been doing it for years. That you made me take your big cock, threatened to hurt me if I didn't. Who do you think Sebastian will believe...me or you?"*

"Jack? What is the matter?"

Lottie's voice wrestled him from the tarpit of shame.

"Nothing. I...I had better get dressed."

He began to pull back, but Lottie wrapped her fingers around his wrist.

"You froze just now. It was as if...as if you were not here." Her clear grey eyes seemed to peer into his soul. "Was it something I said?"

"No, I was just thinking of the time." He forced a smile. "Now that you've gotten me ejected from the premises, I need to pack and arrange for my belongings to be moved to another lodging house before we head to Brompton's."

"You needn't."

He frowned. "After that exchange with Mrs. Clooney, I don't think I can stay here—"

"I meant you don't need to find new lodgings. I was thinking that...that you could stay with me. If you wish to."

Lottie's bottom lip was caught beneath her teeth, and she looked suddenly shy and so sweet that he could scarcely breathe.

"Do you mean it?" he said hoarsely. "What about your reputation? I will not jeopardize—"

"We will have to be careful," she said. "My staff, as you know, is discreet. And you are a spymaster, after all. You've already demonstrated your ability to enter my home without anyone noticing. You will have to continue to be stealthy until we come to a permanent decision about our future. Does the plan suit you?"

"*You* suit me," he said.

He kissed her with all the hope pounding in his heart.

By the time Charlie and Jack arrived at Brompton's, it was near closing time. The manufactory consisted of redbrick buildings surrounded by a wrought-iron gate. A pair of guards flanked the entrance, watching as workers, male and female, filed out.

Jack opened the window when one of the guards stopped the carriage.

"State your business," the burly fellow demanded.

"I am here to purchase matches, good sir." Jack's accent was expansive and suited to his role as a country innkeeper. "In bulk for my business."

To Charlie's surprise, the guard peered into the interior of the carriage with undue suspicion. Out of an abundance of caution, she'd donned a bonnet with a translucent veil, and now she was glad for this layer of protection. To her mind, the visit to Brompton's was rather like searching for a proverbial needle in the haystack. She'd hoped that if they managed to narrow the location where the matches were sold, they might pick up the trail of Tony's killers.

She had not expected that the trail might, in fact, lead to this manufactory. Yet the guard's manner caused a prickling sensation on her nape that she'd learned never to ignore.

"The missus," Jack said jovially to the guard. "She's not much of a traveler. Why, she was ill twice already on our journey from Cheshire, and the London smoke don't help her lungs—"

"Go on through to the office." Clearly wanting to be spared from the loquacious country bumpkin, the guard pointed to an adjacent brick building. "Be quick about it. We close in half an hour."

As the carriage headed through the gates, Jack said under his breath, "All is not what it seems at Brompton's. Wish I'd done myself up a bit more, but I didn't think I would need a full disguise."

"You are playing the role of the innkeeper wonderfully," she assured him. "You'll be careful?"

"Always am, love."

Winking at her, Jack disembarked. Through a slit in the curtains, Charlie watched him inhabit the role of the innkeeper with perfection. His wide, heavy-footed gait and hearty manner went hand in hand with his countrified garb. She admired her lover's ability to slip into the skin of any persona...but it also gave her pause.

She recalled the way he'd grown still back at his rooms. As if he'd been sucked into a thought, a memory that he couldn't extricate himself from. Even as he was sharing more of himself, there were parts he kept hidden. His chameleon charm hid a darker side, and she was determined to know that part of him as well. To know all of him, good and bad and everything in between. Because he belonged to her as surely as she belonged to him.

It hit her then.

She wasn't falling in love with her former husband again.

I am falling in love with him, the real him, for the first time.

The realization percolated through her, leaving exhilaration in its wake.

At the same time, she couldn't shake the nagging feeling that something was not right at the manufactory. Scanning the site through the curtains, she counted a half-dozen rough-and-ready sorts armed to the teeth. Why would a match factory require so many guards?

Raised voices drew her attention. A man and woman were exiting the largest building. The latter was a plump, middle-aged brunette who wore the grey dress, pinafore, and white cap that was the uniform of the female workers. Her skirts whipped around her legs as she tried to keep up with the man's longer stride.

"I'm needing a few minutes o' your time, Mr. Karlsson," she said, panting.

"Not today, Mrs. Sutter." The man was tall, with sparse, fair hair and an air of pomposity. "I have important business to attend to."

"This *is* important business, sir. It's about the unfair fines the foreman is giving us workers. I've been trying to talk to you 'bout it for weeks—"

"Put your concerns in a letter. I'll read it when I have time."

"If I was any good wif pen and paper, do you think I'd be packing matches?" the brunette burst out, clearly at her wit's end.

Karlsson stopped a few feet from Charlie's carriage, and she could see the meanness of his eyes.

"Is this honest work below you, Mrs. Sutter?" he said sharply.

The woman's eyes widened beneath the smudged frill of her cap. "N-no, sir—"

"There are plenty of workers who would be grateful for your job. In fact, they line up outside my office every morning."

"Please, sir. I be needing this job." Mrs. Sutter's chin wobbled. "Me husband broke 'is leg and 'asn't been working, and we've six young mouths to feed—"

"Then I suggest you focus on improving your performance." Sadistic satisfaction curled Karlsson's lips. "Now, out of consideration for your circumstances, I shall only fine you a half-shilling for your insubordination today."

"Insubordination?" Mrs. Sutter said in a quivering voice.

"If you have concerns about the fines levied by the foreman, you should go to him. Not to his superior. I manage this manufactory, which is about to take a great step forward in match production. If I were to attend to the trifling concerns of every worker, how would I perform my duties? You have delayed me, and in doing so, delayed the progress of this business. Half a shilling is a small price to pay for your misconduct. Do you disagree?"

Mrs. Sutter's hands gripped the edges of her pinafore.

"No, sir." Her voice hitched.

"Good. The fine will be deducted from your week's wages."

With that, the factotum left her and strode into the office. Mrs. Sutter wiped her eyes with the edge of her pinafore and, shoulders slumped, walked out the gate.

A few minutes later, Jack returned and muttered something to the driver that Charlie couldn't hear. The vehicle started to move as soon as he boarded and swiftly left Brompton's behind. Lines bracketed Jack's mouth, his expression foreboding.

"What happened?" she asked. "Did you find out anything about the matchbox?"

"To the contrary." He shook his head. "I think I may have alerted the enemies that we are on their trail."

"You think Brompton's is involved with the First Flame?" she said alertly.

"I don't know. But I spoke to the factotum, a man by the name of—"

"Karlsson," she interrupted. "Horrid fellow. I saw him berating a worker before he went into the office."

"He's a cold bastard but also bloody shrewd. At first, I wasn't certain he was buying my story that I was a country innkeeper visiting London who wanted a supply of Brompton's matches to take back for my business. Then, when I showed him the matchbox we found and said I wanted more of the same design, I knew he knew I was lying."

"How?"

"He demanded to know where I'd obtained the matchbox. Said that the design was a special edition for the Great Exhibition and had not yet been released to the public. He was enraged, said that a worker likely had sticky fingers and I was in possession of stolen goods."

"Heavens," she breathed.

"Exactly," Jack said grimly. "I played the gullible bumpkin and said I bought it from a matchgirl on a street corner, the name of which I conveniently couldn't recall due to my unfamiliarity with London. I did not linger to see if Karlsson believed me."

"If the matchboxes have not yet been sold, how did Tony's killers get one? Do you think they work at the manufactory?"

"It is a possibility. Or perhaps a worker did filch and sell some boxes, and the killers happened to buy one." The creases deepened around Jack's mouth. "Something isn't right about the place, though. Did you notice all the guards?"

She nodded. "Ten, at least. Whilst factories often hire protection, that number seems excessive."

"What is Brompton's trying to prevent?" Jack frowned. "The leaking of stolen goods...or of information about the shady activities taking place within?"

"We have to find out," she said.

"Breaking in won't be easy," he said somberly. "The site is gated, and there is no way to approach without drawing notice. With guards everywhere—"

"We're not breaking in." She sat back as the plan took shape in her head. "Tomorrow morning, I will simply walk in."

TWENTY-EIGHT

That evening, it was the first time Jack had enjoyed dining at home with his wife in twelve years, and if asked to imagine it, he would have pictured flowers, candles, and champagne. All of which were present, along with delicious food a stratosphere above his lodging house fare. Yet he didn't notice any of it because he and Lottie had been locking horns since their departure from Brompton's. That had continued until they arrived at her house, and they'd taken a break to change for supper before resuming their battle in the dining room.

Although he couldn't prove that she'd done it to annoy him, she'd placed them at opposite ends of a very long table. He had to peer around an elaborate flower arrangement like a damned Peeping Tom around a hedge just to get a glimpse of her. She looked like Athena at a celebratory banquet after a battle. Her hair was fashioned in a coronet, her bare shoulders exposed by a silver-grey gown that was as cool as her manner. She took a delicate bite of fish as if she hadn't a care in the world.

He grabbed the nearest domed dish, finding delicate beef roulettes blanketed in madeira sauce. At least she'd had the foresight to have supper served *à la française*. As the courses were laid out on the table, she'd dismissed the servants, and they were serving themselves. Unfortunately, they were using the intimate setting to make war, not love.

Just like the old days. He couldn't say he missed this part of their relationship. But he wasn't about to back down when his wife was being irrational and pigheaded.

"It is a terrible idea, and you know it." He sliced savagely into a roulette that was so tender he probably could have cut it with his fork. "If you get discovered, there's no telling what might happen. Members of the First Flame might be working at Brompton's, and if so, I may have inadvertently tipped them off this afternoon. They will be on high alert and—"

"Do I seem incompetent to you?"

Lottie's lofty tone grated on his nerves. Especially since it had to float down the length of the table to reach him.

"Of course not. That is not what I am saying—"

"Did I question your decision to waltz in there as an innkeeper?"

"That was different," he gritted out. "We didn't think the place might be a nest of vipers then."

"I would have supported your decision regardless."

"I am a spymaster. It is my job—"

"And what, pray tell, do you think I have been doing these twelve years past? Hosting tea parties? Parading around in the latest fashions? Twiddling my thumbs, perhaps?"

Her sarcasm chafed at him. When they fought back in the day, her condescension had been tinder to his temper. The haughtier she became, the angrier he got until they had to fight or fuck— most often both—it out of their systems. Whilst he was not averse to plowing his wife, he wasn't about to let her treat him like he was some uncouth idiot.

Stay in control. Don't make things worse by losing your temper.

"I know you run a successful investigative society." He was proud of how reasonable he sounded. "Whilst you have undoubtedly aided many an individual lady, what we are dealing with is a matter of national security. The First Flame regularly slaughters innocents as part of its agenda."

"My Angels and I have dealt with evil in all forms," she said flatly. "We have stopped groups as well as individuals from wreaking havoc on society."

He set down his fork, his appetite lost at the thought of how the First Flame had threatened her in the past. He'd left to protect her, sacrificed twelve years of their marriage. Why couldn't a woman as intelligent as Lottie understand the severity of the risk she was courting and, more importantly, why he couldn't allow her to take it?

"Not like the First Flame." It took effort, but he maintained his calm demeanor. "My team of trained agents has been after them for a decade and a half. Whilst we have won some skirmishes, they've stayed one step ahead of us. Now that there is a chance to put an end to the terror, it is only logical that we—my team and I, that is—should take it. We have years of experience behind us."

When Lottie said nothing, merely sampling another dish, he took it as a sign to push his advantage.

"I will contact Delaney," he said. "She can pose as a worker and infiltrate—"

"Over my dead body will that woman steal *my* plan."

Too late, he realized his mistake. And if he hadn't, the way Lottie shot up from her seat and flung her napkin on the table, with enough force to make a magnificent ring of meringue tremble upon its bed of custard, would have enlightened him. He rose automatically and was treated to the sight of his wife looking like a vengeful goddess. If looks could kill, he'd be seeking passage across the River Styx.

He tried to soothe her. "Delaney is an experienced agent. She has taken countless covert assignments. You have to admit that she is talented: back in Greece, her disguise as Eleni Pappas fooled everyone—even you."

"Yes, she did a singular job convincing the world that she was your lover," Lottie said acidly.

"Well, she wasn't. And that is beside the point," he said in frustration.

"What about after you left me? The pair of you looked quite cozy in the cave."

"Now you're grasping at straws." He clenched his hands, feeling the reins of his self-control slipping. "You know there hasn't been anyone for me but you. Which, by the by, is more than I can say."

"I beg your pardon?"

She crossed her arms, looking at him as if he were a piece of dung that got stuck to her shoe. Her superiority snapped his tether.

"You heard me," he shot back. "I have been faithful to you, but you will not even tell me how many lovers you've entertained in your bed."

"That is none of your dashed business!"

"I am your husband," he roared. "Who you fuck is entirely my business."

She marched over, but he was quicker, and they faced one another, toe-to-toe, near her end of the table. She swiped her tongue over her lips in an angry motion, and he flashed back to the cave. To the way she'd sucked his cock until he lost control, then swallowed his seed. Remembered pleasure and jealousy tightened his scalp, his muscles bunching. Who had taught her that depraved skill? How many men had she taken in that manner?

"*You* left *me*. Made me grieve over your supposed death," she said in scathing tones. "You have not been my husband for twelve years. If I wanted to console myself with five men or fifty, it would be *my* prerogative."

"Five to fifty?" He felt as if he'd been punched in the gut. "That is the range?"

Her chin took a mutinous angle. "I am a widow. I can tup who

I want, when I want, and wherever I dashed well please. In fact, if you hadn't acted like a troglodyte at the Kendall Ball, who knows?" Her smile was sharper than a blade, and that was before she plunged it into his chest. "I might have added an orangery to my list."

Scarlet filtered his vision. In the next instant, he trapped her against the table, wrapping a hand around her nape and forcing her to meet his eyes.

"No other man is touching you again. Ever," he growled.

"You do not get to make that decision."

"The decision is made," he stated. "I don't give a damn if you think I am not good enough for you. If the world agrees that you deserve better. I love you, you infuriating woman, and you are mine. I am *never* letting you go."

Her gaze locked with his. He felt the passionate rise and fall of her breasts against his own heaving chest. Her sensual linen-and-Lottie scent pervaded his nostrils.

He'd never been this hard, this angry.

When she opened her mouth, he grimly prepared to be pushed over the edge.

"I don't think you are not good enough for me." She tilted her head. "Why would you think that?"

Just like that, she cornered him. He tried to think of some excuse but couldn't. Since their reunion, he'd striven to cut through the thicket of lies he'd planted between them, to finally have a clear and honest path to his love. He couldn't bring himself to seed more lies. Not with her.

"I've never felt worthy of you," he said hoarsely.

"But why?"

Fear made him hedge. "I...I am not a true gentleman."

"You've said that before." She sounded impatient. "And I've told you that whatever you've done as a spymaster, whatever secrets you're harboring, you can confide in me. I am not fragile; I will not break. Our relationship, however, is hanging on by a thread, and if you do not show me who you are—who you *truly* are—then it has no chance of surviving."

Christ. *Christ.*

Fear morphed into panic.

His lips formed the words. "I am not Sebastian Courtenay, Marquess of Fayne."

"Yes, I know. You are now Jack Granger—"

"No."

He inhaled, looking into her peerless eyes. Eyes that had the power to judge him and condemn him to perdition. He'd taken on a gang of armed enemies and felt less nervous.

Clenching his hands, he forced out the truth.

"What I mean is that I...I was never Fayne."

TWENTY-NINE

I t took Charlie a few moments to register what her lover was saying.

"Then who are you?" she asked faintly.

"Jack Granger." His eyes were as dark and fathomless as a coal pit. "That was the name I was born with. Everything I have told you about him is true."

"I...I don't understand." She wasn't slow-witted, but this...this was too much to comprehend. "Are you saying that you've been lying to me from the moment we met?"

He gave a curt nod.

"You bloody *bastard*."

Hurt exploded inside her. She tried to get away, but he wouldn't let her. He took her blows to his chest, circling her with his arms, saying roughly, "I am a bastard, it's true. I deserve your hate. But you also deserve to know the truth, and I'll give it to you, if you'll listen."

She struggled to catch her breath and adjust to the topsy-turvy state of her world. Despite everything, she did want to know his secrets. The secrets she'd known he was hiding.

"Let me go," she said in clipped accents. "I am listening."

He released her, taking a step back. "Thank you. I know I don't deserve—"

"You have five minutes of my time. Pray do not waste it."

"Right."

He rubbed the back of his neck, and she hated how his boyish gesture pierced her anger. Her confident, powerful lover looked rather...unnerved. As if he were a schoolboy being summoned to the headmaster's office and expecting the worst.

"I haven't lied to you since my return." He cleared his throat. "I know that doesn't signify much, but I wanted a fresh start with you, Lottie. Obviously, I've had a lot of time to think about all that went wrong the first time, and even though I left to protect you, I think I also left because...because I knew in my heart you deserved better than me."

She refused to let his earnestness affect her.

"How was it possible for you to assume another man's identity?" she asked bluntly. "That of a peer, no less?"

"I was Sebastian Courtenay's servant. I knew him well, probably better than anyone did."

Her shock warred with another feeling when Jack dropped his gaze. He shoved his hands into his pockets, staring at the carpet as he spoke.

"I was only older than Sebastian by two years, and even though I was in his family's employ, we were friends. Strange as that may sound, it's true."

His voice was gruff, as if he thought she wouldn't believe that a lord would be friends with the likes of him.

"Sebastian was an only child, and when he was a babe, he had an illness that made him frail. He couldn't do the things normal boys did, was bullied mercilessly when he tried, and spent most of his days in his chamber by himself. When I came to work as a hall boy at the Fayne estate, he was nearly a hermit. He was desperate for company, and we hit it off. His mother, the dowager marchioness, allowed us to spend time together...probably because Sebastian was happier."

Something surfaced in Jack's gaze—pain, Charlie guessed.

"By that time, Sebastian's constitution was stronger, but he lacked confidence. I got him outside, taught him to play sports. I looked after him and protected him from the local bullies. In turn, he shared his books and lessons with me, showed me a world I didn't know existed. One beyond the drudgery I'd known as an orphan and a servant."

"You were an orphan?" Charlie said numbly.

"My ma died when I was four. My memories of her are fleeting and few, but I remember her as pretty and kind. Loving. She didn't tell me who my pa was." When he spoke again, his voice was pitched low. "She was a prostitute and died of the pox."

"I'm sorry."

"I don't want your pity, Lottie."

"I am too angry to pity you," she said tartly. "I just wish you didn't have to go through what you did. Because no child should be deprived of his or her parents, and I know this from personal experience."

"Of course you do."

His expression softened, but she wasn't ready to mend fences. His deception went deeper than she realized, and until she had the facts and could judge for herself whether she could accept his explanations, she couldn't allow herself to weaken.

"You still haven't explained how you became Sebastian Courtenay," she pointed out.

"Right." He raked a hand through his hair. "As Sebastian came into adulthood, his health continued to improve. He was an idealist who craved the kind of adventure he'd read about in books; more than anything, he wanted to be a hero. He got it into his head that he wanted to buy a commission in the army. But his mama...she still clung to her image of him as a child. She coddled him, wanted to keep him tied to her apron strings, and used guilt and whatever means necessary to keep him by her side." Jack's jaw hardened. "He grew resentful. Eventually, he rebelled and ran off. I was sent after him, and when I traced his steps in London, I discovered that he hadn't joined the army. He'd somehow got himself mixed up in espionage."

She stared at him. "Was Sebastian ready for such an endeavor?"

"No."

The single word sent a chill down her spine.

"But using his family name and fortune, he had bluffed his way in. He traveled to Venice on what was supposed to be a simple mission. Using his name to gain entrée, Sebastian was to attend a house party and deliver a message to an agent about suspected local members of the First Flame. By this time, I had located the spymaster, explained everything, and he agreed to let me extract Sebastian from the mission. I arrived at Sebastian's *pensione* hours before the party...but someone else had gotten there first."

Jack's gaze was blank, turned inward, and Charlie knew whatever he was seeing haunted him even now. She reached for his hand. Feeling how cold he was, she squeezed his fingers, sharing her warmth with him before letting go.

"What happened to Sebastian?" she asked.

It wasn't hard for her to guess, but Jack needed to purge the poison.

"He'd been stabbed. There were no signs of struggle," Jack said tonelessly. "Just Sebastian lying on the floor next to his bed in a pool of his own blood. He barely had any strength left. And he used what remained to shove a crumpled note into my hands. *Finish the job,* he said. *Be Fayne. Show them I'm a hero.*"

"You became Sebastian to finish his mission," Charlie said over the lump in her throat.

The story made sense and fit everything she knew of the man in front of her. A fiercely loyal protector who would sacrifice himself for those he loved.

"That was how it began." Jack's voice was as gritty as sandpaper. "I went to the house party and delivered the note stained with Sebastian's blood. Afterward, the spymaster convinced me that I was needed on his team. That it was my patriotic duty to fight the First Flame—the group that had murdered my friend. Given that the Marquess of Fayne had doors open to him that Jack Granger did not, my superior decided that I should become Sebastian permanently. As Sebastian was the last of his line, the title would die with him anyway. The plan was for me to borrow it instead."

"What about Sebastian's mama?" Charlie lifted her brows. "Did she agree to the plan?"

"That was a sticking point." Jack's features looked hewn from granite. "The dowager blamed me for her son's death, and she wasn't wrong. I should have gotten to Sebastian sooner—"

"The First Flame killed Sebastian, not you." She couldn't allow him to shoulder a burden that was not his. "And Sebastian made the choice to become a spy, knowing the risks. He decided that—not you."

Jack's nod was somber.

"Anyway, my superior dealt with the dowager. He told her he would fund my expenses and not touch a penny of the Fayne fortune. He appealed to the dowager's self-interest: with Fayne alive, she had continued use of the entailed properties, including the country seat where she lived, and access to the funds that came from entitlements. Accustomed as she was to a certain lifestyle, the dowager was loath to give it up. As long as she never saw me—and she never did because I lived abroad—she was content to let the fiction of her son live on."

"That sounds terribly cold." Charlie shivered. "Exchanging your child's identity for money."

"She did not live long to enjoy it. Her heart failed a year before you and I met."

A sudden thought struck Charlie. She was stunned she hadn't thought of it earlier, but she'd been too absorbed in Jack's story, in the secrets he was finally revealing.

"Our marriage. Was it even valid?" she choked out. "You married me under false pretenses."

"I wronged you, Lottie."

Despite her own tumultuous state, she could see his anguish. It was impossible to miss the regret carved on his face, the hunching of his burly shoulders under the weight of guilt. He was tormented by what he'd done...but he had deceived her, made her an unwitting accomplice to his charade.

"How could you do this to me?" Her voice shook.

"I have no excuse for being a scoundrel." He met her gaze squarely, and his smoldering self-revulsion twisted her insides. "When we met in Marseille, I was on an assignment. I was not supposed to meet the bravest, most beautiful woman I'd ever seen in an alleyway. I was not supposed to help her fight off assailants and learn that her guardian was even worse of a predator. Most of all, I was not supposed to fall in love and give her the protection of a name that wasn't even mine."

Her heart was pounding as if it wanted to escape its cage.

"But I did all of those things," he acknowledged, his eyes burning. "And for the year we lived together, though it was the happiest time I'd ever known, the truth haunted me every moment. I wanted so badly to tell you who I was, but how could I? The Marquess of Fayne swept you off your feet, not some nobody named Jack Granger. Moreover, my superior, who was furious that I'd wed without his permission, made me swear that I would never reveal my real identity. At least this way, you had the protection of the Fayne title."

"Which is all I had after you abandoned me," she shot back.

"Do you want to know why I really left?" He shoved a hand through his hair so violently that she was surprised he didn't tear it out by the roots. "To protect you, yes. But also because I *knew*...I knew I wasn't deserving of you. I knew I wasn't good enough to be your husband and that you'd hate me if you found out who I was.

I also knew that loving you made me the most selfish bastard alive. And do you know what?"

"What?"

Yet her retort was without heat. The flames of anger had been dampened by her newfound understanding of Jack. Of his past and why he might have made the choices he had.

"I do not regret it. As sorry as I am for everything else, I will *never* regret loving you," he said with sudden ferocity. "That is why I came back: to fight for another chance to be the man you deserve."

His demeanor had an edge of belligerence, and she realized that she infinitely preferred it to his self-hatred. His chest surged powerfully, and so did hers. Their emotions whipped and crackled like an invisible storm. Standing there, in the center of it all, facing the man who'd made wrong decisions but who was there and would fight to be there with her, she was jolted by sudden clarity.

None of it mattered.

From the moment he had left, she'd been mired in the past. Because of resentment? Partly. A desire for answers? That too. But mostly because...

I love him, and I never stopped.

Despite all his faults, everything he'd done, she loved him. She had never gotten over him and never would. And he felt the same way—couldn't bring himself to regret loving her, even when it had hurt him. Even when he'd punished himself, hated himself, for lying to her. Even when she'd acted cruelly, lashing out, taking out her fears and insecurities on him. Their love was not perfect or without problems. It might take the rest of their lives to sort out their troubles.

None of it matters.

Because they had the one thing that did matter.

Imperfect and irrevocable. Stormy and soul-stealing.

The kind of love that lasted, that never abandoned you, that simply *was.*

"Do you hate me, Lottie?"

Jack's voice was gravelly. He stared at her with hooded eyes, as if he had to have her answer but was also resigned to what it would be.

"Are you planning to lie to me in the future?" she asked.

Brows drawn, he shook his head. "Since my return, I may not have always told you everything, but I haven't deceived you. I have been trying to do the opposite. What I want, more than anything..."

He trailed off, his hands balling, and she felt a fierce pang as she finally realized what stopped him from voicing his desires. What had made him believe that he was not good enough for her. What had prompted him to speak of his love but not ask for the same in return. Born fatherless, raised parentless, then pressed into service at a young age, Jack had occupied the bottom rung of the social ladder. Society had taught him that he and his needs did not matter; he was there to serve, nothing more. A natural protector, he had been shaped by those around him to give even more—to give all of himself, sacrificing his own happiness to do what he believed to be his duty.

Protecting those he loved with his life.

Tenderness washed through her.

"You can tell me," she said steadily. "You have a right to your desires. Even if it feels selfish, even if you believe you aren't deserving, you can ask for what you want."

"*You* are what I want." Hunger and longing blazed in his eyes. "The only thing I have ever wanted as Sebastian or Jack, Fayne or Granger. I love you, Lottie—and even if you want me out of your life, I don't know how I will stay away. Because I knew, from the moment we met, that you are my home and always will be."

Home. What she'd always yearned for. What he had given her with this house but, most of all, with his love.

"I love you." She said the words without fear or hesitation.

His eyes widened, then he squeezed them shut. When he

opened them again, moisture spiked his lashes, and his irises were midnight scattered with bronze stars.

"How...how could you?"

His words, rough with wonder, abraded her heart.

"Because you are a good man, Jack Granger, and deserving of love," she said softly. "You protect those you love, even at the cost of your own happiness. You are loyal and strong, and as long as you promise not to deceive me, for any reason, we can make things work."

"I will never lie to you again," he vowed.

"A wise woman once told me that if there is love, nothing else matters." She gave in to the wifely impulse to straighten the lapel of his frock coat. "I think she might be right."

He placed his hand over hers, pinning it against his chest.

"I love you more than life itself," he said hoarsely. "If you let me stay, Lottie, I will never leave again."

"Stay with me, Jack. Always," she whispered.

She hadn't known that happiness could feel this simple, this freeing. She saw the same incredulous joy on his face. She leaned up and he down, their mouths melding in a sizzling kiss.

THIRTY

J ack didn't understand how it happened. One minute, they were fighting; the next, he'd blurted out the sordid truth of his past. Instead of throwing him out of her life for good, however, Lottie had given him another chance. She'd told him she loved him...the real *him*. Not a marquess, not even a gentleman, just Jack Granger, bastard servant-turned-spy who had nothing to offer but his love.

He'd even told her about how he'd failed Sebastian. While he hadn't revealed all the shameful details, he'd given her the essentials. The truth—he hadn't lied. Maybe one day he could bring himself to talk about Judith...but not tonight. Not now, when he had love and hope and everything good within his grasp.

If life had taught him anything, it was to never look a gift horse in the mouth. Especially when that mouth was as sweet and hot as his Lottie's. He drove his hands into her hair, savoring the fine silk between his fingers while he held her steady for his kiss. He possessed her with his tongue and lips, and she did the same, claiming him for her own.

All I've ever wanted.

The thought made him even hungrier, and he feasted on his

beloved. She kissed him back with equal fervor, her feminine desire driving him mad with wanting. He thrust his tongue deep between her lips, and he groaned when she sucked on his offering, reminding him of her unparalleled oral talents. When her touch feathered across the pulsing ridge of his erection, he tore his mouth from hers with a groan.

"Let's go to your bedchamber."

"I want you now. Here." She closed her palm around his cock, the gentle squeeze making him pant. "This is our home, Jack, and we can do whatever we please."

His breath stuttered. "*Our* home?"

She studied him. "This property was not entailed, which means you purchased this home with your own funds, didn't you?"

Back then, it had taken every penny he'd earned and invested, plus a loan from Primus to secure this house. It had been worth it to give Lottie a place that befitted her.

"I bought a house," he said gruffly. "You made it a home."

"Even though you left, you were taking care of me. Protecting me." The tenderness in her eyes expanded his chest with wonder. "Now you are back, and we are going to share a future together. Make a home...together."

This woman was his every fantasy come true. A goddess whose love made redemption seem possible. A wanton whose boldness made his cock throb to be inside her. A minx whose unpredictability would keep him on his toes for the rest of his life, and he would love every second of it.

His heart pounding, he asked, "Will you marry me, Lottie?"

"Perhaps. If you propose properly." Her grey gaze held a teasing sparkle. "This time."

With a surge of embarrassment, he recalled that his other proposal had been as impetuous as this one. It had happened over their third meal together in Marseille. He'd been so captivated by her that the words, *Will you marry me?*, had popped out of his mouth...and he hadn't come prepared with a ring or flowers. By some miracle, despite his ham-handedness, she'd said yes.

This time, I will do better by her. In all respects.

"I am going to give you the most proper proposal in the history of proposals," he vowed.

"In the meantime," she said, as beguiling as a siren, "you could convince me of your affection in other ways."

His blood went from hot to simmering. "What is your pleasure, my love?"

"I wish to have my dessert," she said playfully. "Will you have a seat, please?"

He managed to pull out a chair and seat himself without stumbling like a love-drunk fool. Guessing his wife's intentions, he left plenty of room between him and the table...and a good thing, too. When she knelt gracefully between his legs, her skirts formed a poofy cloud around her. With her face framed by honey strands he'd dislodged from her coronet and her mouth red and wet from his kisses, she looked like a naughty queen.

She undid his fall, and his cock jutted out in tribute.

"Oh, darling," she murmured. "You are too splendid for words."

Her adoration made him *feel* splendid. It made him feel like a partner who was worthy of her, made him feel like a...a king. The sensation was foreign and potent, and he went with it. He fisted his scepter of flesh, giving himself a slow pump that made her eyelids lower halfway. On the upward stroke, a milky drop beaded on his flared tip.

"You may have a taste," he said.

"Thank you, sir," she said demurely.

He didn't know what aroused him more: her deference or the cheekiness that lay beneath. Her gaze glinted with mischief as she placed that first sweet kiss on his dome. He shuddered at the feather-soft brush against his sensitive crest. Instead of licking off his seed, however, she smeared it over her mouth. Looking in his eyes, she swiped her tongue over her lips, slowly and deliberately. Savoring him and letting him know it.

It struck him, then. In opening himself up to her, he'd paved the way for greater intimacy...in every regard. Their newfound honesty extended to the bedchamber—or dining room, as it were —and he was reaping the rewards. The realization filled him with a heady sense of power. By trusting Lottie, he'd earned her trust in return, and she was showing him by shedding her inhibitions.

Bloody hell, there was something to be said for hashing out their problems.

"Do you like the taste of my cock, sweeting?" he said huskily.

Her delightful blush heightened the vividness of her irises.

"It's not a bad start."

He remembered that he'd once teased her with those exact words.

"Not a bad start, eh?" He raised his brows, tracing her lips with his thumb.

"I have an idea to make it better."

"Why am I not surprised?"

Turning toward the table, she reached for one of the dishes... the floating island. The fluffy poached meringue wobbled on its pool of rich crème Anglaise as she dragged it closer to her. Intrigued, he watched as she took a spoonful of the dessert.

She wouldn't...

"I think this will make things even sweeter," she said.

She upended the spoon over his prick. The meringue plopped onto the dome of his cock, the crème dribbling down the turgid length. With a hum of anticipation, Lottie bent over him and had her dessert. She swirled the meringue with her tongue, making him grunt. Then she sucked, and he grunted louder. She proceeded to enjoy the crème, destroying what was left of his self-control in the process.

She lapped the length of his shaft, consuming every sweet trickle. When she was done, she added another dollop, the cool meringue an erotic contrast to the heat of her mouth. He was beyond hard, the vein that snaked along his shaft pulsing as custard dribbled over his stones, and she licked them clean. He shuddered with pleasure even as he needed more.

She nuzzled his bollocks, licking the swollen curve.

"Tell me what you want," she whispered. "Whatever it is, you can have it."

She was a gift, his Lottie. His mate who loved him no matter what.

He fisted a hand in her hair, directing her mouth back to his tip. "I want you to suck my cock properly. To take me deep into that sweet mouth of yours."

Elation filled him when she gave him what he wanted. Her mouth was bliss beyond compare, but it was the stormy arousal in her eyes that pushed him over the edge. She wanted this—wanted him to take his pleasure, to demand it, to own it. She wanted him to know that his desires were worthy...that he was worthy.

Gripped by emotion, he pressed her head down, groaning as she went readily. He guided her movements, making her take him as deep as she could, reveling in her surrender. She gave him everything he asked for, held nothing back, and when he felt the loving clasp of her throat, he let go. He came with a roar, burying himself in his wife's kiss, emptying himself in long, ecstatic bursts.

She looked up at him with tear-edged eyes. She was smiling. She was so sweet and alluring that his still-hard cock jerked against his stomach.

"Did you enjoy your dessert?" she asked.

"Undoubtedly." He traced the downy slant of her cheekbone. "In fact, I am ready for another helping."

"Jack, that is too wicked. You shouldn't...oh *heavens*."

Her cheek pressed against the table linen, Charlie quivered

with helpless pleasure as she stood bent over the dining table. Jack was behind her, as naked as she was, doing unspeakable things with the butter boat.

"You started it, minx. What is sauce for the gander is sauce for the goose."

Even though she couldn't see his face, his admonishment aroused her terribly. She loved his dominant side, loved that he felt comfortable enough to impose his will. She'd wanted him to know that his desires were important to her...and his actions surely conveyed that she'd succeeded. After she'd enjoyed her floating island, he had decided to have his own feast.

He'd used her like a plate, eating delicacies from every part of her body and then eating *her* until she'd moaned her way through multiple climaxes. Naked and spent, she'd been limp as a rag, but Jack had just been getting warmed up. He'd put her in the current position, and his comment about the proverbial "sauce" hadn't been metaphorical.

She twitched as he dribbled warm butter sauce along her spine, following the downward flow with his tongue. All the while, he kneaded and stroked her muscles until she melted into the table, her eyes fluttering in bliss.

They flew open when warm sauce trickled down her rear crevice. Surely he didn't intend to... She gasped when he spread her cheeks wide, and his tongue delved between. Circling, teasing, licking that hidden rim whilst she squirmed helplessly against the table.

"That's wicked," she breathed.

"Says the woman who licked crème Anglaise from my cock."

"Well," she said after a pause. "You may have a point."

She felt more sauce dripping between her cheeks and shuddered when he thrust his cock against the slickened crack. His rod slid against her forbidden pucker, setting off strange and titillating sensations whilst his stones slapped her swollen folds.

"There's a sight," he said thickly. "I wish you could see what I'm seeing."

She looked over her shoulder, and although she couldn't see their joining, she could see her lover's face. Jack's cheeks were flushed, his eyes hungry and proprietary as he watched himself thrusting against her bottom. His arousal amplified her own; her nipples and pearl tingled as his thrusts rocked them against the wood. But it wasn't enough. Her pussy clenched on nothing, the emptiness a physical ache. She needed more.

"Come inside," she whispered.

"I, er, didn't come prepared." He looked slightly abashed. "Shall we go upstairs?"

"I want you now," she said.

His eyes flared. If he looked hungry before, now he looked voracious.

"Are you certain?" he asked with quiet intensity.

"Are you going to make an honest woman out of me, Mr. Granger?"

"As soon as I can get you to say yes," he said fiercely.

"Then make love to me. I need you, Jack."

In the next heartbeat, he notched his cock to her slit, the wide head pushing into her, spreading her, opening her to pleasure. She gasped at his possession, the fullness of it, the totality. There was no sheath, no barrier to their union, nothing to separate his flesh from hers. His massive cock lodged into the center of her being, and she felt whole.

"This is where I belong, Lottie," Jack growled. "Right here. Inside you."

"Yes, my love. Yes. Give me more."

She pushed back on him, and he responded with a savageness that stole her breath. He withdrew, ramming into her with blissful force. The dishes clattered as he rode her, taking her to a rapid zenith. As heat began streaking through her limbs, she felt his thumb sweeping along her crack, pressing into her smaller passage.

The forbidden thrill catapulted her over the edge, and her entire being exploded with joy.

Pulling out, Jack turned her onto her back and plowed right back into her. Even spent, she felt a frisson of excitement at his lustful intensity. His eyes were half-lidded, his mouth slack, the sculpted muscles of his torso rippling as he pounded into her.

"You have no *idea*." He squeezed his eyes shut briefly, sounding drunk on pleasure. "How good you feel…"

"I have *some* idea." She fitted her legs in the hard grooves of his hips, her heels bouncing against his taut arse. "I am yours, Jack. Whatever you want. Whatever you need."

"You, Lottie. I need *you*."

His movements became savage, his eyes gleaming with a primal prerogative. Looming over her, he claimed her with unbridled vigor, and she loved it. Her nerve endings reawakened, sparking to life with his sensual onslaught. He swooped down and sucked her nipples, tugging on some invisible cord in her pussy. She clenched on his driving rod.

"Just like that," he growled. "Milk my prick, Lottie. Take my seed."

Even if she wanted to deny him, she couldn't resist the seductive strokes of his cock, his persuasive fondling of her pearl. He fingered her bud as he shafted her, setting off deeper, longer tremors. Bliss gushed from her, and he arched his neck, bellowing as he hilted himself, flooding her with tide after tide of his heat.

Breathing harshly, he leaned over and kissed her.

Then he scooped her up and carried her upstairs.

Despite the feast of last night, Jack woke up famished. Lottie's lady's maid, a freckled redhead named Jenny, brought up breakfast. He was pleased that Jenny seemed flustered by the presence of a man in her mistress's bedchamber, which suggested this was an unusual occurrence. From now on, it wasn't going to be: Jack planned to sleep with Lottie as often as possible. In fact, his goal was to never be apart from her again.

Our home. Those had been her exact words. Even though she knew who he was, she was willing to become Mrs. Jack Granger. Bloody hell, how had he gotten so lucky? All he had to do now was give her a proper proposal. He would shop for a ring forthwith. Flowers, champagne, a bloody orchestra...he was going to set the stage with care and do everything right this time around.

He dug into his food with gusto. When he polished off his plate, Lottie refilled it.

"Worked up an appetite, did you?"

Her eyes smiled at him above the rim of her coffee cup. In his estimation, she was always a goddess; when she flirted with him, he wanted to worship her slowly, thoroughly, until neither of them could move.

"I had to satisfy you, didn't I, you wanton minx," he drawled.

"Oh, you did, darling. At least a half-dozen times."

"Splendid, we have a record to beat. Excellence never sleeps."

He raised his cup in a toast, and she did the same, laughing.

While he would love nothing more than to banter and make love to his wife all day, there was pressing business to discuss. Her mien grew somber; knowing she was about to bring up the topic, he beat her to it.

"Let us discuss the plan for Brompton's," he said.

"You cannot stop me—"

"I know." He exhaled. "I don't wish to stop you from being who you are, Lottie. You've accepted me for who I am, and I want to do the same for you. I love *you*—and that includes the brave, bold, and capable lady investigator that you are."

Her eyes shone. "That means everything to me, Jack."

"But even the best investigators need reinforcements."

She nodded slowly. "My society has a motto: *sisters first.* Partnership is what makes us strong."

Relieved that this was going better than planned, he said, "So you agree to have a partner?"

"I do. Unfortunately, it cannot be you. Karlsson got too good a look."

He wanted to kick himself for not choosing a more thorough disguise.

"You couldn't know that Brompton's might be tied up with the First Flame." With her usual acuity, Lottie read his mind. "I will have to bring in a different partner. Since Pippa recently gave birth and Fiona is starting to show, I think they should sit this one out. That leaves Livy and Glory." She hesitated. "And Devlin."

Since he and his wife loved each other and had spent the night proving it, Jack could afford to be magnanimous. Moreover, her safety came first.

"A pair of reinforcements wouldn't hurt," he said. "You and one of the Angels can apply to be factory workers. And Devlin can put in to be a foreman."

Lottie looked pleased. "That is a capital plan. After breakfast, I shall gather my team."

"And I will contact mine. We are going to dig into the background of Brompton's," Jack said with resolve. "If the company is abetting the First Flame, we'll need proof before we take them down."

THIRTY-ONE

After breakfast, Charlie decided to stop at Glory's home first. The residence was in the East End, a starkly elegant compound where Glory's husband, Wei Chen, ran a clinic that specialized in Chinese healing arts and *kung fu*. An elite martial artist, Master Chen had become a sought-after *shifu* for gentlemen eager to improve their health through his remedies and physical exercises.

Thus, it was no surprise that the courtyards were already packed with pupils when Charlie arrived. They were practicing drills on wooden dummies, honing their punches, kicks, and other maneuvers. The majordomo took her through to a private building at the back of the compound, where Glory and Master Chen received her in a spacious hall that served as an all-purpose entertaining area.

"Good morning, Lady Fayne." The master bowed, the clipped waves of his raven hair gleaming. "To what do we owe the pleasure?"

Although he often dressed in the English style, when at home Wei Chen wore the traditional Chinese tunic and trousers. The elegant simplicity of the steel-blue fabric suited his noble features and lean, wiry build. Handsome yet reserved, Chen was not an easy fellow to read...except when it came to Glory. When his eyes alighted on his new bride, they gleamed with the depth of his emotion for her.

Standing beside her husband, Glory looked equally content. In fact, she was quite radiant in her high-necked lavender gown, and there was a telltale glow on her cheeks that Charlie had seen in her own mirror this morning. Nothing like an early morning romp to get the blood pumping.

"I am afraid this is a matter of business, not pleasure," Charlie replied.

They took their seats at a round rosewood table, and Glory passed out porcelain cups of jasmine tea.

"Is this about the case?" Glory asked. "Fi and I haven't finished surveying the site of the Great Exhibition—"

"A more pressing situation has arisen."

Charlie explained her plan to infiltrate Brompton's manufactory with a partner. Given Glory's zeal for investigation, she'd expected the other to volunteer immediately. Instead, Glory bit her lip and exchanged a look with Chen.

Charlie frowned. Of all the spouses, Glory's was typically the least likely to interfere with Angel business. Not because he was any less protective than the other men; in fact, he was capable of incapacitating anyone who even looked askance at his wife. The reason that he could be more relaxed about his lady's participation was because he'd personally taken her on as a pupil. Whilst all the Angels had been trained in combat, Glory was learning martial arts as well. When she demonstrated her "lightness" *kung fu*, a technique that enhanced her natural speed and agility, Charlie had marveled along with the other Angels.

"I was thinking you could accompany me, Glory." Charlie arched a brow. "Unless there is a problem?"

Glory cleared her throat. "It's not a problem, exactly. Mr. Chen and I were going to wait to share the news, but, um..."

She hesitated, but Charlie already knew.

"My wife is with child." Master Chen did not hesitate, his manner one of fierce and quiet pride.

"May I offer my congratulations?" Charlie said sincerely.

"Thank you, Charlie." Glory was beaming. "I plan to continue my work as an Angel during my pregnancy—"

"Little tigress, we talked about this," her husband said under his breath.

"*But* I did promise to take extra care," she amended. "This morning, when Mr. Chen was taking my pulse, he noticed a slight disturbance. It's probably nothing, but to err on the side of caution, I should rest a day or two."

"Possibly three." Chen's tone was dry. "If you can remain still that long."

Glory rolled her eyes. "Being still isn't that hard."

"For you it is." His mouth tipped up, as if he were recalling something satisfying. "Luckily, you have me to guide you."

Whatever the private memory was, it turned Glory's cheeks apple-red.

"I am sure I will be fine by tomorrow—" she began.

"Do not worry about it. I will ask Livy." Charlie patted Glory's hand. "Get some rest, dear."

Jack met his subordinates in their usual spot. Given a recent haul from the Smithfield market, the back room of Mr. Campbell's shop was filled with carcasses awaiting preparation. Sawdust covered the floor, soaking up but not hiding the dark stains of butchery.

Delaney, a redhead today wearing a washer woman's garb, issued her usual refrain.

"We really cannot find a better place to meet?"

Jack took a drink of the butcher's tea. "It's not that bad."

"The animal corpses or the tea?" Delaney wrinkled her nose. "I don't know how you can stomach Campbell's brew."

"Let's get this over with." Laurent swatted flies with a handkerchief. "You called the meeting, *mon ami*. What have you got for us?"

Jack explained the situation at Brompton's.

"The First Flame and a match manufactory, eh?" Laurent scratched his head. "Bit on the nose, as the English say."

"Or they're thumbing their noses at us," Delaney grumbled. "The bastards think they're untouchable."

"They are if we cannot get evidence of wrongdoing." Jack shoved his hands in his pockets. "Lady Fayne is infiltrating the manufactory as a worker."

Calderone let out a low whistle.

Laurent quirked a brow. "You're letting her go in?"

"My permission was inconsequential," Jack said wryly. "I trust her, however. She knows what she's doing."

"Primus isn't going to like this," Delaney predicted darkly. "After Hastings, he wanted you to shake her loose. He was not pleased when she absconded with the clue. Got an earful about it, didn't I. As if I had anything to do with it."

"I am not shaking Charlotte loose," Jack stated. "We are getting married again."

Which reminded him: he needed to find time to stop at Rundell, Bridge & Co. to commission a ring for Lottie. The jewelers catered to the upper crust and had fashioned the Imperial State Crown worn by Her Majesty the Queen at her coronation. He hoped they could get the order done quickly because he wanted to propose to Lottie the moment this mission was over.

Delaney crossed her arms over her chest. "I want to be a fly on the wall when you tell Primus."

"My private life is none of Primus's business. In fact..." Jack hesitated before giving voice to the decision that had been forming in his head. "In fact, after this case, I am out. For good."

The other spies stared at him. Even though Jack could not say they were close, they were the nearest thing to family he had. He felt a tug akin to loss that he was closing this chapter of his life. But he was ready, more than ready, to move on.

To start a new life with Lottie, unfettered by secrets.

Well, there was still one. He told himself that what happened with Judith had no bearing on his marriage and his future. He might work up the courage to tell Lottie about it one day...or maybe he wouldn't. Either way, he wasn't lying to her. He was just keeping his disgrace where it ought to be. Dead and buried.

"*C'est bon*," Laurent said finally. "Good for you."

"At least one of us is making it out alive." Calderone sent Laurent a meaningful look.

"Congratulations." Delaney's expression was sullen. "All the best and whatnot. Who is going to take your role as the spymaster of our little ring?"

"I won't leave the team in the lurch," Jack promised. "Perhaps one of you would care to put your name forward?"

Laurent shrugged. "If we stamp out the First Flame this time around, we may render ourselves superfluous. Then we will all be happily unemployed. So, what do you want us to do now?"

"Dig into Brompton's. Find out everything you can about the owners, their finances, and relationships. Look for any possible connections to the First Flame, no matter how seemingly insignificant. We must leave no stone unturned."

"It is not our first voyage, you know," Delaney groused.

"In the meantime, I am off to Chancery Lane." Jack grimaced. "To locate the deed of ownership for Brompton's manufactory."

"Clerks and chancery rolls, two things guaranteed to bore a man to death." Shuddering, Calderone slapped him on the shoulder. "Maybe you won't make it out alive after all."

THIRTY-TWO

When Jack entered her bedchamber from the adjoining room, dressed in a simple black dressing gown, Charlie couldn't resist teasing him. She dismissed Jenny, who'd been helping her with her evening ablutions, and twisted around in her chair.

She said demurely, "How was your day, dear?"

He raised his brows. "Has my Lottie been replaced by an impostor?"

"I am trying on domesticity for size," she said with a laugh.

He came to stand behind her at the dressing table. His eyes met hers in the looking glass, and he rested his hands lightly on her shoulders.

"How does it fit?"

She thought about it. "I do not think we are going to be like other couples."

"That ship has long sailed, my love." He studied her. "Do you mind that we are different?"

"No," she said honestly. "I think I am better suited to unconventionality."

Leaning down, he kissed her with seductive thoroughness.

Heavens, how could she have gone years without this man when a few hours of separation now felt too long?

He nuzzled her throat. "You smell nice."

"It is my face cream. I have it specially blended."

"No, it's you." He kissed the curve of her neck. "Your skin smells like clean sheets."

"Perhaps you just associate me with a bed."

"There is no perhaps about it."

In an easy motion, he swung her into his arms and carried her over to the furnishing in question. He deposited her, crawling over her like a playful bear whilst she giggled. Smiling, he kissed her softly on the nose and mouth. Then he sat up against the headboard, gathering her in the crook of his arm.

"Tell me about your day," he said.

She snuggled against him. "I have good news and bad news."

"Why can't it ever just be good news?" he asked of no one in particular.

"The good news is that I got the job at Brompton's and start tomorrow."

"Well done." He quirked a brow. "The bad news?"

"Livy did not get hired."

"What happened?"

"The foreman thought she had the look of a troublemaker and would be a bad influence on the other workers. Livy was furious." Charlie smiled, recalling her charge's indignation. "It did not help that Hadleigh was waiting in the carriage, and when she told him what transpired, he guffawed and said the foreman was a good judge of character."

"His Grace will be sleeping in a cold bed tonight." Jack smirked. "And Devlin?"

"I have no idea what sort of bed he'll be sleeping in."

"Very amusing." Jack gave her a squeeze. "Did he get hired?"

She nodded. Before recruiting Devlin to the mission, she'd informed him of the state of affairs between her and Jack. To her relief, he'd taken the news well and acted like the professional he was.

"He was gloating because his wages will be much higher than mine," she said with a huff. "He will be standing around telling us workers what to do whilst I actually make the boxes for the matches and pack them. I even have to supply my own glue and string."

"Grossly unfair."

"It is a man's world, but one day it will change," she predicted. "In the meantime, women will continue to get things done as they always have. Livy gave the liquid to her uncle, by the by. She said he should have some answers for us in the next day or so. Glory and Fiona are making progress on their surveyance of the Great Exhibition. And I've told Pippa to redirect her efforts from finding the matchbox design to gathering any information on the streets about the First Flame. Thus far, she says the larks haven't picked up any news."

"You have had a productive day," Jack said. "Better than mine."

"What did you discover?"

"That I despise bureaucracy. I spent six hours being passed from clerk to clerk. At this rate, I am better off making a visit to the Public Records Office tomorrow night."

She canted her head. "You would break into a government office?"

"It wouldn't be the first time."

"I shall come with you," she decided.

"After your shift at the manufactory, you'll need your rest. One of my colleagues can come with me."

"Miss Delaney, by any chance?"

The words slipped out, and Charlie wished they hadn't. Jack had told her he had no interest in his fellow agent, and she believed him. Yet her insecurities continued to nibble at her for no good reason.

"I'll ask Laurent," Jack said.

Not only did he let her unwarranted jealousy slide, but he also made things easy for her. His high-mindedness shamed her, for her nature wasn't as generous. For instance, even though he had asked, she hadn't yet shared how many lovers she'd had during their separation. She'd withheld the information partly on principle—he'd left her, made her think he was dead. But now she realized with uncomfortable clarity that she might have also held back for another reason: to punish him. To pay him back for hurting her. The recognition made her feel very small.

"There was only one," she blurted.

Jack drew his brows together. "One...what?"

"One lover. During the time you were gone."

He said nothing. His only reaction was his arm tightening around her.

"Given how I thought our marriage ended, I was not exactly eager to get involved with another man," she went on. "Time passed, and when I returned to London and started my society, I began to feel more myself, more in charge of my own destiny. I was ready to pursue physical intimacy once again. At the risk of sounding immodest, I had my choice of lovers—"

"That is hardly surprising," Jack muttered.

"Yet I was cautious. I did not want a repeat of what I believed to be my past failures."

"I am sorry, love. The fault is mine for making you feel—"

"No, Jack." She placed a hand on his chest and felt the potent throb of his heart. "You've made your apologies. Repeatedly. But I have yet to take responsibility for my part in the collapse of our marriage."

"Because you have none," he said with a savage shake of his head. "I was the one who deceived you. Who left you, for God's sake."

"Yes. But I wasn't exactly honest with you either." She sighed. "I *knew* something was wrong, but I was too afraid to ask you what it was. Instead, I bottled up my fear, assumed the worst, and investigated you. Then I lashed out at you, didn't even give you a chance to explain."

"It does not make it right that I left."

"It doesn't," she agreed. "But it makes it more understandable why you thought leaving might be the best thing. We were fighting all the time, even before I thought you were unfaithful. And I had a part in that, Jack. The entire time we were together, I had this constant fear that our happiness wouldn't last. That you would betray me—tire of me and leave."

"I will never tire of you," he said fiercely. "And I won't leave again."

"I know that now." She gave him a tremulous smile. "The benefit of age and experience. If we are to start afresh, we need to be honest with ourselves and one another. I don't want us to repeat our mistakes. You needn't take the blame for everything, and I needn't accuse first and ask later."

"Do you know," he said huskily, "how damned much I love you?"

"Are you going to show me?"

His kiss was far more persuasive than words. He rolled over her, taking her down to the pillows, their mouths clinging. Tender and sweet, hot and possessive, their kiss mirrored their love, and she luxuriated in the drugging warmth of his lips, the muscular length of him pressing her into the mattress.

He lifted his head. "I have a question."

"Yes, darling?" She sifted her fingers through his hair.

"Why only one?"

Rolling her eyes, she said, "Is this to satisfy your male vanity?"

"Since we are being honest...yes."

Beneath his cocky smile, there was a hint of vulnerability. A past like his didn't exactly foster self-worth. With a pang, she realized that while he'd expressed his devotion freely, she hadn't done the same.

"Fine. You ruined all men for me." She pretended to huff. "Does that make you happy?"

"Perhaps merely relieved that I am not competing with five to fifty lovers." He was smiling, but his eyes were serious. "I cannot deny that I am a possessive bastard where you are concerned. But you are a passionate woman, Lottie, and I am sorry that you went without sensual pleasures for so long."

"Who says I went without? During our separation, didn't you take matters into your own hands?"

He cleared his throat. "Well, yes."

"Why wouldn't I do the same? A woman's needs are no less than a man's."

"How?"

"I beg your pardon?"

"How," he murmured, "did you pleasure yourself?"

She refused to blush. "In the usual manner."

"Did you pet your sweet little quim with your fingers? Use a device made for that purpose?"

When she didn't answer, he said in a low voice, "Both?"

"Really, Jack—"

"I want to watch."

Despite her best efforts, she couldn't prevent heat from flooding her cheeks.

"No," she said.

"Please?"

His lopsided smile, paired with the wicked gleam in his eyes, was irresistible. And the rogue knew it. The moment she hesitated, he pounced.

"Is the equipment in your wardrobe?" he guessed.

He *would* have a spymaster's knack for finding hidden things.

He flashed a devilish grin. "I shall fetch it for you."

Before she could protest, he was off. She sat up, her heart thumping, wondering if she could go through with this. Her nervousness heightened when he returned carrying the familiar wooden case in one hand...and a stack of books in the other.

Botheration. Her face flamed.

"Interesting reading material you have here." Smirking, he read the spines. "*The Amorous Tales of an Abducted Lady?* Or, better yet, *Submitting to My Lord and Master: A Diary of Marital Lust?*"

"Those aren't mine." To her chagrin, she sounded like a criminal caught in the act. "That is, I bought them whilst I was in disguise tracking down Miss Loveday. I didn't choose them for myself...oh, never mind."

"We can consult the books later if we are in need of inspiration."

He set the books aside and joined her on the bed, placing the rosewood case between them.

"Open it." His eyes dared her.

On principle alone, she couldn't back down. A woman had a right to pleasure as much as a man, and she refused to be embarrassed about it. To do so would undermine the philosophy of female independence upon which she'd built her society. Even so, she fumbled with the brass clasp before she got the lid open. Nestled in blue silk was a set of five ivory phalluses, ranging in size from small to large...although not quite as large as Jack.

From his smug expression, he'd obviously made the comparison.

"You have quite the collection of dildos," he said.

"*Godemiche,*" she corrected. "They are French."

"*Bien sûr, madam.*" His eyes gleamed. "Why don't you show me which one is your favorite?"

Jack didn't know whether he found Lottie's loftiness more amusing or arousing. Only his wife could act like a queen when confronted by her collection of dildos—or *godemiches*, rather. He wanted to laugh, and even more he wanted to see the brazen minx pleasure herself with one of the fake pricks before he gave her the real thing.

Part of his lightheartedness stemmed from the fact that Lottie had only shared herself with one other lover. One who hadn't made much of an impression, apparently. Whilst it undoubtedly proved that he was the cave dweller she accused him of being, he reveled in the fact that he'd ruined her for others. As silly as it seemed, he knew such a thing was possible because she'd done the same to him.

Me for Lottie, her for me.

The way it was meant to be and would be, from here on in.

Seeing his spouse bite her plump bottom lip, he felt his temperature rise another notch. He adored her contradictions, especially the way her principles were battling with her natural modesty. As enjoyable as her rare moment of indecision was, he decided to nudge her along.

Taking her hand, he placed it on a medium-sized *diletto* (yes, he knew what the Italians called it, too). "Why don't you start with this one?"

She narrowed her eyes at him. Then she snatched her hand away, grabbing hold of the biggest rod. It was a good seven inches and hefty too. It didn't rival him, however...not that he was comparing.

"This one will do," she said boldly.

"Let us get you ready then, hmm?"

He tumbled her onto the mattress. He took his time winnowing pleasure from her until she writhed, gasping his name. Beneath her robe, he discovered a scrap of a negligee that made his cock harder than the dildo she'd released in favor of clenching her hands in his hair.

"How much do you like this negligee?" he asked.

"Don't you dare."

He hid a smile as she helped him yank the garment over her head.

And there she was...his Lottie. Creamy curves, elegant lines, aroused and defiant eyes. In that moment, he realized that she owned every part of him: his brain, his heart, his jutting cock.

She knew it, too. In that instant, the tables were turned. Her smile seductive, she reached for the dildo.

"Watch," she said throatily.

He observed from the foot of the bed, riveted by his wife.

She brought the dildo to her lips. He swallowed as she licked the broad dome. When she traced the carved vee on the underside with her tongue, he could feel the sensual caress on his own throbbing head. Slowly, she pushed the rod betwixt her lips, making it disappear inch by inch. Her eyes on his, she hollowed her cheeks, and he groaned, his cock responding to that phantom suction.

When she pulled the instrument out, it was shiny and slick. She trailed the dildo down her throat and over the rounded mound of her breast. His lungs seized as she traced the dome over the stiff pink buds until they, too, were glistening.

"Tell me what you're thinking," he said reverently. "What you fantasize about."

Her eyes were smoky with passion. "Right now, I am imagining this dildo is your cock."

Christ. He leaked more seed as she dragged the dildo down the center of her body.

"Your skin would feel so soft against my prick," he rasped.

"I am even softer here. Wetter, too."

She spread her knees, giving him a view that made his blood steam in his veins. And that was before she brought the dildo to her dewy pink crease and rubbed the head against her pearl.

"Do you like it when I tease your pussy that way?" He took up her fantasy. "When I rub my cock against your stiff little bud?"

"Yes," she breathed. "It feels lovely."

His nostrils flaring, he watched her diddle herself with lazy strokes. Unable to resist, he shed his robe, wrapping a hand around his enormous erection. Lottie's gaze locked on his cock, and she whimpered, frigging herself harder.

He pumped himself slowly. "Where else do you want this?"

"Inside." She sighed. "Inside my pussy."

"Put it in."

His cock twitched in his fist as she slid the dildo into her quim.

"How does that feel?" he asked.

"Like I would rather have the real thing."

Her pout made his cock quiver with anticipation.

"You'll have it soon enough, sweetheart," he promised. "After you play with yourself."

She did as he asked and gave him a show, working the dildo into her pussy, arching her hips in rhythm to her thrusts. He was fascinated by his opposing reactions: burning lust and irrational jealousy...over a fake cock, for Christ's sake. Yet Lottie was his, and he wanted to be the one touching her, pleasuring her.

She caught her bottom lip beneath her teeth, and he knew the dildo alone wasn't enough to bring her over. Leaning forward, he skated his thumb over her pearl, and she jerked, moaning. He frigged her harder, pressing her bud against the gliding ivory. She liked his petting well enough, but it didn't make her spend.

"What do you need, love?" he asked intently. "Tell me, and I'll give it to you."

"Make love to me," she whispered. "I want to come with your cock inside me."

Who am I to resist such a summons?

Tossing aside the dildo, he got on his back, hauling his wife atop him. She gasped as he pulled her down on his stiff flesh. He could feel her passage stretching to take him.

"You wanted my cock. Take it," he ordered. "Deep into that needy pussy."

She trembled at his command. Whimpering, she impaled

herself inch by inch until her cunny kissed his stones. She felt like a lush, pulsing glove around him, and he gnashed his teeth in bliss.

"Christ. You feel so bloody good."

"You feel better than good." She framed his face with her hands, looking deep into his eyes. "You are the best, Jack. The only man for me."

At her avowal, his throat got scratchy and his eyes hot. Not knowing what to say, he cupped her nape and pulled her down for a kiss. Then he made love to his wife all night long, intent upon proving to her—and himself—that she was right.

THIRTY-THREE

"You ain't done this before, 'ave you, Mrs. Gibson?"

Charlie stopped fumbling with the matchbox she was attempting to put together and faced Molly Sutter. She'd deliberately chosen the spot at the end of the table closest to Mrs. Sutter, hoping to strike up a conversation. From what she'd seen of the encounter between the worker and Mr. Karlsson, the former would be a fount of useful information.

"It's my first time." Today Charlie was posing as Laura Gibson, a pleasantly rounded and bespectacled mother of three. "'Ad to find work after my old pot and pan left me 'igh and dry."

"Men." Mrs. Sutter snorted. "Can't live wif 'em, but it ain't much easier living wifout 'em. My 'usband broke 'is leg."

"Must've been a bad fall," Charlie said sympathetically.

"Down a gin bottle. The bastard's lucky I don't kick 'im out for good," Mrs. Sutter said with a huff. "Now we can't be caught palavering, or we'll be fined for certain. Just watch what I'm doing and follow along. You don't want to waste the glue you're paying for, and you'll need to work quick to meet the quota. Wif the way the place is managed, we'll be lucky if we take 'ome wages at the end o' the day."

Mrs. Sutter cast a nervous glance around even as she deftly constructed the matchbox. The manufactory was lined with rows of tables. Different sections were set up according to the task being performed by the mostly female workers. One section sorted out the imported Lucifer matches from large bins, tying them into bundles of twenty. Another section was responsible for cutting the cardboard for the boxes to the correct dimensions. Charlie and Mrs. Sutter were in the final assembly area, where they constructed the boxes, affixed the labels, and packed up the matches.

Foremen strutted up and down the rows like cockerels guarding their coops. When Charlie signed on, she'd been informed of the manufactory's copious rules, which included dressing in the proper uniform and not socializing with other workers. Any violation of the rules resulted in fines levied by the foremen.

Luckily, Devlin had managed to get assigned to Charlie's section. He, like her, was in disguise, and he acted the part well, barking at a worker for pasting on a crooked label. Although he did not make eye contact with her, she knew he was giving her the opportunity to pump her coworker for information.

"If things are so bad, why do you stay?" Charlie whispered.

Mrs. Sutter's resentment outweighed her fear of fines.

"It weren't always like this. Since the Bromptons decided to produce matches instead o' just importing 'em, things 'ave gotten worse. They plan on making us fuss wif white phosphorus and other nasty chemicals." Mrs. Sutter placed a finished matchbox in a basket and started on the next one. "They brought in Mr. Karlsson, who used to run a works in Sweden. 'E's supposed to 'modernize' us and is working on some newfangled machines in the building behind us. None o' us workers are allowed inside, and 'e hired those brutes on patrol to keep us out."

That explains the guards. Are the new "machines" for the purpose of modernizing matchmaking...or could they have a more sinister purpose?

"Surely someone has seen inside that building?"

"Not a soul. And don't go putting your nose where it don't belong," Mrs. Sutter warned. "There's no saying what Karlsson's brutes are capable of."

Charlie finished her matchbox. It was a bit misshapen, but when Mrs. Sutter gave a nod of approval, she placed it in her basket.

"Is Karlsson the only one in charge?" she asked. "What about the owners?"

"When I started 'ere three years ago, it was Mr. George Brompton wot ran the place. Salt o' the earth and always took care o' 'is workers, God bless 'im. Well, 'e passed last year, and his son Emmett took the reins. Then things took a turn for the worse." Mrs. Sutter pitched her voice to a whisper. "Rumor 'as it the junior Mr. Brompton loves the cards, but they don't love 'im back. 'E's a cheeseparer when it comes to us workers. 'E's the one who 'ired Mr. Karlsson."

Could Emmett Brompton be involved with the First Flame? Did they pay his debts and control him—the way they did Tony Quinton? I need to find out more.

"Does Mr. Brompton come to the factory?"

"Not the way 'is pa did. Old Mr. Brompton was the first to arrive and last to leave." Mrs. Sutter tossed another box into her basket. "The new one drops by every now and again when the fancy strikes. Last time was, oh, a month ago at least. 'E were showing off the factory to a couple o' high-kick friends...as if 'e knew the first thing about running this place."

Before Charlie could ask if Mrs. Sutter knew the names of Emmett Brompton's friends, a voice cut in.

"You ain't getting paid to flap your lips." One of the foremen, a corpulent fellow with beady eyes, lumbered toward them. "You know the rules. That'll be a fine o' three pennies apiece."

"But Mr. Smith, Mrs. Gibson 'ere is new, and I was just showing 'er—"

"Shut yer gob, or it's another penny off your wages," Smith snarled.

Mrs. Sutter's face reddened. She looked angry and on the verge of tears.

"It were my fault," Charlie said hastily. "I couldn't get an edge o' the box straight and asked Mrs. Sutter for help. The fine should come out o' my wages."

Smith looked her up and down. Despite her wig, spectacles, and ample padding, Charlie felt naked beneath his salacious perusal.

"Perhaps we can work somefin' out, Mrs. Gibson." He leered at her. "Come to my office after your shift."

Disgusting pig.

"What seems to be the problem 'ere, Smith?" Devlin cut in. "This is my section."

"The problem is that your hens are clucking and setting a bad example for the others," Smith said righteously. "Someone 'as to keep 'em in line, so I gave a fine and a warning."

"Neither are yours to give in the area I supervise," Devlin said. "I'll take care o' it."

Smith opened his mouth to argue, but eyeing Devlin's pugnacious posture, clearly thought better of it and stalked off.

"Back to work," Devlin clipped out. "Or I'll be deducting your wages myself."

Mrs. Sutter sent Charlie a relieved look, and they both got back to making boxes.

Returning home that evening, Charlie was satisfied with the day's work. She had learned some important information, especially about Emmett Brompton. Although Mrs. Sutter hadn't known the name of Brompton's friends—a "well-heeled gent and lady"

was all she recalled—she had provided details that the Angels or Jack's team could investigate further.

During Charlie's break, she had also snuck out to surveil the building where Mrs. Sutter had said the "machines" were stored. The wooden structure stood two stories tall with shuttered windows. There were exits at the front and back, guards posted at each. A pair also patrolled the grounds; when spotted by them, Charlie had pretended to be lost.

Her instincts told her Brompton's manufactory was hiding something sinister. She would convene with Devlin and figure out a plan to get into that mysterious back building tomorrow night. Although Mrs. Sutter had mentioned that the guards worked in shifts around the clock, between Charlie, Devlin, and Livy, they could create a distraction and get inside.

Charlie entered her bedchamber, more than ready to unwind with a bath and supper. Packing matches was hard work; her feet were killing her from standing all day. Moreover, Jack had been keeping her up at night. As much as she hated to admit it, he was right that she was in no shape to accompany him to the Public Records Office this evening. She would catch a few winks before he returned in the wee hours.

She rang, and her lady's maid came in a few minutes later, holding a package.

"This came for you, my lady," Jenny said.

Charlie took the parcel. Wrapped in plain brown paper and tied with twine, it felt solid...like a book. "Who delivered this?"

"That was the strange thing, my lady. Someone rang the bell and left the package on the doorstep."

Unease prickled Charlie's nape.

"Thank you, Jenny. Please have a supper tray readied."

After Jenny exited, Charlie sat down on her settee. She stared at the object in her lap, then took a breath and unwrapped it. Inside was a letter and volume bound in cognac leather.

She unfolded the missive. The handwriting was feminine,

embellished with swirls and curlicues. As she read the perfectly rendered lines, her blood turned cold.

To Whom It May Concern,

This is a true statement written on the 12th day of November, in the year of our Lord 1838.

I am Judith Courtenay, the Dowager Marchioness of Fayne, and I attest that a man named Jack Granger is responsible for the death of my son, Sebastian James Courtenay, the fifth Marquess of Fayne.

Mr. Granger entered my home as a servant and used his wiles and animal magnetism to take over my household. My family fell prey to his powers, and we did not realize the extent of his manipulation until it was far too late. He pretended to befriend my son Sebastian, a frail boy who was vulnerable to Mr. Granger's dominant and persuasive personality.

Prior to Mr. Granger's arrival, Sebastian and I had a close and affectionate relationship; by the time Mr. Granger left, he had caused a painful rift between my darling son and me. He sowed seeds of rebellion in Sebastian, causing him to leave home in a reckless, precipitous fashion once he reached his majority. Preying upon Sebastian's sense of honor and duty, Mr. Granger encouraged my son to engage in perilous espionage activities with the purpose of getting Sebastian killed.

How do I know Mr. Granger's intent? Because after Sebastian's death, Jack Granger assumed the identity of the Marquess of Fayne to enjoy the privileges of the esteemed title. He lived abroad to prevent his fraud from being detected. And, to guarantee my silence, he blackmailed me using as his weapon the greatest shame of my life. But for the sake of my son's memory and my own conscience, I can no longer keep quiet.

Mr. Granger seduced me. I have no excuse for my behavior except for the loneliness and isolation I suffered as a widow. As any

*who know Mr. Granger will attest, he is a charismatic man, and
he used his animal powers upon me. For five years, I was helpless to
his lustful advances. When I finally worked up the courage to resist,
he forced himself upon me. Repeatedly.*

*As a female in a world dominated by men, I know I am not
likely to be believed. Nonetheless, I have enclosed my diary which
faithfully documents my encounters with Jack Granger, which
ended when he left a year ago. I pray the world will see him for the
monster and murderer he is. He killed my son, ruined and abused
me, and stole a noble heritage. He must be prevented from manipu-
lating and controlling others for his own nefarious ends.*

Only then will my son rest in peace.

Lady Judith Fayne

Numbly, Charlie stared at the diary. It was unassuming and
ordinary...like an explosive device the instant before it detonated.
She tried to think, but her mind felt frozen and sluggish. *As a
female in a world dominated by men, I know I am not likely to be
believed.* Judith's words hit a chilling nerve of truth. Even so, a part
of Charlie wanted to trust Jack. Another part flashed to his past
deceptions, his betrayal, and the niggling feeling that she'd ignored
yet again: he still had secrets he wasn't telling her.

*Could Jack have done what Lady Judith Fayne claims? Could he
be...* She swallowed, forcing herself to confront the possibility. *A
rapist and a killer? Judith was his best friend's mama and the
woman he worked for, yet he has never spoken of her by name.
Because he's innocent...or because he has something to hide?*

Charlie had to find out. She'd dedicated her life to helping
women gain justice, and she couldn't resort to denial for the sake
of her own happiness. Because she was afraid to discover the true
nature of the man she'd fallen in love with.

With trembling hands, she opened the diary.

THIRTY-FOUR

It was past three in the morning by the time Jack returned to Lottie's. For the sake of caution, he came in through the back. He didn't want to risk being seen and doing damage to her spotless reputation.

A reputation that had been fairly earned.

You are the best, Jack. The only man for me.

As he walked through the darkened corridors, a foreign sense of pride rolled through him. Despite everything he'd done and his ignoble origins, Lottie accepted him. He couldn't wait for this business with the First Flame to be over so that he could propose and, hopefully, get her to say yes. To be his wife again, in name and forever.

For once in his life, things were going smoothly and according to plan. Yesterday, he'd told Primus about his plans to remarry Lottie and retire from espionage. The spymaster had disagreed, of course, with Jack's decision.

"After everything you have achieved, all my efforts to train you to become the spy you are today, how can you even consider giving it up for a woman?" Primus had snarled.

Easily and readily.

For the first time, Jack had not backed down to Primus. Not even when Primus reminded him of his shameful affair with Judith. That, he realized, was Lottie's effect on him. She made him recognize his own desires and needs, made him feel worthy of having them. She forgave his mistakes and did not use them as a weapon to coerce him...something that, he now painfully recognized, his mentor had no trouble doing.

Yes, he could not wait for the mission to be done with. To avenge Sebastian and do his part in eradicating evil. The discoveries he and Laurent had made brought them closer to tracking down the First Flame, and he hoped Lottie was awake so that he could share it with her.

And, admittedly, so that he could make love to her. The thrill of success made him randy as hell. He mounted the steps to her bedchamber, counseling himself to be considerate. If Lottie was asleep, he should let her rest. He would wait and bid her good morning with a lusty plowing.

That didn't stop his cock from stirring when he saw that her light was on.

A post-mission tup it is.

As the door was ajar, he didn't bother knocking. To his surprise, Lottie wasn't in bed but perched on the settee in the sitting area. She rose when he entered, and there was a guardedness to her expression that gave him pause.

Perhaps she was tired; it was late, after all.

"You did not have to wait up for me, sweeting," he said.

He went over, intending to kiss her.

She took a quick step back, evading him, and his unease grew.

"Did you have relations with Lady Judith Fayne?" she said coldly.

Jack's blood turned to ice. "How did...why are you asking me this?"

"Answer my question. Were you, or were you not, bedding Judith Courtenay for years?"

His gut seized, forcing bile up his throat. He couldn't answer her.

"Did you seduce her, Jack?" Lottie hissed. "Did you surprise her in her bath? Take her in the stables? Did you fuck Sebastian's mama in front of him to drive a wedge between the two?"

The memories crashed over him in a tide. He couldn't breathe. Then the undertow came—the guilt, the unrelenting shame pulling him under.

"What the bloody hell is going on?" Sebastian standing at the entry of the stall, yelling, the horses neighing. *"Get your hands off my mama, you dirty bastard!"*

Judith sobbing. *"Jack seduced me, I swear it. I told him it was wrong. I would never hurt you, my darling boy..."*

And Jack himself, naked, frozen, helpless. Knowing there were no words to take the pain and disgust out of his friend's eyes. To drain it from his own soul.

I didn't want this. I wanted it to stop. Being with her always felt wrong.

Who would believe a bastard like him? Who had ever believed in him?

Did he even believe in himself?

Realizing that his silence was damning, he swallowed back his self-loathing and tried to explain. "I didn't mean...I didn't want Sebastian to see us."

"But you were tupping his mama. For years."

Lottie's flat tone made him shrink inside.

He couldn't lie to her, didn't know what else to say. He gave a terse nod.

"And when she wanted you to stop, you forced yourself upon her." Her gaze hardened with revulsion. "You raped her."

"No." He had enough wherewithal to deny the false accusation. "I swear I never forced her. She wanted it. She was the one who—"

"I have heard that excuse before," Lottie snapped. "What about Sebastian? Did you kill him?"

The guilt that cinched his throat was more suffocating than shame. What made it worse was the horror in his beloved's gaze. The condemnation.

"I told you he died because of me," he said tonelessly. "I didn't lie to you."

"But you omitted some key truths."

Her voice trembled with pain and anger, and he couldn't blame her. Because even though he'd told himself he wasn't lying, he hadn't been honest either.

"After Sebastian found me in the stables with Judith, he understandably became enraged. He wanted nothing to do with either of us and ran off. He'd been going through his papa's effects and found certain coded missives that convinced him that his papa had been an agent for the Crown. He'd also found the name of his papa's contact and went to find him in London. That man, my spymaster, agreed to train him as a spy...and, well, you know the rest."

He stood, shoulders hunched, awaiting his wife's judgement. Wishing he had some way to convince her he was worthy, knowing that he was not. Knowing that he'd been fooling himself that he could ever be deserving of her.

"Why did you never mention Judith to me?" Lottie interrogated him as if she'd already found him guilty. "Was it because of what you did to her?"

Lottie stabbed a finger toward the settee, and such was his state of mind that he only now noticed the volume on the cushions. He recognized it immediately. Judith's diary—the one she'd created for the express purpose of blackmailing him. She'd wanted to use it as leverage to keep him as her own personal stud and sexual servant. In the end, Primus had obtained the vile journal at a great cost.

Jack knew, then, who was behind Lottie's newfound knowledge, but in that moment, it didn't matter. Because he'd read that diary from cover to cover and knew the despicable version of events Judith had penned. His gut lurched as if he were about to be sick: Lottie had read that toxic mix of twisted words and spiteful lies, and she...she had believed them.

Believed that he was a monster.

"It is not what you think." His tongue felt heavier than lead. "She made me...it wasn't what I wanted."

"She wrote about every encounter you had with her." Lottie's eyes were bright with contempt. "The depraved things you did to her. And when she wanted to end the affair, you assaulted her."

Although the diary was mostly fiction, there was a core of truth that made his insides writhe with shame. He *had* bedded Judith, his best friend's mama. He had done it for years. Even if he hadn't wanted to, he had done filthy things to her and let her do filthy things to him in return. His palms turned clammy, his insides roiling with humiliation and confusion.

I tried to end it, he wanted to say. *I didn't like the way she made me feel.*

But Judith purred in his ear. *See how hard you are, Jack. You want this. You cannot get enough...*

A man owns up to his mistakes. Primus's voice. *You let lust get the better of you, and now you must deal with the consequences.*

Numbness spread through Jack. The detachment was as familiar as an old blanket. Wrapping himself in it felt better than the bullies' fists, Judith's debased games, Sebastian's last gurgling breaths. It had even allowed him to endure twelve years of separation from his beloved...but why wasn't it helping now?

"What I did was wrong," he said dully.

"Your contrition means nothing," she said bitterly. "I cannot trust you, Jack. And what you did to Judith, to Sebastian..." Loathing contorted her features. "You disgust me."

That makes two of us.

"I love you. If you would let me explain..."

He hated the edge of desperation in his voice, but he couldn't give up. Not when she was the one thing—the only thing—he'd ever wanted for himself. He willed her to understand, to give him a chance...

"Get out," she said flatly.

"Lottie—"

"You've promised me time and again that the best is still to come. But it *never does*. It is over between us—this time, for good."

The finality in her voice gutted him.

"You will leave my home now, and you will not return." Her eyes gleamed, not with loving wisdom, but with the steely armor of animosity. "For the remainder of this mission, kindly direct all communication through another member of your team. And when this is over, I never wish to see you again."

THIRTY-FIVE

"You look like hell," Delaney said.

Laurent gave her a nudge; she nudged him back with enough force to make him grunt.

"What?" she challenged. "That carcass over there looks livelier."

Jack and his team were at the butcher shop. Mr. Campbell had ushered the four of them into the back room with his usual boisterousness. It was shy of nine in the morning, and Jack hadn't slept. Since Lottie had kicked him out in the middle of the night, he hadn't found lodgings yet and was too miserable to look.

It's over. What I thought was a new beginning was merely the end of a dream I held onto for twelve years too long.

He was who he was. A depraved and selfish bastard who hurt people time and again and deserved what he had coming. He'd done the right thing in leaving Lottie the first time; his mistake was returning. In believing, for even an instant, that he was worthy of her...of happiness. Anguish welled inside him, but numbness came to the rescue again. With practiced ease, he shut out the demons roaring in his head and focused on the mission.

"*Niños.*" Calderone stepped between Laurent and Delaney. "Must we bicker at this ungodly hour?"

Laurent cleared his throat. "You do look rather worse for the wear, Granger. Too excited to sleep after our successful foray last night?"

"What did you discover?" Delaney demanded.

"Just that the property upon which Brompton's Works is built was sold to a company called Wilmer Upholsteries." Laurent buffed his nails against his lapel.

Delaney frowned. "What would an upholstery business want with a match factory?"

"After the Public Records Office, we stopped by Wilmer's warehouse in Spitalfields to see if we could find out," Jack replied. "We let ourselves in and found nothing of note, except receipts indicating that they do business with the London Joint Stock Bank on Princes Street. I will go there today and see if I can get information about the account holders associated with Wilmer."

"I hate bankers. They're like clams," Delaney muttered.

"In the interim," Jack said, "I need one of you to report this new development to my...to Lady Fayne."

His colleagues exchanged a look.

Laurent spoke first. "Er, did you not inform her when you saw her last night?"

Might as well get this over with.

"I am no longer a guest of Lady Fayne," Jack said flatly. "And whilst she will continue to work on the mission, she has requested that someone other than myself act as liaison for our team."

"*Problemas en el paraíso,*" Calderone murmured.

"That's colder than a whore's farewell." Delaney slapped her hands on her hips, her brows arched. "What did you do, Granger?"

"Why do you assume he did anything?" Laurent said.

"Because he is a man, obviously."

"Maybe his lady changed her mind. Since she is a woman, obviously."

"Stop it, you two." In no mood for their bickering, Jack cut to the chase. "Lady Fayne learned something of my past that changed her opinion of me, and rightly so. That is all I will say. Now who of you will be the liaison?"

"Your lady would prefer one of them." Delaney jerked a thumb at Laurent and Calderone.

"Laurent it is," Jack said shortly. "Now, what progress have you made on the Bromptons?"

"Quite a bit," Delaney said smugly. "Turns out Emmett Brompton, the heir apparent to the company, is a neck-or-nothing cove, especially when it comes to cards. Half the moneylenders in London held his vowels at some point, but something changed in the past year."

Jack's nape prickled. "His debts mysteriously got paid off?"

"Exactly," Delaney replied. "But now that we know Wilmer Upholsteries owns the Brompton's Works, it's not a mystery after all. He sold the property without telling anyone, and they've let him stay on as if nothing had changed."

"This bears similarities to Tony Quinton's situation," Jack said. "We have a gambler whose debts are paid off by a mysterious benefactor. The fellow then becomes beholden to said party. The party then uses the man toward their ends: in Quinton's case, his skill as a sailor to bring in some sort of cargo. In Emmett Brompton's case, they wanted his match manufactory...but why?"

"Perhaps Lady Fayne might know based on her surveillance of the factory?" Laurent suggested.

Bloody hell, Laurent was right. Last night, things between Jack and Lottie had disintegrated to such a degree that they'd forgotten about work. Not only had Jack destroyed his marriage, but he was also bungling up the assignment as well.

"I shall relay her a message," he said tersely.

"One more thing." Delaney held up a finger. "Emmett Brompton might be missing."

Laurent's brows elevated. "Might be?"

"I overheard his maids saying that he hasn't been home in five days. He didn't take a bag or his valet, so he's not on a trip. It's possible that he's holed up in a brothel somewhere. Apparently, he has a penchant for the birch."

"Brothels and flagellation, eh?" Laurent smirked. "I volunteer to look for the cove."

Jack nodded. "Good idea. Brompton may be able to tell us what Wilmer is up to."

Calderone sighed. "I had better accompany Laurent. No telling what trouble he may get into otherwise."

The pair departed.

Delaney, however, remained. And she was staring at Jack in a manner that made him feel as bare as the de-feathered fowl swinging from hooks.

"If you find yourself with idle time," he said curtly, "you can help me dig into Wilmer's financials—"

"You did this the last time," Delaney said.

"Did what?"

"Ran away. From your wife."

Emotion rammed against the numbness in his chest.

"I did not run away," he said tightly. "I corrected a mistake that I should not have made."

"Semantics." She shook her head. "You never learn, do you?"

"What the bloody hell is that supposed to mean?"

"What was the mistake you made, Granger?"

"I married Charlotte. Dragged her into the mess that is my existence. Something I had no business doing."

"Wrong." Delaney braced her hands on her waist. "How long have we known each other?"

"Too long, obviously," he muttered. "If you feel entitled to pry into my affairs."

"Fifteen years," she said as if he hadn't spoken. "In all that time, how often have I seen you happy?"

The feelings inside him swelled, his throat constricting.

"Two times," she informed him. "The first time was when you wed your lady. The second, when you returned to her. In between, you were bleeding miserable. Half-alive, going through the motions like a blasted automaton."

Delaney wasn't wrong.

"I don't deserve her," he said tautly. "After the things I've done—"

"You, me, Laurent—we've all done things. As nasty as those things might have been, they were done in the service of good."

"I meant even before the espionage."

Delaney squinted at him. "Did Primus tell you that?"

"Tell me what?"

"Did he sell you the notion," she said succinctly, "that you had to redeem your past by working for him?"

Feeling a fissure in his numbness, Jack shifted on his feet.

"He did. Blooming hell, you didn't actually *buy* his snake oil, did you?"

"I committed an unpardonable sin," Jack said gruffly. "Primus gave me a way to better myself."

"No, Granger. Primus gave *himself* a loyal and obedient underling to do his bidding. That is what we are to him, you know. Useful pawns in his game."

Cracks spread through Jack's wall of detachment. Because she was right. Primus *was* ruthless and expedient, and Jack had always known this. In fact, he hadn't been surprised that Primus had sent Lottie the diary. The spymaster used everything at his disposal—including those who worked for him—to achieve what he wanted.

"Why do you continue to work for him?" Jack asked suddenly.

"Because I use Primus as much as he uses me." Delaney spoke as if Jack might lack basic intelligence. "The codger has made me rich, helped me hone my natural talents, and freed me from boredom—and by that, I mean a life where I must answer to a husband and have a brace of brats hanging on my apron strings. Marital bliss ain't for all. In return, I help Primus battle evil. Seems like a fair exchange; I might even come out ahead. But you..."

"What about me?"

But Jack already knew. Feeling was seeping through, a wash of scarlet over his senses.

"Primus is using you, and you're too decent a fellow to use him back. For you, the scales will never be balanced. You are also his favorite and second-in-command, which means Primus will do whatever it takes to keep you under his thumb."

"I told Primus that I was getting back together with Lottie," Jack bit out. "That I was leaving espionage behind. He turned around and instigated a rift between her and me."

"Ingenious but unsurprising." Delaney quirked a brow. "What are you going to do about it?"

He shoved a hand through his hair because he didn't know. Didn't know how he could convince Lottie that while he was far from perfect, he wasn't the monster Judith made him out to be. But he did know one thing.

"I am not going to run away," he said with sudden clarity. "Not this time. Even if I have to spend the rest of my life proving to Lottie that I am worthy of her, I will."

Delaney cuffed him on the shoulder. "That's the spirit."

He looked past the hardness in her eyes and saw kindness.

"Thank you," he said.

"Thank me by never mentioning this conversation again." She headed for the door, slamming it behind her.

Jack was about to depart when Campbell appeared, steaming cups in hand.

"Thought you could use a cup o' my brew before you go," the butcher said.

"That is kind of you, sir." Gratefully, Jack downed the strong, bitter tea.

"That'll put hair on your chest, eh?" Campbell clapped him on the shoulder. "Everything all right? You look a might worse for the wear."

"Just a temporary problem. One I plan to fix." Jack set down the empty cup. "Thank you for the tea."

THIRTY-SIX

That evening, Charlie headed over to the Hadleighs' home to prepare for the night's expedition. She was exhausted for she hadn't slept after the confrontation with Jack. After a bout of crying, she'd pulled herself together and left for the manufactory. She'd wanted to count the guards and observe their patterns in preparation for tonight. Truth be told, she'd also needed the distraction.

The last thing she wanted was to be alone with her thoughts.

Or to be alone at all...which, it seemed, she was destined to be.

She shut out the morose thoughts. She wasn't going to allow Jack to send her into a spiral of grief and loss again. How could one grieve a lover one had never really known? The Jack whom Judith Courtenay had accused of being a rapist, manipulator, and murderer was not the man Charlie thought she knew.

Even with all the damning evidence, she had expected, nay prayed, that he would have some explanation. Some perfectly reasonable response to it all. Instead, he hadn't denied any of it... well, except for forcing Judith. Yet his claim that "she wanted it" was too familiar to Charlie: it was the refrain of men who blamed their victims for the assault.

All these years of running an investigative society has obviously not improved my judgement. The irony curdled her stomach. *I was the one who was taken in, over and over. Who was played a fool. Who fell in love—again—with a man who may be a predator.*

While Charlie struggled to believe that Jack was capable of evil, why would Judith lie? At this point, Charlie was too drained to sort fact from fiction; she needed to get through the mission tonight. Arriving at the Hadleighs', she managed to put on a smile. The smile became genuine when she saw Livy and Hadleigh's pretty dark-haired toddler, Esmerelda, clinging to her papa's knee.

"Esme was supposed to be off to bed," Livy said. "But she insisted on staying up to say goodnight to her Aunt Charlie."

Charlie bent to be eye-level with Esme.

"I am honored, Lady Esme," she said.

Esme's eyes, green like Livy's, studied Charlie.

"Aunt Char-wee go bed too," Esme announced. "She look ti-werd."

Out of the mouths of babes.

"All right, dearest," Livy said hastily. "It's off to bed with Nurse now."

"Want Papa." Esme held up her arms to His Grace. "Papa read *best* story."

Smiling, Hadleigh scooped her up and tossed her into the air, to her giggling delight. With a stab of pain, Charlie realized she'd had daydreams about this sort of scenario with Jack. In her fantasies, he'd been a doting papa, one determined to give his children the paternal love that he, himself, had never known.

"One story, poppet. Then it's bedtime."

"Two," Esme wheedled as Hadleigh carried her out. "I want two stories, Papa!"

"She is a handful," Livy said ruefully.

"She is adorable and takes after you."

"That is what Hadleigh says." With an impish grin, Livy said, "Let us get ready upstairs."

They headed to Livy's spacious sitting room, where a table had been set up with a generous supper collation. Beneath her cloak, Charlie had on dark, masculine attire suitable for the mission, and Livy quickly changed into a similar outfit. This left them with time before Devlin arrived. He and Hadleigh would be escorting them to Brompton's. The plan was for the men to divert the guards whilst Livy and Charlie searched the building.

"Aren't you going to eat something, Charlie?" Livy asked.

"I am not hungry, dearest." Charlie poured herself a cup of tea. "Please help yourself."

Livy brought a plate over, joining Charlie on the settee. "Are you all right?"

Charlie had made it a rule not to lie to her Angels.

"No," she admitted. "But you needn't worry. My personal affairs will not interfere this eve."

"By personal, are you referring to Mr. Granger?" Livy ventured.

"I would prefer not to discuss it."

"But discussing it might make you feel better." Livy popped a bite-sized sausage roll into her mouth, golden flakes raining over her plate. Swallowing, she said, "That was true for me when Hadleigh and I were first getting together."

Charlie smiled. "You were a debutante in the first blushes of love; it was natural for you to solicit the advice of friends. I am a widow, however, a woman of experience who should be able to handle her own affairs."

"A woman needs friends at any age," Livy said stoutly. "You've taught us that sisterhood is key. Being independent doesn't mean being an island; it means being strong and wise enough to rely on your friends when needed."

Charlie bit her lip; Livy was right.

"Even though you are my mentor, Charlie, you are also my friend," Livy went on earnestly. "I would trust you with any knotty issue, and I hope you feel the same about me."

"I do." Charlie sighed. "It's complicated. Between Mr. Granger and me."

"Love is seldom anything but," Livy said sagely. "I know this from personal experience."

Because she knew that Livy's road to love had had its share of twists and turns, Charlie gave in to the need to confide. She gave a condensed but accurate version of her relationship with Jack, from the first time they met to the last.

Livy's eyes were rounded. "Do you believe Lady Judith Fayne's claims about Mr. Granger?"

"He did not deny them," Charlie said flatly. "Except the charge of assault. To which he replied, *She wanted it.*"

"I see." Livy furrowed her brow. "How old is Mr. Granger?"

"Thirty-five. What does that matter?"

"Well, I am trying to understand the timeline of events," Livy said in her logical way. "The way I do with a case. It often gives me insights I might have otherwise missed. If Mr. Granger is currently thirty-five, then when he and you met he was, what, twenty-three?"

Charlie nodded slowly.

"When did Judith pass away?"

An unpleasant tingle crossed her nape. "A year before Jack and I met, I believe."

"And the letter she wrote. When was it dated?"

"That same year. 1838."

"Right. And at that time, Mr. Granger would have been..."

"Twenty-two." The realization rammed into Charlie like an oncoming carriage, knocking her breath from her. "He was only twenty-two. And in the letter, Judith claimed he'd left a year before that."

"Which made him twenty-one when the affair ended. Since she wrote that their relations lasted for five years, it must have started when he was sixteen."

Sixteen. Just a lad.

"How old was Judith at the time?"

"I...I am not sure. But her son was only two years younger than Jack."

"Wait, I've got it. I'll be right back." Setting down her plate, Livy dashed off.

Charlie remained where she was, mired in panic and self-recrimination.

How could I have overlooked this? How could I have assumed the worst of Jack when I did not have all the facts? But why did he not speak up?

She shut her eyes then, remembering. Remembering that he had tried.

It is not what you think, he'd said. *It wasn't what I wanted.*

Livy returned, lugging a massive red leather volume.

"I knew I had a copy of Debrett's. Esme was using it as a step-stool." She sat next to Charlie, leafing through the pages. "Ah, here it is. The Fayne family tree. Judith Alice Courtenay, nee Berry, born 1800."

"She was sixteen years older than Jack." Charlie's heart splintered as the facts sank in. "If he was sixteen when their relationship began, she was thirty-two. A woman who'd been married and had a child. He was her servant, a poor orphaned bastard starting his first job. Whereas she was his employer, twice his age, and a wealthy woman of privilege. Between them, she was the one with more power."

"It seems unlikely that Mr. Granger had the clout to force Lady Fayne into anything. Or that she was innocent in all of this," Livy said thoughtfully. "But why didn't he counter her claims?"

"He tried to." Charlie's eyes heated with shame. "I wouldn't listen. After reading that noxious diary, I was so distressed I wasn't thinking properly—"

"It's the work we do," Livy said. "The darkness predisposes one to think the worst. Many of our clients are victims of the crimes Judith described. Since you've made it your purpose to help those women find justice, it is natural that you would give credence to her assertions."

While this was undoubtedly true, Charlie knew it did not excuse her behavior.

"I jumped to the worst conclusions about Jack," she said with self-loathing. "It's true that he didn't tell me about Judith, but I can understand why he didn't."

From everything Charlie knew of Jack's character, he was a protector who put everyone before himself. Indeed, he had left her because he thought she would be better off without him. Yes, he hadn't always been honest, but that had been part of being a spy. His intent was to do good and avenge his friend, whose death he felt responsible for even though it wasn't his fault. He couldn't control Sebastian's actions any more than he could those of Sebastian's mother.

Yet that was Jack: noble and selfless to a fault. If Lady Judith Fayne had seduced him, an impoverished, young lad, then *he* was the victim and not her. But Jack wouldn't see it that way. He would blame himself—as was his habit—and Charlie had inadvertently reinforced his erroneous belief.

"I thought he was a monster." A tear spilled over, wending down her cheek. "I didn't give him the benefit of the doubt, a chance to tell his side…"

"Given what you read in the diary, your reaction was understandable," Livy said gently. "Judith seems quite clever, twisting the narrative to suit her purpose. She used her position of privilege to her advantage. Even if Mr. Granger countered her version of events, who would take the word of an orphaned bastard servant over that of a marchioness?"

"I would. I *should* have," Charlie said fiercely. "The reason I started the Angels was to serve those who have been subjected to abuses of power—no matter who the abuser is. You know we have stopped both male and female predators. We protect those who cannot protect themselves. That is the true mission of our sisterhood."

"Do you know why Judith might have wished to discredit Mr. Granger?"

"I have a few ideas," Charlie said grimly.

According to Jack, his superior had negotiated with the woman to gain her acceptance of their plan for him to become Sebastian. She'd agreed out of self-interest: to continue living in the style to which she was accustomed. It was no stretch to assume that a mama who would sell her dead son's name would have little difficulty fabricating a diary to use for extortion. For more money or some other sort of leverage.

Livy nodded. "And have you thought about who sent you the diary? Clearly, he or she wanted to create trouble between you and Mr. Granger."

"Jack's superior comes to mind," she said flatly. "He probably sees me as a threat to Jack's career, especially since Jack proposed again."

"Oh, Charlie. I am so happy for you!" Livy clasped her hands in delight. "Will the Angels and I be your matrons of honor?"

"If there is a wedding." A spasm hit Charlie's chest. "After how I've acted, I don't know if Jack will forgive me. If I *deserve* to be forgiven."

"Love is about forgiveness," Livy said. "I deceived Hadleigh for most of our courtship. Look how well that turned out."

Charlie gave her protegee a wry look. "Are you certain that is the lesson of that experience?"

"My point is, Hadleigh forgave me my ruse because he understood me. And I forgave him his boorishness because I know him. That is the power of love."

"I hope you are right."

After tonight's excursion, Charlie would search Jack out. Apologize. Then she would do what she ought to have done in the first place: listen and try to understand.

Half past midnight, Charlie and her team landed on the grounds of the manufactory.

Charlie had scouted the front entrance; seeing only a pair of sleepy-looking guards posted at the gate and no patrolmen, she'd revised the strategy. Instead of creating a diversion, Devlin and Hadleigh accompanied her and Livy, the four of them scaling the back wall. Now they were on the grounds, the buildings looming beasts in the darkness, drifts of fog heightening the eerie scene.

"It is too quiet," Devlin murmured. "Where are all the guards?"

Charlie did not like it either. "Stay alert, everyone. We stick to the plan. Devlin and Hadleigh will cover Livy and I whilst we get into the building."

Both men nodded, their weapons drawn.

She led the way to the building, Livy following close behind. They stuck to the shadows and blended into the night. As they neared their destination, the moon shone through the fog, plating the front door in bright silver.

"It's too exposed," Charlie whispered. "We'll go around the back."

Livy nodded, and they moved stealthily to the rear of the building. Again, there were no guards. Using her lock picks, Charlie gained access. She pushed the door open, freezing at the slight squeal of hinges. When no patrol rushed over, she and Livy slipped inside. The gloom of the cavernous space was broken by ribbons of moonlight slipping through the shutters.

Charlie lit the candle she'd brought with her. Holding it up, she circled the room in case she was missing something. There were only a few scattered tables, their surfaces bare.

"There's nothing here," Livy said, her voice hushed.

At the soft scrape of footsteps, Charlie whirled around, yanking out her pistol. Livy's blades flashed in her hands as she, too, faced the newcomers. But it was Devlin and Hadleigh...and a woman Charlie recognized immediately.

What is Maria Delaney doing here?

"It's Granger," the spy said grimly. "He's been taken."

She handed Charlie a note, and Charlie's heart lodged in her throat.

Stop meddling in our affairs, or Granger dies.

THIRTY-SEVEN

Charlie convened an emergency meeting at eight o'clock that morning.

Her worry for Jack had made it impossible to sleep during the few hours since her return home. A part of her had wanted to rally the forces and comb London in search of him. But Maria had told her not to waste her energy.

"We don't know where to look," the spy had said. *"Turning London inside out will accomplish nothing, except maybe endanger Granger's life. For now, he is the First Flame's bargaining chip, which means he's safe as long as the bastards believe we are backing off. To find him, we need to find* them, *and we need to be stealthy about it. Which means we need a plan."*

Realizing that Maria was right, Charlie had put a lid on her panic. She'd summoned the Angels and their husbands whilst the other had gotten the word out to her team. Laurent and Calderone had arrived early and were making inroads into the breakfast offerings on the sideboard. Primus had yet to show, and Maria was not confident that he would. She characterized her leader as ruthless and expedient, to the extent that Jack's abduction might not be sufficient for him to compromise his cover.

Whilst Maria and her colleagues were there for Jack, they also remained mum on Primus's identity. The spies might be hardened by life, but they were loyal. Charlie found herself warming to them, Maria especially. Without the distorting veil of jealousy, she could admire the woman's pluck and no-nonsense attitude.

Charlie tapped a glass, drawing everyone's attention to start the meeting.

The door swung open, and Livy and Hadleigh hurried in.

"Apologies for our late arrival," Livy said breathlessly. "We have news!"

Hope pounded in Charlie's heart. "Tell us."

"I heard from Uncle Harry this morning," Livy said excitedly. "He's identified the solution as a combination of white phosphorus and carbon disulfide. He said both substances are volatile on their own. Combined as they are, all it takes is exposure to air and..."

She moved her hands outward, her breath whooshing out in an explosive sound.

"White phosphorus is used in making matches," Charlie said alertly. "That explains why the First Flame wanted Brompton's."

"Perhaps Tony Quinton was shipping in carbon disulfide from France," Maria postulated.

"According to Uncle Harry, a sufficient quantity of white phosphorus and carbon disulfide could create a fiery explosion," Livy said. "One that would burn down a city block."

The room grew hushed as everyone took in the enormity of the situation.

"We must warn the authorities," Fiona declared.

"I will send word to my contact at the police," Charlie said.

"The police are already on alert." This came from the Earl of Hawksmoor. "Given the crowds here for the opening of the Great Exhibition, their resources are stretched thin just keeping the peace. They need more than a possible weapon and a shadowy anarchist group. They need to know when and where the attack will take place and who is behind it. It is my understanding that Her Majesty the Queen and His Royal Highness Prince Albert have been advised on the situation but are refusing to change their plans for the opening day ceremony. The purpose of the exhibition is to demonstrate the power of progress, and they will not bow down to terror."

"How is it that you know so much about these affairs, my lord?" Laurent asked shrewdly.

"The same way, I imagine, that you do, sir." Hawksmoor's countenance was bland. "I will add that several searches have been done of the Crystal Palace. No threats have been found."

"The security forces are forewarned, but we need to give them more," Charlie said with determined focus. "Which brings us to Wilmer Upholsteries."

Livy drew her brows together. "Is *upholsteries* a word?"

"It's plural," her husband said. "For *upholstery*."

For his helpfulness, the duke received an exasperated sigh from his duchess.

"What does an upholstery company have to do with anything?" Fi wanted to know.

Charlie turned to Maria. "For that, I shall give the floor to Miss Delaney."

Maria, who'd been leaning against a wall, straightened to address the group.

"Granger and Laurent discovered that Wilmer Upholsteries purchased the match manufactory. Now we know why—to gain access to the white phosphorus. We also know that Emmett Brompton probably sold his inheritance to pay off his gambling debts."

"If we interrogate Mr. Brompton," Glory cut in, "maybe he can tell us who owns Wilmer Upholsteries."

"We'd have to find him first," Maria replied. "He hasn't been home for days. Laurent and Calderone checked all his usual places, too."

"No one has seen Brompton," Calderone said. "We think he has gone for a swim in the Thames."

At the euphemism for murder, the room went silent.

"That is no coincidence," Charlie said quietly. "He knew too much, and they got rid of him."

"Wilmer is key to all of this," Maria agreed. "Granger was digging into the ownership and financials of the company yesterday, and we were supposed to meet up, but he didn't show. Instead, I found that note threatening his life if we didn't stand down."

Charlie fought back the surge of anxiety. Told herself that Jack was a seasoned spymaster, a survivor, and could handle himself. Her job was to find the people who'd taken him—

A sudden, obvious thought struck her.

"Is Wilmer's presenting at the Great Exhibition?"

The words had barely left her when Glory visibly jolted, causing FF II to leap from her shoulders and seek refuge with Chen, who stood behind her chair.

"Do you know the answer, little tigress?" Chen said attentively.

"No, but I know where to find it." Glory rummaged through the large satchel she'd brought with her, pulling out a red volume and waving it triumphantly. "I managed to get a copy of Routledge's guide to the Great Exhibition before it sold out. Not only does it have a map of the Crystal Palace, but it also has a list of all the exhibitors."

Charlie and the other Angels gathered around her as she flipped through the pages.

"Ah, here is the section on fabrics and textiles," she exclaimed. "And an alphabetical listing of the exhibitors..."

Charlie's breath held. *If only it could be this easy...*

"Wilmer Upholsteries is not listed." Glory blew out a breath. "So much for that idea."

"Disproving a theory is as important as confirming it." Chen gave her shoulder a consoling squeeze. "Now we know Wilmer will not have a booth showcasing explosive material."

"Was that a pun, old boy?" Hadleigh said with faint humor.

"Let us refocus," Charlie said resolutely. "We need to find out who is behind Wilmer."

Fi canted her head. "Why don't you ask Bernadette? She seems to know everything when it comes to fashion and society. And she owes you a favor."

"That is a *brilliant* notion." Excitement flooded Charlie. "I'll go to her straightaway."

"Who is Bernadette?" Maria asked.

"A friend of ours," Charlie said smoothly. "She writes articles for a magazine that covers the latest trends in fashion."

"As fashion is not my forte, I'll leave it up to you. Laurent, Calderone, and I will pick up where Granger left off and try to track Wilmer's financials to its owners." Maria pursed her lips. "I don't need to say this, but we must all be discreet. If the First Flame discovers that we are not standing down, they will not hesitate to retaliate."

At the word *retaliate*, Charlie had to draw a calming breath.

"As to that," she said. "I have been thinking that the First Flame seems to be one step ahead of us. How did they know to empty the manufactory? How did they know about Jack?"

Maria narrowed her eyes. "You are saying there is a leak."

"I am saying the First Flame seems to have first-hand knowledge of our plans."

"Are you accusing one of us?" Laurent said tersely.

He and Calderone flanked Maria.

The Angels moved closer to Charlie, but she waved them back.

"I am saying that, twice now, the First Flame has anticipated our moves," she said evenly. "And I do not believe there is a problem on my end."

Maria's eyes flashed. "How dare you—"

The door opened.

Charlie was stunned to see Sir Hewitt Lancaster strut into her drawing room.

Why would the butler let him in...?

The realization hit her at the same moment that he spoke.

"My apologies for my tardiness," he said brusquely. "I'm afraid I had a problem with a pest."

"Pest, sir?" Maria tilted her head at her superior.

"A mole," the spymaster replied. "I have taken care of it."

The meeting ended on a note of hope.

There was a plan in place to find Jack. His colleagues were pursuing Wilmer via a financial angle; Charlie was investigating a social one via Bernadette. Livy and Hadleigh would surveil the match manufactory for any leads. Pippa and her husband, Timothy Cullen, were leading a team of mudlarks to keep watch for suspicious activity around the Crystal Palace. Fi and Glory, along with their spouses, were analyzing what they knew about the First Flame's explosive weapon and the exhibition to determine the most likely scenarios for the attack and how to prevent, or at least contain, the possible damage.

Although her business with Bernadette was urgent, Charlie had another matter to attend to first. She faced Sir Lancaster in her study, and neither of them bothered to sit.

"Thank you for meeting with me," the spymaster said. "Given the pressing situation, this will necessarily be brief."

"Yes, it will," she said with disdain. "For Jack's sake, I am cooperating with you. But my tolerance of your presence does not signify trust or respect, and I think you know why."

"The diary." Sir Lancaster's craggy features showed no remorse.

Maria is right. The bounder has no conscience or care for anything but his mission.

"I admit it was a mistake," he said.

"Your *mistake* nearly destroyed my relationship," she shot back. "If not for your poison, Jack and I would not have fought. He might have been in a better state of mind—perhaps he would not have been taken. But that is not the only reason why you've earned my hostility, sir."

Sir Lancaster waited with the patience of a cat preparing to pounce.

"You knew what happened to Jack, and you didn't help him." Her voice throbbed with emotion she couldn't, and didn't want to, hold back. "Instead, you used his situation to manipulate him and make him into your soldier."

"That is untrue," Lancaster said rigidly. "I gave him a chance at *redemption*."

"He did not need redemption!" Tears blurred her vision, and she was too angry to care. "I know Jack, and I don't believe he did anything to Lady Judith Fayne. The accusations of rape, murder... she made those up for her own gain, didn't she?"

"Yes," Lancaster said with distaste. "Lady Judith Fayne was a vile, self-serving female. Granger, however, bears fault as well. He had the poor judgement to have an affair with her. For years."

"He was an *adolescent* who was preyed upon by a woman sixteen years his senior. A woman with power and wealth who coerced her teenaged servant."

"No woman could physically force Granger, even at that age—"

"Coercion has many forms, not just physical force," Charlie retorted.

It is not what you think, Jack had said. *She made me...it wasn't what I wanted.*

Charlie's heart clenched with remorse. "I would wager this house that Jack tried to end the affair, but Judith used emotional manipulation to trap him. And instead of helping him, you blamed him. To suit your purposes, you gave him a new identity because you knew he despised himself enough to go along with your plan. You, sir, are as much a predator, a monster, as Lady Judith Fayne."

Her chest heaving, she was glad to see animosity spark in Lancaster's dark eyes. She wanted to do battle, to draw blood from this bounder who had hurt her Jack.

"That is bloody nonsense," Lancaster snapped. "I saved Granger. Even if he was less experienced than that woman, he should have exercised better judgement. A man must take responsibility for his actions. For his mistakes. If he allows a woman to manipulate him, then he must accept the consequences. The only way for him to redeem himself is by correcting his mistakes, by whatever means necessary. Whatever it takes, he must do it."

Despite her fury, Charlie noted the flush on Lancaster's jowls, the balling of his hands.

And she knew.

"Are you speaking about Jack," she said coldly. "Or about yourself?"

Demons surfaced in Lancaster's gaze. The next instant, he locked them away.

"I helped Granger," he said in clipped tones. "If it weren't for me, he would be a nobody—a servant who'd stupidly swived his own mistress. Because of me, he is a man of wealth and skill. I showed him his true calling as a spymaster."

"Because of you, his life is in jeopardy," Charlie retorted. "When this case is over, know that I will do everything in my power to protect Jack from *you*. If he wishes to continue working as a spymaster, that will be on his own terms. Not because he is manipulated and coerced into it."

Lancaster sputtered, "I never coerced—"

"I do not have time to argue with you," she said. "I have to find Jack."

He glared at her; she returned his look with a steely one of her own.

She knew she won that battle when he stalked out, slamming the door behind him.

THIRTY-EIGHT

J ack awoke in suffocating darkness.

He gulped frantically for air, then realized he was gagged. He inhaled through his nose, drawing in acrid air that burned his nostrils. But it eased the straining of his lungs and shocked his sluggish brain into working.

Keep breathing. Stay calm. Figure out what happened.

As his respiration steadied, his senses sharpened. He was lying on the ground, and his hands were bound behind him. There was something gritty against his cheek. He maneuvered himself into a sitting position and heard the clank of chains. A shackle weighed down his right ankle.

The pungent smell in his nostrils was ubiquitous: coal. The damp air and relentless gloom felt subterranean...a coal cellar. As his eyes adjusted to the dimness, he could make out lumpy piles along the walls. He listened intently, but all he picked up was the scurrying of vermin. No voices or footsteps. None of the hustle and bustle of London streets.

Where is this cellar? How did I get here?

A wave of dizziness swamped him, and he fought to remain clear-headed. To remember. He'd had a cup of tea with Campbell, then hailed a hackney to London Joint Stock Bank. But the hackney had taken a wrong turn into an alley and stopped. Brutes had emerged from nowhere, and he'd tried to fight them off, but he'd been weak, dizzy for some reason...

The tea. Bloody hell.

As the betrayal sank in, his first thought was for his colleagues. If Campbell had been compromised—if he'd found a way to eavesdrop on the team's meetings—then the First Flame knew everything. It explained why the bounders had remained a step ahead.

Christ, I have to warn the others—to warn Lottie.

Determination cleared his head. To help them, he had to get himself free first.

Bracing his back against a wall, he managed to get to his feet. He took a few measured steps to ascertain he had his balance. Then he set about getting his bearings. The chain only allowed him to take four steps in any direction and was connected to a ring embedded in the brick wall. He tested his cuffed leg, trying to see if the chain might give. No such luck.

Suddenly, he remembered.

The Quintons' pen.

Obviously, whoever had abducted him had taken his weapons; did they bother to take the writing instrument in his inner coat pocket? He couldn't reach to see if the pen was still there, but he thought he felt its scant but precious heft. If he could free his hands, he could use the lock picks to unlock the manacle and find a way out.

How do I cut the rope binding my wrists?

He felt his way along the wall, trying to find a nail, anything with a sharp edge. He got to a section where the coal was piled too high, blocking his access to the wall. He used his feet to clear the area. He was near the bottom of a pile when his foot encountered something solid. At first, he thought he'd hit the ground, but when he kicked it again, the object shifted, coming loose from the depths of coal.

It felt heavy against his foot, the shape of...a coal shovel.

Thank you, God.

He crouched, feeling for the shovel with his hands. His fingers brushed a metal edge. It was blunted from years of use, but it might be enough to saw through the ropes. His ears pricked at faint noises. They grew louder...descending footsteps. Hurriedly, he rose, kicking coal over his buried treasure as fast as he could.

Keys clanged on a ring, and the lock clicked.

He whirled to face the opening door, the sudden flare of lamps blinding. He squinted, glimpsing four silhouettes. One of them stepped forward.

"Welcome back, Mr. Granger," she said.

Bernadette did not prove easy to find. Charlie first checked at the offices of *The Englishwoman at Home*, where one of the other writers thought the American was out researching the latest fashions in millinery. Visiting each of the suggested shops, Charlie came up empty and decided to wait at Bernadette's lodging house by Earl's Court. Just when she was about to move on, Bernadette showed up.

Since boarders filled the parlors, Bernadette suggested they take a stroll, and Charlie readily agreed. They found a bench in a nearby square to talk.

"We are lucky we nabbed this bench," Bernadette said. "With the Great Exhibition opening tomorrow, the crowds are everywhere. I couldn't even get a seat on the omnibus...but I presume you haven't come to make chitchat. What can I do for you, Lady Fayne?"

"I have come to seek your professional knowledge. About a matter of some delicacy."

"Delicacy?" Bernadette waggled her brows. "Oh, goody. I sense a juicy story. But never fear, my lips are sealed."

"I need information. About a company called Wilmer Upholsteries."

"What about them?" Bernadette said promptly.

"Anything you've heard could be useful. In particular, I wish to know who owns this company and how they came to be so popular in a short time."

"You and every upholsterer in the business," Bernadette said with a snort. "A few months ago, Wilmer came out of nowhere and became an overnight sensation. To do research on the latest household décor, I went to their warehouse. I wanted to speak to the person in charge but kept getting passed from clerk to clerk. It was like one of those Russian dolls. I finally got to a supervisor, a fellow named Mr. Russell, who told me that the Wilmer family spent most of their time abroad and to direct any questions to him."

Charlie made a mental note of the supervisor's name.

"A strange way to do business," she said. "Do you know how they gained popularity?"

"I think they were quite clever, actually. They understood that there is a prosperous, if not quite wealthy, middle class hungering for fashionable goods that don't cost an arm and a leg. Upholstery that looks good and is of sufficient quality to pass muster. At the same time, you can afford to replace it when the next trend comes along."

Charlie nodded slowly. "They found an audience hungry for their goods. But how did news spread about their products?"

"As far as I can tell, the usual way. By word of mouth," Bernadette replied. "In my experience, a craze is started by a select few. Arbiters of fashion, if you will. Once those with social influence are seen with the item—be it a frock, wallpaper, or, in this case, furnishings—the rest follow like lemmings."

"Who made Wilmer fashionable?"

"Oh, let me see." Bernadette tipped her head, as if running through mental notes. "There was Ginny Farnsworth—of the mining Farnsworths. She was one of the first to own a Wilmer brocade set. But she told me she'd first seen a settee in the home of her friend, Anne Marks, the wife of the wine merchant. And Mrs. Marks, who is a bit of a fussbudget, gushed over the quality of her Wilmer damask and said she'd first seen a Wilmer at the home of... oh, who was it... Right. It was Isadora Rigby, wife of Ellsworth Rigby, industrialist extraordinaire."

Recognition tickled Charlie's nape.

The Rigbys have enough money to front an operation like Wilmer. To buy a manufactory.

"Strange that she'd prefer middling goods when her husband's rich as Croesus," Bernadette went on. "I've only met Mrs. Rigby once, at a tea. I took her for a proud lady who made it a habit to do as she pleased."

"What else do you know about her?"

Bernadette pursed her lips. "She's half-French, I believe. She met Ellsworth Rigby abroad, and after he made his fortune, they bought that estate in Hamstead. They travel most of the time, so it is unusual that they've been in London these past few months. Then again, most everyone is here for the Great Exhibition—"

"I must go." Charlie shot up. "Thank you, Bernadette."

"I am happy to help." The American rose as well. "Given your interest in Wilmer, you might want to check out their displays at the Crystal Palace."

Charlie froze. "What displays? I was told that they are not exhibitors."

"Not officially. I believe I mentioned I was granted early access to the exhibits? Well, last week, the superintendent, Mr. Owen Jones—no relation—gave me a tour. He told me that the banners intended to decorate the balconies had been lost in a fire at the supplier's warehouse. A real tragedy and no one knows what happened. Mr. Jones was quite frantic. Luckily, Wilmer stepped in and offered to provide banners in the same pattern and color as the originals. At cost, too. Mr. Jones was ever so relieved."

Dear Lord. Wilmer has access to the exhibition.

"Is everything all right, Lady Fayne?" Bernadette stared at her, looking faintly alarmed.

"Thanks to you, it might just be."

Charlie hurried off.

Keep going. Almost there.

Gritting his teeth, Jack worked the edge of the shovel against the ropes binding his hands. He'd managed to prop the tool up against the wall; sitting, he sawed at the ropes with the dull edge. Each movement aggravated his bruised ribs and assorted injuries, a gift of Isadora Rigby's brutes.

"It will get much worse for you, darling," she'd cooed. *"If your meddling friends don't leave us alone."*

"We will never stop hunting you," he'd spat.

She'd laughed, the ruthless glint in her eyes oddly familiar.

"Who is the hunter, and who is the prey?" She'd made a tsking sound. *"Hewitt Lancaster—Primus to you—thinks he is in charge, and he's fooled all his dutiful minions to believe the same. But I will let you in on a secret."*

She'd leaned closer, running a pointed fingernail along his cheek. He'd forced himself not to cringe, refusing to give her the satisfaction of a response.

"I am my mother's daughter. He seduced her, a revolutionary dedicated to the cause, then betrayed her. He used her to get to her people—militants fighting for la liberté. *Then they turned their backs on her too. For the rest of her life, ma mère lived as an outcast, shunned by everyone. She whored herself, and still we were so poor we foraged in rubbish heaps, slept buried in garbage for warmth. But I grew up knowing the truth, and I promised her that I would never forget. There is no such thing as justice. No such thing as loyalty. Liberté, Egalité, Fraternité—pah, nothing but an illusion to soothe the masses. The only thing that exists is power, and I will use that*

power to show the world what life is truly about: chaos and destruction."

The ruthless conviction in her dark gaze made something click in Jack's brain.

"You are Sir Lancaster's daughter?" he'd said, stunned. *"Does he...does he know about you?"*

"He soon will. As will the world."

Even her smile had been like her father's—cold and predatory. A sadistic gleam had lit her eyes when she'd turned her brutes on him for a final round.

"Have fun, but don't kill him yet. Wait until all goes smoothly in a few hours. After that, slit his throat and dump him in the Thames."

"Hurry up, my dear, or we shall be late." Ellsworth Rigby appeared. He flicked a glance at Jack, then said to his spouse, *"Let the guards amuse themselves. We have work to do."*

The couple departed.

The brutes left Jack on the floor, battered and unconscious.

He didn't know how long he'd been out, but the moment he was able, he'd crawled back to the place where the shovel was buried. Fear pushed back his pain, drove him to find his makeshift weapon and get to work. He had to get free—warn his team that Isadora Rigby was behind the First Flame, and in addition to her goal of destruction, she had a personal vendetta.

Against Hewitt Lancaster, her father.

Christ.

Jack worked at the ropes with savage force, cutting his hands in the process. After what seemed like an eternity, he felt the individual cords snapping, the rope weakening. He sawed some more, then yanked his hands apart as hard as he could, and the rope broke.

Finally.

He reached into his inner pocket, exhaling when he found the pen. He uncapped it, removing the nib and drawing out the lock picks secreted within. Fumbling in the darkness, he managed to insert them into the cuff around his ankle, working by feel until he heard a click. He removed the manacle and got to his feet, his body protesting at the movement.

Nothing seemed broken at least. He wasn't in the best shape to fight his way out...and maybe there was a better way. It was a coal cellar; cellars had chutes. He walked the perimeter of the space, searching for a shaft through which the coalmen would dump the fuel. The darkness impeded his vision. If only he had a light...

Then he heard it: a faint whistling sound...wind passing through a gap overhead. He followed the noise to its source. Stretching his arms up, he found the chute, feeling his way around it. The rough brick passage would be a tight squeeze for his large frame, but it was his best option.

Even if it's going to bloody hurt.

Gritting his teeth, he dug his fingers into the brick and mortar and pulled himself up.

It took him several tries before he got purchase inside the chute, his ribs shouting all the while. The passage was even narrower than he anticipated; sweat glazed his forehead at the tightness of the space. Using his hands and feet, he inched his way upward, praying he would not get stuck. Then he hit a barrier—the door to the chute.

Air whispered through the crack between the double panels. He pushed; the panels were locked together from the outside. Pressing his ear to the wood, he listened for voices, any sign that there might be guards waiting outside. Hearing nothing, he took a risk and rammed himself into the door. He paused, waiting for a reaction from the outside. When none came, he clenched his jaw and did it again. And again.

The panels bulged outward, but the lock didn't give. He kept at it until he heard a splintering sound...one of the panels had partially separated from its hinges. He focused on that panel, slamming his shoulder into it repeatedly until it flew off its anchors.

Shoving aside the remaining panel, he hoisted himself through the opening and onto a graveled surface.

Catching his breath, he got to his feet and staggered to the nearest wall, using it for cover. He was at the back of the house, windows shedding pale light on the manicured garden. Beyond the groomed space was a wooded area, which would conceal his escape. But he would have to get through the garden first, which was exposed save for some low hedges and statuary. He scouted the darkest path to the woods, then made a run for it.

He moved with rapid stealth. Even so, the crunch of gravel and his harsh breaths were deafening in his ears. With each step, his pulse thudded with the fear of discovery. He reached the trees, and enveloped in the shadowy copse, he exhaled with relief.

A rustle sounded behind him.

He spun around, muscles bunched in readiness.

"*Jack.* Thank heavens you are all right!"

His wife threw herself into his arms.

THIRTY-NINE

Lottie had brought a team comprised of the Angels and Jack's own colleagues to rescue him.

Together, they surrounded the Rigbys' mansion, swarming the entrances. They searched the entire house, but the Rigbys were gone, and their remaining servants either refused to say where they'd gone or simply did not know.

"It doesn't matter," Delaney said dourly. "We know where the bastards will show up."

"We haven't much time." Lottie consulted her pocket watch. "The opening ceremony is in five hours. We'll have to head directly there and meet up with the rest of the team."

At Jack's questioning look, she said, "I'll explain everything on the ride over."

He nodded, turning to Delaney, Laurent, and Calderone.

"I need to talk to Primus," he said. "It's urgent."

"Lancaster will be at the Crystal Palace."

To his surprise, the clipped words came from Lottie. He looked at his colleagues, who shrugged as if to say, *She knows everything.*

"You met with him?" he asked with care.

"Yes, he and I exchanged a few words." Her tone indicated that the discussion hadn't been pleasant. "He and the others are making preparations at the exhibition, and we will meet them there."

"Since there are no secrets." Jack exhaled, realizing that his duty to his team and to the greater good outweighed his personal allegiance to Primus. "Isadora Rigby told me she is Lancaster's daughter."

"What?" Delaney gasped.

"Apparently, in his younger days, he seduced a French revolutionary to infiltrate her group. He abandoned her after the mission, but Isadora was the result," he explained. "I'm uncertain if he knows of her existence or that she is behind this. I thought you should know because in addition to Isadora's desire to cause destruction, she is also hell-bent on personal vengeance."

"If he knew and did not tell us..." Delaney said with a growl.

Her anger was reflected in the faces of his other colleagues.

"That would be the end of the road for me," Laurent said.

"Have we not reached that point already, *mi querido*?" Calderone murmured.

The men exchanged a look that Jack understood. He felt the same way. He was done with espionage—with the deception and darkness and filth. He wanted to spend the rest of his days in the light...with his love. If only it were possible.

He gazed at her, and by some miracle, what he saw in her eyes gave him hope.

She slipped her hand into his, and he held on tightly.

"All right, lovebirds. Can we save the billing and cooing for after we defeat the villains and save the world?" Delaney inquired.

She was right. They had work to do.

"Let's get to it," Jack said.

🦅

He went with Lottie in her carriage. She fussed over his injuries despite his assurances that he was fine. They didn't have much time before they reached Hyde Park, and she filled him in on everything he'd missed. Since she did so whilst tucked against him, he couldn't say he minded.

Lottie summarized the findings concerning Wilmer Upholsteries.

"After Bernadette told me about Wilmer supplying the drapery and banners, I rushed to the exhibition. Hawksmoor has, ahem, contacts with the police and authorities involved in national security, and he convinced them to listen to me. We tested one of the banners. The result was terrifying." She shivered. "The fabric had obviously been treated to enhance its flammability. The white phosphorus and carbon disulfide solution ignites when exposed to air; if the mixture had been thrown on the banners, the entire building would have been on fire within seconds."

"But it won't be. Because of you," Jack said admiringly.

She shook her head. "I am not deserving of your praise, Jack. Not after what I've done."

Shame crept over him. "If you are referring to our last encounter, your reaction to the diary was completely understandable—"

"*No*, it wasn't." She turned to face him. "I should have given you the chance to explain what happened with Judith. To listen to your side of the story before I attacked you. Above all, I should have known that you would never force her or any woman."

He was grateful and humbled by her belief in him, yet he had to tell her everything.

His chest tight, he said, "Judith lied about the assault. In fact, most of that journal is a fabrication. She created it to use as leverage. She wanted me to...to continue having relations with her."

"She was coercing you," Lottie burst out.

"Yes and no." A sigh shuddered from him. "I did have an affair with Judith. Willingly. It lasted for years. It was wrong, and I knew it, but even though I wanted to stop, I...I couldn't."

He hated his weakness. Hated how confused he'd been by the pleasure and the pain.

"It was not your fault." Lottie framed his face with her hands, holding his gaze. "You were sixteen when the relationship started?"

He gave a terse nod.

"She was sixteen years your senior. An experienced woman and widow. Not to mention, she was also your employer and had power over your livelihood and future. Think about it, Jack: in that situation, who had the power? Who seduced whom? Who was in control?"

The memories slithered through his head. Judith's touches, seemingly innocuous at first. When he fetched her something, she would brush his hand with her fingers. Or, several times, she'd "accidentally" bumped into him, pressing her breasts against his chest. And the incident that had started it all: he'd been whipped by the butler for breaking something, and she'd treated his wounds with a tenderness that had filled him with bewildered gratitude.

Gratitude that had turned into something else, something that had twisted his insides with heat and confusion, when she'd reached between his legs, saying, *I'll make everything feel better, dear...*

Yet he couldn't deny that he had reacted physically to her.

"She may have instigated the affair," he said gruffly. "But she didn't force me into it. I was grown by then, big for my age—"

"Who told you that? Judith?"

Lottie's acuity took him aback. Judith had told him what a man he was, and he'd liked it at the time. Liked feeling mature and worthy of a woman's attention.

"There are many kinds of coercion," Lottie said quietly. "Physical force is but one. Preying upon another's needs and weaknesses is a form of coercion as well."

It sickened him to recognize that Judith *had* done that. That he'd given her the power to do so.

"A man must take responsibility for his actions," he said stubbornly.

"And that little gem came from Lancaster, no doubt," Lottie said.

His surprise must have shown, for she smiled humorlessly.

"During my chat with your leader, I gave him a piece of my mind for not telling you what I am telling you now. What you should *know*. Instead of helping you see that Judith was the bloody predator, that she manipulated you for her own selfish reasons, Lancaster did the *same*. He used your guilt and shame, your dashed noble nature, to convince you that you needed to redeem yourself by following his orders."

Awareness spread through Jack like dawn breaking outside. The way Lottie explained things made them seem obvious. Yet they hadn't been to him until now.

"Delaney said that Primus uses us for his own ends," he said. "And I shouldn't fall for it."

"Then I like Miss Delaney even more," Lottie declared.

At that, he had to raise his brows.

"Perhaps I let jealousy get the better of me in the past," she allowed. "But I am turning a new leaf. And so should you, darling. Stop punishing yourself for what happened—with Judith and Sebastian. You are not to blame. I *know* you, and if I hadn't been blinded by my own pain and prejudices, I would have seen that diary for what it was: an evil woman's attempt to twist the situation to her advantage."

Her words held the wisdom of a goddess and granted him the absolution he'd been searching for.

His eyes heated. "You truly believe that, Lottie?"

"I love you, Jack Granger. Even if you've concealed things from me, you have never hidden yourself," she said fiercely. "The loyal, protective, and good man that you are. And I would be proud to be your wife, to stand by your side for the rest of our days, if you still want me."

"I love you," he said raggedly. "I never stopped, and I never will. Because of the woman you are. My wise goddess who isn't afraid to fight for good. My beautiful wife who makes me feel alive and whole, like the luckiest bastard in the world. I cannot wait to officially make you mine again."

Her eyes shone with the brilliance of her love. "Then kiss me, my darling. Before we go and win our final battle."

She tipped her head up, and he brought his mouth to hers, coming home at last.

FORTY

C harlie and Jack arrived at the Crystal Palace two hours prior to the opening. The crowds were already gathering, filling the park, clamoring to see the promised wonders of the modern world housed within the glass walls. Charlie and Jack were let in through a back entrance. They met with the rest of the team in a private area. All the Angels and their spouses were present, and standing with them...

With a cry of delight, Charlie hurried toward the couple. She exchanged kisses on the cheek with the dainty brunette, then clasped the paw-like hand of the large, dark-haired gentleman. She smiled fondly at her former butler and housekeeper, now the Duke and Duchess of Ryedale, noting the positive changes that marriage had wrought.

"What are you doing here, Your Graces?" she said.

"There'll be none of that," the Duke of Ryedale chided her. "We'll always be Hawker and Mrs. Pea—Mrs. Reid, that is"—he cast a proud look at his duchess—"to you."

"The Angels wrote us saying you were in trouble," Pearl Reid, the Duchess of Ryedale, explained. "We came as quickly as we could. When we arrived this morning, your staff said you would be here. Glory spotted us, and here we are."

Hawker sized up Jack, his expression thunderous. "Is this the bastard who laid hands on you?"

Charlie made to intervene, but Glory got there first.

"It wasn't Mr. Granger who hurt Charlie," she said hastily. "We, um, got it wrong when we wrote you that letter. As it turns out, Mr. Granger is Charlie's, um, old friend."

"Her fiancé, actually." Jack bowed, winking at Charlie. "Pending a proper proposal."

Charlie stifled a grin.

Hawker continued to look suspicious. Pearl, however, scrutinized Charlie, then Jack, and after a moment, she beamed.

"Congratulations to you both," she said warmly.

"Thank you, my dear," Charlie said. "But I am afraid a proper reunion must wait until after we defeat the First Flame. How are preparations going?"

"We removed all the articles supplied by Wilmer," Fiona said. "The superintendent arrived and put up a fuss about what the bare spaces did to his design. Until Glory demonstrated to him exactly how bare the place would be if we allowed him to keep the banners."

"I snipped off a teensy corner of a banner and put it in a large bowl before I set it on fire." Glory shrugged. "It was quicker than arguing with him. Also, Livy had her uncle's special powder handy."

"Special powder?" Charlie quirked a brow.

"It is a formula Sir Harry developed to put out fires."

It was Hadleigh who spoke, as his duchess was preoccupied. Livy was sitting in a corner, scribbling in a small notebook, muttering to herself. Earlier, the Angels had said she was "working on something," and recognizing Livy's look of intense concentration, Charlie knew to leave her be.

"Since Kent created the powder at the behest of his wife, he submitted the patent under the name, *Tessa's Friend*." Hadleigh smiled wryly. "He gave us his entire supply so that we may all have some on hand."

"That is a relief," Charlie said. "Even though we've removed Wilmer's products, there are plenty of flammable objects around. If the First Flame succeeds in unleashing even a few vials, we will have a disaster on our hands."

"Since you informed us that Isadora and Ellsworth Rigby are behind this attack, I've made sketches of them," Pippa put in. "I've given copies to the mudlarks, guards, and police. Everyone is on the lookout."

"Good work," Charlie said.

"They will be in disguise, so everyone's eyes must be sharp," Jack said somberly. "And there will likely be multiple attackers, not just the Rigbys. The guards and police must be prepared to detain anyone who looks suspicious."

"That is a tall order," Hawksmoor said. "The crowd is larger than anyone anticipated. Upward of twenty-five thousand people."

"*C'est impossible.*" Laurent shook his head. "That is too many to search."

"We shall have to do our best." Charlie chewed on her lip. "With its three stories, the exhibition occupies nearly a million square feet. It is too massive an area to monitor, even with our group and the police combined. Fiona and Glory, in your analysis, did you come up with likely areas for the First Flame to strike?"

"We've circled them on this map." Glory unrolled a plan of the exhibition on the table, pointing to the places circled in red.

"We prioritized the areas that were most likely to draw a crowd," Fi explained. "The Koh-I-Noor diamond, the Tableau of Exotic Beasts, that sort of thing."

"We also included anywhere Her Majesty and His Royal Highness—"

"*By Jove, I've got it.*"

Everyone stared as Livy leapt up, throwing her arms up in what could only be described as a victory pose. Looking amused but unsurprised by his duchess's antics, Hadleigh walked over and chucked her under the chin.

"What has your clever mind figured out this time, little queen?" he asked.

"From the moment I saw the words *Wilmer Upholsteries*, I knew something was off," Livy said breathlessly. "It just didn't look right, if you know what I mean."

Since no one had any idea what she meant, they waited for her to explain.

"It niggled and niggled at me. And just now, I figured it out. It's an *anagram*."

She grabbed the notebook, holding it up.

Beneath a jumble of scribbles and crossed-out letters, she'd written in bold:

WILMER UPHOLSTERIES = PROMETHEUS WILL RISE

Charlie's breath caught; even Jack's jaw slackened.

"Prometheus—that's what people are calling the giant elm tree by the Crystal Fountain, isn't it?" Livy said. "What if the First Flame is planning on setting the tree on fire? It would provide the ultimate fuel source."

"The symbolism of such an act of terror is befitting of the First Flame." Lancaster entered the room; his gaze flitted to Jack before returning to Livy. "They think of themselves as Prometheus, the architect of mankind. Like the god, they plan to give fire to the world—but they will use that fire not to build but destroy."

As much as Charlie despised the spymaster, his analysis had the ring of truth.

Glory gasped, her gaze on the map. "The dais where Queen Victoria and Prince Albert will be conducting the opening ceremony is next to Prometheus. And suspended over the dais is a huge *baldacchino*."

Master Chen's brow furrowed. "What is that, little tigress?"

"It's a fabric canopy used for ceremonial purposes," Glory explained. "This *baldacchino* has been dubbed the *Canopy of Crowning Glory*, given its elaborate design."

"If it caught a spark from the tree, it would be the *Flaming Canopy of Death*," Maria muttered. "Can we get it down?"

"It is suspended from the tallest point of the ceiling, over a hundred feet up. We don't have time to get it down." Glory nibbled on her lip. "We didn't think to remove it earlier because we were focused on Wilmer's goods."

"There is nothing we can do about it now." Charlie consulted Hawksmoor, who would be working covertly as part of the Queen's security detail. "Will Her Majesty agree to have her guards establish a perimeter around the tree and the dais?"

"I will convince the powers that be of the necessity," the earl said.

Charlie nodded. "We will concentrate our resources in the same area. Work in pairs, and don't lose sight of your partner. If you see anyone acting suspiciously, investigate; if necessary, apprehend. Any questions?"

When no one spoke, she added, "Before we go, we Angels have a motto that I think is fitting in these circumstances."

The Angels formed a circle, and the others joined.

Charlie put her hand out in the center. Livy, Pippa, Fiona, and Glory placed their hands on top of hers. The others followed suit.

Charlie looked at the Angels, and they chorused as one.

"Sisters first!"

Whilst Lottie and her group disguised themselves as ratcatchers—rather apropos—Jack pulled Primus aside and told him about Isadora Rigby.

Seeing resignation, not surprise, on the spymaster's face, he felt a jolt of rage.

"You knew," he said with revulsion. "You knew who was behind this, but you didn't tell us? You sent all of us into danger to clean up the bloody mess you made?"

"I didn't know. I only...suspected." Lancaster's tone was leaden—perhaps with guilt, if the man had enough conscience to feel such a thing. "When I left Colette, I knew she was with child. But the mission was done, and she was a bloody anarchist, Granger. How could I be with her?"

"She was also a woman, a human being, whom you used for your own ends. Whom you abandoned after you destroyed her life." As Jack said the words, he was filled with clarity. "The only one who has ever needed to repent his sins is you, Lancaster."

"I didn't know that Colette's offspring would grow up to be a monster." Lancaster shook his head. "But when we came to London, and I met Isadora Rigby, there was something...well, familiar about her. Something about the way she looked at me, as if she knew me. Something I couldn't put a finger on."

"Perhaps you didn't want to know," Jack shot back.

"Perhaps you are right." For the first time, Lancaster's age showed, and he looked weary. "Even though I had no reason to, nothing but an instinct to go on, I investigated her background. The more I looked, the less there was to find. I knew only that she was French, born in the same year that my child with Colette would have been. That wasn't enough, Granger, to pin her as a notorious criminal."

"Maybe not, but it was more than enough to share with us," Jack said flatly. "Your team. The people you ought to have trusted and protected."

"I have my regrets—"

"It is too late now. After this, I am done. We all are."

Turning, Jack walked away.

People swarmed the exhibition, eager to see what was inside the glass structure that had been tantalizing them for months. *Oohs* and *aahs* were a refrain as they wandered through the sweeping hall of delights. They examined curious and precious objects, stopping to peer up at the giant trees, which had seemed ordinary in the park but had a magical presence inside this astounding glass box.

Everywhere, people of all classes saw wonders.

Everywhere, Charlie saw danger.

She was posted on the second-floor balcony, across from Prometheus. It gave her a bird's-eye view of the dais and crowd below. The Angels and Jack's colleagues were circulating amongst the visitors, subtly and effectively monitoring the area. Pippa and Cullen had brought whistles that made a distinctive bird-like sound; if anyone spotted trouble, they would blow the whistle, so to speak.

Policemen were posted along a perimeter around the dais and elm, yet they had to be careful. Given clashes with authorities in the past, crowds were generally not fond of law enforcement; one wrong move, even in this celebration of civilization and progress, could turn the happy visitors into a mob. Which was exactly what the First Flame would want.

Charlie saw Jack circling Prometheus along with Maria. Thanks to Master Chen, who'd bound his ribs and applied a healing salve to his wounds, Jack was moving well. In fact, despite his recent ordeal, he appeared his usual virile, outsized self.

Because he is a survivor. A warrior. My hero.

His gaze met hers, and his lips curved in a smile that was only for her.

A buzz came over the crowd, signaling the arrival of the royal family. Her Majesty the Queen and His Royal Highness Prince Albert, accompanied by their eldest children, the Prince of Wales and the Princess Royal, came down the aisle of red carpet leading to the dais. A coterie of guards proceeded and followed them. As the family advanced, regally waving and nodding to the adoring hordes, Charlie saw Hawksmoor and his fellow agents moving alongside them in the crowd.

At that instant, her gaze snagged on a familiar figure farther up ahead. A tall man with thinning fair hair...when he turned his head, she saw his face clearly beneath the brim of his hat. *Karlsson.* She blew her whistle, the sound loud enough to draw the attention of her team but fading into the cacophony for everyone else. She caught the Angels' gazes, pointing at the target. Livy, who was closest, scampered through the crowd toward Karlsson, as nimble as the ratcatcher she was supposed to be.

Charlie's heart thumped as the royal couple continued down the aisle. In a few feet, the Queen would directly pass by Karlsson —did he intend to mount an attack? If he used the vile potion, he could set the carpet on fire, endangering the lives of everyone packed into the building. She gnawed on her lip as he reached for something in his pocket.

Livy dodged through the crowd, closing the gap between her and Karlsson. Luckily, Her Majesty stopped to exchange greetings with a child, and Livy passed her, reaching Karlsson with moments to spare. With a deftness that did her training proud, Livy pretended to run into the bounder, tripping him in the process. He went down with a shout, and she landed atop him. Hopping up, she took off again, squeezing through the throng.

Karlsson rose, his furious expression turning into one of comic surprise when he reached into his pocket and found it empty. He swung his head in Livy's direction, stalking after her, shoving startled people—including women and children—aside. He was intercepted by a pair of policemen. They dragged him off to the cheers of the crowd who had no tolerance for uncouth behavior.

One down.

Charlie continued scanning the path toward the dais. An unsavory-looking fellow caught her attention, especially when he bent to reach for something. As she was about to sound the alarm again, he straightened, a little girl in his arms. He hoisted her onto his shoulders, beaming with fatherly pride at her delight. Charlie looked beyond them...and saw Pippa whisper something to Glory. An instant later, the pair was on the move.

It took Charlie a moment to recognize whom Pippa had spotted. Ellsworth Rigby had transformed himself into a pearl-wearing matron in a plaid dress. He stood near the end of the carpet, as close to the dais as the public was allowed to be. He clutched a beaded reticule as if his life depended upon it. Pippa approached him with a flirtatious swagger, and he looked taken aback, but he retained a tight grip on his bag. Behind him, Glory set FF II loose from her pocket. The ferret made a beeline for Rigby, darting beneath his skirts.

Whatever FF II did caused Rigby to emit a yelp so high-pitched it sounded convincingly female. The reticule flew from his hands, and Charlie's breath lodged as the dangerous cargo went flying. If there was a vial inside that bag and it broke... Glory sprinted after it, her lightness *kung fu* a thing to behold. She leapt into the air, twisting elegantly, catching the reticule's strings in her fingers. She landed easily and, catching Charlie's gaze, gave a thumbs-up.

Charlie let out a breath as a struggling Ellsworth was led away. There were two other incidents around the dais, the would-be perpetrators foiled by Fiona, Hawker, and Mrs. Peabody. Queen Victoria and Prince Albert finally arrived at the dais, mounting the steps, their guards forming a protective barrier. Even so, unease slithered through Charlie. The royal family was literally and figuratively on the world's stage: there was no better time for Isadora Rigby to send her message of destruction.

Where is she?

The ceremony began. Prince Albert read the Report of the Royal Commissioners to the Queen, the *baldacchino* swaying overhead. The crowd quieted, their attention rapt upon their reigning family. Jack, who'd been roving around Prometheus, suddenly halted. Reading his rigid body posture, Charlie followed the line of his gaze.

A grey-haired lady wearing a lavender hat and promenade dress had slipped through the policemen's perimeter. Since she was bent over, using a cane to shuffle along, they had probably assumed she was harmless. She carried a knitting bag and approached Prometheus. Everything seemed to happen in slow motion. Jack was already running over, Chen and Cullen doing the same from different directions. Charlie blew the whistle...but it was too late.

Reaching inside the bag, the old lady pulled out a fistful of glass vials and threw them at the base of the tree. The glass shattered, liquid splashing the trunk. Instantly, flames roared to life. Jack, Chen, and Cullen arrived a second later with bags of *Tessa's Friend*. They threw the powder at the tree, extinguishing some of the rising flames. They were joined by the Angels and Jack's colleagues, whose contribution of powder put out the rest.

All of this happened in mere moments. Riveted by the ceremony, the audience seemed to take no notice of the near calamity. The team was preoccupied with putting out the fire and did not immediately give chase to Isadora Rigby, who made a run toward the nearest exit.

Charlie abandoned her watch and dashed for the stairs.

By the time she made it outside, she saw Jack several yards ahead of her. He was pursuing Isadora through the field of waiting carriages that stood between the back of the Crystal Palace and a nearby pond. Coachmen, grooms, and servants milled about. Isadora used the horde and conveyances to her advantage, ducking in and out of sight. Jack ran into the next aisle, and Charlie followed.

As Jack was faster, the distance between them widened. Charlie lost sight of Isadora, but Jack broke into a sprint. Then she saw what he did: Isadora leaping into the driver's seat of a carriage.

The passenger compartment was filled with crates, more strapped on top and to the back. And Isadora's alternate plan became clear.

With that amount of explosive material, she could take out the entire building.

Isadora steered the carriage into the aisle, heading straight for the Crystal Palace. Panic gripped Charlie as she yanked out her pistol. She raised it, her arms shaking with indecision. If she shot at Isadora, and the carriage crashed into the others, the explosion would result in significant fatalities. But if Isadora managed to drive the carriage into the exhibition...

At that instant, Jack turned, his gaze meeting Charlie's. Her panic turned to horror when she realized what he meant to do. He mouthed the words, *I love you*.

Then he ran toward the oncoming carriage.

There was no choice but to gain control of the carriage.

Any other option would lead to a heavy death toll, and Jack could not let that happen.

You can do this. Jump into the driver's seat and grab the reins. Also, don't die, or Lottie will never forgive you.

The rush of battle cleared his head as he neared the accelerating vehicle. He saw the malicious glee on Isadora's face as she prepared to mow him down. At the last moment, he swerved and jumped, grabbing onto the side of the carriage and pulling himself into the driver's seat.

Isabella yowled with rage as he fought for the reins. They tussled, Jack yanking fiercely to prevent the horses from running into a group of footmen playing dice. The carriage slowed as he and Isadora continued to grapple, and he almost had the upper hand when Isadora suddenly let go. He saw the blade flash in her hand; it was too late to dodge.

He angled away as best he could, bracing for the strike.

Isadora screamed.

Lancaster had jumped into the driver's seat on her other side, grabbing her wrist and disarming her with a ruthless twist. The three of them jostled against one another as the horses, realizing no one was in control, neighed wildly and started to gallop.

Jack had to use one hand to grip the side of the perch, and his remaining grip on the reins was slipping.

"Sir," he shouted. "I can't hold on—"

"Then let go." In the throes of wrestling with Isadora, Primus met Jack's gaze. "A man must take responsibility for his actions."

Then Primus gave Isadora a shove that catapulted Jack from the perch.

Jack hit the ground hard. As he rolled, his body was a pulsating mass of pain. He fought the swamping darkness. A rumble went through his body, a deafening blast making his head pound even more. Was that the smell of burning...brimstone?

Was this death? Had he died and gone to hell?

"Jack. Jack, my darling. Don't you dare die on me—"

Lottie? His goddess. If she was here, he couldn't be in hell.

He forced his eyes open and saw his beloved's anxious face above him. He glimpsed the Angels, keeping the crowd at bay.

"Not dead," he croaked.

"Yet," she said in a suffocated voice. "I may murder you for risking your neck like that."

It came back in a rush. He tried to sit up.

"Don't move, darling. You may have broken—"

Lottie's warning came too late as fresh pain erupted through him, and the world spun.

He fell back, panting. "Wh-hat happened?"

"Lancaster fought Isadora for the reins," Lottie said. "She was aiming for the exhibition, but he got the upper hand. He drove the carriage into the pond, and there was a small explosion."

"Lancaster?" he said hoarsely.

But he knew. Even before Lottie shook her head somberly, he knew.

A man must take responsibility for his actions.

"Hawksmoor and the police are attending to the scene now," she said. "As for you, I am taking you home and keeping you there."

Home. With his Lottie. *Heaven*.

He pushed back the encroaching oblivion. Dazed as he was, he knew there was another question he needed answered. His life depended upon it.

"I have something to ask you," he managed.

"Yes, dearest?"

"Will you marry me?"

Lottie started laughing.

His vision wavering at the edges, he pushed out, "Is that a yes?"

"A resounding yes to your very proper proposal, my love."

"You've made me...the happiest..."

He gazed adoringly at his Lottie...at *both* of her faces?

Then he passed out.

EPILOGUE

SIX WEEKS LATER

With infinite satisfaction, Jack carried his wife over the
threshold of their bedchamber.

"This is hardly necessary," Lottie said with a laugh.

"I told you I would do things properly this time around."

Despite his botched proposal at the Crystal Palace—which he
chalked up to his head injury at the time—Jack had made good on
his promise. He had proposed to Lottie again, this time on bended
knee and with the ring he'd commissioned for her from Rundell,
Bridge & Co. Flanked by a pair of diamonds, the dazzling sapphire
in the center had a rare quality: depending on the light, it shifted
hues from vivid blue to rich grey. As Jack set his bride down, he
saw how the ring on her finger nearly matched the brilliance of her
eyes.

He took a moment to memorize how stunning she looked in
her mazarine blue wedding gown trimmed with lace. Then again,
he'd stared at her throughout the intimate wedding ceremony
held at their home, secretly wishing their guests would leave so
that he could have her to himself. His behavior had earned him

knowing chuckles from the Angels' spouses. He enjoyed the camaraderie of the fellows, who'd welcomed him into their circle.

"A husband of an Angel needs the support of cronies," Hadleigh had said. "Trust me on this."

Jack had a feeling the duke was only half in jest. Nonetheless, the men had looked on with fierce pride as their ladies, one by one, preceded the bride down the aisle. Then Lottie appeared, and Jack had lost track of everything else. Her gaze met his, her smile as vibrant as the bouquet of specially chosen flowers she held. The daffodils, she'd explained, symbolized their undying love, whilst the asters stood for their new beginning.

With Lottie, Jack had found just that: a fresh start. She helped him to see his past through new, wiser eyes. He began to recognize which burdens were his to carry...and which were not. Together, they had burned Judith's diary. Afterward, emotion had overwhelmed him, yet knowing that his wife was there—that she promised to be there always—he had allowed himself to feel and to heal.

They also discussed other painful subjects: the mistakes they'd made during their first year of marriage, Lottie's relationship with her papa...no topic was forbidden. Their intimacy flourished, supported by a maturity that neither of them had possessed the first time around.

In fact, the fresh start extended to all areas of Jack's life. Delaney, Laurent, and Calderone had attended the wedding ceremony, and afterward, he and his former team had shared a few toasts in private. They drank to Jack's marriage and his decision to leave espionage. They celebrated Calderone and Laurent's purchase of a beautiful vineyard on the island of Mallorca. They toasted Delaney, who had been promoted to Primus's position. Lastly, they held a moment of silence for their former spymaster, choosing to forget his transgressions and instead honor his self-sacrifice.

"As the English bard says, *all's well that ends well*," Laurent had murmured.

Through a combined effort with the police and the Queen's guards, the First Flame's plot had been hushed up. The incident with the carriage had been chalked up to the tragic actions of a madwoman, who in a delirium had driven away in the wrong carriage, one which happened to be carrying fireworks. She had been stopped by two brave bystanders, Granger and Lancaster. Thus, when history books discussed the Great Exhibition, there would be no mention of terror, only the miracles of progress and modernization.

After the wedding ceremony, Delaney, Laurent, and Calderone had slipped away like the spies they were. Jack wasn't sure when he would see them next. But he was glad they were each on their own path to happiness...just like he was.

Lottie wound her arms around his neck.

"How does it feel to be a husband again?" she teased.

"I've always been your husband." He cupped her cheek. "Now, however, I get to enjoy the privileges."

Her smile was sultry. "Are there any particular *privileges* you would like this eve, my love?"

At her offer, he grew instantly hard. Then again, he'd been battling arousal all bloody day. He couldn't believe that his Lottie was finally *his* again.

"Why don't I help you out of your gown, and we can find out?" he murmured.

"Hurry," she said.

Whilst he had planned to take his time on their wedding night, his bride was having none of it. She tore at his clothes with a lusty enthusiasm that matched his own. Christ, he loved her hot-blooded nature. Within minutes, they tumbled naked onto their bed, their mouths passionately fused. She rolled on top of him and began kissing her way down his chest.

Tangling his fingers in her honeyed tresses, he halted her progress.

"Ladies first," he insisted.

Her pout made his prick weep with anticipation.

"But I want to taste you, Jack."

"And you will, love. *After* I eat your pussy."

She drew her brows together. "Are we really going to fight about this?"

"No." He decided creativity was in order. "We'll compromise."

Grabbing her hips, he spun her around so that she was still atop him, but now her cunny was over his mouth and his erection beneath hers. He smirked at her sound of surprise. He'd been meaning to experiment with this position and what better time than their wedding night?

"Together, darling," he ordered.

With an excited gasp, Lottie obeyed. Her kiss sucked a groan from his chest. Her tongue did wicked, delightful things. He returned the favor, eating her cunny like a man starved, relishing her wanton squirming against his face. Parting her with his thumbs, he speared her with his tongue. He stabbed inside her clenching passage and heard her whimper around her mouthful of cock. The stimulation brought him to the edge too quickly.

He tried to pull away, but Lottie wouldn't allow it. She dove on him, and when her throat closed around his tip, squeezing enticingly, his eyes rolled back in his head. Knowing that resistance was futile, he redoubled his efforts, frigging her pearl whilst he licked her slit. He was drunk on her flavor, her abandon, how wild they made one another.

"Come in my mouth, wife," he growled. "I want your cream on my tongue. *Now.*"

He'd discovered that Lottie enjoyed his authority...in sexual situations, at least. With a breathless cry, she gave him what he wanted. The taste of her pleasure triggered his own release. He buried his groans in her sweet cunny and his seed betwixt her loving lips.

He cuddled her close, and they shared a hot, tender kiss.

"If this is how we settle disagreements from now on," his wife murmured, "I see a bright future ahead of us."

"Compromise is key, I always say."

"When did you get so wise?"

"You must be rubbing off on me." He thumbed a speck of his seed from the corner of her mouth, and his voice thickened with renewed lust. "Or am I rubbing off on you?"

"Why, Mr. Granger." Lottie caressed his cock, and it was no longer stiffening but hard as a rock. "I do believe you are ready for another round."

"With you, Mrs. Granger? Always."

His eyes holding his wife's, he entered her with a deep, soul-satisfying thrust.

"Christ, I love being inside you," he said with fervor.

"You belong here," she said tremulously. "You always have."

His voice vibrated with the force of his emotions. "You're my home, Lottie."

"And you are mine, Jack."

"I love you."

They said the last together. It echoed the vows they'd exchanged earlier. They lost themselves in their joining, their bodies surging toward the ecstasy that their hearts had already found.

A few weeks later, Charlie watched on with pride as Jack prepared to receive his knighthood.

The investiture ceremony was taking place in the Throne Room of Buckingham Palace. Against the regal backdrop of crimson and gilt, the recipients of the honor knelt one by one before Her Majesty the Queen, whose plush throne was shaded by a lavish gold-fringed *baldacchino*. His Royal Highness Prince Albert stood to her right. As the Grand Master of the Order of the Bath, he pinned the insignia on the ceremonial coats of the newly made knights, and both he and the monarch offered words of congratulations.

Then it was Jack's turn. Although he was receiving the honor as a civilian—his past as a spymaster and the attack by the First Flame had to be kept secret—he had the bearing of a warrior. Prior to kneeling before Her Majesty, he turned his head and met Charlie's eyes. The wink he gave her during this solemn occasion was nearly scandalous.

Charlie hid a grin. Her husband had always lived by his own rules. It was one of the reasons they were a perfect match. Jack got down on one knee, his hair gleaming like armor beneath the chandeliers, and was made a Knight Commander of the Order of the Bath.

Afterward, there was a reception, and Charlie and Jack were joined by Livy, Pippa, Fiona, Glory, and their spouses. Everyone wore formal court dress—extravagant white frocks for the ladies, dark coats and breeches for the gentlemen—and looked as proper as could be.

This might be, Charlie thought with amusement, *our finest disguise*.

"Congratulations, old boy," Hadleigh said.

"Well done," Chen agreed.

"How does it feel to be Sir Jack?" Cullen asked.

"The same as when I was a plain mister," Jack replied.

The men guffawed.

"I noticed the prince murmured something to you during the ceremony." Livy aimed a curious glance at Jack. "Is it something you feel free to share?"

"His Royal Highness thanked me. For protecting those most dear to him: his wife and children."

Jack slid an arm around Charlie's waist, and she leaned into his solid strength.

Hawksmoor cleared his throat. "If you are interested, sir, my team has an opening."

"No, thank you."

Jack meant it. Charlie knew this because they'd spent hours discussing what he wanted to do with his future. She feared he was giving up espionage for her, but he had assured her otherwise.

"I want to make maps," he'd said firmly. *"I want to explore new lands and chart the progress of existing places. Most of all, I want to help people find their way home."*

With her full support, Jack had accepted a cartography commission in Greece. The visit was going to double as a wedding trip, and Charlie couldn't wait for her first vacation in years. After many interviews, she had hired a partner whom she was confident would keep her society running smoothly whilst she was away.

A hush came over the crowd, which parted like the Red Sea at the approach of the royal couple. Their group bowed and curtsied, and the Angels and their husbands made space for Queen Victoria and Prince Albert to have a private moment with Jack and Charlie. Whilst His Royal Highness conversed with Jack, Her Majesty addressed Charlie.

"Lady Granger, we understand that your husband is not the only one we must thank today."

Charlie met the monarch's clear blue eyes. The queen was a petite woman with glossy chestnut curls and porcelain skin. Her serene decorum made it easy to see why she was a symbol of propriety and domesticity.

Charlie wondered how much the monarch knew about her society's involvement at the Crystal Palace. According to Hawksmoor, the Angels had been omitted from the official reports to protect their reputations. And, perhaps, to spare the royal sensibilities.

"I endeavor to be a support to my husband, Your Majesty," Charlie said demurely.

"While we find that commendable, we wish to express our gratitude for your efforts not as a wife but as a champion of women."

Charlie stilled. Her heart began to race.

Queen Victoria leaned forward. "Several friends have told us about your society, and we are quite intrigued."

Charlie gulped.

"Whilst history may erase your contributions—and, indeed, those of most women—we know what the Angels have done, and we offer our sincere appreciation for your service."

"Th-thank you, Your Majesty," Charlie stammered.

Mischief glinted briefly in the monarch's eyes. "And we have forewarned dear Albert: should he stray, we know who to seek out."

The prince finished his conversation with Jack, and the royal pair moved on.

"What did Her Majesty say to you, love?" Jack asked.

Charlie widened her eyes. "She *knows*. About my society."

"Is that a bad thing?"

"I don't think so." She furrowed her brow. "She thanked the Angels for our service."

Jack let out a bark of laughter. "Perhaps she will grant your society a royal warrant. That will be sure to drum up business."

"Very amusing." Charlie's lips curved. "It is nice, however, to know that one's efforts are appreciated."

"I am constantly telling you how much I appreciate your efforts. In fact, I recall doing so last night." He raised his brows. "Repeatedly."

Charlie's cheeks flamed as she recalled her husband's wicked praise in bed.

"Don't get me into a lather now," she scolded. "The reception won't be over for hours."

His eyes smoldered. "We could sneak out—"

"Absolutely not. This is the greatest honor of your life, and we are not leaving early."

"It's not," he said.

"Not what?"

"My greatest honor. That happened when I made you my wife."

Her heart melted at his tender look. "Which time?"

"Both times. Nothing makes me prouder than being your husband."

"I know something that might come a close second."

Jack's shoulders went rigid. When he spoke, he sounded like he was holding his breath.

"Are you saying what I think you're saying?"

She nodded. "The physician confirmed it. I am with child."

The wonder and joy that blazed across her husband's face was everything she'd hoped for.

"Every time I think you could not possibly give me more," he said with gravelly emotion, "you find a way to prove me wrong."

"I didn't know I could be so happy," she confessed giddily.

With no care for where they were, he pulled her into his arms and kissed her.

Then he said the words he'd proved, time and again, to be true.

"The best is still to come, my Lottie."

The Angels will return...

Author's Note

I must confess I have been eagerly awaiting the arrival of 1851 in my book universe so that I could write about the *Great Exhibition of the Works of Industry of All Nations*. I have always imagined the Crystal Palace as a magical place, full of the wonders of the world at that time. In writing the scenes that take place at the Great Exhibition, I tried to incorporate as many authentic details as possible (e.g., the *baldacchino* and giant elm appear in drawings and daguerreotype images of the event). I did, however, take some artistic liberties: the afore-mentioned *baldacchino* was never at risk of being known as the *Flaming Canopy of Death*...or was it? Lol.

After the exhibition ended, the Crystal Palace was relocated to Sydenham Hill and rebuilt in an expanded form. Visitors today can still see the beautiful park that was designed to surround it. The venue itself was used for many shows and concerts until it burned down in 1936.

Speaking of burning, I based the weapon used by the First Flame on the "Fenian Fire" made infamous by the Irish Republican Brotherhood in the 1860's. Although my story occurs a few years earlier, both white phosphorus and carbon disulfide were already being used, so I didn't think it was too far-fetched for my villains to have discovered their volatile properties when combined.

ACKNOWLEDGMENTS

First and foremost, thank you to my readers! This series about intrepid lady detectives has been so much fun to write, and I could not have done it without your support and encouragement. I remain ever grateful for my amazing book family for allowing me to run wild with my imagination and write stories from my heart.

The creation of every book takes a village, and I am so fortunate in mine. Thank you to my writing group: Barbara, Anne, and Veronica, you inspire me so much, and I love hanging out with you. To my editor, Peter, thank you for your insights and for understanding my zany ideas. To my proofreaders Faith and Alyssa, you are gems and make my books shine.

To my family, 2023 brought some choppy and unexpected waters. Through the ups and downs, I was always happy to be on this journey with you. Love you.

About the Author

USA Today & International Bestselling Author Grace Callaway writes hot and heart-melting historical romance filled with mystery and adventure. Her debut novel was a Romance Writers of America Golden Heart Finalist and a #1 National Regency Bestseller, and her subsequent novels have topped national and international bestselling lists. Her writing has also received critical acclaim. She is a three-time recipient of the Daphne du Maurier Award for Excellence in Mystery and Suspense, the Maggie Award for Excellence in Historical Romance, and the Passionate Plume. Her other awards include the National Excellence in Romance Fiction Award, the Golden Leaf, and the National Excellence in Storytelling Award.

Growing up on the Canadian prairies, Grace could often be found with her nose in a book—and not much has changed since. She set aside her favorite romance novels long enough to get her doctorate from the University of Michigan. A clinical psychologist, she lives with her family in Northern California. Her hobbies include dancing, dining in hole-in-the-wall restaurants, and going on adapted adventures with her special son.

Keep up with Grace's latest news!

Newsletter: gracecallaway.com/newsletter

facebook.com/GraceCallawayBooks

bookbub.com/authors/grace-callaway

instagram.com/gracecallawaybooks

amazon.com/author/gracecallaway

Made in the USA
Columbia, SC
20 March 2024

33389385R00226